THE *Royal* HOUSE OF NIROLI

## SEMPRE APPASSIONATO, SEMPRE FIERO

*Always passionate, always proud*

**The richest royal family in the world—
united by blood and passion,
torn apart by deceit and desire**

Complete your collection with all four books!

**The Royal House of Niroli:
Scandalous Seductions**

**The Royal House of Niroli:
Billion Dollar Bargains**

**The Royal House of Niroli:
Innocent Mistresses**

**The Royal House of Niroli:
Secret...**

## WELCOME TO NIROLI!

Nestled in the azure blue of the Mediterranean, the majestic island of Niroli has prospered for centuries. The Fierezza men have worn the crown with passion and pride since the Middle Ages. But now, as the King's health declines, and his two sons have been tragically killed, the crown is in jeopardy.

The clock is ticking—a new heir must be found before the King is forced to abdicate. By royal decree the internationally scattered members of the Fierezza family are summoned to claim their destiny. But any person who takes the throne must do so according to 'The Rules of the Royal House of Niroli'. Soon secrets and rivalries emerge as the descendants of this ancient royal line vie for position and power. Only a true Fierezza can become ruler—a person dedicated to their country, their people…and their eternal love!

# THE *Royal* HOUSE OF NIROLI

## Billion Dollar Bargains

### CAROL MARINELLI
### NATASHA OAKLEY

Harlequin Mills & Boon Limited, Eton House,
18-24 Paradise Road, Richmond, Surrey TW9 1SR

THE ROYAL HOUSE OF NIROLI: BILLION DOLLAR BARGAINS
© by Harlequin Books SA 2011

*Bought by the Billionaire Prince* © Harlequin Books S.A. 2007
*The Tycoon's Princess Bride* © Harlequin Books S.A. 2007

Special thanks and acknowledgement are given to Carol Marinelli and
Natasha Oakley for their contribution to The Royal House of Niroli
series.

ISBN: 978 0 263 88946 8

011-0211

Harlequin Mills & Boon policy is to use papers that are
natural, renewable and recyclable products and made from
wood grown in sustainable forests. The logging and
manufacturing processes conform to the legal environmental
regulations of the country of origin.

Printed and bound in Spain
by Litografia Rosés S.A., Barcelona

# Bought by the Billionaire Prince

CAROL MARINELLI

# CHAPTER ONE

'Is he good-looking?'

Meg felt her teeth literally grind together as her travel companion, Jasmine, repeated the question for the hundredth time. Here they were docking in Niroli, which was undoubtedly the most beautiful island Meg had seen on her travels to date, and all Jasmine wanted to talk about was potential men.

Coming from Australia, where everything was comparatively new, Meg was in awe of the past that drenched each place she had visited on her travels through Europe, reeling at the ancient architecture and glorious tales of times gone by and, for Meg, Niroli had it all! To the South of Sicily, the island of Niroli, according to the travel guide Meg had devoured on the boat trip, was steeped in history, its colourful past filled with rivalries and wars dating back centuries and still playing out today. They'd just passed the tiny island of Mont Avellana, which, as recently as two decades ago, had been ruled by Niroli, and now they were coming into Niroli's main port. Meg stared in wonder as they approached—sandy beaches rapidly giving way to a lush hillside, which was like a fabulous tapestry, with thick forests, and edged by vineyards that laced neatly around the sprawling town. But a grand castle set on a rocky promontory was for Meg the main focal point, standing tall and proud, looking out towards the ocean, as if somehow guarding it all.

'That's the palace,' Meg pointed out to Jasmine excitedly, checking with the map to get her bearings, 'and over to the right there's a Roman amphitheatre….'

'There's a casino,' Jasmine said, peering over Meg's shoulder, 'oh, and a luxury spa!'

'We can't afford luxury.' Meg smiled. 'We're backpacking!'

'Then we'll just have to find someone who can!' Jasmine countered, her mind flicking back to the inevitable. 'So what sort of doctor is he?'

'Who?' Meg asked, then let out a pained sigh as Jasmine's momentary interest in her surrounds rapidly waned. 'Alex is a surgeon,' Meg admitted, then wished she hadn't, noting Jasmine's eyes literally light up at the prospect of dating a rich surgeon—well, she could dream on. Alex was the least money-minded of persons and would see through Jasmine in a flash.

If only she had, Meg inwardly sighed. At first when Jasmine had befriended her, Meg had been only too glad of the company, only lately the very qualities that Meg had admired had started to repel. Jasmine's impetuous nature, her carefree attitude and her obsession with men were starting to irritate, and Meg was actually looking forward to cooling off the friendship a touch—ready now to complete her journey alone.

Backpacking through Europe had seemed the most unlikely of adventures for Meg to embark on. Routine was the key in Meg's life—routine was what saw her through. Routine was the only way she could control her life and the emotions that had overwhelmed her as she'd struggled to come to terms with her difficult childhood.

But now here she was, twenty-five years of age and ready to start living; ready to let go of a difficult past and truly embrace a world that had at times been so very cruel. Backpacking through Europe was the final self-imposed step in her recovery. Casual work, casual clothes and casual meals had at first been a huge enigma for Meg, but gradually she was starting to relax—that knot of tension that had been present for as long as she could remember was slowly unravelling and, as she stepped off the boat and took a deep cleansing breath, closed her blue eyes and turned her face up to the warm sun Meg knew there and then that she had been so right to embark on this journey—could hardly wait to tell her brother just how far she'd come.

'Where is he?' Jasmine's hopeful face scanned the crowd for a first glimpse of a suitable good-looking surgeon. 'Does he look like you?'

'Not in the least.' Meg laughed but didn't elaborate. Alex Hunter was as dark as Meg Donovan was blond, his eyes black where Meg's were blue. They looked nothing alike and with good reason—both were adopted, Alex when he was a toddler, Meg when she was twelve years old. But despite their differences, despite not sharing one shred of DNA, they were as close as any blood brother and sister.

'Does he know what boat you're coming on?'

'I told him ages ago.' Meg frowned. 'Well, I emailed him with the details.'

'And he got it?' Jasmine checked.

'Yes, I'm sure he got it,' Meg answered, but a trickle of unease slid down her spine. 'He *should* be here.'

'Well, it doesn't look like he is,' Jasmine pointed out as the crowd started to disperse. 'Maybe he's stuck at the hospital.'

'Maybe,' Meg answered, but she wasn't convinced. It

was *most* unlike Alex to just not turn up; if he couldn't make it himself then he'd have sent someone. 'Though I haven't checked my emails for ages. Maybe he's been trying to get hold of me.'

'So what do we do now?' Jasmine asked, her eyes scanning the notice boards. 'They said at the youth hostel there were usually loads of signs advertising for seasonal workers, but there doesn't seem to be any—not that I fancy fruit-picking!'

'It sounds fun. And you *do* need the work,' Meg pointed out. Jasmine wasn't just down to her last Euro, she was dipping into Meg's carefully planned budget and, frankly, Meg was tired of hearing Jasmine say she'd pay her back as soon as she got some work.

'Well, I think fruit-picking sounds awful.' Jasmine pouted, but soon cheered up, cheekily ripping down a notice and then pocketing it. 'This is more me. They're looking for casual staff at the casino and there's discounted accommodation—ooh, look, there's even a courtesy bus.'

'I think that's for the clientele,' Meg said as some holidaymakers who certainly weren't backpackers were escorted into the luxury vehicle.

'So?' Jasmine shrugged and pulled on her backpack as she called to the bus driver to wait for her—Meg couldn't help but smile; Jasmine was like a cat who always landed on her feet. 'Come on, Meg.'

'I don't think so.' Meg shook her head. 'A casino is the *last* place I want to be. All that noise and bustle…'

'All those rich men!' Jasmine giggled and even Meg managed a laugh. 'Come on, Meg, hold off on your search for inner peace for a few days and come and have some fun at the casino. We can share a room.'

'It's really not me.' Raking a hand through her blond hair, Meg felt the salt and grease and almost relented—given Alex wasn't here, that long soak in a bath she'd been looking forward to wasn't going to eventuate and accommodation at the casino, even if it was budget accommodation, was surely going to be better than some of the hostels she'd stayed in. 'I think I'll head over to the hospital.' Meg checked out her map. 'It isn't very far. Maybe he *is* just caught up at work. You'd better go or you're going to miss that courtesy bus.'

'Well, if it doesn't work out with your brother, you know where I am.'

'Thanks.' Meg grinned, watching as her friend climbed on the bus and waved her off, wishing, *wishing* she could, even for a little while, be as happy and as carefree as Jasmine—could relax just a little bit, could have just a fraction of her confidence. The universe itself seemed to provide Jasmine with her assured nature.

Meg watched until the tiny bus disappeared from view, filled with something she couldn't define—a hunger, a need almost for familiarity, to be able to let down her guard a touch, to be with someone who knew how hard this was for her, someone who knew that this so-called trip of a lifetime, this carefree existence, was in fact an agonising journey for her.

Where the hell was Alex?

The last e-mail he'd sent, he'd confirmed her date and time of arrival, had told her he couldn't wait to catch up, had huge news to share. Surely if his plans had changed he'd have contacted her?

But how?

Meg closed her eyes against a temporary moment of panic. She hadn't been near a computer for the last couple of weeks—happy the next leg of her tour had been arranged, she'd decided to cut loose for a while—and look where it had got her!

The taxi rank had long since closed, so, consulting her map, Meg set out on foot towards the Free Hospital where Alex had told her he was working. The midday sun combined with her heavy backpack made the relatively short distance seem to take for ever. How she'd have loved to have lingered and wandered through the pretty shops, but a backpack and a pressing lack of accommodation for the night didn't allow for such luxuries, so instead Meg stopped at one of the pavement cafés and ordered a quick coffee. Watching intrigued as the town seemingly prepared for something—shopkeepers were draping their stores with huge vines, hilarity ensuing as a few vocal locals strung banners and lights across the street, calling to each other in their colourful language as children watched on gleefully.

'Is there going to be a party?' Meg asked one of waiters whose English was better than most.

'A bigger party than you have ever seen!' Filling her cup he elaborated, 'The Niroli Feast starts tomorrow—we party for the next few days and celebrate the treasures the rich soil gives us.'

'Here?' Meg checked, gesturing to the street they were in, but the waiter just laughed.

'The whole island celebrates—you *must* stay for it,' he insisted as only the Italians could. 'I ask you—why would anyone not want to stay a while in this wonderful place?'

Why indeed?

Boosted from her shot of coffee, Meg made her way more briskly to the hospital, hoping against hope that Alex would be there and trying to fathom what she'd do if he wasn't.

\* \* \*

'Dr Alex Hunter!' Meg tried to keep her voice even, trying not to show her frustration as she said her brother's name for perhaps the tenth time. On perhaps the eleventh, the receptionist nodded her immaculately groomed head.

'*Sì*, Alessandro Fierezza!' Eagerly, again she nodded, tapping details into her computer. 'He no here, I have no contact for him. Try *palazzo!*'

*Help!*

Meg grabbed her long hair into a tight fist and let out an exasperated breath as the receptionist called on a colleague, who spoke even less English, listening to their vibrant discussion peppered with the names Alex and Alessandro and wondering what on earth she should do.

'Your brother marry.'

'But my brother is not married, he's not even engaged!' Meg gave a helpless laugh, then shook her head as in broken English the two women attempted to explain the impossible.

'*Matrimonio,*' the receptionist said firmly, nodding as Meg frowned. 'Your brother, Alessandro—'

'Alex,' Meg corrected, then slumped in defeat as the receptionist forced her to admit the truth—even if they had got the names mixed up, the simple fact was if Alex was in Niroli then he'd have met her at the port; her careful plans for the next couple of weeks flying out of the window courtesy of three little words—

'Your brother gone.'

# CHAPTER TWO

JASMINE HAD BEEN RIGHT—there *was* work at the casino.

Lots of it!

Working her way through mountain after mountain of white china plates, Meg tried to block out the noise of a busy kitchen—the chefs screaming at each other like proud cats fighting over territory, waiters collecting elaborate dishes, swooshing out of the swing doors only to return moments later, laden with half-eaten dishes to add to the pile Meg had been allocated. Not that Meg minded hard work, she'd been more than prepared for the back-breaking work of fruit-picking, but being shut up in a kitchen, her face red from the heat, her blond hair dark with sweat, was a million miles from what she'd envisaged from her time in Niroli.

Almost as soon as she'd found Jasmine and filled in an application form, Meg had been given a list of shifts. Six till ten o'clock each evening, paid in cash at the end of each of shift, which meant Meg had the whole day for exploring Niroli, and it paid well, *much* better than fruit-picking, which meant, Meg realised, if she was careful and perhaps worked a couple of extra shifts she could treat herself to a day at that luxury spa.

With renewed enthusiasm Meg tackled the mountain of

plates—the last hour of her shift made so much easier by fantasising about being smeared in the famous Niroli volcanic mud she'd read about and being thoroughly pampered and spoiled for a day!

'Faster now!' Antoinette, her colleague for the night who was rinsing and stacking the plates that Meg was washing, egged her on in her broken English, but kindly. 'We need empty sink for next staff. Or else they…' She didn't finish what she was saying—in fact a ream of sentences and orders around the kitchen remained forever incomplete, broken off midword for a reason Meg couldn't yet fathom—the swing doors opened and an immediate hush descended on the busy kitchen as a group of dark suits entered.

'Ah—sir!' The head chef jumped to nervous attention as he approached the foreboding-looking men that had entered, yet he addressed only the leader.

And even if he hadn't uttered a single word, even if she had no idea who he was, Meg knew that he was very much in charge. His jet hair was a head above the rest of them, but it wasn't just his height that set him apart—there was an authoritative air about him that would hush any room, an intimidating and overwhelming presence that had everyone in the kitchen, Meg included, on heightened alert.

'Who is he?' Meg whispered to Antoinette as slowly he toured the kitchen, talking with the staff as he did so. There was a slightly depraved look to him, a dangerous glint in those black eyes as he worked the room.

'That,' Antoinette said, in broken English, 'is the boss, Luca Fierezza. He owns the casino. A prince.'

For a simple woman like Antoinette, Meg reasoned, such an enigmatic personality *would* seem like a prince. Not for a second did it enter her head that *nothing* had been lost in translation.

He was over at the far end now, talking with some of the kitchen staff, and Meg quickly realised that this was far more than a cursory appearance by the owner, that he was actually listening to what they were saying, taking in every word and relaying them to one of his sidekicks who was faithfully writing down each word.

'He comes often,' Antoinette said. 'He make sure that everything work okay. See, now Mario tell him the trouble we are having with the shrimp—the yield was low this last two days….'

'Is that his concern?' When Antoinette frowned Meg attempted to make herself clearer. 'Isn't that a problem for the kitchen?'

'He makes it his concern,' Antoinette said, an almost proud note to her voice as she did, letting Meg know she had understood her the first time. 'This casino is the best place to play and to work—Luca makes sure of that. I work here under four different owners and he is the best.

'Come—' she nudged Meg '—work now. He is coming.'

Meg could feel him making his way over, feel the thick tension in the air as he worked the room, the raucous sound of the earlier kitchen replaced now by the quiet hum of ordered efficiency.

'Antoinette!' he greeted the elderly lady by her first name. *'Come stai?'* How are you?

*'Molto bene, grazie.'* Very well, thank you. Antoinette carried on working as she spoke, kept her head down as she addressed her boss, but, Meg noted, even if his greeting had been personable and friendly, Antoinette was keeping her respectful distance, a clear pecking order on display.

Meg glanced over as he walked past, gave him a brief polite nod as he did the same, and then picked up a plate, swishing the cloth over it, waiting for him to move on—a casual kitchen hand undoubtedly didn't merit Antoinette's more familiar greeting—only he didn't move on! Meg could feel him standing over her shoulder; feel the burn of his eyes on the back of her neck as he questioned Antoinette.

Antoinette introduced Meg and he asked something in Italian, his rich, fluid voice prompting Meg to briefly turn around.

'She's a good worker,' Antoinette responded to his question as Luca ran a dismissive eye over her, and, turning her back on him, Meg plunged her hands back into the soapy water, her skin red—not from heat or exertion, instead embarrassment, humiliation prickling every nerve as they openly discussed her without inclusion.

She was beautiful.

Luca had noticed her the second he'd walked into the kitchen, her blond head amidst the many dark ones immediately drawing his attention, her tall, willowy body forcing his gaze.

She didn't belong in the kitchen—that tall, delicate frame would wear the finest of gowns with ease; those long, delicate fingers should be wrapped around the silverware on the other side of the door; those full lips should be tasting the delicacies produced here, not clearing the aftermath. Yet she clearly thought otherwise. There was nothing martyred in her stance as she worked on, unlike some of the foreigners who came to the island—he had met one just moments before. Bold as brass, she had deemed herself too good for the manual work behind the scenes.

Only *this* lady *was* too good for this.

Too good for here, only she didn't know it yet—and now she was turning her back on him.

Luca felt the discomfort of his staff around him, registered the appalled look on Antoinette's face as this *Meg* broke with protocol as she turned her slender back to him and proceeded to work on, but instead of feeling enraged, instead of demanding that she face him when he spoke, unusually he smiled and took a step closer to her. For the first time he inhaled the scent of her and it was like pulling the stopper on a fragrance bottle, a heady rush of femininity filling his nostrils, his first instinct to touch her shoulder, to turn her around to face him, but he resisted. Instead he clenched his fingers into his palms—there would be time for that later.

*There would be a later.*

Luca knew that with the certainty of a man who always got his own way. A combination of wealth, power and devilish good looks were a heady cocktail no woman had ever refused—at least not for long. The pleasure of pursuit was a skill Luca never needed for more than the short-term. But chatting up a lowly kitchen hand was far from Luca's style, so quickly he came up with what *he* deemed a suitable solution, addressing her for the first time in English.

'We need blondes out on the casino floor. You come and see me tomorrow and we can discuss something—'

'No, thank you,' Meg interrupted, still keeping her back to him, still not looking at him, but at least she was moving now—quickly washing the dishes, anger fuelling her, appalled at the gall of him.

'I am offering you a promotion.'

'And I'm declining,' Meg answered through gritted teeth,

her hand reaching for the hose to rinse the plates and sorely tempted to turn it on him, but Luca wasn't about to be dismissed, his voice authoritative, almost daring her to defy him.

'You will turn around and face me when I speak with you.'

Oh, she'd face him, all right, Meg decided, swinging her *blond* head around, more than ready to give him a piece of her mind, more than ready to tell him just what he could do with his blatant chauvinism, but again she hadn't counted on the effect of Luca up close and personal.

He was savagely good-looking.

Savage, because the effect of him close up was utterly brutal—like staring into the sun. His beauty, his presence was so dazzling, so blinding that, though the sensible thing to do was surely tear her eyes away, to shield herself from his effect, Meg found it impossible. Instead, she took in the impeccable attire, the raven hair without even a fleck of silver, and his exquisitely chiselled face that hadn't met with a razor for the last couple of days, the dark stubble of regrowth giving him a bandit-like appearance.

Danger!

Her mind was screaming it, playing out the message in stereo in her head, yet for once her body wasn't listening. Instead it was flaming into a wicked response caused by a mere look from him and now burning with awareness as his eyes leisurely worked her, leaving Meg to beg the perilous question as to how she would respond if he so much as touched her.

'I'd prefer to work in the kitchen…' Her voice was a croak, her protest pathetically weak compared to the one she had intended, but Luca wasn't listening anyway.

'You work where I tell you to. Nine o'clock tomorrow.' His thickly accented voice clipped his order and Meg stiffened. 'You come and see me then, tell the security staff who you are when you arrive and they will show you where to go—oh, and wear something nice.'

'Lucky you.' Antoinette beamed as Luca stalked out of the kitchen followed by his entourage, but normal services were definitely not resumed, every member of the kitchen crew staring at her, awaiting her reaction as Antoinette excitedly chatted on. 'Tomorrow you will be working on the casino floor—'

'I don't want to,' Meg broke in. 'I've already told him that!' But Antoinette firmly shook her head, her voice more insistent now.

'You will do as Luca says. You *have* to go and see him—he has ordered you.'

'He can order away,' Meg said grimly, peeling off her drenched apron as Antoinette did the same, the long, exhausting shift over, and even as they took their work cards to the management and were paid for their time, somehow Meg knew that tonight had been her first and final foray as a kitchen hand at the Niroli casino, that when she didn't turn up tomorrow for *promotion*, her services would no longer be required.

But it wasn't a lack of work that was troubling Meg.

It was the effect *that* look had had on her—the fact that, despite her brave words, despite his appalling rudeness, she was actually *thinking* of going to see him again tomorrow.

Meg practically ran back to her hotel room, ran as if the devil himself were chasing her, but she couldn't outrun her feelings, shocking emotions beating her to her door.

With one look, one brief exchange, it was as if he'd somehow reached inside and flicked a switch, aroused feelings that were so deeply buried Meg was barely aware of their existence—till now. It was as if he'd undressed her right there in the kitchen with his black, knowing eyes, as if in the two seconds he'd graced her with, somehow he had peeled away every layer of clothing, leaving her vulnerable and exposed. And if ever it were possible to make love to someone and never even touch them, then that was surely what had just happened.

Tomorrow morning she'd pack her things and head to Mont Avellana, look for work in the vineyards or orange groves. She was tired of Jasmine anyway; it wasn't running away, Meg countered her own question as her shaking hand put the key in the lock.

It was about staying in control.

# CHAPTER THREE

'COME ON, Meg—loosen up and live a little!'

Since Meg had arrived back from her shift Jasmine had been attempting to persuade her to dress up and venture out to explore the night life on their doorstep, but it was positively the *last* thing Meg felt like doing. They'd been travelling since the early morning, she'd worked in the hot kitchen and that was all on top of the disappointment of missing Alex. Stepping out of the shower and falling into bed were the only things on her mind; except it was their last night together and *loosen up and live a little* had been the exact reasons for this trip. Though she might be travelling lightly, Meg's emotional baggage was weighty and few would ever know the supreme effort it took for Meg to give a casual shrug of her shoulders and finally nod in agreement. 'Just for a couple of hours,' Meg warned, peeling open her backpack and peering inside.

'Well, hurry up and don't take for ever deciding what to wear!'

Which was a joke only backpackers could understand! In an attempt to travel lightly, Meg had packed only one outfit suitable for a glamorous night out—which on the positive side removed the usual angst of what to wear, whilst on the down side…

What had she been thinking when she'd packed it?

The short black tube skirt had seemed a good choice when packing as it took up a mere square inch of her backpack, and the crushed silk azure top took up even less space; only they showed off way more of her body than Meg really felt comfortable with—the confident, assured woman she had envisaged wearing these was probably a few weeks further into her getting her life together.

Stepping back, Meg stared at her reflection, took in the slender, tanned body, her hair scooped up and twisted into a casual but elegant style. Her face that had been void of make-up for her entire trip seemed unfamiliar now—her blue eyes sparkling vividly with the help of shimmering eye shadow and a slick of black mascara, high cheekbones accentuated with a hint of rouge and her lips plump and full with the help of some lipstick. But despite the vision that stared back at her, despite the transformation that had taken place in the small, cramped bathroom, still Meg eyed herself critically, fighting the urge to rip off the clothes, to rub off the make-up, to dive into her bed and pull the sheet over her head. She almost *hated* the woman who stared back at her, the confident, feminine, sultry image that belied the terrified child inside, her exposed flesh, the curves on her body, the jutting, high breasts, provoking terror within her. She knew that tonight she'd turn heads, that men would look at her, men like Luca….

Her throat felt tight as she swallowed hard, forced herself to relive that brief encounter. She could feel his eyes burning her skin all over again, the shock of sexual awareness fizzing through her body no matter how she'd tried to douse it. Since she'd first glimpsed him, since first he'd stepped closer into her personal space, Meg had felt unsettled, as if he'd taken some imaginary spoon and skillfully stirred her some-where deep inside.

He was beautiful—even that blatantly obvious acknowl-edgement was a monumental feat for Meg, a step forward even. Too many times in the past she'd buried her feelings, refused to examine them, but standing there staring at her re-flection, her knuckles white as she gripped the sink, Meg forced herself to stay with her feelings for a moment—to *explore* them. Those dark, liquid silk eyes had caressed her, the deep drawl of his voice had moved her, and Meg ac-knowledged how much she *had* wanted to take him up on his offer, and find out what exactly he had in store for her…to see him again!

'*No!*'

She said the word out loud, pulled the window shut on the thoughts that were flittering in. He wanted her for how she looked—could look; he'd made that blatantly clear. Men like Luca were used to getting what they wanted, most women couldn't resist their charms.

Only she wasn't like most women.

'You look fantastic!' Jasmine thrust a glass of cheap wine into her hand as Meg stepped out from the bathroom. 'I adore your top. Where did you get it?'

'At a craft market in Queensland.' Meg attempted girl-talk, tried and wished to be as happy and carefree as Jasmine as they discussed her top; mind you, it was divine. The deepest azure, it scooped into a halter neck and from the front it looked elegant and simple, but it was rather more daring from behind, its low cut making the wearing of a bra impos-sible and instead revealing the vast expanse of her golden sun-kissed back and almost the entire column of her vertebra.

The crushed silk fabric was caught at the bottom and ruched together in a glittering butterfly encrusted with glass beads and semiprecious stones. The moment Meg had set eyes on it she'd wanted it—one of the few impulse buys in her life.

'Well, you look stunning,' Jasmine affirmed with a slight hiccough as she forced down her wine. 'Why on earth do you hide yourself away all the time?'

'I don't,' Meg clipped, refusing to accept the compliment and certainly not answering the question. Instead, she took a sip of the drink and screwed up her face, wondering how Jasmine managed to drink it as if it were flavoured water. Her heart rate seemed to be topping a hundred and Meg knew that if they didn't leave now, then she'd surely change her mind. 'Come on, Jasmine—let's hit the town!'

The casino was everything Meg had expected it would be and more. The white marble of the floors and walls in the vast foyer, where Jasmine and Meg stood getting their bearings, was no doubt a cool respite from the activity in the gaming rooms.

Despite the lateness of hour, it hummed with activity, elevators pinging regularly as winners and losers spilled out, heading to the bars and restaurants eager to spend their winnings or drown their sorrows, the sound of machines an ever-present backdrop. Jasmine and Meg wandered a while, peering into the designer shops, noses pressed against the windows like children at a toy shop.

'He's going to buy it for her!' Jasmine breathed, watching as a rather ancient gentlemen leant heavily on his walking frame with one hand as his other retrieved a wallet, peeling off one of many credit cards and handing it to a pouting redhead who was young enough to be his granddaughter. 'He's actually going to buy that diamond ring for her! Lucky, lucky thing!'

'Lucky?' Meg screwed up her nose in distaste, not sure who to feel sorry for—the woman who would later *pay* an extremely high price for her gift or the man who was being fleeced.

'Let's go in.' Jasmine nudged Meg, pressing the intercom and waving at the assistant who gave a snooty frown as she looked over.

'I somehow don't think we're the kind of clientele they're looking for,' Meg said, turning to go, but just as she did, surprisingly the assistant came over, gesturing to a security guard who opened the heavy glass door. Like a puppy chasing a ball, Jasmine leapt inside as Meg rather more hesitantly entered.

'Is there anything in particular you are looking for?' The assistant spoke fluent English and directed all of her questions at Meg. Embarrassed, Meg shook her head.

'We're just browsing—if that's okay?'

'Of course!'

But browsing in an exclusive jewellery shop in the Niroli casino was nothing like the high-street stores Meg usually frequented. In fact, it was like nowhere Meg had ever been in her life. Once inside, the rather snooty demeanour of the receptionist faded—slivers of bitter chocolate were offered and refused, but a glass of champagne thrust into her hand while *looking* was apparently non-negotiable—but Meg couldn't relax and enjoy. Excruciatingly aware of the security cameras whirring and homing in, and more than aware she couldn't afford as much as a keyring, all Meg wanted was out.

But Jasmine had other ideas. 'Oh, would you look at these? Have you ever seen anything as beautiful?'

*Never.*

Peering into the glass display cabinet, even Meg, who was itching to escape, was momentarily transfixed; on simple black velvet hung a pendant and earrings and, even to a novice like Meg, their worth was clearly more than the entire shop put together.

'They are very beautiful, yes?'

'Stunning!' Meg watched as her breath fogged up the glass, eyes widening as the assistant pulled out a key from her belt and opened the display cabinet.

'Clearly you appreciate the finer things—these are pieces from some of the Niroli royal family's collection. You can hold them for a moment—but that is all.'

'We can actually hold them?' Meg blinked.

'The king tries to make things more…' The assistant snapped her fingers as she attempted to locate the word she was looking for, and then settled for a longer version. 'He tries to let his people closer to the family—these are not the best pieces, of course.'

And this wasn't your average jeweller's, Meg thought. They were locked in, cameras were everywhere, but even so holding such treasures even for a short while was a rare treat.

'How much are they worth?' Jasmine asked as the assistant placed the jewels in Meg's hands, the cool of the perfect stones heavy in her heated palms, and Meg knew the answer before the assistant even spoke.

'They are not for sale. We are honoured to have them for a short while.'

'They must be insured for a figure,' Jasmine rudely pushed as Meg handed the treasures back.

'Their street value is not relevant,' the assistant answered tartly. 'These jewels stay within the royal family.'

\* \* \*

'Snooty madam!' Jasmine declared once they were outside. 'I wonder what they are worth…'

'What does it matter?' Meg asked. 'I can't believe we actually got to hold them—I wish I'd brought my camera.'

'You probably wouldn't have been allowed to use it,' Jasmine pointed out. 'Right, enough of window-shopping. I'm tired of looking at things I'll never be able to afford!'

'Let's go and buy a drink,' Meg suggested.

'Let's not!' Jasmine laughed, steering a bemused Meg out of the shopping mall and through a gaming room towards a bar. Supremely self-conscious, Meg took a seat on a bar stool, pulling her skirt down over her thighs, then fiddling with her earrings, aware that they had been noticed. More than a few heads had turned as they'd walked into the room but, instead of boosting Meg's confidence, it merely heightened her already nervous state, especially when Jasmine assuredly summoned the bartender and loudly ordered two glasses of their most expensive champagne.

'We're on a budget,' Meg whimpered, aware that the slender glass the waiter was pouring the pale golden liquid into was undoubtedly worth her entire night's spending money.

'Relax, will you?' Jasmine giggled, pulling a sequinned purse out of her evening bag, but before she'd even opened the zipper, before the drinks had even been put down on the placemats, the bartender halted her.

'It has already been taken care of.' He gestured to a nearby table, where four middle-aged businessmen sat, staring openly at them with knowing smiles.

*'Salute!'*

'Cheers!' Jasmine held her glass up in acknowledgement

to the nearby table, then winked at an appalled Meg. 'Come on, drink up. There'll be plenty more where that came from.'

'At what price, though?' Meg bit the words out—she could feel the colour mounting on her cheeks, torn between wanting to send the drinks back and not wanting to make a scene. 'Jasmine, they're going to want something….'

'Oh, for heaven's sake, Meg! Will you loosen up? For God's sake, they bought us a drink. Can't you just say thank you? It's just a bit of fun.'

Only it wasn't.

As Meg had predicted, as soon as the glasses met their lips the men made their way over, sleazy chat-up lines were followed by sleazy chat-up lines, a bottle of champagne soon appeared, and all she wanted was to get the hell out, knowing the money that was being spent on them had nothing to do with their engaging conversation, nothing to do with a man wanting to get to know a woman. It had been a mistake to come—a horrible, horrible mistake.

'They want us to play the tables!' Jasmine said gleefully as Meg bit back a smart retort. 'Come on!'

She was tired of pointing things out to Jasmine—tired of acting like a boring big sister when Jasmine clearly didn't want to hear what she had to say.

'I'm going to bed.'

'Bed!' Jasmine gave her a wide-eyed look. 'It isn't even midnight. Come on, Meg. It will be fun.'

'It's not my kind of fun,' Meg answered. 'Look, Jasmine, I'm tired and I don't particularly like the company we're keeping. If you want to stay on, then that's up to you. Just be careful.'

'Five minutes,' Jasmine pleaded. 'Then slip away— pretend you're going to the loo or something.'

They were already at the gaming area, Jasmine's eyes glittering from the champagne and attention as Meg attempted her excuses. There was nothing subtle now about the men's advances—one of them offered her a chip to play the roulette table, which Meg refused, a prickle of fear running down her spine as Jasmine accepted. Things were really starting to get out of control.

'Thirty, red.' Jasmine kissed her chip and placed it on the table as Meg watched on. She'd never played roulette. Oh, she'd seen it on films, but she had no idea of the rules and absolutely no desire to find out, but her escort was insistent, pushing the chip into her hand.

'No!' Meg almost shouted the word and flung the beastly chip at him. She wanted nothing from him, nothing at all. And, boring or not, she was going to get Jasmine out of here and tell her she was flirting with danger. Once this beastly game was over, even if she had to frog-march her to the toilet, *that* was what she was going to do!

'Your bet, please.'

As the businessman who had latched onto Meg pushed the chip back into her hand, Meg again shook her head, but table etiquette demanded she now play, and if Meg didn't want to make a scene then she had no option but to place her bet. 'Black seventeen,' she said, plucking a number from midair and pulling out her purse, refusing to baulk when the croupier informed her of the minimum bet and handing over her entire night's wages plus a touch more.

Meg barely watched as the wheel spun. Her eyes were seemingly on it, but her mind was elsewhere. Sensing the leering stares of her companions, feeling a hand lingering too long as it brushed her back, she wished this moment over, willed the ball to stop anywhere, for this awful night to end.

Tomorrow she was leaving…. The wheel was slowing down as her jumbled thoughts assimilated into some sort of order, her mind calming as she worked out a rudimentary plan: her job in the kitchen was over, when she didn't show up in Luca's office tomorrow she'd be out on her ear anyway, and tonight Jasmine had delivered the last straw. She was tired of Jasmine, tired of Niroli come to that—she'd had nothing but trouble and disappointment since she'd arrived. First thing tomorrow she'd head to back to the port, catch a boat to Mont Avellana perhaps. She'd heard there was seasonal work there…. Only the ball was moving now, rattling around the stilling wheel and even though the tension at the table was building, now she had a plan, for Meg it was abating….

Until the ball landed in its slot and all hell broke loose.

Black, seventeen!

# CHAPTER FOUR

'TABLE FOUR; move in closer!'

Luca's order was swiftly obeyed, the security camera zooming in on the minor commotion in the general public gaming room, the winning figure being relayed to Dario, his Chief of Security, through an earpiece and passed on to Luca, who didn't bat an eyelid. It was small pickings compared to the figures he dealt with on a daily and nightly basis and, more to the point, in a few hours the winnings would most probably be fed back into the casino. No, it wasn't the money that intrigued Luca, it was the reaction of the women that held his attention now. One was jumping up and down, accepting champagne and kisses in all directions, and for a moment Luca thought the information he'd been given must be wrong—that surely she must be the winner—because the other woman stood apart, her stance almost disappointed at her sudden fortune.

'Closer!' Luca snapped his fingers impatiently, his eyes narrowing as he recognised one of them. The bold kitchen-hand that had approached him earlier this evening and asked to be considered for work out on the casino floor. He'd declined her instantly and if her behaviour now was anything to go by then he'd been right to do so. But who was the other woman?

Could it be her?

Shamelessly he ordered the camera to focus in on her, and his staff complied, more than used to Luca taking his rich pickings: zooming in on the prettiest girl in the room and observing her for a few moments before making his move. As if he were a lion stalking his prey, this was his domain and everyone present knew it.

It *was* her! Luca's eyes narrowed as he focussed on her image. He'd been right with his first assessment—she didn't belong in the kitchen scrubbing dishes—but neither did she belong down there being fawned and harassed, and now that she had won some money she was even more of a target. He knew how this place worked, knew that the euphoria after a win was a dangerous time, that those men would take full advantage…and it made him feel sick to the stomach.

'Who are those guys with them?' Luca asked his staff.

'Some businessmen they picked up earlier. We've been watching them for the last hour or so—they've been buying the girls drinks and now they're giving them money to play the tables—the usual.'

Which it was—this type of thing happened every hour of every day in the casino; Luca knew that more than anyone. So why, then, did he feel so disappointed? Why, then, did he feel as if he'd just been punched in the stomach?

'She paid for her own bet, though,' Dario added, listening to some information being relayed through a head piece, and, if it was seemingly a useless piece of information, it was relevant on two counts for Luca. On a professional level it made things easier for the security staff to deal with—her escort had no claim on her, there could be no pointless argument about whose money had aided the bet—but for far more personal reasons, for reasons he could barely fathom, somehow, to Luca it mattered.

It mattered a lot.

'The croupier just let us know—things are starting to get out of hand.' Dario ground out the cigar he had been smoking and focussed more cameras on the area. 'She's trying to leave, but the men insist that she stay and celebrate with them—the croupier wants the floor security to come over.'

He could sense Meg's nervousness. Those gorgeous eyes were darting, glancing around the room as if hoping to be rescued, flicking to the surveillance camera for a single second, holding his gaze without knowing it, seemingly asking him for help.

'Do it.' Luca snapped his fingers impatiently, watching on another screen as almost instantaneously the security guards made their way through the busy gaming room, the well-oiled machines of the casino moving into swift action—any potential *situation* swiftly dealt with before it escalated. Luca knew his hand-picked staff were more than capable of dealing with this, knew that in a matter of moments things would easily be brought discreetly under control and the small crowd dispersed, so why then was he pulling on his jacket, filled with something, a need almost to get out there and help her himself?

He snapped his fingers again—ordering his cheque-book and writing out a figure in his impressive violet scrawl, then stalking out of the room as his bodyguards followed without a word. They were more than used to Luca Fierezza's routine when a pretty girl won: most of her winnings would be delivered personally by cheque, so that she couldn't spend it, which got him straight to second base because it showed her he was looking out for her best interests—first base had

already been passed courtesy of his stunning good looks—
and for the final run, with the percentage of cash he handed
her, he'd invite her to join him in the high-rollers club.

Home run.

'Congratulations!'

His voice was instantly recognisable—and Meg started
in recognition as she heard it, her startled eyes swinging
round to his, actually grateful for his presence. Since her
number had come up the table had been a frenzy of activity,
everyone around her eager to celebrate, pressing her to join
in, to carry on and party into the night, when all she wanted
to do was disappear, for the glare of the spotlight to dim from
her—and now it had.

Luca was the only one who held the spotlight, the only
man in the place who could instantly regain control by his
mere presence, and regain control he did. Meg's unwelcome
companion actually melted away without even a murmur of
protest as Luca ushered Meg over to a quiet table, pouring
her a glass of water, which she accepted gratefully, before
handing her her winnings.

'Most of it is in a cheque—you can come tomorrow
morning and cash it.' He smiled at her frown. 'People often
blow their winnings, by tomorrow morning you will be more
restrained.'

'I'm more than in control now.' She gave a tight smile.
'In fact all I want to do is get the hell out of here. Is it always
so…?' She fumbled for a word for a moment and failed to
come up with one, but Luca, even with his rather more
limited disposal of the English language, found the one she
was looking for, or at least one that came close.

'Frenzied?' he offered as Meg gave a nod. 'Always.

Especially when a…' His voice trailed off as he realised somehow that she'd had an earful of shallow compliments tonight, that telling her she was beautiful was probably the last thing she wanted to hear right now. 'Join me upstairs.' He watched her eyes widen, and smiled. 'I mean, there is a quieter gaming room upstairs—a little more civilized, perhaps…' She knew where he meant—the high-rollers club. She'd seen it when she'd arrived, the elevator neatly roped off with security ensuring that only the richest and most beautiful went there, but it held little appeal for Meg.

'I'm actually really tired, but thank you for the offer,' Meg politely declined. 'I think I'll just go to bed.'

'Meg!' She hadn't realised Jasmine was standing behind her, but her indignant wail alerted Meg, followed by a very harsh whisper in her ear. 'You simply cannot turn down an invitation like that. Come on, please say yes—I don't know how to get rid of these guys!'

*The same guys she's been accepting drinks and gambling chips from all night,* Meg thought, but she felt herself relenting; as much as Jasmine had provoked things by accepting so much hospitality, she couldn't just turn her back on her. Maybe a quiet escape to somewhere more *civilised* would give her a chance to talk to Jasmine and tell her how precarious her situation was with those guys, and surely one drink with Luca couldn't hurt….

Who was she kidding?

The memory stick of her camera was full of photos of her travels, packed with exotic locations she'd wanted to capture for ever, but nothing came close to the man sitting opposite her at the table—whether she went for a drink or not, already his image was branded in her mind. As arrogant, as presumptuous as he'd been earlier, still she hadn't been able to shake the feeling he evoked.

'Can my friend Jasmine come?' Meg watched as his eyebrows furrowed slightly, wondered at the thought process behind the tiny gesture.

Luca didn't want her *friend* to come, didn't want the brash woman to join them—strange, he'd actually thought till now they might be sisters. They were both blond, both fairly tall, only this Jasmine was like a crude caricature of Meg. She had none of her delicacy, none of her subtle beauty and her conduct certainly wasn't befitting of the high-rollers club—yet Luca knew it was the only way he could get Meg to join him, that if he didn't act quickly, at any moment she was going to terminate the evening, so, forcing a smile, he gave a small nod.

'Of course!'

But, for once, Luca had misread a woman, because it wasn't Jasmine forcing Meg to take Luca up on his invitation, it wasn't some misguided sense of duty that had her standing up and heading towards the velvet rope that was pulled back as Luca approached.

It was something else propelling her tonight—something Meg usually chose to ignore. Whether it be hunger or emotion, it was something she usually stifled—only not tonight.

Feeling his hand on the small of her back as Luca guided her into the exclusive VIP lift, Meg acknowledged what she was feeling….

Want.

And this was a *want* she somehow couldn't deny.

Some friend, Luca thought scornfully as within seconds of arriving Jasmine disappeared into the thick fog of smoke, her inbuilt radar homing in on the richest, loudest table, and, frankly, Luca was happy to see the back of her, more than happy to turn his attention to the rather aloof woman who sat before him.

'Normally people smile when they win.'

'I was actually hoping to lose.' Meg gave a small laugh at his bemused frown. 'I wasn't particularly enjoying myself!'

'You don't like my casino?'

'No,' Meg admitted, but softened her rather brittle response with a smile. 'Though don't take it personally—I'm not really a big fan of clubs and bars, people shouting over each other just to be heard…' Conversation here was surprisingly easy. After the noise from below, the exclusive upstairs area was quieter with no gaming machines. Luca had selected a secluded area for them at a low couch well away from the tables, but it wasn't just the ambience that made talking easier—without his entourage, seated beside her, those brooding eyes and haughty features softened by the dim lighting, he was far less intimidating. In fact, after the pandemonium of before and the unwelcome company she'd been keeping, Luca Fierezza's controlled demeanour was a refreshing change—only it wasn't relaxing for Meg. Far from it!

The seedy attempts at chat-ups Meg had encountered downstairs had made her uncomfortable, ill at ease, but she didn't feel like that with Luca. Unsettled was how he made her feel. Though he hadn't lifted so much as a finger in her direction and his conversation had been supremely polite, there was definitely an awareness, a tension between them, and she knew he was biding his time, felt as if he was slowly, mentally circling her, waiting to make a move. She knew that it wasn't by accident she'd ended up at this casino magnate's table.

For the second time that night a bottle of champagne

appeared without order, only this time Meg found it easier to decline. 'I'd actually prefer some water.'

'Of course—would you like something to eat? We can—'

'I'm not hungry,' Meg interrupted quickly, but as he sent the waiter away with a flick of his wrist and proceeded to pour them both water she rather regretted her haste. Not just because she was, in fact, hungry, but because part of her wanted to stay, to linger a while longer in his presence…to simply relax and enjoy the company of this astonishingly beautiful man. Even his hands were sexy, neatly manicured fingers, olive skin contrasting with the heavy white cotton cuffs of his shirt, but Meg's forehead knitted in concentration as she glimpsed his gold cufflinks, trying to place where she'd seen the image before. Engraved on the heavy gold was the image of an orange tree surrounded by vines… She tried in vain to place them, giving in when Luca distracted her with a question.

'Are you on holiday?' Luca checked and Meg nodded.

'I'm backpacking around Europe. I've been away from home for three months.'

'And are you enjoying yourself?'

Meg hesitated a fraction too long before nodding, and Luca must have noticed the tiny pensive pause because he dismissed her enthusiastic response with an observation.

'You don't look like a backpacker.'

'What do backpackers look like?'

'Carefree,' Luca mused, 'out for fun—they certainly don't normally decline the offer of a free drink.'

'And you must know so many,' Meg responded with a heavy dash of sarcasm. Luca Fierezza's world was light years away from the one she'd inhabited these last months and she was annoyed at his assumptions—that she was some starving wretch who would jump at the chance of a free meal and an expensive drink.

He ignored her sarcasm. 'We have many backpackers that come to Niroli—some to holiday and enjoy the magnificent beaches, others for casual work.'

'It is a beautiful island,' Meg admitted. 'Well, from the little I've seen of it. I was looking forward to exploring it and…' She didn't continue, just snapped her mouth closed, realising she'd given him an opening, and Meg felt a stab of disappointment when instead of pouncing on it he instead asked a question. 'So how long do you intend to stay in Niroli?'

'I'm not sure,' Meg admitted. 'I actually came to Niroli to meet up with my brother, but there was a miscommunication. I was thinking of leaving to see if I can find work.'

'You already have a job,' Luca pointed out, for the first time acknowledging their encounter in the kitchen. 'And tomorrow you will have a better one.'

'Tomorrow I might decide to dye my hair.' Meg didn't bat an eyelid, stared coolly at him as she spoke. 'Then I won't be blond enough for you.'

'I was trying to help….' Luca attempted, but Meg shook her head at his attempt at an excuse.

'Well, you didn't,' she bristled. 'Tell me something— how come you didn't ask me to join you for dinner back in the kitchen?'

'I don't understand?'

'Oh, I think you do,' Meg said shrewdly. 'Anyway, it's irrelevant. Tomorrow, I'm going to head to Mont Avellana and look for some seasonal work.'

'Mont Avellana?' Luca sneered. 'Why would you possibly want to go there?'

'I've heard it's beautiful.'

'It is nothing compared to Niroli,' Luca derided in distaste. 'Full of gypsy *Viallis*—there is nothing for you there!'

'I'm sure they speak highly of you!' Meg made a flip comment and instantly regretted it, watching as his face darkened.

Oh, she'd read about the battle between the islands—knew that Mont Avellana was now a republic and that there was still simmering resentment between the two islands—but the way Luca was talking told Meg that this was more than just patriotism. This was hatred born from the cradle and taken to the grave. 'I'm sorry,' Meg offered, unable to comprehend that it was so, so... *personal* to Luca, but realising she had hit a raw nerve. 'I've clearly no idea what I'm talking about.'

It took a moment for him to translate her vague humour, but he accepted it with a gracious smile, swiftly changing the subject as only he could!

'Anyway—you can't go to Mont Avellana tomorrow—you are meeting with me.'

'I said no, remember.' Meg smiled, but it died on her lips as she caught his eyes. They weren't touching, a generous few inches separated them on the sofa, but she could sense his body, feel the heat of him next to her. It wouldn't have mattered where they were, whether in a busy kitchen or the luxurious surrounds of the high roller club, because again it was just the two of them—the subtle, almost indefinable process of man and woman gauging each other, that delicious heightened awareness when every move, every gesture, revealed itself in slow motion. As her tongue bobbed out to moisten her dry lips Meg knew, *knew*, he was imagining the taste of her, knew that in this volatile climate even that tiny gesture could be construed as provocative...because it had been. He provoked her, in the most unsettling of ways. He made her dizzy. It was as if she were riding on a carousel, snatching images as she whirred ever faster; images not just of the man sitting before her now, but dangerous glimpses of where this night could lead—that full, sensual mouth pressed onto hers, the feel of his hard, toned body pressed against hers. Never had a man moved her so—never had she felt such a compelling attraction to someone, never had she been more tempted to throw caution to the wind, to let some romance into her ordered life….

*To loosen up and live a little.*

Till he spoke!

'I'm sure *whatever* job you want, it can be accommodated.'

Never had she been more grateful for the dimmed lighting as a dark, burning blush swept up her neck and over her cheeks, her mouth dry all of a sudden, her heart hammering in her chest, unsure if she'd misinterpreted and appalled if she hadn't—was he offering her a job in his casino or in his bedroom?

'I speak no Italian.' Giving him the benefit of the doubt, Meg chose her words carefully. 'I don't really see what sort of work…'

'It doesn't have to be in the casino; perhaps you would like to spend your time in Niroli with me?'

'With you!' She let out a shocked gasp at his directness. 'You're offering me a job as your escort!'

'Meg—' immediately he shook his head '—I think you misunderstand. I am requesting your company for a period of time. I would like us to have a chance to get to know each other better. As you will understand, I'm sure, I am not permitted the luxury of casual dates—I am not able to suggest we meet tomorrow afternoon for coffee or a chat, or a wander on the beach—'

'Because you're too busy?' Meg interrupted scornfully. 'Too busy to deal with something as trivial as getting to know another person—oh, but if they look okay, if they can string a sentence or two together and are impressed enough by your status, then you'll simply bypass the superfluous and cut straight to the chase.'

Her angry words didn't faze him—anything but. A smile on his lips revealed very white, very even teeth. 'I think you're overreacting.'

'Do you!' Meg gave him a wide-eyed look—she really couldn't believe the audacity of him. Yes, he was stunning to look at, and, yes, she conceded, they were attracted to each other, but to have the nerve to sit there and offer to *buy* her company for a few weeks made her blood boil—that he was so pompous, so full of his self-importance to think he was *above* the social niceties, infuriated her.

'As I said, you misunderstand….'

'I don't think so.' For the first time in a long time, instead of holding it in, Meg let it out—disappointment, embarrassment all aiding her in a very few choice words. 'I'm surprised you offered dinner. Why don't we just go straight upstairs to your luxury suite?'

'Excuse me?' For the first time she startled him—a flicker of confusion in his eyes as she confronted him.

'Your luxury suite. I'm sure you've got one waiting—and given that you're clearly too busy and important for something as trivial as romance or dating, and given that I'm too tired for a late night, why don't we just go straight up there and get it over and done with?'

As his face darkened for a second Meg thought she'd gone too far—questioned the wisdom of speaking in such a manner to a man she barely knew, her feisty, sarcastic tones maybe open to misinterpretation, but as her words hit home his anger faded. The smile that had been on his lips before returned with vengeance now as he threw back his head and laughed out loud, until Meg actually managed a reluctant smile of her own.

'You are always this angry?'

'Only when I'm mistaken for a prostitute!'

'Never!' His thumb and finger found her chin, lifting her face so her eyes were level with his—touching her for the first time, the shock of contact with him tumbling her into confusion because despite her angry words before, despite the sarcasm that had laced them, she wanted him—wanted what she had moments before scorned.

Wanted him to make love to her.

'Eat with me,' Luca offered again and it was sheer self-preservation that made her shake her head, determined to politely end the conversation and just get the hell out before she did something stupid—something she would surely regret. She was here to sort her life, not complicate it further, and being a paid mistress to this man was surely a recipe for disaster!

'No.' Meg dragged the word out, jerked her chin away to break the contact as, reaching down, she picked up her bag and stood up. 'As I said, I'm very tired. Thank you for your hospitality.'

'You haven't allowed me to show you any hospitality.' He stood up as she did, clearly taken aback by her abrupt change of mood. 'But that is your choice.' He gave a brief shrug. 'I will walk you back.'

'I don't need to be walked back,' Meg declined, but Luca begged to differ.

'Your friend appears to be busy and those men are no

doubt still downstairs. It would be better if I walk you back to your room.'

If it had been anyone else offering it would have made sense. Meg had no desire to run into that group again, but neither did she want to walk with Luca. It wasn't that she didn't trust him—not for a minute did she imagine him forcing himself on her as that creepy businessman had before—but he had made his intentions exceptionally clear and so now must she.

'Thank you for the offer, Mr Fierezza, I mean, *Signor* Fierezza, but I'd prefer—'

'Luca,' he interrupted.

'I'd rather keep things formal,' Meg said crisply back, but she couldn't look at him, instead staring down at the ground, ready to turn on her heel and walk off.

'Well, in that case, my correct title is: His Royal Highness Prince Luca of Niroli.'

As her startled eyes shot up to his, despite the twist of a smile on Luca's lips at her reaction, she knew in an instant he was speaking the truth. Antoinette *hadn't* got her words mixed up, those cufflinks he was wearing, Meg realised in a flash, were actually the Niroli coat of arms she'd seen in her guide book, but it wasn't just that that convinced her, it was his sheer arrogance, the absolute confident way he carried himself—which told her he would never stoop to lying to impress a woman.

'There will be no discussion. I *will* walk you back to your room.' His hand touched her elbow and she practically shot into orbit at the contact, any argument fading on her lips as he guided her to the opening door.

'Oh, and Meg…' as the elevator glided open, as he

declined the escort from his bodyguard, Luca managed to elicit a smile from her shocked lips '…you can call me Prince for short.'

As they walked through the casino, his hand still on her elbow, Meg's mind was whirring. They made their way swiftly—he didn't need to guide her through the throng of people because they all stepped back for him, heads turning, couples nudging each other as they passed, and Meg started to understand what he had been trying to tell her. A prince couldn't date in the usual way, couldn't walk into a bar unrecognised or linger over a coffee as he got to know a virtual stranger, and those thoughts were confirmed when finally they left the crowds behind and walked the long corridor to her room.

'You didn't know?'

'No,' Meg admitted. "Antoinette, the kitchen hand, did say something, but I thought she was…' She gave a helpless shrug. 'Shouldn't you be locked away in a palace or something, with bodyguards protecting you?'

'I should be according to my grandfather—the king,' he added as Meg blew a breath skywards, the entire conversation so bizarre she couldn't believe it was taking place. 'But it is not how I choose to live; I like to work—to run my businesses. Here I get a shot of a normal life.'

'Normal!' Meg gave a wry grin. 'Even before I heard your title, Luca, you didn't fit into that description.'

'I have a comfortable life—but I work hard for it. Yes, I can afford many things, and maybe I could just live off my title, but I still take pride in my work, my business ventures—that is why I mainly choose not to use my title, why here I prefer to be called just Luca, though naturally most people know who I am.'

They were at her door now and Meg wished they weren't, wished somehow she were staying in some remote cottage at the end of a very long beach, instead of a shared room a mere ten minutes away…

She didn't want the night to end—even though she'd terminated it, now she wanted to prolong it and it had nothing to do with his royal title, more the fascinating man behind it, the man she was starting to glimpse.

'Thank you,' Meg said simply.

'For what?'

'For coming over when you did. Things could have got out of hand otherwise.'

'You have to be careful, Meg. Your friend is not much of an escort for you.'

'I don't need an escort,' Meg answered stoutly, but Luca remained unmoved, shaking his head at her proud words.

'Tonight things could have been very different—I see a lot of things that go on. Buy your own drinks, Meg, and hold onto your glass. Don't let it out of your sight.'

'You sound like my father.' Meg rolled her eyes as she chatted. 'When I say my father, I mean my adopted father. I had all the lectures before I set off on my trip—'

Her voice halted abruptly; she was stunned at her own words, at how easily she'd revealed a piece of herself to Luca. She'd been with Jasmine for weeks yet she had never revealed this, yet here she was, an hour into Luca's company, and she was opening up like a flower in the sun with him. But Luca didn't seem to notice the revelation, just carried on the conversation where she had so hastily left it.

'I would not like to be your father.' He gave a wry smile. 'I am sure the man must never rest, worrying about his beautiful daughter.' He'd called her beautiful and instead of flinching or refusing to take the compliment she absorbed it, even felt a little bit beautiful. Luca stared thoughtfully back at her. 'You're not going to come tomorrow?' When she shook her head he pushed for a reason. 'Can I ask why?'

She paused for a moment before answering, wondered how on earth she could explain that, though she wanted to, though she was more attracted to him than she'd ever been to *anyone*, it was just too dangerous, too damned scary to let him into her life. 'I don't want to complicate my life; the reason I'm travelling is that I'm actually trying to sort a few things out….' Meg answered as honestly as she could without telling him her painful truth. 'And, somehow, I don't think spending time with you is going to help me achieve that.'

'It might.'

'I doubt it.' Meg gave a rueful smile. How could a holiday romance with a royal prince possibly help her find the peace she craved? But never had she been more tempted to relent, the rigid self-discipline she usually lived by treacherously displaced by his presence. 'It's been nice meeting you, Luca.'

'May I kiss you *goodbye?*'

She'd been about to shake her head, to refuse his request for a kiss goodnight, but his choice of words had her hesitating.

It really *was* goodbye.

A chance encounter that would never in her life be repeated—men like Luca didn't come around twice in a lifetime—and Meg bit down on her lip, torn between fear and want, sensing the danger yet lusciously curious.

'I don't think that's a very good idea,' Meg breathed, her hormones weeping in protest as she denied them the goodies that were clearly on offer as her mind scrambled to regain control. 'Anyway, I thought it was supposed to be the other way around.' He was watching her mouth as she spoke, as she attempted a joke, attempted to delay the inevitable. 'We're supposed to kiss and *then* you turn into a prince!'

'For you, maybe there is better.' His hand was on her cheek, his thumb playing with her lower lip. 'You *deserve* better,' Luca elaborated. 'Maybe your kiss would make me a king.'

She didn't know if he was joking, didn't know if it was just a light-hearted response, and frankly she didn't care—Luca was as skilled at flirting as he was at manipulating. His mouth was just inches away, teasing her with his breath as he spoke, honing in on her distraction, asking for something only moments ago she wouldn't have considered.

'Don't go to Mont Avellana tomorrow—spend the day with me instead.'

Breathless, dizzy and deliciously disorientated, she struggled with what now seemed a straightforward question, her mind trying to recall the reasons she should decline.

'The day?'

'I'll show you Niroli—and maybe then you'll decide to stay on for a while, maybe you can find the peace you crave here.'

She opened her mouth to protest, to remind him why she couldn't stay, but with a few words Luca had made the impossible suddenly feasible. Taking a strand of hair, he brushed it behind her ear, all the while staring into her eyes. 'We are two very different people but with one constant.' He didn't need to elaborate, their arousal, their attraction achingly evident, but Luca broke the contact, stepped back into the hallway and asked her a very pertinent question. 'Did refusing my kiss give you peace?'

She didn't say anything but Meg's answer was obvious, her whole body screaming a protest at Luca's rapid withdrawal.

'I will be in the foyer tomorrow at nine.'

He walked away then—Luca's bid clearly in, leaving it

for Meg to decide. He didn't even offer a backward glance as he walked back along the corridor, leaving Meg jumbled and confused, fumbling in her bag for her keys, then entering her room and sitting on the bed, somehow trying to make sense of all that had occurred.

They couldn't last.

That much Meg understood.

But they couldn't end yet either, Meg realised; the attraction was too strong, the emotion too intense to just walk away.

Pulling out her purse, Meg slid her fingers into the wallet and pulled out a well-worn picture, one she hadn't looked at in weeks, but occasionally, at times like this, when decisions needed to be made, it was called upon. Even though she'd seen it a thousand times, even though she'd *lived* it, still the image shocked her.

Pained eyes in a gaunt face stared back at Meg, her skeletal frame engulfed by a wheelchair, a nurse at her side holding her hand as she struggled to come up from her lowest point.

There were a million reasons to set her alarm for six and get the hell out of Niroli, to organise her backpack and literally run for the hills.

But there was one very good reason to stay. Falling asleep with the photo still in her hand, Meg was only vaguely aware of Jasmine bumping around in the night, her mind focussed on one thought only.

Tonight, for the first time in her life, and only with Luca, she'd actually felt beautiful.

# CHAPTER FIVE

'I'M GLAD YOU decided to stay.'

As Luca joined her in the crowded foyer, Meg was glad she'd decided to stay too. The hour between waking and seeing him had plagued Meg with doubt and indecision. She was almost sure that her vision of the man she had met last night wouldn't stand up to the scrutiny of the morning glare, that somehow seeing him again could only taint the delicious memory.

Wrong.

If anything, Luca was more stunning.

Dressed casually in dark denim jeans and a black T-shirt, unshaven and unkempt, he looked even more ravishing, but there was no time for awkward small talk, no time for anything at all really, as Luca took her by her arm and shepherded her out the foyer and straight into the luxurious confines of a sleek silver sports car.

'I thought today was supposed to be relaxing!' Meg attempted as the car sped away from the casino.

'Now, it will be,' Luca said cryptically, glancing in the rear-view mirror and finally slowing down. 'I'll ring Luigi now and tell him I haven't been kidnapped.'

'Your bodyguard?' Meg checked as Luca nodded and

punched in speed-dial. Even if her Italian was extremely limited, it soon became clear that Luigi was less than impressed at his boss's hasty exit.

'Sorry about that.' Luca grinned when the call ended. 'Luigi is supposed to accompany me whenever I go outside the casino or palace. I do not like it.'

'I wouldn't either.' Meg smiled, glancing shyly over to him. 'I'm glad it's just us.'

'Me too.' Luca nodded. 'You look wonderful!'

'Er, I doubt it.' Meg grimaced. Never had her backpack's offerings appeared more measly. She'd been hoping to spend yesterday getting acquainted with a washing machine, but for the biggest date of her life she'd been left with no choice other than faded denim shorts and a pale lemon halter-neck. Still, given it was Luca, she'd bypassed her runners for some gorgeous leather sandals she'd purchased in Rome, and instead of scraping her hair back into its usual sightseeing fare of a pony-tail had blow-dried it and left it down. 'I wasn't exactly inundated with choice.'

'Inundated?' Luca checked.

'Spoilt…' Meg attempted to no avail. 'I don't have many clothes to choose from—I've tried to pack something for most eventualities, but a day trip with royalty wasn't something I'd planned on!'

'We may not get into the restaurant I wanted to go to for lunch—I don't think they allow shorts…' Luca shrugged '…but that's no problem.'

'Sorry.' Meg flinched.

'I tease you.' Luca laughed. 'There are some perks to being a prince—you could be wearing nothing more than a bikini and we would get the best table. I meant what I said—you look wonderful.'

She did.

Luca, too, had been wondering what to expect this morning. So many times before the raw beauty he'd witnessed in a woman had disappeared the second she'd found out *who* he was—commandeering the salon, spending up in the boutique. He'd almost resigned himself to greeting a stranger this morning, yet here she was, more beautiful, more vibrant, more sexy than the woman he had met last night—acres of soft, browned skin on show, her hair a blond fragrant cloud, and just a slick of gloss on those incredibly kissable lips….

'Where are we going?'

'Does it matter?'

Turning his attention from the road for a second, he held her gaze and Meg bit down on her lip, processing his question for a moment before answering, her single-word answer the boldest thing she'd ever said.

'No.'

In fact, if they never set foot out of the car, Meg wouldn't have minded. Dressed more casually, and well away from the extravagance and decadence of the casino, Luca was infinitely more relaxed, his company engaging. But Luca actually did have plans for the day. He wanted to show her all that Niroli had to offer and show her he did, gliding the sleek car through the steep hills, at every turn the view even more stunning.

'No more!' Luca grinned when Meg begged him to stop for yet another photo shoot. 'Or you will run out of space—wait till we get to the ruins. We stop now at one of the wineries and I'll ask them to make us a picnic.'

Which, when it was Luca Fierezza asking, meant that a blanket was included, the hamper groaning under the weight of Niroli delicacies, and Meg wanted to taste them all, only not just yet—first they spent a sun-drenched day exploring. Luca steered them well away from the usual tourist haunts in the south of the island and instead headed north where he showed her the ancient Roman ruins, regaling her with tale after tale, making her privy to information that could never be gleaned from a history book. But as excellent a tourist guide as he made, as much as he seemed to enjoy showing her Niroli, the day was about them—the sultry air thicker somehow when blended with desire, awareness thrumming as they explored, not just the temple and amphitheatre, but each other's minds. And by the time Luca spread out the blanket and they shared their picnic, Meg knew a single day could never be enough to scratch the surface of all it had to offer—only she wasn't thinking about Niroli!

'Here,' Luca said proudly, pouring her an icy glass of champagne as she gazed around the amphitheatre. 'There are often concerts held here—there will be one this weekend....'

'For the Feast?'

'You have heard about it?'

'One of the shopkeepers told me.' Meg gave an abstracted nod, biting into slivers of bitter orange dipped in dark chocolate and closing her eyes as she relished the taste. 'This,' she declared, 'is the nicest thing I've ever tasted.'

'You said that about the olive dip, and then the cannoli. It is good to see someone who likes their food.' Luca frowned at her reaction. 'Why does that make you laugh?'

'It just does.' Meg's answer was evasive, a first date not really the best time to slip in the little gem of the eating disorder that had ruled her for years, but, closing her eyes, Meg lay back and smiled as the warm sun bathed her, relishing the moment, his casual observation a revelation. Here, away from it all, for the first time in the longest time, she'd actually forgotten her problem, *had* just enjoyed food as it should be enjoyed. Oh, she was long past the frantic calorie counts, way, way past controlling every morsel she consumed, but to simply *enjoy*… Luca could never have even hazarded a guess as to how much this moment meant to her.

'You are having a good time?' Luca enquired, lying down on the blanket beside her, his body just inches away, so achingly close all Meg wanted to do was reach over and touch him. She could feel the hum of sexual energy between them, his masculinity bathing her now, only with more ferocity than the sun, her skin tingling as even with her eyes still closed she could feel him watching her.

'It's been great.'

'It has…' Luca let out a long sigh, his body so close she could feel his chest move beside her. 'It is nice to relax.'

'I don't suppose you get much chance,' Meg offered. 'What with work and…' She gave a tiny frown, peeped her eyes open to look at him. 'Do you have to do all the ceremonial, well…stuff?' She gave a helpless shrug but thankfully Luca understood.

'Always there are commitments. Take this weekend—there will be many events I have to attend as a royal prince.'

'You don't sound as if you want to?'

'It is not about want, it is about duty,' Luca explained. 'It is what is expected of me—and lately…' He didn't finish, just shook his head, but Meg's curiosity was piqued now.

'Lately?' she pushed.

'You ask too many questions. It is not correct.'

'Excuse me?' Meg's eyes were wide open now as Luca attempted to put her in her place.

'You should not pry so much. I will tell you what you need to know.'

'I don't *need* to know anything.' Meg gave a shocked laugh. 'I was asking because I *wanted* to know. And don't pull rank on me when it suits!'

'It is not about pulling rank—when you are out with royalty—'

'But I'm not,' Meg broke in, disarming his rather terse response with a smile. 'I'm out with Luca—remember? That was the reason you left Luigi behind, that was the whole point of today—to get to know each other a bit better away from it all.'

'Are you always this argumentative?'

'Always.' Meg smiled as Luca's face blackened. 'Now, if there's something you'd prefer not to discuss, then you just have to say so, but, please, don't hide behind your title!'

Closing her eyes, she lay her head back down and even though her heart was hammering in her chest at the small confrontation, she certainly wasn't about to let him know that. If Luca thought he could talk to her like that, then he'd better do a quick rethink! And, Meg decided, if he didn't break the angry silence, then she certainly wouldn't—she'd start snoring if she had to!

'When I was younger I…' as Luca conceded, as he struggled to find the right word, Meg felt her heart soar as she opened her eyes and looked over to him '…was a little wild.'

'A little?' Meg checked.

'A lot,' Luca admitted. 'Always I was in trouble. Now I stay out of trouble, but the king has a long memory and so do the people of Niroli. He spoke to me recently—told me I have to…' He gave a frustrated shrug. 'Now, I prefer not to discuss family business.'

'Fine.' Meg smiled. 'That's all you had to say.'

'So, now it is my turn—why did you come?'

'Because you asked me to.'

'Not here.' Luca shook his head. 'Why did you choose to travel? You said you were here to sort things out. Can I ask what?'

And maybe this was one first date where she could reveal, because, in that second, it didn't feel as if they'd only just met. Her eyes were looking straight into his, the sun blocked out by his presence, it didn't feel as if there were a million barriers between them—it felt as if they were one, as if she were looking at a man she'd always known, just hadn't really met yet.

'What?' Luca pushed, just a touch too soon, the brave leap she was about to take thwarted by impatience, and Meg recoiled back into herself, shaking her head as if to clear it, stunned at how close she had come to letting him in—letting *anyone* in.

'I'd prefer not to say.'

'You confuse me, Meg. One minute you are so strong, so sure, yet the next…' He gave a helpless shrug. 'You are very complicated, yes?'

'Yes.'

It wasn't the answer he was expecting, perhaps a small admission, a revelation, but when there was none forthcoming Luca, surprisingly, graciously conceded. 'Perhaps we need to get to know each other even better,' Luca suggested. 'Maybe one day isn't enough for us?'

'Maybe,' Meg gulped.

'So…' his voice was slow and measured, cautious this time as he approached '…will you stay a little longer? More than just this day?' His face was moving in closer as she toyed with her answer, but he didn't wait to hear it. 'Maybe this will help you decide.'

She'd been so sure he was about to kiss her, so absolutely

sure, it was *all* she could think about, so when his hand lightly dusted her stomach, when his warm fingers brushed the gap between her shorts and top, her body tightened in delicious confusion. Meg could almost hear the reverse sirens sounding in her brain as it instructed her neural pathways to move their guard, that she was being attacked from a different angle, but even as her stomach tightened in reflex Luca changed tack, his mouth moving in, and Meg closed her eyes as his hand snaked around the back of her head. He moved a fraction closer, his breath warm on her cheekbone, making her wait, her lips twitching in nervous expectation, anticipating the feel of his mouth on hers, her breath held in her lungs as so slowly he moved in, but nothing in her imagination could ever rival the true feel of him, the heat of his mouth when it met hers. Like a reflex action her lips parted, his kiss as direct as his approach to her had been, his tongue sliding in offering a simultaneous taste of champagne and power.

*Such* power, his kiss utterly potent, making mockery of any past efforts, turning the few men she had dated into mere boys as his skilled mouth searched hers and his arms wrapped fiercely around her body. For ever he kissed her, drenching her with his passion, banishing reticence, pressing himself so hard against her it was as if they were one person, his lips first paying her mouth the most thorough of attention, then blazing a trail down her neck, kissing her exposed shoulder deeply, his tongue moving up to the base of her neck and then back again. It was to die for, so erotic, so, so shatteringly sexy Meg had to remind herself to breathe.

As Luca's hand cupped her bottom he pressed her heated groin into him, his erection wedged against her. It was Meg kissing him now, hungry lips meeting his scented neck, tasting

Luca's warm flesh as her fingers knotted in his hair—the salt of his skin on her tongue, his cologne filling her nostrils as his other hand moved to the front, the pad of his thumb plying her swollen nipple through her top. With each measured move he spun her ever faster, whirring her mind, her body, into one giddy blur—his hands touching her where her body needed it, *before* Meg even *knew* it herself. How easy it would be to just let go, to give in and follow to where he was taking her, to let this vortex consume her, but so ingrained was her control, so fearful was she of losing it, that with supreme effort Meg pulled back, the ground coming up to meet her as she jumped off at the last moment, staring at him with stunned, fearful eyes as the world carried on spinning.

'We can't!' The words she gasped out were more directed at herself than Luca; she was stunned at what had just taken place, at her body's perilous response to him, but Luca's reply just confused her further.

'We won't,' he murmured, moving in, kissing her again, only more tenderly now. 'We wouldn't,' he said between breathless mouthfuls. 'Not here…not somewhere so public. Now, we just kiss.'

*Just* kiss!

His comfort offered no solace. If, for Luca, that was just a kiss, then what would it be like to be made love to by him, if that was what he could do to her with his mouth…? Meg's mind begged quiet, needed him to stop, her ingrained restraint so violently compromised it actually scared her.

'Please, Luca…'

Something in her voice reached him, his mouth stilling, those black eyes surprisingly tender as he stared down at her.

'I have upset you?'

'No…' She was biting down on her lip in an effort to stop

crying, every emotion she'd ever suppressed clamouring for freedom as somehow Luca unleashed her. 'It's just too soon…' Her eyes pleaded with him for understanding, for Luca to realise that it wasn't sex she was talking about here. 'It's too soon to be feeling like *this!*'

'Then stay,' Luca said simply, holding her in his arms, only more tenderly now, letting her catch her breath as everything calmed down. As the world came back into focus, almost the same as when she'd left it…only somehow different now.

'Now, I'll take you to the beach.' After a few moments in Luca's arms, when still Meg hadn't responded to his suggestion, Luca decided on a change of scene and Meg was surprised how relieved she felt that their date wasn't over yet. But, as nice as he could be when he remembered, as engaging and charming as he was without even trying, every now and then Meg was reminded of his station in life—Luca Fierezza was so thoroughly spoiled, so impossibly arrogant at times, sometimes Meg honestly thought he was joking.

He wasn't!

'Niroli has the most beautiful beaches,' Luca elaborated, offering his hand to help her up.

'I don't have my bathers with me.'

'Bathers?'

'A swimming costume,' Meg attempted, but Luca screwed up his nose at the Australianism.

'They are horrible words—I like women to wear bikinis! Come,' he said impatiently as Meg started to clear up the picnic. 'Just leave it.'

'You can't just leave it! What about the blanket, the basket…?' Meg insisted, but Luca had other ideas, striding off towards the car and clearly expecting her to follow.

'If they want it, then they can come and find it!'

'What's wrong?' As Meg climbed into the car, almost immediately she realised something was up, Luca frowning into the phone as he checked his messages.

'I'm not sure,' was Luca's distracted reply, his face rigid as he replayed his voicemail message, before finally he turned around and faced her. 'I have to go back to the casino. It would appear I am needed.'

'That's fine.' So riddled with doubt was Meg, she was sure he was making it up, sure that her little exposé before must have put him off, but, forcing a smile, she tried not to let her disappointment show as they drove towards the casino in silence. When he didn't elaborate further, didn't suggest that they meet up later, Meg could sit on her hands no longer.

'Luca.' Taking a deep breath, Meg decided to bite the bullet, almost managed to convince herself that she was imagining the sudden tension between them. It was only since the phone call the mood had changed—maybe he was worried about work. 'Tomorrow, why don't we—?'

'Let's just wait and see, shall we?' Luca snapped out his response, lifted his hand from the steering wheel and flicked away her attempt. For Meg it was like being slapped, her face burning as he declined her brave offer, her voice when it came again as tense and as strained as the expression he was wearing.

'Would you be able to drop me off at one of the beaches…?' She didn't even get to finish, Luca flicking on the indicator and pulling over before the sentence was even over, and for Meg it was the final straw, everything that had been before evaporated into thin air as she opened the passenger door and stepped out, the atmosphere so suddenly vile, she didn't even bother to say goodbye….

And neither did Luca.

# CHAPTER SIX

'YOU'RE SURE?' A muscle was pounding in Luca's cheek as Dario fiddled with buttons and the grainy CCTV footage came up on the screen.

'Here we see the girls looking at the jewellery, now she is handling it—the staff kept a close eye on them, of course.' Luca didn't say anything, his black eyes narrowing, watching as Meg held the earrings in her hand, then handed them to her friend, who held them up to her a moment before handing them back to the assistant. 'Here, four hours later, the footage isn't as good—the main camera was on the front desk—but you see she came back with the man she had been drinking with in the gaming room and asked to see the jewels again. This is when the man she was with suddenly collapsed.'

Luca snarled. 'It was a distraction technique; a ruse to keep the main camera on the front desk and distract the staff.'

'*No.*' Dario shook his head, extremely experienced in all aspects of casino security; he was one of the few people who could disagree with Luca and get away with it. 'I also thought it might be a distraction technique, but I have checked with the hospital—he is in the coronary care unit after suffering a major heart attack.' The security chief's words were delivered in rapid Italian, but his voice was non-chalant—theft was a common occurrence in the casino, but with the security so tight it was quickly and easily dealt with. 'Here you see her more clearly now. I don't think she planned it, just saw the opportunity and got greedy.'

Even though he'd been told the facts, even though Dario rarely made a mistake, still he hoped it would be Jasmine that would appear on screen, that somehow Dario had mixed up the two women, but despite the grainy footage, even if Meg's face never fully came into view, there was no mistaking the unique, stunning top she had worn last night. Luca sucked in a deep breath, his teeth gritting together. What the hell did she have to go and do that for? He'd have given her anything she wanted, anything at all. Hell, he'd been so smitten, if she'd wanted some damn jewellery he'd have bought it for her without batting an eye, and now here she was, a woman he'd actually thought different, a woman he'd respected, showing her true colours—stealing his own family jewels.

It made him sick—sick to the stomach, yet he was also filled with a strange, hollow sadness, not just for what he had lost, but because he knew what he had to do. There was a strict one-strike policy at the casino, with no exceptions—even if he had thought for a short while that this Meg was one.

'You've spoken to the friend?'

'When we searched the room. Apparently Miss Donovan was in and out last night.' Dario gave a shrug. 'The jewels were wrapped up in the top Miss Donovan was wearing and had been stuffed in the backpack—we've got all the evidence we need to call the police.'

Luca stared at the frozen image on the screen, trying to relate the deceitful, shady character to the woman he thought he had glimpsed, the woman he had held in his arms and kissed, the proud, dignified woman he had wanted to get to know.

The woman who had duped him.

'Do it, then.' Luca stared one more time at the image frozen on the screen, then gave a terse nod as, on his command, Dario picked up the telephone. 'Tell the police you will let them know when she returns to the casino.' It was said entirely without feeling, his orders exactly as they would be for any other common thief who attempted to get one over on Luca Fierezza, but if Dario had looked up as Luca stalked towards the door he might have noticed the rigid shoulders and bunched fists as his boss made to leave the room. He *did* look up, though, as Luca turned and gave one unusual final instruction. 'Page me when she arrives—this I want to see.'

Luca was used to burying himself in work, the casino just one of his many business ventures, each one demanding scrupulous attention to detail, ruthlessness and resolute indifference, so why couldn't he concentrate? Why was it that, over and over, he kept staring at his phone, checking his pager?

*'Concentrarsi'*. He snapped the order to himself, answered a red-flagged email, and with a few strokes of the keyboard gave the order to fire one of his CEOs in the UK as well as ordering an internal audit on one of his growing business ventures on the Gold Coast in Australia….

Where Meg was from….

What was it with her? *Dio!* She wasn't the first woman he'd met who'd shown her true colours and it certainly wasn't the first time he'd had to have someone arrested, so why, no matter how hard he tried not to think about her, did every road, every thought he had lead to Meg?

Burying his head in his hands, Luca sucked in air and, closing his eyes, he gave into a rare moment of introspection.

*She* wasn't the problem, Luca decided; it was the rather confronting talk he'd had with his grandfather, King Giorgio, just a few days before that was making her attractive—making this thief who came in the night the ultimate forbidden fruit.

"Stay out of trouble, Luca.' The king's voice, though weak from his declining health, hadn't wavered as he'd delivered his order for Luca to keep his nose clean—to stand up and face the fact that he was a potential heir to the Niroli throne.

And though he'd been born a prince, though technically the chance he might one day rule Niroli had been explained to him as he'd grown up, deep down it had never really seemed plausible. Two years ago he'd been way down in line to the throne—the king had had, as the saying went, an heir and a spare: his first-born son, Antonio, and then Luca's father, Paulo, and any possibility of one day ruling Niroli had seemed far away in the distance.

Then the accident had happened.

Two years ago the royal house of Niroli had been thrown into turmoil when a boating accident had claimed the life of the immediate heirs. Antonio and his wife Francesca, along with Luca's father, Paulo, had been tragically killed. While any family would have struggled to come to terms with such loss, for a royal family it threw up more issues, which, with each passing day, were becoming more pressing.

Since the accident, King Giorgio's health had deteriorated rapidly—a proud man, he did not want to rule from his sickbed and was determined to provide his people with a fitting heir before his abdication. The people of Niroli had mourned along with the royal family, had suffered with them through the bad times, and now it was time to pave way for the new. Summoning the family members from around the globe, the king had informed them of his plans to find Niroli's new ruler from amongst them—one in keeping with The Rules, a strict set of orders that the ruler must live by.

Raking his hands through his jet-black hair, Luca tried and failed to imagine himself as King.

He loved his country.

He'd die for his county—and that wasn't an idle statement: the neighbouring island of Mont Avellana had once been under Niroli's rule, but after a bitter battle, control had been lost and it had become a republic. Even today, there was still rivalry and resentment. Unlike the extinct volcanoes that existed on Niroli, there were grumblings of discord that could spill over at any given time—and Luca knew, without a flicker of doubt, he'd be in the front line if he was called.

Yes, Luca sighed, he'd die for his country, but could he live for it?

*Live only for it?*

'No more scandal, Luca.' The king had waved a thin, gnarled finger at him—that one gesture, that short sentence, summing up a colourful life. Luca's teenage years had been mired in petty crime and scandal not befitting a royal prince; it was a life the tabloids had gleefully dissected over the years and like vultures still they wanted more scandal— scandal that somehow Luca had always provided. 'Niroli has given you a good life—fast cars, beautiful women—and over and over our beloved people have forgiven your mistakes, always loved you, so now it is time for you to pay your debt, to put that life behind you once and for all. Now is the time for you to maybe become more than a man—you are in the running to be King. So, think of settling down, winding down your business interests and keeping more suitable company. You owe it not just to me, but to our people, to stay out of trouble, Luca, to give them something back, something they can enjoy—a wedding, perhaps!'

'You're telling me to marry?' Luca couldn't believe what he was hearing—couldn't believe what was being asked of him—but the king had stood his ground.

'I'm telling you that your reckless days are over—that a suitable bride might prove a better escort than some of the women you choose to date. The people of Niroli need to see that you have grown up and a good wife would be a fitting gesture.' As Luca had opened his mouth to put his point the king overrode him, his frail voice gaining momentum, reminding Luca, even if he didn't need it, that this wasn't a grandfatherly chat—Giorgio was, for now, still King! 'I am not asking you, Luca, I am ordering you. I do not want to open a newspaper again and see a slur with your name attached to it. Those days are gone—for ever!'

Staring blindly out at his luxurious office, the king's words still buzzing in his ears, Luca felt the prison gates slowly closing behind him. He glimpsed a future he couldn't fathom: his business interests slowly wound down to accommodate a more royal schedule; performing his duties with a beautiful nameless face on his arm. A privileged lifestyle many would hanker for, but for Luca it felt as if he were about to be delivered a life sentence.

'You were born for this,' Luca said sharply to himself, heaving aside his doubts, forcing himself out of his introspection and facing facts. He couldn't help Meg—even if he wanted to, his hands were tied. It wasn't just the king who had spoken, but history itself! As if the first of The Rules of the Royal House of Niroli had been decreed with him in mind:

*The ruler of Niroli must be a moral leader for the*
*people and is bound to keep order in the Royal House.*
*Any act that brings the monarchy into disrepute*
*through immoral conduct or criminal activity will rule*
*a contender out of the succession to the throne.*

There were ten rules the leader of Niroli must abide by,
but this was the first—and this was the one that Luca had
failed on many occasions. His playboy reputation was legendary on the island, and back when he was a teenager he'd
had a few run-ins with the police himself, arrested for petty
theft and several other misdemeanours. And though charges
had never been laid, and technically there was no criminal
record—the people of Niroli's memories were long. As the
king had pointed out, Niroli had been more than good to him
and now they needed a leader.

Now it was Luca's time to abide by the rules.

Meg was on her own.

So why, instead of turning off his pager and getting back
to work, did he jump when it bleeped? Why, when he was
informed by Dario that Meg was approaching the casino, did
he head down towards the entrance?

Why did this woman still move him so?

'Signorina Donovan?'

So deep in her own thoughts was Meg as she wandered
back from the beach that the police cars screeching alongside, lights and sirens blazing, at first jolted rather than
alarmed her. She was sure there must have been an accident,
an incident taking place perhaps, certainly something that
didn't concern her—until they said her name....

'Alex?' It was her first thought. The most reliable, trustworthy man she knew hadn't turned up yesterday and now the police were calling her by name. Meg's heart lurched with all the fear of the innocent—something terrible must have happened to Alex. 'Is he okay?'

But her question was never answered, instead she was shoved against a wall, her head hitting the rough stone. Pain coursed through her. Merciless hands ruthlessly searched her, groping her, pressing against her shorts, shamelessly lingering a little too long over her flimsy top, and Meg felt her fear, her panic, subside into revulsion…into dread.

'Get off!' Pale lips attempted to get the words out, blood was trickling down from her head. 'Get your hands off me…' But it was like being trapped in a nightmare, her mouth forming the words, her brain screaming them, only no sound was coming out, like some horror movie on mute. She could feel inappropriate hands still groping her, still touching her, still *violating* her as people gathered and watched. She could smell the stale breath of the police officer as the crowd called out insults in Italian.

'Don't!' It was all she could manage, the one word that did come out, her slender hand clasping the fat, podgy fingers as they slid up her thigh, her lips snarling in disgust, distaste as she saw his leer, the beads of sweat on his upper lip. Meg decided she wouldn't give him the satisfaction of her fear, wouldn't give the gathering crowd the show they so clearly desired by fighting with this brute. Instead she stopped struggling, just leant against the wall with her eyes closed till it was over, till she felt the cool of the handcuffs as they were snapped on her wrists and she was unceremoniously spun around and marched towards one of the waiting police cars. The ideal world she had so briefly glimpsed just a few hours ago was suddenly frightening and confusing.

First Luca's brutal rejection, now flashing lights and sirens and jeers from the crowd, but she refused to cry, refused to let anyone see how much this was hurting her, refused to look at anyone—until her eyes caught sight of him....

Luca Fierezza standing there, despite the forty-degree heat, impassive and cool, watching the proceedings from a slight distance, his face unreadable as he registered her plight. Meg's first instinct was to cry out to him, to ask him for assistance. She knew somehow that he was the one person who could help her, but even as she opened her mouth to call out to him she choked her plea back. The black eyes staring at her held none of the warmth she had briefly witnessed, the mouth that had kissed her was now pressed in the same firm, grim line it had been when she'd left him, and somewhere deep inside Meg knew, just *knew* this was his doing, knew in that instant that he wasn't going to help her.

Well, she wouldn't let him see her pain—wouldn't let him know any of her agony. Whatever twisted game he was playing, she wasn't going to partake in it! And though the fight in her might have appeared to have died—her body seemingly weak and pliable as the police officers roughly shepherded her into one of the cars—inside she was regrouping, stronger perhaps than she had ever been in her life. Pressed against the door, she pulled her thighs away so there was no contact with her captor, closed her mind to his angry words. Meg hunched herself forward, watched as blood dripped from her face to her legs, and ran a dry tongue over her bruised and swollen mouth. Taking slow, deep breaths as the car careered through Niroli at breakneck speed, she tried to somehow regain control when there appeared to be none.

She would call the embassy—whatever mess she was in it would soon be sorted. There were rules for this sort of thing, procedures in place for tourists in trouble abroad—she had nothing to fear.

Despite the direness of her predicament, Meg felt her fear abate a notch, the steely grit that had got her through her difficult, difficult life coming to the fore when she needed it most, but it wavered a touch as she recalled Luca's hostile stare—the man she had almost trusted, nearly let into her life, causing her more pain than the injuries and indignity she had so recently suffered.

Well, she'd learnt her lesson.

For the first time she'd let down her guard, trusted that the world could be kind and gentle if only she let it, and look what had happened....

Never again.

Meg held her head high now, stared out of the window as they turned a corner and the Niroli palace came into view, its impressive walls burnt orange in the late afternoon sun, its beauty mocking her as the car halted and she was roughly pulled out, the sight of the palace her last image of the outside world as she was frogmarched into the police station and forced to endure another degrading search before she was bundled into a tiny, dimly lit cell.

No one would hurt her again.

# CHAPTER SEVEN

SHE DESERVED IT.

Scribbling his signature on a thick pile of correspondence, Luca tried and failed to put the image of Meg from his mind. Since her arrest, Luca had made several impromptu checks on various areas of the casino, taken care of endless phone calls he'd long been putting off, and, for the first time since he'd taken the business over, cleared his overflowing correspondence tray, but nothing he did managed to fully erase the image of Meg's stricken face as the police had led her to the car.

Where had he seen that expression before? His mind started to drift, to search the recesses of his mind in an attempt to match the image he was seeking, but Luca abruptly halted it there.

*Forget about her,* Luca demanded of himself. Forget about the wretched thief, the woman who could have brought him shame and scandal when he needed it the least. Glancing at his watch, Luca saw that it was nearly midnight. Glad that this vile day was nearly over and with a shake of his head, he stood up, deciding to head to his suite and shower and change, then head to the bar, end his wretchedness with a stiff drink and perhaps some company. Only despite his best efforts, still Luca's thoughts reluctantly turned to her....

She hadn't even put up a fight, Luca scorned—if she'd been innocent, surely she'd have been enraged, hissing and spitting like a kitten. No, it was almost as if she'd been expecting it, had *known* what the police were there for.

'A call for you, sir.' Despite the lateness of the hour, his secretary buzzed the intercom—her day not over until Luca discharged her.

'No more calls,' Luca snapped. 'I'm finished for the day—you can go home now.'

'It's Her Royal Highness.'

And if it had been any other minute of any other day, Luca would have taken the call without hesitation, his mother, Laura, the one woman whose calls weren't screened, who was usually put through without hesitation—just not this time.

'I said no calls,' Luca barked. But instead of marching out of the office, instead of heading to the bar where it would be so, so much safer to go, he sat back down in the darkness, black bile churning in his stomach as a piece of this reluctant puzzle slotted into place....

Unwelcome, seldom-visited memories pelted his mind like a sudden hailstorm—a storm so violent, so forceful, so rapid in its arrival that there was no time to seek cover, no time to shield himself from its onslaught, so that all he could do was wait, sit at his desk with his head in his hands and ride out the storm in the hope it would quickly pass.

It didn't.

Each memory lashed him more fiercely.

Watching again his father's fist slam into his mother's face, her long black hair, taut in his fingers, as over and over she took the beating, never once crying out—just as Luca hadn't.

Peering into the room that hateful night he had stifled his screams by instinct, something telling him, even at this tender age, that what he was witnessing must never be acknowledged.

He'd tried, though. Ramming his knuckles into his fist, Luca felt the slap of his mother's hand again on his cheek; felt the confusion, the bewilderment all over again as she'd later denied what he had seen take place, told him off for even *thinking* such filthy things.

But he *had* seen it, had seen his mother, despite the indignity, somehow still proud, somehow stronger in her passiveness than the brute that beat her.

He'd seen that expression once in his mother, her face etched with stricken dignity as that bastard had laid into her, and he'd seen it again today—with Meg.

It was a fifteen minute drive to the palace, but Luca did it in eight—his silver car rattling around the tight bends at breakneck speed. Instead of turning off into the guarded private road to the palace, he carried on to the prison, not even taking the keys out of the ignition before he strode in.

'Where is she?'

The guard jumped to his feet, recognising Luca instantly and fumbling to cover his sordid trail—stubbing out a cigarette and ramming a bottle into a drawer.

'In the cell.' He gave a low laugh, which revealed black, rotting teeth. 'She says she wants a lawyer. I told her all the lawyers in Niroli are retained by you!'

'What else has she said?'

'She's crazy.' He tapped the side of his head a couple of times. 'She refuses her meals, refuses to sleep, or to put on the clothes we give her. She went crazy in there before—like an animal, pulling off the mattress, kicking at the walls, throwing her meal when we gave it to her. Now she says she is sister to Prince Alessandro....'

'What?' Luca barked. 'What exactly did she say?'

'That she came to the island to meet her brother—she gave his other name—the one he had before....'

'Alex Hunter?' Luca frowned, his mind racing. Was that what had happened—had the attraction that had flared the second he'd laid eyes on her actually been recognition?

Alessandro was his cousin—they shared the same grandfather, so if somehow he had a sister...?

'I want to talk to her.' It wasn't a request, it was an order, Luca's urgent words delivered almost in anger, and the guard knew better than to question it—just a slight raise of untidy eyebrows as he shrugged and led Luca to the cells.

She was adopted! As he followed the guard down the dank stairwell he replayed their earlier conversation over, recalling the details, and relief flooded him as he remembered what Meg had said. Even if she *were* somehow related to Alessandro, then it wasn't by blood—but it was a royal prince's sister who was locked up in a cell and about to be charged with theft—a scandal the family could do without just now.

For the old king's sake—for the honour of the family—the fact Alessandro's sister had been arrested for the attempted theft of the Niroli jewels, no less, was something that had to be kept quiet.

'*Aspetta*—wait!' Despite Luca's haste to get to her, there was one unsavoury duty that needed to be performed first—one last court with disaster before the king made his decision. Pulling out his wallet, Luca delivered his orders to the guard, hoping to God as he did so that the half-drunk bottle of whisky he had seen him shove into the drawer would be empty by the morning—that this blurry exchange would be nothing but a distant memory by dawn.

The cells were mainly empty apart from a couple of drunks sleeping it off, but the pubs and clubs hadn't closed yet. Luca knew that by morning the place would be rank with Niroli's low life. As he entered the dreary area that housed Meg, Luca knew that it wasn't duty that was driving him—as he made his way in, his eyes taking a moment to accustom to the dim lights, Luca knew it was her he was truly there for.

She was sitting on the simple metal bed, back rigid, staring fixedly ahead, not even turning as they approached, and Luca knew, quite simply, that she didn't belong in such a rank place.

Whatever emotions he'd been feeling before were paltry compared to what he felt now. He'd thought her beautiful, but realised it was a shallow description. Here, with her hair dark from sweat, her face a mess of dried blood and grime, and her top torn, sitting on the bare metal frame of the bed with a rudimentary attempt of a meal upturned on the floor beside her, he witnessed something in Meg far deeper and longer lasting than beauty. Despite the chaos of the room there was an elegance to her that seemed to reach some-where deep inside him and twist his stomach, something about her that tugged at him. He'd always liked women, always enjoyed their company, but this ran deeper. This feeling Meg stirred wasn't about him, but instead about her and what he could do *for* her—only she mustn't know.

*This isn't your doing!*

There was an attempt at reason, to remind himself that it was her actions that had put her in this place—but it was futile. Whatever her reasons, whatever had driven her to steal last night, he wanted to know them—wanted so much more from Meg than he wanted from most women.

He wanted to get to know her….

Good or bad—he wanted all of her.

*'Alzarsi!'* Meg's grasp of the Italian language might be less than basic, but as the guard entered her cell and pulled her to her feet there was little room for misunderstanding and Meg did as she was told: she stood up. But nothing more— refusing to turn her head, refusing to acknowledge Luca Fierezza as he stepped into the tiny cell.

She'd known he was here—had heard his deep, angry voice for the last few moments—but whatever his reason for coming, it was too little, too late. The last couples of hours had been a nightmare: no one spoke more than a few words of English and, combined with Meg's few words of Italian, the police and guards had seemed to take pleasure in the chaos it had created. Taunting her when she'd asked for a lawyer or for them to contact the embassy, laughing in her face when Meg had written down Alex's name for them and tried to explain that until recently her brother had worked at the hospital. Then, after a rough body search, she had been thrown in the tiny, damp cell—which for Meg was the worst part of all, the tiny cell, the isolation, so reminiscent of her younger years it was impossible not to compare, not to relive the virtual prison of her childhood, impossible for it not to provoke a reaction. The guard bringing her a meal, ordering her to eat, had, for Meg, been the final straw and now, exhausted from her outburst, amidst the chaos she'd created, she stood before Luca.

'Meg, are you okay?' It was such a relief to hear English, her determination not to look at him, not to talk to him, weakened a touch, but she held on—still, even at this eleventh hour, trusting that order would prevail, that a lawyer, an official, *someone* would come and sort out this chaos.

'Meg, talk to me,' Luca insisted. 'I can help you.'

Her top lip sneered in disgust and somehow Luca knew she wasn't going to accept his offer of help, that, even if she was the guilty one, somehow it was he, Luca, she mistrusted. *'Aqua,'* Luca snapped to the guard, thinking on his feet, trying somehow to get her to realise that he was on her side. He barked orders in Italian to the guard, demanding he get food and something to clean up Meg's face with. Only when they were alone did he approach Meg, but she recoiled as if he were poison and with supreme effort he halted, stifling the instinct to take her in his arms and soothe her. 'Meg…' He stared at the paltry room, took in the upturned meal on the floor and struggled to find what to say, how to reach her. 'You should eat something….'

'I'd rather starve than eat what they bring me.' Even if it was laced with venom, at least she was talking, Luca conceded.

'You could be here for some time—you should change out of these dirty clothes, get some sleep. You need to eat—'

'Why?' Angry, defensive eyes turned to him. 'Why should I wear their clothes or sleep or eat at their command when I have done nothing wrong? Anyway, what is it to you? What exactly are you here for, Luca?'

'As I said, I am here to help you.'

He thought she might spit at him—her face was so sour with contempt she was barely recognisable.

'More likely, you're here to make sure that your handiwork has been carried out properly. Well, as you can see, it has been. Is this what happens when you refuse to sleep with the prince of Niroli?'

'It has nothing to do with that!' The guard was back and, taking the bowl of water and cloths he'd brought with him, Luca dismissed him, leading her to the bed where she reluctantly sat, examining the small cut in her eyebrow. 'I will clean your face. It is dirty in this cell—the wound will get infected.'

'I'll clean it,' Meg snarled, but he didn't listen, just calmly dipped the fabric into the water and bathed her wounds as the first sting of tears since her arrest reached her eyes. His hand was so supremely gentle, so tender, she couldn't help but compare it to the treatment the guards had given earlier, and for a second it was just easier somehow to let him help, to close her eyes as gently he removed the dried blood and dirt before pulling out of his pocket a heavy silk handkerchief and telling her to press it to her face.

'You will need a stitch or two. Do you know if the guard has arranged a doctor?'

'I'm sure that he has it on his list of people to call for me.'

Her sarcasm wasn't wasted on Luca, his eyes shuttering closed for a moment and she hoped it was in guilt, guilt for what he had done to her, but in that second he changed, his demeanour shifting from tender to practical.

'You stole from me, Meg—I saw the evidence myself. I had no choice but to call the police. You are here because you are a thief. Now we have to work out what to do with you.'

'Do with me?' Meg gave an incredulous laugh. 'And what the hell do you mean that I stole from you?'

'I've seen the evidence, Meg.'

'How?' She balled her fists to her temples in an attempt to calm down, the whole thing getting more ludicrous by the moment. She'd realised the guards thought her a common thief, that much she understood, but hearing it from Luca, realising he thought that of her, was almost more than she could take. 'How could you have seen something when it didn't even happen?'

'The jewels that were found in your bag are the Niroli family jewels, so, yes, you stole from me. Why you would do such a thing I do not know. Whatever trouble you are in I will try to help, try to understand, but it is imperative—'

'Luca—I am not a thief,' Meg broke in. 'I have no idea what you're talking about. All I want is a lawyer, someone to ring the embassy so that this mess can be sorted. I've never stolen a single thing in my life.'

It was like rewinding his life—watching the woman he adored furiously denying what he had witnessed—only this time he wouldn't back down. He was a man now—not a confused child. He was a royal prince and he would not be lied to, would not just *choose* to believe her because it was easier to.

'Don't lie to me!' His words were a roar, his six-foot-two frame jumping from the bed and towering over her. She was so convincing, so utterly, utterly convincing that if he hadn't seen the evidence himself, he'd have believed her—wanted to believe her—wanted to be taken in by this vixen's lies.

'I will not be lied to,' Luca repeated, but more calmly this time, speaking to her now as he would any of his staff that had overstepped the mark and needed to be pulled swiftly back into line. 'I am here to try to help you, but how can I do that when still you lie to me? I saw it with my own eyes, Meg. I saw you taking the jewels from the display—they were found in your backpack, wrapped in the top you were wearing last night.' On and on he went, each word damning her, each word confusing her further, because he clearly believed them, and all Meg knew was that it was imperative that Luca believe in her.

'I don't know what you saw or what you've been told, but

you're mistaken.' She stared right at him as she spoke. 'If you can't or won't believe me, then can you please just call a lawyer or the embassy for me in the morning?'

'It's Saturday tomorrow,' Luca pointed out, 'and it is a long weekend for the Feast—there can be no officials contacted till Tuesday, perhaps even Wednesday.'

'Then can you please try and get hold of my brother for me…?' Meg gulped back tears, her voice wobbling with fear as she realised that this nightmare wasn't anywhere near over and, though she was loath to ask Luca for any assistance, it was infinitely preferable to staying here. 'His name's Alex Hunter. He was working at the hospital—'

'Alessandro Fierezza is on his honeymoon,' Luca interrupted, 'on his way back to Australia. Alessandro is not going to be able to help you now.'

'Alessandro?' Meg gave a bewildered shake of her head. 'I don't know any Alessandro. I'm asking you to find my brother—'

'My cousin,' Luca brutally cut in, taking no pleasure as her proud face literally crumpled before his eyes, but his face remained impassive. He knew she needed him to be strong, that this fiery, independent woman wouldn't take a grain of his sympathy. 'Your brother is my cousin—get it? Alessandro is a royal prince—'

'No!' It didn't make sense, nothing today made any sense. Alex was a doctor, her brother, the most honourable man she knew, if he'd had news this big he'd have told her himself, face to face….

*He'd wanted to.*

The truth, however unpalatable, was starting to sink in. Alex had said the news was *huge*; could this have been it? Like Meg, Alex had been adopted, only at a much younger age, so his past was vague, but he was of Italian descent and the receptionist at the hospital had used the same name Luca was using now—Alessandro Fierezza…

Burying her face in her hands, Meg struggled for control, tried to glimpse some way out of this hellish mess. Drunken, loud voices were coming from upstairs, the tiny cells starting to fill with undesirables, and she was trapped here till God knew when….

'I can sort this mess out for you, Meg.'

'How?' Peeling down her fingers, Meg stared up at him.

'I just can….' Luca's Adam's apple bobbed as he swallowed hard, unsure how Meg would react to what he had done, but somehow guessing she wouldn't take it particularly well. 'I can make this go away.'

'You mean you'll bribe someone!' Appalled, Meg shook her head, but Luca was insistent.

'You are the sister of a prince—therefore you do not belong here. The family cannot afford the scandal at this time.'

'The only scandal is that I've been locked up and accused of a crime I didn't commit,' Meg retorted. 'I don't need you covering my tracks, Luca. It's your family that will suffer if I stay here.'

'It will cause shame for your brother,' Luca pointed out. But Meg wasn't about to be subdued.

'Then you clearly don't know Alex,' she flared back. 'He'd tell me to fight my case. Unlike you, Alex would believe a woman who was speaking the truth.'

'Then your brother is a fool,' Luca retorted. 'We both know you lie, we both know the truth. You can stay here and rot, then. I have offered assistance. I have done the right thing by Alessandro. It is not my fault if you will not accept it!'

This was getting nowhere; Luca had quickly realised that. He could hear the processing of the new prisoners taking place upstairs, knew that at any given moment he might be recognised. If Meg didn't come with him now, he would have to leave her here to fight her case alone.

Staring down at her, defiant, wary and so very, very scared, Luca knew what he had to do, knew that she was too proud for charity, too proud to back down—so he did what he did best.

Cut her a deal—Luca style.

Let her think she had a choice, let her think she had a chance of winning.

'Maybe there is another way,' Luca mused out loud. 'Last night I said I wanted to spend time with you; last night I explained I wanted the pleasure of your company....'

'You had that today,' Meg attempted, but Luca shook his head.

'Forget today, Meg. Now I know how low you stoop, the offer drops. I will not bribe the guard, but I *will* pay your bail—I will assure him that I am taking care of you and that you will return for your hearing with suitable representation.'

'And in return?' For the first time since he'd arrived Luca actually smiled. 'You mean you want me as your *puttana*,' Meg spat. It was one of the few Italian words she did know—she had heard it several times since she'd been locked up, and it was one of the few words that needed little translation. He was literally offering to buy her company. 'You're not doing this out of some false sense of duty to Alex, you're offering this because of how I look!'

'Well, you don't look very good at this moment,' Luca retorted, 'but I think you will scrub up very nicely. This is a good offer, Meg,' he continued. 'You can stay here and take your chances with the guards and your fellow prisoners, or

I will pay your bail and you can come with me and stay in luxurious surrounds until Tuesday, when I will arrange full access to one of the best lawyers on the mainland.'

'And for the privilege—I'll have to share your bed!'

'Of course.' He stared down at his watch, tapped an impatient foot as he awaited her decision, and her first instinct was to slap him, to spit on his arrogant face and tell him where the hell he could put his offer, but something held her back. Realisation sank in that she was here for the duration. Her passport had already been taken, her belongings locked away. Here she had no rights, no possessions, but as the prince's mistress she would be afforded decent legal representation—could get out of this mess through the correct channels instead of offering some sleazy bribe.

She still had a choice.

She would *choose* to eat at his table, *choose* to share his bed, but she wouldn't share her heart…. Luca Fierezza had enough money and power to buy her company for a short while, but he would never hold her heart.

# CHAPTER EIGHT

THEY DROVE IN SILENCE to the palace, Luca's car hugging the beach road, the palace easily visible thanks to a vast moon hanging low in the sky, but despite the warm night air as she'd stepped from the prison to the custody of her new jailer, Meg had started violently shivering, so she sat now huddled in the passenger seat wearing Luca's jacket.

'Why aren't we going to the casino?'

'You will be recognised at the casino—you are on the black list. Until we can arrange for some new clothes, your hair to be done differently, you will have to stay away from there.'

'But surely…'

'The staff at the palace are discreet—that is why I am taking you there.'

'Won't they at least want to know who I am?'

'Why would they?' Luca shrugged and she glanced over at him, taking in his perfect profile, the sheer maleness he radiated, the absolute arrogant beauty of him, and the unpalatable truth was further affirmed. They wouldn't ask questions because this was clearly a regular occurrence—oh, not the rescue from the jail, but clearly the palace staff were more than used to Luca arriving home at all hours with a woman in tow! 'I will arrange a doctor to come and tend to your cut.'

'I don't need a doctor, and anyway,' Meg added, 'surely *he* would ask questions.'

'Why would he? I pay for his discretion,' Luca responded with all the arrogance of the truly rich, but he did at least concede that her arrival might cause some issues, because as the gates to a private road slid open and the car approached he momentarily stopped and, with the engine idling, he turned to face her.

'This is what we do. I tell my family the truth—you are Alessandro's sister, you came to the island to look him up not realising he had already left. That is why I am taking care of you.'

'So am I here as Alex's sister or your mistress?' Meg quipped, but Luca, as always, had an answer.

'Both.' He turned and gave her a dry smile. 'Just remember, though, your first duty is to me.'

'And the cut?' Meg snapped. 'Did that come in the line of duty?'

'Jet-skiing.' Luca gave a rare smile—clearly happy with his fabrication. 'You had an accident jet-skiing today when you were exploring. You were hoping your brother would be able to patch you up.'

'That's not the truth,' Meg pointed out.

'Oh, but from now on it is.' Black eyes bore into hers. 'You really don't expect me to tell them you were attempting to steal the Niroli jewels, do you?'

'No, because that isn't the truth, either.'

He didn't respond, just pulled off the handbrake and drove along the stretch of road towards the palace, orange groves flanking their progress. Despite the vile day, despite an exhausted mind that just wanted to switch from all that was happening, Meg couldn't help but be impressed at the sheer splendour of the building she'd till now only glimpsed from a distance. A huge fourteenth-century castle, it stood proud on the edge of the ocean as if carved out of the rocks itself, and Meg could scarcely believe that this was where she would be calling home for the next few days.

Even before the car had slid to a halt, despite the lateness of the hour the door was opened by waiting staff, but Luca barely greeted them, just exchanging a few words with a burly, suited gentleman before taking a stunned and shivering Meg by the arm and leading her to a side entrance, which Meg soon realised was the access to the palace's private apartments.

'That was my bodyguard, Luigi,' Luca needlessly explained his earlier conversation. 'He is annoyed that again I did not tell him I was leaving the casino. I will speak with him in the morning—if you need to leave the palace for any reason, he is to drive and accompany you.'

'I don't need an escort,' Meg responded tightly.

'Perhaps not,' Luca answered as he pushed open the door to his apartment, 'but since I signed your bail papers you are my responsibility. I want to be sure I know where you are— and, more importantly, that you will return.'

She was too tired to be indignant or even attempt a smart retort. She stepped inside Luca's luxurious apartment. Someone on the gate must have alerted the staff, because even though it was only a matter of minutes since the car had entered the palace grounds there was a fire taking hold in the magnificent marble fireplace and the lights were all on. A large whisky had been poured and set on an occasional table, which Luca downed in one gulp while Meg still stood at the doorway taking in her surrounds. Lavishly furnished, the apartment had been exquisitely refurbished—somehow managing to combine the fourteenth-century décor with *all* the luxuries of the twenty-first century. Vast high walls were broken by voile curtains that swept the shuttered windows, a papal purple carpet runner softened the cool Italian marble floor. The apartment was a virtual treasure trove of antiques and under any other circumstances Meg would have been thrilled to explore, but all she could do was stand and shiver, overwhelmed with fatigue, and Luca, for the first time since the prison, was gently perceptive, guiding her limp body across to the warmth of the fire.

'Even in summer the castle is cool at night,' Luca explained, but there was a worried edge to his voice, his hand running over her forehead as if she were a child and he were checking her temperature, 'The doctor will be here soon.'

'You've called him?' Meg frowned, worried that she couldn't remember, but Luca shook his head. 'I told Luigi to take care of it.'

There was clearly no trouble arranging a rapid house call when you were Niroli royalty, and the doctor arrived shortly afterwards. Any worries Meg might have had about explaining her injuries were quashed when Luca did what little talking was required.

'You need two stitches on your...' Luca tapped his own eyebrow by explanation, then gave a small wince as the doctor said something else to him. 'He says he can give you an injection to make it numb before he stitches you, but that will hurt as much as if he just goes ahead and puts in the stitches without it.'

'No injections!'

*'Il donatore il suo anestetico locale.'* Luca fired at the doctor in rapid Italian. Too quick for Meg to grasp.

'What did you say?' Meg asked as the doctor nodded.

'I said that he was to numb it first for you.'

'Well, that's not what I want. Can you please tell him to just go ahead and do the stitches?' Meg countered.

'But it will hurt.'

'So will the anaesthetic,' Meg pointed out, 'and next time you decide to act as a translator for me, please, allow me to answer for myself!' As Luca opened his mouth to argue, Meg got there first. 'What is he saying now?'

'That he will use the finest silk, and that with make-up the cut will not show. After he has tended your wound you are to bathe and sleep…' He checked his understanding of the order of events with the doctor, who was setting up his tools, then elaborated. 'You are to bathe, have a light supper and then sleep—he will come and check on you again some time over the weekend. I'll have the house-keeper run you a bath.'

'I'd prefer a shower.' Meg screwed her eyes closed as the doctor poured out antiseptic and proceeded to clean her wound.

'Would you?' Luca snapped. 'Or are you just determined to contradict everything I say?'

'Yes to both,' Meg answered cheekily. As Luca let out a hiss of indignation, she caught his eyes and gave him a tiny glimmer of a smile, which, after a beat of hesitation, he reluctantly reciprocated. 'Let's just get this over with.'

The stitches hurt, though not that much, and Meg bit hard on her lip as the needle went in and out. When Luca reached for her hand to comfort her, she pulled it back, preferring to see this through by herself.

'You are very brave,' Luca commented once the doctor had gone and finally they were alone. 'Not many people would sit there so still. In fact…' His voice trailed off—the only other person he could think of who would react as Meg had, who would barely offer a reaction as their wounds were tended, was his mother.

'Can I have my shower now please?' Supremely polite, she evaded comment on his observations.

'Of course.' Luca nodded, attempting normal, trying to blot out the pictures that were forming in his mind, to stifle the wells of emotion she produced in him without even trying.

What had happened to her?

The question buzzed in his mind as he led her to the bathroom. There was no need to check that she had everything she needed when she was in the Niroli palace—the sparkling bathroom had every luxury required for an unexpected female guest—Luca's thick, white fluffy towels were warming on the heated rails, new toothbrush still in its wrapper, expensive moisturisers and rich, handmade soaps. But her weariness troubled him and Luca, for the first time ever, turned on the taps for a shower he wasn't invited to partake in.

'Call if you need anything,' Luca offered, though he knew that she wouldn't.

Who *had* hurt her?

Heading into the lounge room, he stood as the supper tray was delivered and the maid poured him another shot of whisky. He raised the glass to his lips once she stepped outside, but instead of drinking it, instead of taking refuge in the sharp, sedating liquid, with a curse, a howl of pain almost, he hurled the glass into the fireplace, watching the heavy crystal crack and splinter, not even blinking at the flare of blue light as the alcohol momentarily ignited.

What was it with this Meg woman?

This thief who had crept into his heart—what was it with

her that moved him so, unleashed something within him, forced him to examine the murky waters of his own life? She was like a drug—like the most dangerous of drugs, one taste and he had been reeled in, hooked by an internal craving for something he couldn't define, something that could surely only end in grief if it was sustained. And like any addiction it was mired in secrets. There was no hearing on Tuesday—the guard had been easily paid off, Meg's belongings put in the back of the car—but if she knew that, she'd be gone in an instant. She was only here because he'd supposedly paid for her, the woman he was starting to know was way too proud to accept a sympathy vote....

He must treat her as he would any mistress—demand of her what he did of all his women: engaging company, immaculate presentation and a healthy dose of sex to boot—then get her off the island, purge her from his mind once the festivities were over.... Clenching his fists beside him, Luca blanched at that prospect of losing her, whilst simultaneously baulking at the prospect of keeping her.

She was trouble.

No, Luca corrected, with sadness—she was troubled.

'Are you okay?'

Strange that it was Meg asking him the question, that someone so fragile, in such dire straits, was asking someone so seemingly strong. But there she was standing with her hair dripping, wrapped in a huge bathrobe, her fingers pulling the wrap of the neckline tighter; vulnerable, nervous and, Luca realised, utterly, utterly adorable.

'I'm fine.' Luca nodded. 'There is hot chocolate and sweet breads… I don't know what you would call it,' he attempted, expecting her to refuse, quietly pleased when she tentatively sat down, taking a sip of the warm sweet drink before parting the pastry with long, delicate fingers, then hesitating.

'Come on, eat,' Luca prompted, frowning as her body stiffened and she dropped the pastry down onto the plate.

'I'm not hungry.'

'You didn't eat in the prison,' Luca pointed out. 'You remember the doctor said that you should have some supper.'

'So?' Meg shrugged. 'It was a suggestion, not a prescription.'

'Suit yourself.' Luca gave a tight shrug, but he was getting rattled now; he had rescued her, brought her here to his apartment, arranged a doctor, in fact he had done more for this woman in the few hours he had known her than he *ever* had for anyone before. Yet, far from being grateful, she had the audacity to speak back at him. In fact, Luca realised, he was no closer to her now than he had been back in the Niroli kitchen. Again she was keeping him at arm's length, treating him with mild disdain as if *he* somehow wasn't good enough for *her*. 'Is there anyone you would like to ring?'

'I don't fancy my chances of getting a lawyer from the embassy at this hour of the night.'

'They will tell you exactly what I have—until your case is heard you are not entitled to your passport. What about your parents?' He was holding out the phone to her, offering her a link to the outside world, his hand completely steady as Meg's reached out for the phone, but if Meg had looked up she'd have seen his nervous swallow. 'I mean your adopted parents….'

'*They* are my parents,' Meg corrected hotly, but the fire in her died a bit as, after a brief hesitation, she pulled back the hand that had reached out, curled up tighter on the chair and started to comb her damp hair. 'I don't want to worry them.'

'That is surely their job—to worry!'

'As you said—there's nothing anyone can do. Calling my parents isn't going to make a scrap of difference. Once I've spoken to a lawyer, once I know what's happening, *then* I'll let them know.'

Never had she wanted her parents more. The thought of ringing them, hearing their reassuring voices amidst this blizzard of confusion, to ask for their guidance, their assistance, was a temptation that was almost impossible to resist—but she couldn't do it to them…again.

Combing her hair furiously, Meg recalled how they'd worried about her travelling. It had taken weeks, no, months to reassure them, to tell them she was ready for this, to assure them she'd be okay. Meg closed her eyes, imagining the ringing of the phone piercing their afternoon—they were probably out on the decking, enjoying the last of the sunshine before evening descended. The thought of spinning them into anxiety, of *again* being the source of their pain, was the only reason Meg refused Luca's offer.

'You look a lot better,' Luca observed as she finished combing her hair.

'I feel it,' Meg admitted, making the stilted conversation just a little easier. 'I was already desperate for a shower by the time I got to the casino, covered in suntan oil and sand. It seems like ages ago….'

'A lot has happened since then.'

'I still can't believe it about Alex.' Meg gave a bewildered laugh. 'Though I actually *do* believe it.'

'You are adopted also,' Luca said. 'Who knows? Maybe you are royalty, too—isn't that every adopted child's dream?'

'Not mine.' Meg took a nervous sip of her drink. 'In fact, I spent most of my childhood *hoping* to find out I was adopted.' When Luca gave her a curious look, Meg reluctantly elaborated. 'I was adopted when I was much older than Alex.'

'How old?'

Meg gave a tight shrug. 'When I was twelve.'

'What happened to your parents?' Luca's voice was curious rather than sympathetic. 'Were they killed? Did they—?'

'My *biological* parents are alive and well—physically anyway.'

'I don't understand.' Luca frowned, treading carefully now, hearing the emphasis on the word biological and realising there was considerable pain behind the tight, rigid expression Meg was wearing. 'When you say physically…'

'Some people should never have children,' Meg said firmly, then pushed the conversation firmly back to its original direction. 'You say that Alex is married?'

'Very happily,' Luca replied, 'and very quickly! She's a nurse, her name is Amelia.'

Which ended that conversation. The tension was increasing as she put down her empty cup, her drink finished, her wounds tended, the doctor's orders loosely followed all bar one….

'It is time for bed,' Luca said, stating the inevitable.

'Okay.' Her voice was small, a flash of nervousness darting in those gorgeous blue eyes as she stood up and, though Luca had never wanted her more, wanted so much to take her in his arms and kiss away all the horrors of the day, he also knew that wasn't what she really needed and, for the first time in his spoiled life, Luca pushed his own needs aside.

'I will sleep on the couch.' Luca broke the interminable silence. 'The doctor said you needed to rest.'

'I thought…' Meg gave a nervous, embarrassed swallow,

incredibly grateful for the reprieve, but confused all the same. 'I thought that I was supposed to be—'

'My mistress?' Luca finished the difficult sentence for her, his voice suddenly harsh. 'I don't think somehow you fit the bill tonight—did you not think to look in the mirror when you left the bathroom?'

She was too damned exhausted to be cross, too damned grateful not to have to be involved in some extended sexual marathon to answer back. The bed was soft as she climbed in, the heavy Italian linen cool on her aching limbs, her exhausted body stretching out gratefully, but still she couldn't relax, the whole day just too bizarre, too overwhelming to switch off just because she closed her eyes. She tried, tried not to think about all that had happened, her mind buzzing like a chainsaw till finally a fitful sleep descended, only there was no solace there—back in a prison cell, only the walls were different; pretty, pale-pink walls, the grimy, grey prison blanket replaced now by a soft, pink one, toys smiling down at her from the wall.

Back in the bedroom of her childhood—seemingly perfect; sinister in its deception.

But unlike then, this time when she cried out in her sleep it didn't go unheeded; this time, when she called out in terror, someone answered….

For Luca it wasn't an effort to hold her and not intimately touch her. Meg could never have known the supreme effort it had taken him to be so cruel to her before she'd gone to bed. Holding her in his arms now, shushing her back to a sweeter sleep, for the first time he was in bed with a woman and it wasn't sex that was on his mind, but the woman herself.

Tonight he would hold her, Luca decided, breaking his

promise, slipping dangerously off the wagon as he pulled the sheets around her slender shoulders, breathed in the sweet scent of her damp hair; tonight he would allow himself the luxury of looking after her…then, tomorrow, it was back to business.

# CHAPTER NINE

'BREAKFAST IS HERE!'

A sharp rap at the door and Luca's even sharper voice had Meg waking with a start and the mother of all mortification.

If she'd made wild passionate love to him she'd have felt better—but waking up in the empty bed, gradually orientating herself, piecing together the previous days, Meg cringed with embarrassment. Not at being labelled a thief or finding herself locked up, nor at the shame of being arrested in front of a crowd of curious onlookers, but at what had taken place long after the day was over: crying out in her sleep—reaching out to Luca when he'd come, holding onto him throughout the night….

Letting out a low moan, Meg rolled over, inhaling his heavy, unmistakable scent that lingered on the sheets, seeing the indent in the pillow, the bed still warm from where he'd lain beside her—wondering how she could summon the nerve to head out to the lounge and face him….

'Good morning!' Wearing a false smile brighter than the sun blazing through the windows, Meg breezed into the living room, curiously deflated that her grand entrance was masked by the vast broadsheet he was engrossed in as he sat at a beautifully decorated table. The heady scent of fresh flowers that hadn't been there last night mingled with the aroma of coffee. There were crisp white napkins and heavy silver cutlery fit for a five-star restaurant—a world away from the backpacker hostels that had been home for the last few months.

'Buongiorno.' He flicked a hand in the vague direction of a vast silver trolley that had been wheeled into the room. 'Help yourself to breakfast.'

It wasn't just the table that was elaborate—clearly room service took on a whole new meaning when you were living at the palace. Meg would have quickly helped herself had there been anything as straightforward as cereal, but the trolley groaned under the weight of various hams, sickly pastries and an array of olives and syrupy fruits. What was it with the Italians that their breakfasts looked more like an evening meal? Meg had loved France with the crusty rolls and hot chocolate breakfasts, but this was all way too much.

'If you would prefer a cooked breakfast I can call the chef.'

'No, no.' Meg shook her head, her stomach curdling at the thought. Even though she was well into her recovery, Meg was still nervous of eating in front of strangers, especially at this hour of the morning—so, bypassing the meats and oil-soaked delicacies, she fashioned something similar to the breakfast she had enjoyed in France, taking a thick slice of olive bread smothered in rock salt and adding a dash of coffee as thick as treacle to a glass of warm milk poured from a heavy silver jug.

'Come!' Impatiently Luca gestured for her to join him. 'I have to go into work shortly—is that all you are having?' He frowned. 'It's no trouble to call the chef….'

'I'm fine—thank you.'

'Tonight we eat out,' Luca said. 'Away from here, away

from the casino—there is a nice bayside restaurant I will take you to. There they do the best rainbow mullet you will ever taste. It is the island's speciality dish….' He frowned at her lack of enthusiasm. 'Is there a problem?'

'Of course not.'

'Only you do not seem particularly talkative.'

'It's seven in the morning,' Meg pointed out. He might be paying for her company, but surely he didn't expect an all-singing, all-dancing production at this hour. 'I'm never particularly talkative this early.'

But, clearly, he did.

'Well, I'm sorry to have woken you!' Luca's sarcasm was biting. 'Perhaps tomorrow you can ensure it's the other way around.'

Clearly, Luca liked his women bright and breezy and ready to entertain at all hours. Picking up his newspaper, less than amused, Luca didn't look up as he spoke. 'I will arrange for a stylist to come over this morning—do you have any preferences?'

'Preferences?' Because he wasn't watching now, Meg dipped her bread into her coffee. 'I can go out and get some clothes this morning.'

'Dressed in your robe?' Luca peered over his paper. 'Or rather, in my robe? And tell me—how do you intend to pay for your purchases? You could always cash your cheque, I guess, or sell a few jewels. Oh, sorry, I forgot—all your belongings have been impounded!' With a dry smile he returned to the business page. 'Oh, and I'll send someone from the hair salon too,' he added as an afterthought. 'Your hair really does need attending to—it is very brassy.'

Where, Meg wondered, had the tender man who had held her, comforted her last night disappeared to? But then again she was almost relieved to see the back of him. This version of Luca she could deal with—life was so much easier when she could hate him!

'Anything else?' Meg checked, bristling at the insult—brassy it might be, but that was from swimming in the ocean and hours in the blistering sun. She'd never dyed her hair in her life. 'Is there anything else you'd like me to fix so I look the part for you?'

'That is women's business.' Luca shrugged. 'You can surprise me—speak with the beautician. She can do the wax or whatever you need—I do not need to know such things.'

'What about a lawyer?' Meg watched as his knuckles tightened around the newspaper, practically curling it into a ball as she spoke on. 'While you're on the phone arranging my minimakeover, could you find the time to arrange the lawyer we'd agreed to?'

'*Public holiday.*' Luca shrugged.

'You know—' Meg put down her mug '—your English is incredibly bad when you want it to be.'

'And your manners are appalling when you think no one is watching.' Luca finally deigned to put down his newspaper, catching her red-handed as she dunked her bread once again. 'And when you date royalty, someone always is—it would serve you well to remember that.

'Right, I will put all the arrangements in place and my mother will come with you to the day spa.'

'Your mother?' Meg gave an incredulous grin. 'It's a bit early to be meeting the in-laws, isn't it?'

'Don't be facetious!' Luca reproached. 'You are Alessandro's sister, of course I would introduce you to her. Anyway, tomorrow the formal celebration for the Feast of Niroli takes place. There will be a ball here in the palace. I expect you to attend. My mother will tell you how to behave. She knows how a lady should act—it would be useful for you to listen.'

'I thought you wanted to keep things quiet,' Meg attempted. 'What if someone recognises me?'

'Believe me, Meg—' Luca gave a tight smile '—once you are groomed and more suitably dressed...no one will recognise you. I can also assure you my mistresses do not spend their time *sitting* around to fill the hours.'

'Of course not,' Meg challenged. 'They're too busy preening themselves and voiding themselves of any opinions in preparation for the master's return!' She'd gone too far—at least further than Prince Luca's women usually did, because his swarthy skin was pale as he turned to face her, his eyes black as coal as he silenced her with a look.

'I make no apology for liking beautiful women, Meg.' His eyes narrowed as he walked towards her, his fingers reaching out and cupping her chin, assessing her, appraising her, as if he were purchasing some sort of show pony. 'You know, for someone so very pretty you spoil it with your bitterness, your—' With his free hand he snapped his fingers, summoning a word that wouldn't come, and settling for one that hurt way more. 'You *infect* yourself with your anger, your animosity.

'Remember—if it wasn't for me, you would be rotting in jail for the next week or two.'

'I've survived worse,' Meg retorted, defiant perhaps, yet speaking the truth, but Luca shook his head.

'You were scared when I came and rescued you—and the night hadn't even started. You want to go back, then I will take you there now—just say the word.'

He would, Meg knew that, and she also knew that if jail had been hell before it would be worse on her return. She could almost feel the rough, greedy hands of the guard on her and her eyes widened in terror, her brow beading with sweat. Luca must have seen it, because somehow he changed, the anger replaced by confusion.

'Here you have everything—the best of everything—and still you fight me,' he said.

'I won't… I'm not.' Her breath was coming out fast and rapid, the thought of returning to the cell filling her with horror. At least here she had relative freedom, and there was a chance she would get a decent lawyer, but, more to the point, here she knew she would be looked after, that somehow Luca Fierezza, with all his pompous arrogance, would take care of her. 'I'm not fighting you, Luca. I'm looking forward to getting dressed up. I'm looking forward to the Feast.' And she expected a gleam of triumph in those angry black eyes, but he blinked in confusion at the change in her, the hand gripping her face loosening. 'I won't let you down.'

Within an hour of Luca leaving, as promised, there was a knock on the door and a middle-aged woman entered, her greeting brief but effusive, kissing Meg on both cheeks and introducing herself as Laura.

'Luca's mother?'

'That is right.' Her English wasn't as good as Luca's, but she explained she was here to help her with her choices. Just as Meg was about to ask what she meant, the question was answered by the arrival of not a dresser with a couple of samples wrapped in a carry suit, but endless racks being wheeled into the apartment, and not just dresses either— underwear, bathing suits, shoes, nightdresses.

'My son, he thinks of everything,' Laura said proudly as

Meg rather timidly approached the clothes. 'Come, Meg,' Laura said impatiently. 'We set to work!'

That was the understatement of the millennium. Clearly any mistress of Luca's, however temporary, was expected to look the part—and once her closet was filled with the smartest Italian fashion pieces and Meg was rather more suitably dressed, a car was summoned and Meg was being whisked to the day spa at breakneck speed, only the lights and sirens missing, in an effort to repair her 'brassy' hair.

'Don't worry.' With Meg placed in front of a mirror, a hairdresser tutting as she examined Meg's split ends, Laura gave a sympathetic smile and delivered the most stunning backhander. 'She is a miracle worker, I tell you. She can fix anything!'

Clearly used to being thoroughly spoiled, Laura had a facial as Meg's hair was 'dealt with', and at first they chatted amicably. Thankfully Laura didn't ask too many questions about Alex or her arrival in Niroli, just gave Meg a few tips on dealing with her new status as the sister of Niroli royalty.

'Luca will look after everything—the best thing you can say if the press ask a question is nothing.'

'I'm sure no one's really that interested in what I have to say,' Meg answered as Laura gave her a questioning frown.

'Come—you are surely not that naïve. Any woman on my son's arm generates interest, especially now he might become King.'

'Luca?' The hairdresser stepped back as Meg's head spun around.

'The king's health is failing,' Laura responded. 'Why not Luca? Your brother, he chooses his career over his country—

so now the attention turns to my son—' knowing eyes held Meg's '—and, of course, his beautiful bride-to-be."

'I'm not Luca's bride-to-be.' Meg jumped as if she'd been branded. 'We've only just met—it's hardly—'

'I tease you.' Laura smiled but it didn't quite reach her eyes. 'Still, that is what the press will say. When Luca is seen with anyone there is always speculation, but especially now. That is why it is imperative you behave properly. After we are finished here we have lunch back at the palace—I tell you then how you should behave with Luca.'

There was little chance of anyone at the casino recognising her, because back at the apartment, staring into the magnificent antique mirror over the fireplace, Meg barely recognised herself.

Her sun-bleached hair was but a memory now. Superbly toned down to a soft caramel-blond, it fell in a thick, straight, glossy curtain. Her complexion was smooth, her cheekbones impossibly visible thanks to the skill of the make-up artist—and she truly was an artist. With each stroke of her brush, with each dab of her finger she had sculpted Meg's face till it was almost unrecognisable—her blue eyes huge now, her already full lips glossy and pouting like a fashion model on the cover of a magazine. Even her body seemed to have changed. The dresser had crowed in delight at Meg's tall, svelte figure, but now as she stood and stared in the mirror, as perfect as the image supposedly was, Meg couldn't help but feel disappointed. The soft curves she'd fought so hard for had been all but eradicated in the simple, elegant shift dress, her legs impossibly long and slender in the highest of sandals.

'Pour his drink.' Laura's words echoed in her head as Meg followed protocol. 'Welcome him home with a smile.'

\* \* \*

What the hell had he done?

Walking into the lounge, for once Luca was lost for words. Oh, he was used to beautiful women, perfect make-up, perfect hair. That was what he liked—that was what he insisted on, after all; but watching Meg walk over, holding out his drink to him, a smile forced on her made-up mouth, softly enquiring about his day, it was almost grief that hit him. Where was the feisty, independent lady he had left here this morning? Where was the tender, fragile woman he had held in his arms last night?

'How was work?'

'Long.' Luca flashed an on-off smile. 'How did you get on today?'

'Great, the day spa was wonderful…'

'And my mother?'

'Charming.' Meg's smile was as stilted as his, but then she relented a touch, offering an observation, even if it wasn't expected from her.

'She was lovely, actually—she clearly adores you.'

'She can be a bit overbearing, but she means well.'

'I like her,' Meg mused, 'or I think I would if…' Her voice trailed off as she remembered her place—remembered there would be no getting to know anyone. Neither time nor protocol allowed. 'What time is the restaurant booked for?' Meg forced an even bigger smile. 'I'm really looking forward to dinner.'

'Dinner,' he said stoutly, 'will be served when I choose to arrive.'

'Perfect.' Meg's smile barely moved.

Whistling through his teeth, Luca picked up the telephone and ordered his bodyguard to meet with them, wondering again what the hell he had done.

* * *

'Just smile,' Luca said taking her arm as they approached the restaurant. 'If anyone tries to stop and talk just smile graciously and keep moving.'

'Of course.' Nervous and trying not to show it, Meg took in a deep breath as the restaurant doors opened, hearing the gasp of delight from the clientele as their hefty dinner bill was more than justified—a night dining in the same restaurant as Luca Fierezza giving all present a tale to be regaled later.

'The food here is superb.' Luca chatted on as if it were just the two of them, clearly used to waiters flitting around and his bodyguards seated at the next table, clearly not minding a jot that the whole restaurant was watching—but for Meg it was a living hell, each morsel of deliciously prepared food like a dry rock in her throat, each attempt at meaningless conversation drying up by the second sentence.

'Really superb,' Meg agreed, cutting up the damned rainbow mullet and rueing the fact it was an Italian prince she was with—they were only starting the main meal and were already four courses in!

They'd started with antipasto, but like no other Meg had experienced. Each mouthful had been a taste sensation; in fact, Meg had never tasted an olive that tasted so much like an olive—though she hadn't attempted to explain that to Luca, just demurely murmured her approval when the plate was removed. Then had come shrimp salad, which Meg had actually enjoyed, the salad drizzled in Niroli Virgin Olive and Orange Oil—a local delicacy, Luca had told her, and she could see why. If Australian customs had allowed, Meg would have been sorely tempted to blow her budget and ship a lifetime supply home.

For Meg, though, the real hard work started when the pasta arrived.

Three huge squares of ravioli, each packed with gourmet fillings and drizzled with thick cheese sauce.

'These are my favourite.' Luca smiled as he poised his knife and fork. '*Salute!*'

'*Salute.*' Meg beamed, taking a hefty slug of water and bravely soldiering on.

'Is there a problem, Meg?' Watching her push her food around the plate, Luca frowned.

'None at all,' Meg said brightly. 'It's delicious. So, how was your—?'

'Four times tonight you have asked about my day,' Luca broke in, 'and three times you have said my mother is charming. We have discussed the weather, the food, even the rate of exchange—'

'I'm sorry you find my company boring.' Meg flashed her eyes at him.

'I didn't say that.' Luca's voice was irritated. 'I just—'

'Just what, Luca?' Putting down her knife and fork with a clatter, Meg struggled to keep her voice down, the strain catching up with her, the disappointment in his eyes as he looked over at her choking her. Yet no one, not even Luigi sitting a mere table away, could have guessed the conversation was anything but amicable, her rigid smile still in place as she told Luca exactly what she thought. 'You rudely tell me I don't look the part, you tell me I am too angry and hostile, you tell me I have appalling manners—so now, when I'm dressed appropriately, when I'm speaking dutifully and keeping my elbows well off the table, suddenly you're bored! Now, if you'll excuse me, I'm going to the bathroom.' Placing her napkin on the table, Meg excused herself, then changed her mind, her voice deathly quiet, but loud enough that Luca could hear, her smile still in place but her eyes saying otherwise. 'Just what is it that you want me to be? You keep changing the rules, Luca. I am doing what was asked of me—tonight I look the part, tonight I am good enough to share your bed and dine at your table—'

'And purge afterwards—' Gripping her wrist, he caught her as she turned to go, almost immediately realising he'd gone too far because the look of sheer horror on her face could never be manufactured, her voice hoarse with emotion when finally she found it.

'Can we leave now please?'

'I'm sorry.' They were being driven from the restaurant, Meg's face flaming beneath her foundation as they headed back to the palace. 'It was just an off-the-cuff comment—I was angry. I had no idea it would upset you so much.'

'You don't know me at all, Luca.'

She felt like asking to be let out, asking Luigi to stop so she could run, just take her chances and run as far away from everything as possible, claustrophobic at the prospect of returning to the vast palace with him, whilst conceding there was no space big enough to allow her to hide from Luca. It was as if he could see inside her, every word he uttered exposing more and more of her, peeling her away till there would surely be nothing left.

'We will walk the last part.' They were inside the palace grounds now and Luca helped her out of the car, speaking in Italian to his guards while Meg stood gulping in the cool night air, grateful when the car slipped away into the darkness. 'Always I have to tell people where I go.' His deep voice had a low growl to it. 'I am in my own home, yet still I have to give my route. I tell them we walk along the beach. Is that okay?'

She gave a silent nod.

'I hate having to account for every move—that is why I prefer normally to stay at the casino. Not that I will be able to if I become…' He didn't finish, and, according to the rules she'd been privy to today, Meg should have left it there, should have known better than to pry or prolong a conversation he wanted to terminate, but it was so much easier to talk about him than her now, so much easier to dwell on his problems than her own.

'Will you have to give up the casino, then, if you become King?'

For the longest time he didn't answer, just walked on in silence, till they came to a gorgeous stretch of beach, Luca waiting as Meg took off her sandals. 'You can leave them there,' Luca said when she picked them up to carry them. 'No one will take them; this is a private beach.'

'It's stunning,' Meg breathed. She'd seen plenty of beautiful beaches both at home and on her travels, but if there was a piece of paradise on earth then this surely was it—the most beautiful land reserved for the most beautiful people. White sand as soft as powder dusted beneath her bare feet, the castle a stunning backdrop, the sea warm as occasionally it lapped at her feet.

'And it could all be mine.' Instead of staring out to the ocean Luca stared back at the island, but there was no expectancy in his voice, just weariness…. 'I could rule it all.'

'Do you want to?'

'Would you?

She thought long and hard before answering, the question so hypothetical it was almost impossible to imagine how she might feel in the circumstances. Only it wasn't hypothetical for Luca. She glanced over at his brooding face and tried to fathom for a moment his existence—one where every movement, every action was open to scrutiny, tried to fathom the price he paid for his lavish existence.

'I wouldn't want it,' Meg admitted finally. 'But then I'm such a private person, I just couldn't imagine being such…'

'Public property.' Luca chose the words for her. 'I was born into this, I have lived all my life in this goldfish bowl, yet it has taken till now for me to accept it. Now I have the casino, now I have a chance to be just Luca for a few hours, it is manageable—but if I become King then all that goes.'

'Does it have to?'

'There are rules—if you are a prince there are always rules.' Despite several thousand dollars of Italian silk suit, Luca lowered himself and stretched out on the sand, gesturing for Meg to join him. 'I ignored them when I was younger, of course—' he gave a rueful smile '—but now I try—if I become King, though—'

'There will be even more rules?' Meg offered.

'Many more.' Luca nodded. 'And running a casino conflicts with many of them. Your brother, Alessandro, would have had to give up his profession to be King—the ruler of Niroli must dedicate their life to the kingdom.'

'Alex would never give up medicine.' Meg knew that instantly. 'It's his life, but…'

'Running a casino is not so noble, huh?' Luca gave a weary shrug. 'It is not about what I want—I have been brought up to know that. When you are royalty, you know from an early age that things are different. I have always known there was a chance that one day I might be King. The fact I hoped it would never happen is irrelevant. It is what is expected, how I have been raised.'

'What does your mother say?'

'She is proud.' Luca shrugged. 'What mother wouldn't want her son to be King?'

Plenty that Meg could think of, but she didn't say that, of course, the abyss between them widening. Luca's world was just so far removed from hers, but something Luca had said didn't sit right. Meg could still hear the bitter note in Laura's voice when she'd spoken of Alex, was sure that, despite what Luca said, Laura was far from happy at the prospect of Luca ruling Niroli.

'What about your father?' Meg ventured. 'What would he have said about all this?'

'Nothing.' Luca's voice was black with bitterness. 'By this time of night he would be too drunk to form a sentence.' He gave a tight smile at her shocked expression. 'There—you have a story you can sell afterwards!'

'I would never do that. When you say—'

'Enough about me.' Luca rolled onto his side and stared over to where she sat, hugging her knees, gazing out to the ocean as she pondered his impossible life. 'Tell me something about you.'

'Like what?'

'What work do you do? Why did you leave your family to travel? As you say, I know nothing about you.'

'Me neither.' She smiled at his frown. '*That's* why I'm travelling. I work as a receptionist at a hotel in Queensland.'

'Do you enjoy it?' Luca enquired.

'Not really.' Meg shrugged. 'I like it, I suppose, the staff are nice and it pays the bills, but it's certainly not what I want to do for the rest of my life.'

'What work would you like to do?'

'I'll send you a postcard when I've worked that one out.'

'And in Australia, is there a boyfriend?' There was a

slightly hesitant note to his voice as if her answer actually mattered, but, Meg checked herself, a mere detail like that wouldn't matter to Luca. He wanted one thing and one thing only from her, and she'd better not forget it.

'No, well, no one special.'

'Has there been?' Luca asked perceptively. 'Is that what you are running away from?'

'I'm not running away,' Meg said defensively, 'and, no, there hasn't really been anyone special.'

'No children?'

'Of course not.' Meg laughed. 'I just told you I don't even have a boyfriend.'

'You never know in these times.' Luca shrugged. 'Would you like children some day?'

Meg gave a low laugh. 'Your mother told me to keep the conversation light....'

'My mother is not here.' Luca rolled his eyes. 'Well, would you?'

'I don't know.' Meg stared out into the distance—funny that the questions Luca was asking were all the ones she was asking of herself. 'Again—when I've worked out the answers I'll send you a postcard.'

He couldn't help but reach out and touch her.

Despite the closeness of their bodies, despite the conversation, as he stared at her, Luca felt as if he were watching from a distance, standing on the balcony of his apartment and watching this troubled lady sitting on the beach. Her loneliness was so palpable he wanted to end it, wanted to reach out and hold her, but as he did, as his hands reached for hers she jumped as if she'd been burnt. But Luca wasn't daunted, capturing her hand again and holding onto it, despite her resistance, feeling the pounding of her radial pulse beneath his fingers from just the tiniest contact and as slowly it settled, that troubled heart beating a more regular rhythm, Luca was filled with something akin to pride....

She *was* like a kitten. Oh, not the cute cuddly kind, more like the feral one who had come at night to the castle when he was younger, crying and meowing to be let in, then hissing and spitting when you approached.

His mother had put out scraps.

Luca could still remember her, dressed in her finest, jewels around her throat, a tiara in her hair, placing a saucer outside.

*'Perché?'* He could hear his youthful voice ask why? Why would she care about this tiny wild creature that didn't even want her help? Why would she come out into the cold for something so wild and ungrateful? But now he understood the rewards that came from the most unexpected of sources.

The noise of the casino, the endless demands on him had been no different from the thousands before, only today it had grated. For the first time he had actually wanted to come home, wanted to see her, *needed* to know more about her.

'I was angry at the restaurant,' Luca admitted, surprising himself with his honesty. 'Angry because all day I have looked forward to seeing you—and when I came home it was as if *you* had vanished.'

'You told me to.'

'I know....' He ran a confused hand over his forehead, intoned the words over and over. 'I know, I know...Meg, I do not know what is happening here—I just know that it cannot!'

'I know too.' Meg gulped, because she did. They were light years apart—two distant stars colliding, impossible in the present with the fallout yet to come.

'What I said—about your eating—I am very sorry. It was careless and thoughtless.'

'It was,' Meg said, then relented a touch, hearing the genuineness in his apology. 'I used to have an eating disorder. I don't actually do all that any more—I haven't in years....' She gave a pensive smile. 'You've no idea how good it feels to be able to say that.'

'You are better now?' Luca asked. 'Recovered?'

'Recovering,' Meg corrected. 'You never fully get over something like that—it's there with you always. Oh, nothing like it was—I don't panic about food all the time. I actually enjoy eating now....'

'Just not eight courses.' Luca winced.

'And not with an entire restaurant watching on!' Meg smiled at his discomfort.

'I truly am sorry,' he offered again.

'You weren't to know.'

'Can I?'

Even though his question wasn't particularly well phrased, Meg knew what he was asking and her first instinct was to change the subject, stand up perhaps and walk away....

Only she didn't.

Staring at the vast moon hanging like a paper lantern over the inky ocean, she sat in grateful silence for a moment until the flutter in her stomach stilled a touch, waited for the knee-jerk reaction to abate, and when it did Luca was waiting, patiently waiting for her to tell her story, if she so wanted.

And for the first time she did; she actually wanted to share this vital piece of herself with Luca, for no purpose or gain that she could fathom, other than that he was here—that, however unwittingly, he'd exposed her secret and that he mattered; to Meg, he mattered, *this* moment, however fleeting, really mattered. She turned and looked at him for a sliver of a second, then turned back to the beach, drinking in the view, searing it in her mind, knowing that if it ended, *when* it ended, this slice of time would be forever important.

'I was the biggest mistake of my parents' lives.' She didn't look at him as she spoke, didn't want to see his reaction, see the shock of sympathy in his eyes as she told her tale.

'Your parents?' Luca checked, watching her stiffen, then rephrasing his question. 'Your biological parents?'

'They'd never intended to have children and they never let me forget it even for a moment. They led this bohemian lifestyle, drifting from one place to another, which sounds romantic, only it wasn't….' Meg paused for a moment, arching her neck backwards and staring higher into at the sky as if searching for answers. 'I didn't fit into their lifestyle. Apparently I was a needy, very demanding baby.'

'Aren't all babies?'

'Perhaps,' Meg conceded. 'I think any demand on them from me was too much. If they hadn't had me they could have travelled more, had their all-night parties with their hippy friends—that's what they said anyway. All I know for sure is that they wanted me to disappear so in the end I did.'

'You ran away?'

'No, I just ceased to exist.'

'I don't understand.'

'You never could,' Meg said quietly. 'In all my childhood I can't remember one cuddle, not one kind word—not one,' she reiterated. 'Sometimes I wish they'd beat me—'

'Don't say that,' Luca interrupted, but Meg refused to back down.

'As I got older I tried to help them, tidying, cooking, cleaning, but nothing I did worked. All they wanted was for me to stay in my room, so in the end I did. I came out when they weren't there, used the bathroom before they got home so I wouldn't disturb them, ate whatever they'd left out for me…by the time it finished I wasn't allowed in the fridge or pantry. I was just left scraps.'

'How?'

Meg turned in surprise as he asked the question.

'How were they found out?' He frowned quizzically at her response. 'Did I say something wrong?'

'Most people ask who did I tell, or why didn't I say something…?'

'You were a child,' Luca said. 'They were your parents. How could you know it was so very wrong?'

'I didn't,' Meg sniffed, swallowing back tears, astounded by his insight, that this arrogant, seemingly insensitive man could, when it really mattered, say the very right thing. 'I just knew I felt bad, knew that my family wasn't normal, it was like this dirty secret and there was no one I could tell….'

'I know.'

Glassy eyes jerked to his, her first thought to scoff, to tell him he couldn't possibly know, but as she looked over, saw the pain in his eyes, Meg realised that he did, that somehow Luca, this royal prince, this man with the most privileged of backgrounds, somehow had visited the dark hole she was clawing her way out of.

'How *do* you know?' Meg whispered, the derision that would have been in her voice a mere few seconds ago completely absent. 'What happened, Luca?'

'It is not my tale to tell.' He shook his proud head. 'But I know what you say when you describe keeping a secret. I know how I felt in school, seeing my family in the newspaper in the morning, on the television some evenings, being told over and over how lucky, how privileged, how very noble…' He didn't finish, *couldn't*, Meg realised. Instead he asked a question of his own. 'If your parents didn't feed you, wouldn't you want food even more so now?'

'I wish!' She gave a small laugh, but it wasn't mocking, knowing no one could understand, that even she couldn't truly understand it. 'My parents *forgot* to enroll me in high school, eventually the welfare system caught up and, to cut a long story short, I was adopted by the two most wonderful people. Suddenly I had everything, parents who adored me, a brother, a beautiful home, food prepared for me… I just couldn't accept it. I kept waiting for it to all just disappear, sure that if I put a foot wrong, somehow they'd hate me too. I hit puberty, suddenly I was growing up, I suppose food was the only thing I thought I could control….'

She stopped then, utterly drained from her revelation, and even if there was loads more to say, right now she simply couldn't manage it, wondering now his take on all this. She turned shyly to face him, bracing herself for shock or sympathy in his eyes from her sorry tale, that maybe he'd parcel her off, return her from whence she came, like shop-soiled goods, but his eyes were now adoring her, his want for her never more visible, and for Meg it was a revelation. She was stunned that, after she'd given him the very worst piece of her, somehow, he considered her beautiful. And best of all he didn't try to end the conversation with trite words or well-worn clichés when none of them could have helped. Instead, reaching over, he kissed her softly, delivering a tender touch when she needed it the most.

'Come,' Luca said, pulling away, and Meg knew he was struggling, knew that the kiss they had just shared had been meant as a display of compassion, but with the energy between them it was a dangerous move. Like a match tossed onto parched bushland as he stood up and offered his hand, the whole place, Meg knew could ignite at any second; the tension as they headed towards his home was palpable.

'I am tired of staying at the palace.' It was Luca that filled the strained silence and Meg looked up at the castle and saw through his eyes, perhaps, the imposing walls that shadowed them.

'You hate it, don't you?'

'No,' Luca said wearily, 'but no matter how many times I walk this path I never feel I am going home. After the Feast we will move back to the casino,' Luca said decisively. 'There I can relax.'

'Why?' She knew she was pushing, knew she was asking more than he was prepared to give, but still she persisted, guilty almost at having revealed so much of herself, needing him to do the same. 'Why doesn't it feel like—?'

'Leave it, Meg,' Luca growled, his hand tight around hers, but just as he warned her away he let her come a little closer, slowing the pace till finally they stood facing each other. 'I never feel like I belong there—it is hard to explain. I am told I was born to all this and yet sometimes I feel like a stranger… Enough!' He walked on more purposefully now, letting go of her hand as she went to retrieve her shoes, and she wished she knew what to say, wished she knew the questions to ask, but instead she concentrated on the tiny buckles of her sandals, her hand shaking so much she could barely manage the simple task, so conscious now of his presence. When she stood she knew he'd be there waiting, knew they wouldn't be walking a step further.

'Oh, Meg…' Luca's lips crushed hers as his hungry mouth sought hers. This wasn't anything like the kiss they had shared back at the casino. That had been about lust and attraction; this one was more, so much more.

It ached of need, of want, of something she had never felt, his kiss so overwhelming, so demanding, so consuming that it was all she could think of, all she wanted to think of. Kissing off her lipstick, devouring her, he was pushing her down onto the sand, yet supporting her at the same time, her body sinking backwards as somehow he broke her fall, lowering her onto the sandy floor, his body on top of her, the weight of him exquisite, the *feel* of him pressing into her, wedging her beneath him. His hands dragged over her, his fingers pressing into her breast, searching for the side zipper and locating it, moaning as his fingers met her warm, ripe flesh, and to an onlooker it would have looked like an attack, but the apparent suddenness, the haste, was a mirage. It had been building since he'd come home, since their first kiss, since they'd laid eyes on each other, and Meg knew he somehow needed this, that whatever dark place he'd just visited in his mind, this was what he needed to chase it away, and she gave it to him gladly, gave it because she needed it, too.

Needed to escape for a moment as well.

His rough jaw scratched at her chest, his mouth searching and claiming her nipple, sucking her sweet flesh as his hands slid up her dress, cupping her bottom, his erection pressing against the satin of her knickers and she wanted him.

Wanted him.

Meg's body was responding without her orders, bold in a way she'd never been before. As he slid down his own zipper, her hips lifted to welcome him, his manhood still pressing into her knickers as she slid provocatively beneath him, rueing the strip of satin that parted them, losing herself in the delicious friction. His needy fingers were tearing at the flimsy material and, panting with expectancy, she knew the second he tore them free he would be inside her, knew from his rasping breath, his jerking motions, that he was as close as her, and the first flicker of Meg's orgasm was aligning, at the greedy thought of him spilling as he entered her....

'I have wanted this—' as he tore off her knickers Luca's arbitrary words were those of a lover in the throes of passion '—since I first saw you. This, this is what I wanted.'

Sex.

This wasn't the deal they had struck—sex, yes, but not this! Not this wild abandonment, not giving herself to him so completely, so fully, letting him take such supreme control, and something in her died, the motions purely mechanical now as Luca positioned himself to enter her. But he pulled back, his voice hoarse with question as he sensed the rapid change in her, felt the body that had been so closely meshed with his unyielding now in his arms. 'What is wrong?'

'Nothing,' she whispered, closing her eyes, willing the moment over, wanting him to just take her and be done, but that wasn't enough for Luca. He'd tasted her fervour and wanted more, his confused eyes searching hers for an answer.

'What just happened there?'

'Nothing,' she attempted, tried to pretend that everything was okay, but the passion of before wasn't one that could be manufactured, the sheer assault of emotion that had hit her not one that could be faked, and Luca knew it.

'One minute you are alive in my arms, one minute you are crying out my name, then this! I need to know what happened, Meg.'

'I changed my mind!' Embarrassed, confused, she found

it was easier to shout than cry, easier to attack than back down. 'I am allowed to, you know.'

'You really should be more careful how you tease men.'

'I wasn't teasing….' Tears were threatening but she gulped them back, Luca's brutal response stinging with each sharp word.

'Much more careful!' he reiterated loudly. 'When I met you, you were accepting drinks off rich businessmen—I should have known better.'

'I'm not like that,' Meg insisted, but Luca wasn't to be swayed by her pleas.

'Aren't you?' he demanded. 'Well, if you're really not then here's a piece of advice: lying on a beach half naked with your legs wrapped around me is not the wisest time to change your mind. Not all men are as honourable as me!'

'I know.' Her teeth were chattering so violently she could barely get the words out. He had every right to be angry, every right to be confused; Meg was herself. It wasn't sex that was the problem, it was the feelings behind the act—how could she possibly tell him it was *how* much she wanted him that scared her the most? 'Maybe we should just…' Her mind searched for answers and desperate times called for desperate measures, and not all of them wise. Leaning forward, she pressed her mouth to his, kissed him with all the false passion she could mount, screwing her eyes closed in shame and mortification as with an enraged howl he pushed her aside.

'Get it over with!' He finished the unspoken sentence for her, and added his own crude twist to the end. 'Do it like dogs in the street then walk away. I am a prince!' Angry, dignified and straight to the point, he stood up and arranged his clothing as Meg did the same. 'I have absolutely no need to accept your charity.'

# CHAPTER TEN

THE TENSION had been unbearable since they'd returned.

Luca, refusing to spend two nights on the sofa, had thrown her out a blanket and one of her very new nightdresses, then commandeered the royal bed, clearly with no expectation of her joining him, and Meg had spent the night staring into the dying embers of the fire.

She wanted him.

More times through the night than she could remember she'd stood up, wanting so badly to go into his room, to explain that her change in mood had been nothing to do with him and everything to do with her, but she'd baulked at the final hurdle. Hand gripping the door handle, ready to knock, over and over she'd padded back to the couch.

'I am late!' Bristling with rancour, Luca stalked into the lounge dressed in nothing but black boxer shorts and a foul mood. Picking up the phone and demanding coffee, he turned his angry mood back to her when she tried to talk to him.

'Luca, about last night…'

'There's nothing to discuss,' Luca dismissed, 'and could you please at least put on a robe? Don't display what's not for sale, Meg.'

'You put out this nightdress for me, Luca,' Meg argued. 'What else was I supposed to wear? I'm not trying to tease you. I'm trying to talk to you!'

'I don't need to hear it,' Luca roared. 'Since the moment I set eyes on you, you have caused nothing but trouble— reeling me in with your lies, with your sob stories. Well, not any more. Now you are in my palace and you will act by my rules.' He disappeared for a moment, then came over, stood over her, his black eyes filled with contempt as he picked up her arm as if she were a belligerent child, dressing her in a robe and bundling her onto the sofa. 'For two more days you are in Niroli—and then, I want you out of here.'

'Fine!' Meg snapped—and it should have been. He wasn't sending her back to prison. In two days she would be out of here, and clearly from Luca's reaction he didn't expect her to sleep with him now. She'd got exactly what she wanted— so why did she feel like crying?

'Now I must go to mass—I am expected to go at Feast weekend.'

'Do I have to come?'

'Please,' Luca snorted. 'Only a lady would join me at mass, only a woman who was considered suitable to be my wife would come with me—and you, Meg, are neither. This morning, apart from the staff you will have the palace much to yourself—the family will be at various celebrations for the Feast. This afternoon you will make full use of the staff that come from the spa to do your hair and make-up, and then you will escort me to the ball tonight.'

'I'm surprised you'd want me to,' Meg bit back, close to crying and trying not to let him see.

'The place settings are done—your name is already down, I need an escort and I have neither the time nor inclination to find another. You will be there with me.' A knock at the door heralding the arrival of his coffee didn't stop his sharp tongue. 'I can bring any tart to that!'

She was tempted to stay in the room after he'd left, to just hide herself away, but his acrid words played over and over in her mind and in the end Meg was grateful to leave the apartment for a while. She found herself walking along the marble corridors; the staff were everywhere, busy arranging vast floral arrangements, polishing the marble floors, giving her curious looks as she passed. Meg felt like an intruder and a fraud. As if she'd been locked in some luxurious department store—all the treasures on show, but nothing she could ever own.

'Can I get you anything, *signorina?*' One of the maids approached as Meg stood gazing out at the sparkling pool and, because she was in a palace, because incidentals like heading back to her room to collect the new bathers she'd chosen yesterday didn't matter here, Meg, for the first time, utilised her temporary privileged position.

'I'd like to swim.'

'Of course.' The maid smiled. 'I'll send someone to collect your things—this way.' She led Meg through to the changing room. In a matter of minutes the small gold-thread bikini she had chosen had arrived. And by the time Meg had stepped out poolside, a jug of iced lemonade and a fruit platter were waiting for her.

'If you need anything else just pick up the phone.'

'I won't,' Meg said, thanking her.

The bliss of the cool water on her body was unsurpassed. Sliding through the still, azure pool, she found it was easy to forget the turmoil of her life, the chaos that had brought her to this point, but real life soon invaded. The maid's white shoes were waiting for her as she breathlessly came to the edge and, squinting into the sunlight, Meg shielded her eyes and looked up as the maid informed her that a visitor had arrived for her at the palace.

'Who?' Meg asked, her mind galloping hopefully—a lawyer, perhaps, or even Alex—frowning when she heard who it was.

'Jasmine—she says she is a close friend. Would you like Security to let her through the gates?'

'Jasmine?'

It seemed a decade since she'd seen Jasmine, so much had happened since that night at the casino, and Meg's heart soared—finally someone who could help her sort this mess out. Finally someone who would be able to help her clear her name.

# CHAPTER ELEVEN

ACID CHURNED in his stomach.

For Luca, disgustingly healthy with the constitution of an ox, the overwhelming nausea that struck him as he left the church was an enigma. The blistering sun on the white tombstones was too bright this morning, the noise from the jubilant crowd just too loud. Despite the heat of the morning, the sweat that broke on his brow was icy cold. For a moment, as he excused himself, put on dark shades and darted around the side of the building, he thought he must have food poisoning.

'*Ke che*, Luca?'

It was his mother, her face etched with concern, her hands reaching up to pull off the dark glasses and try to fathom what was wrong.

'*Dove* Meg?' As direct as her son, she asked Meg's whereabouts, frowning as Luca gave a casual shrug. 'Why didn't you bring her with you?'

'Why *would* I bring her here?'

'Because she is Alessandro's sister,' Laura answered carefully.

'She is not his blood.' Luca shrugged. 'It is up to the king to introduce her if he sees fit. Anyway, she is just visiting Niroli for a few days; it's no big deal.'

'That's not how it seemed to me yesterday.' Laura frowned up at her son. 'Yesterday you asked me to take care of her, to look after her as if she were family. I got the distinct impression you like her.'

'She is just a girl, just a woman I met a couple of days ago. If I bring her here to the church…' He gestured to the crowds of well-wishers, waiting for a glimpse of their beloved royal family, the press with their cameras ready, all descending on Niroli in expectation of the grand ball to be held tonight.

'People might think it is serious?' Laura finished for him.

'Exactly.' Luca nodded, glad that his mother got it. 'It would be all over the papers tomorrow.'

'You have to live, Luca.' Laura pointed out. 'The press are always going to jump to conclusions, whatever you do or don't do—they will make their own story. You know how it is.'

'Meg doesn't, though.' Luca shook his head. 'I don't think she'd…' He gave a helpless gesture with his hands. 'She is not like most other women; she would not like the scrutiny.'

'So you want to protect her?' Laura asked softly, her knowing eyes taking in the grim set of her son's mouth.

'It's not that simple.' Luca gave an impatient shake of his head, but Laura wasn't to be deterred. Despite the dark glasses, despite the sheer height of him, Laura confronted him, tried to get him to express the problem.

'Feelings never are, Luca.' She put a hand to his arm. 'This is the first time I have heard you talk about a woman like this, the first time I have seen you worrying about what the press might do to her. I would say that Meg is *not like most women* in more ways than one for you.'

*She was.*

Meg wasn't like most women he had dated, in fact Meg wasn't like any woman he had ever met.

She was *more* of a woman—as if the essence of femininity had somehow been distilled, the mere scent of her provoking a need, a want, that was unsurpassed—yet she enraged him.

Her carelessness with herself, her recklessness—his anger at her this morning had been more at himself than at her. How could he explain to his mother—to anyone—that the woman back at the palace had stolen, not only the Niroli jewels, but his heart as well?

*Dio*, what did this woman do to him?

'It does not matter how I feel.' Still Luca resisted the temptation; still he refused to fathom the possibility. 'She leaves on Tuesday anyway.'

'Then talk to her now, Luca,' Laura urged. 'Spend time with her while you have it.'

'I have things to do today.' Luca shook his head at the hopelessness of it all. 'Commitments, you know that.'

'You will always have commitments, Luca,' Laura answered hotly. 'As long as you are a prince, duty will always be calling you, and if you become King—' She took a deep breath and steadied herself because no elaboration was needed; they both knew what lay ahead if that was the path laid out for him. 'You must learn balance—' her voice was softer, but no less urgent '—to survive in this family; sometimes your first duty must be to yourself.'

'Yours never was.' Seeing the warning look in his mother's eyes, Luca snapped his mouth closed and gritted his teeth—the subject he had touched on was still barred after all these years, but the churning feeling in his stomach was back, the *rage* he felt rising again, and for the first time ever, he had his say.

'I saw what that bastard did to you.' As his mother opened her mouth to protest, to shush him, Luca overrode her.

'Don't ask me to be quiet again. Don't tell me I have no idea what I'm talking about.'

'This is surely not the place, Luca.'

'Where is?' Luca continued. 'Back at the palace in front of the staff, or maybe we should go to the local Niroli psychologist.'

'Luca, please…' Laura begged, but he was beyond reason.

'I tried to help you! After, when I came to see if you were okay, you slapped me, you told me I spoke filthy lies, that I imagined things. But what sort of sick person would make that up?'

'Luca, you didn't make it up…' Tears spilled out of his mother's well-made-up eyes. 'I am so sorry I confused you, slapped you… Can you understand that I was trying to protect you?'

'How?' The noise from the gathered crowd, cheering as the royal family left the church, drowned out his wounded roar, the Niroli church bells peeling out to celebrate the Feast as Luca raged at the world he had witnessed as a child. 'How can you say you were protecting me, by denying what I know I saw?' He thought he might actually vomit, right there at her feet as the filth of the past spilled out. 'He beat you, slammed his fist into your face over and over. I saw him kicking you, beating you—that man was my father who I was supposed to respect and obey. That bastard would have been King. Where do the Niroli Rules apply here, Mother? Where was his honour when he did that to you?'

'Don't be angry, Luca,' Laura pleaded. 'Let it pass—let it rest now. He is gone.'

'Yet still you defend him,' Luca croaked, still breaking the rules, stepping in territory that was as forbidden as it was new. 'By pretending you were happy, by pretending you had choices, he is not gone—still he is here, still he has the power over you.' He almost expected to be slapped—for her hand to silence him again just as it had all those years ago, the one time he'd confronted her—and again he'd have taken it, for his mother he'd have taken it, but instead he was stunned to see that through her tears she was smiling; a soft, pensive smile that only confused him.

'I *was* happy, Luca.'

'How?'

'I took the advice I just gave you—I learnt balance. I learnt that, to survive, sometimes my first duty was to myself. Luca, what happened was wrong, but that is not the entire picture— it is not *all* that our marriage was. Let your father rest, Luca. Don't waste your life hating what you cannot change.'

'Is that what you did?'

She didn't need to answer, the answer was there for him to see—and even if he didn't understand, he accepted it, believed it, because for the first time he looked, really looked at his mother—saw the serenity in her face that surely only came when one was truly at peace with themselves—and he saw what was missing in Meg.

'I have been told by the king there is to be no more scandal.' Luca dragged in a breath, wondered whether to go on, but the honesty of before had forged a new path and, after a moment's hesitation, Luca continued to lead the way, a tiny smile twisting his tense mouth as he tried to sum up Meg to his mother. 'She is trouble!'

'You were trouble,' Laura pointed out. 'And if this Meg were straightforward she would not hold your interest for long, Luca.' Laura smiled too, revelling in the new closeness, even managing a small joke of her own. 'Then you'd end up getting divorced and what a scandal that would be—better to get it over with now, perhaps? The people of Niroli can forgive an honest mistake.'

'What about a dishonest one?' Luca watched as his mother winced, but she quickly recovered.

'Talk to your lady, Luca—whatever the problem, surely you, of all people, can work it out.'

Maybe he could.

Driving back to the palace, Luca was filled with possibility. He had paid the guard off—that drunk wouldn't remember anything anyway, would never put the two women together. Despite what he'd told her, Meg didn't need a lawyer—her things were in the boot of his car. Pulling over, he ripped open the backpack—her passport, her clothes were all there, and he would offer her them now, give her the chance to leave the island if that was what she wanted—but first he'd ask her to stay.

The magnitude of what he was proposing to do dawned on Luca then—she was a liar, a thief, a commoner and clearly she had issues. She was the last person a prince, a future king should be dating, but then again...

Picking up the sheer top she had worn that fateful night, remembering the feel of her in his arms, the *instant* attraction that had propelled them—forced them—to this point, Luca realised she was the *only* person he could be dating, that whatever her problems, whatever had happened in the past, he wanted to help her, to release her from whatever prison she was in.

Burying his face in the soft silk, Luca knew he could no more walk away now than he could have done when he'd found her in the cell.

Taking a deep breath, he closed his eyes in expectation, waiting for the heady, feminine fragrance that was so much Meg to drench his senses, frowning at the cheap, musky scent that filled his nostrils.

Unfurling the top in his hand, he noticed the wine and food stains on the delicate fabric—realising then the horrendous mistake he had made in not trusting her!

And for the first time in the whole sorry saga he cried.

# CHAPTER TWELVE

'SURELY HE MUST have given you some money?' Jasmine's voice was angry and desperate as she refused over and over to accept that Meg could give her nothing. Since the moment she'd teetered to the poolside, hung-over and bitter, Meg had realised it was a mistake to have let her in.

One of the maids was cleaning nearby windows, frowning at the disturbance by the pool, Jasmine's greedy requests getting louder by the minute, her anger escalating, the situation rapidly getting out of control.

'I think you should leave now, Jasmine.' Meg tried to keep her voice controlled and even, tried not to show the anxiety she was feeling as her supposed friend overstepped all the boundaries.

'Why?' Jasmine shouted. 'Are you worried that I'll embarrass you in front of your new posh friends? You didn't mind me when I was getting drinks bought for us all night, did you?' She was walking over now and Meg blanched at the stench of stale alcohol on her breath, knew that at any minute Jasmine might even hit her, and that there was absolutely nothing she could do except suffer the indignity of a so-called cat fight in Luca's beautiful home.

'I think you've outstayed your welcome, Jasmine.'

It wasn't just Luca's unexpected presence that had Meg jumping, but the absolute loathing in his voice and, despite their row and the harsh words that had been uttered just a couple of hours ago, she'd never been so relieved to see him. Jasmine was out of control and things were turning nasty, but so commanding was Luca's presence that within seconds Jasmine had picked up her bag.

'I was just leaving!'

'I didn't mean just here at the palace.' As Jasmine flounced off, the thunder of Luca's voice momentarily stopped her in her tracks. 'I want you out of Niroli.'

'Luca!' Despite her relief that the situation was under control, Meg thought he was being a bit harsh by demanding Jasmine leave the island, but clearly, whatever Meg thought, she actually knew nothing, because suddenly Jasmine was running, her stilettos not the ideal footwear for a quick poolside getaway, but Luca didn't chase her. He didn't move an inch, just stood as two of his bodyguards caught the woman in a rather undignified tussle.

'What's going on?' Meg begged, startled eyes turning to Luca, then widening in horror as realisation dawned even before Luca had a chance to explain.

'Your *friend* was the thief.' Luca's lips sneered the words out as he glared over at Jasmine. 'Your *friend* borrowed your top and when she sobered up and realised how *stupido* she'd been to attempt to steal from the Fierezzas she decided to get rid of the evidence—in your bag!'' He didn't await Meg's reaction, just strode along the pool to where Jasmine stood, her drunken bravado gone in the face of such power, Luca clearly someone no one would choose to mess with. 'My staff will take you to the port and see you onto a boat. If you choose to stay, then that is your right, but know I will press charges. I will use all my might, and, believe me, it is plenty, to see that you are prosecuted to the full extent of the law. My family writes the rules of Niroli, Jasmine, and I will make it my business to see that they are followed to the letter!'

'How?' Meg was sitting on the bed in her bikini, still trembling from the vile confrontation with Jasmine, and reeling from the shock of Luca's revelation. Still burning from his horribly hurtful words to her this morning. 'How did you know? Have you always known it was her?'

'I found out about ten minutes before you did.' Luca sat down beside her, went to put an arm around her to comfort her, to stop her shaking, but Meg brushed him off. Feigned affection was not what she needed now. 'I am sorry for not believing you.'

'I presume I'm free to go.' It wasn't a question, but a statement. Meg stood on rather shaky legs and tried to locate her robe, suddenly conscious of her lack of attire.

'Your things are in my car.' Luca couldn't look at her, actually had to divert his eyes. To see her so stunned and still so very proud, to see that gorgeous body barely dressed and know he had no claim on it was killing him inside, and because it was a morning for being honest, and lies had got him nowhere, he told Meg the full truth. 'They have always been in my car. The night I came to the jail—I didn't pay your bail. I bribed the guard. There were no charges being laid, no need for you to contact a lawyer—'

'There was no need for me to be here at all really,' Meg bitterly broke in, fruitlessly searching for the blessed robe as she digested his words, not realising she'd left it down at the pool. 'You didn't even get sex!'

'I don't want sex from you, Meg,' Luca said wearily.

'Well, if you've quite finished completely humiliating me, could you possibly arrange to get my things sent up from the car and then I'll be out of here?'

He found his *own* robe for her, handed it to her, summoning the strength to say what he felt as she put it on. It was way too big for her, smothering her slender body, her hands trembling with fury and indignation as she did up the tie.

'I want you to stay, Meg.'

'Why?' she snapped. 'Now I'm not a common thief I'm suddenly more acceptable? Well, guess what, Luca—nothing's actually changed. I never was a thief, I never deserved to be spoken to in the way you did before—'

'I understand that,' Luca interrupted. 'And this has nothing to do with what I have just found out—even before I realised Jasmine was the thief I was on my way home to ask you to stay.'

She didn't buy it, just didn't get it, shaking her head as he surely heaped lie upon lie. 'Would you please just get my things?'

'Only when you listen to me.' Luca was talking over her now. 'Only when you hear what I have to say.'

'There's nothing *to* say,' Meg interrupted furiously. 'You've kept me a virtual prisoner here—'

'I understand you have been treated badly…' His accent was thick with emotion. 'And I also now understand why you did not want to sleep with me; without trust it is nothing.' The directness of his statement silenced her, silenced even Luca for a moment, honesty a breath away and both terrified to hear it, scared of saying the wrong thing, of blowing out the tiny flicker that still existed between them. 'You gave me all of you—told me about yourself, asked me to believe in you—yet I gave you *nothing* in return. I do not want just sex from you, Meg, I want the passion, I want the woman I held in my arms before, I want you crying out my name because you need to hear it—and I understand now why you felt you could not give that piece of yourself.'

'I just wanted you to trust me.'

'I know,' Luca said softly. 'And for that I will always be sorry, but will you believe me when I say that through it all I never stopped trusting *in* you?'

'That doesn't make sense.' Meg frowned, trying to work out the translation, but this time Luca hadn't made a mistake.

'Always I have trusted in you. Trusted that you were a better person than the one I was seeing, trusted that there was more to you than the woman that was being revealed to me.'

He had. With blinding clarity, Meg saw that, despite everything, *always* he had been there for her—always he had believed that she could be so much better. He just hadn't known that she already was.

'You asked that night in the restaurant what I wanted you to be. Had I not made that stupid comment you would have heard my answer—what I wanted was the you I knew was in there. Somewhere between the grubby little thief I first brought home, and the polished mannequin I took out that night. *That*, I believe, is the real Meg, the one I was desperate, *am* desperate, to get to know—if you'll let me.'

She didn't know how to respond, so he did it for her.

'I understand this is a lot to take in. I just ask that you do not leave in haste.'

'You have to go…' Confused, she shook her head. 'You have the parade, duties to attend.'

'They can wait,' Luca said firmly.

'The king said there must be no more scandal.' She

actually wanted him to leave, wanted some time alone to draw breath, to assimilate her jumbled thoughts into some sort of order, to process all that he was saying. 'You can't just let everyone down....' She was fumbling for excuses. At this, the most important moment in her life, she was practically throwing him out, pointing out why he couldn't possibly stay, and Luca saw through her in an instant.

'Do you want me to leave, Meg?'

'No.' Like a driver swerving to avoid a child, her first reaction was pure instinct, but as she slammed her foot on the brakes it was about slowing things down, avoiding the impact that was surely inevitable. 'Yes, I think you should....'

'What is wrong, Meg? And don't say nothing.'

'I'm scared,' she admitted, watching his aghast expression. 'Not of you—of me. Luca...' Shy yet brave, she told him her truth. 'Last night, when I stopped, when you thought I was teasing...'

'You don't have to explain.'

'But I do.' Meg gulped. 'I wanted you the first night I met you and every minute since. I want you so much it scares me.'

'You have never slept with anyone?' Luca asked, confused when she shook her head.

'I have, but not like that.' Her eyes pleaded with him to understand. 'Luca, when I'm with you...it's like I lose it, like I have no control.'

'That is what lovemaking is—trusting in each other's bodies, losing your mind, your control and knowing no harm will come. In my arms you would be safe.'

'I don't think I can,' Meg whispered. 'I don't think I can be the woman you want...'

'You already are,' Luca said. 'And one day, you will want

me as I want you, one day you will be ready to trust me—till then I wait.'

He didn't have to—that he understood her fear, that still he stood before her, not judging, just understanding, made her safe, made her sure, and it was Meg now reaching out for him, made bold by his certainty, by his utter faith in all that they could be.

'It doesn't have to be now,' he said.

'Oh, it does,' Meg whispered.

'You want it quickly over and done with?' Luca teased, just enough to eke out a smile. 'I'm sure that can be easily arranged!' But the joking was over then—her honest admission tearing at his heartstrings.

'I don't want to let you down,' she said quietly.

'You never, ever could.'

Tentatively he kissed her and she felt his tender restraint, his hand warming her shivering body, the scent of chlorine mingling with his cologne, and though it had none of the urgency of before, it was so loaded with passion, so full of a deeper desire, it could only gain in momentum.

Her momentum.

Suddenly she was aware of her near nakedness compared to him, instead of being embarrassing, it irritated her. She needed to feel his skin against hers, her impatient hands fiddling with his shirt buttons until Luca halted her.

'Enjoy the journey,' Luca whispered, removing her hands and taking off his own shirt, his own clothes as still he kissed her. 'There is no rush.'

Oh, but there was.

Some people looked better dressed, but not Luca—stunning in a suit, he was absolutely breathtaking naked. Every promise she had glimpsed replayed tenfold when she saw him—exquisitely beautiful, like the Statue of David she had taken her camera to on her trip to Rome, his shoulders wide, a fan of jet hair on his broad chest all tapering to a flat, toned stomach. Until that moment, Meg hadn't thought men's legs could be sexy, only his were. His muscular thighs glimmered. And because she could, because she should, Meg glimpsed the bit that mattered, history rewritten as she defined true masculine beauty—the Statue of David way out of proportion to this Adonis.

Maybe he sensed the shift in her, maybe her fervour was infectious, because it was Luca now calling the shots, his thick arms pulling her towards him, fingers plying her swollen bosom from her bikini top, and then untying the laces of her bottoms, his fingers finding her swollen bud, his tongue dragging from her chest to her stomach, burying his face in her most intimate place, his tongue cooling the heat that flared and simultaneously fanning it.

She could feel her body giving in to him, feel great waves of lust ripping through her, but rather than scaring her it excited her now—as he lay her on the bed her whole body trembled with want, each kiss more intoxicating than the last, his fingers sliding into her, oiling his delicate way, till she was so moist, so ready, there was no fear, just want. The feel of him entering her, inside her, moving within her, was unsurpassed, his skin sliding against hers, his mouth kissing the hollows of her neck. She could have stayed in this moment forever, enjoying the journey as Luca had said, but her body was hurtling towards a new destination, moving to a rhythm of its own, lifting, rocking herself against him, her toes literally curling, her neck arching at the intensity of it all, and for a single second she fought it, tried to hold onto that piece of herself as his body demanded it *all*.

'Let it happen, *mia cara*,' he rasped, and so she did, and realised with shameless delight that it was Luca who was struggling to stay in control—that her body, the one she had so bitterly loathed, was utterly adored. Heat flared inside, rushing up her spine like an electric shock, her whole body stiffening, contracting, dragging him ever deeper inside. She cried out his name as Luca did hers—feeling him bucking inside her, delivering his precious load to her deprived body, and, when it was over, when her body came to a shuddering, exhausted halt, still he was holding her, still he was there, her world a little different now but surely better for what she had achieved.

For what *they* had achieved.

'I never knew it could be that good.' Meg sighed. 'Never imagined it could be so…'

'Neither did I.'

She blinked back at him—his heartfelt words were like blossoms falling, each one paving the way for the fruit that might follow, only Luca hadn't finished yet, offering now the piece of himself he had held back forever, his torrid secret somehow turned into a precious gift.

'I never knew I could want so much to share with another person—but now it is my turn to give that piece of me to you.

'I witnessed my father…' He struggled to continue only he didn't have to, Meg put her hand up to halt him.

'You don't have to tell me, Luca.'

'I want to.' Luca nodded, the gesture more for his benefit than hers, forcing a certainty that wasn't there in his voice. 'He beat her—badly. I saw it happen once when I was a child.'

'It must have been awful.'

'What was more awful was that it didn't happen.' He saw the cloud of confusion pass over her features, infinitely grateful when she didn't speak, just let him explain in his own time. 'I was told I imagined it, that my father was a wonderful man, might one day be King, how could I dare even *think* such things. My mother slapped me when I tried to help.'

It was as if she'd shaken a snow globe, those strong, arrogant features blurring, those knowing eyes clouding at the painful memory, and Meg knew better than to talk, she just held him until the blizzard settled and the features she knew aligned into focus.

'My mother told me I was never to speak of it—that it would cause more damage if anyone knew; that she could handle it. Maybe she was right—truly, I do not know. It happened since they were married. I saw photos of their honeymoon, my mother had a cut over her eye. To this day she swears she had too much wine with supper and tripped on the deck of the royal yacht.'

'Maybe she did?'

Luca gave a hollow laugh utterly void of humour. 'My father often talked of her drinking, her clumsiness, the staff did too. I guess it's easier to question the morals of the wife than those of the heir to the throne. You know, I have never seen my mother have more than one drink to be polite at a function; the clumsiness stopped the day my father died.'

'That's why you went off the rails when you were younger,' Meg offered. 'If a possible future King of Niroli could act like that, then what the hell?'

He smiled. Painful and loaded it might be, but Luca actually smiled, holding her hand back now.

'How did a little thing like you get so wise?'

'Group Therapy.' Meg even laughed as she said it. 'And a lot of it—I've heard tales that would make your hair curl.'

'Always in my life there have been duties, obligations, and for a long time I chose to ignore them.'

'But not now?' Meg ventured.

'Now I respect them,' Luca offered. 'Now I see that the rules I once snubbed, the laws I rebelled against, are actually there for a reason. To rule Niroli it is not enough to merely live by the laws of the land—a king has to live beyond them, adhere to a strict code of conduct, not just for his peoples' sake but for himself and the people he loves.

'Over and over the subjects of Niroli have forgiven me—"he is young, a little wild"—but now the excuses run out. Now I have to make a choice.' Black, agonised eyes found hers.

'Do you want to be King?'

'I don't know.' For the first time ever he sounded confused—this beautiful, strong man actually bewildered. 'You said on the beach you couldn't do it…'

'This isn't about me,' Meg urged, but it fell on deaf ears, Luca hushing her so that he could continue.

'All I know is this—you matter. You matter more to me than I can even understand. For the first time I think of someone else first. I have known you such a short time yet I feel as if you are a part of me. Does that sound mad?'

'Yes—' Meg smiled through her tears '—but, then again, I think I'm going crazy too. Luca, I cannot be a part of your decision.'

'If we stay together, Meg, if I become King, this *will* be your life—this is what you have to understand.'

'We don't have to make any choices now,' Meg insisted, but she could hear the fruitlessness of her words. As he'd explained on the first night, his status didn't allow the luxury of normal dating, and whether their relationship lasted a week or a lifetime, from the moment they stepped out together *everything* would change.

'You've been through so much.' His own torrid memories were pushed aside, his hand reached out and captured her cheek, and it was so tender, so filled with understanding. Meg rested her head in his palm, for the first time really let someone take the weight from her shoulders. 'I'm scared of what it would do to you.' His statement was as confronting as it was honest. 'The scrutiny, the constant glare of the spotlight...'

'I'm not some fragile flower, Luca.'

'You are to me,' he said softly. 'You are beautiful and precious and delicate. Meg, I have been brought up with this, yet still, sometimes when I read the papers, whether it is lies or truth that they print, it is as if acid is being thrown in my face.'

'I could handle it,' Meg insisted.

'All of it?' Luca softly checked. 'Your family, your friends, your past all fodder...' He watched as she winced, as that strong, proud face disintegrated under the weight of truth.

'I don't know,' Meg admitted.

'Then we find out,' Luca said decisively. 'Tonight we see how hot the water is.'

'Sorry?' Meg frowned, then actually managed a small laugh. 'You mean we *test* the water!'

'I prefer my own version,' Luca answered. 'Tonight you come with me.'

'As your tart?' Meg threw back his earlier statement, taking some solace in his visible wince, but Luca quickly recovered.

'Your language needs some serious work,' Luca teased, 'but, no. I am not just asking you to escort me at the ball— I am asking you to come with me.'

'There's a difference?' Meg frowned.

'A big one.' Luca stared back at her. 'Tonight I ask that you join me on the palace steps.'

# CHAPTER THIRTEEN

'READY?' LUCA'S soft knocking on the bathroom door, though expected, still made Meg jump. The prospect of the ball and facing Luca's relatives, the people of Niroli, were all such alien territory, she could have spent a year preparing and still it would be too soon.

Luca had been obliged to go out in the afternoon, greeting some of the more prominent dignitaries as they arrived at the tiny Niroli airport, leaving Meg at the disposal of a myriad staff—their expressive Italian voices becoming more gleeful as, bit by bit, they transformed her into a date worthy of Prince Luca Fierezza on such an important night for Niroli.

Like a prize racehorse being prepared for a race, her body had been buffed and polished so that every inch of exposed flesh glowed with healthy vitality. Her thick straight hair was coiled into a million tiny glossy ringlets and piled high on her head, but the seemingly effortless cascade that escaped had, in fact, been painstakingly cajoled into place then vigorously pinned.

And as for her make-up!

Her complexion was flawless, her teeth whiter somehow behind her glossy lips, her blue eyes so enhanced by the smoky-grey eye shadow that to Meg it looked as if she were wearing coloured contact lenses. Even her toes were unrecognisable—Meg glanced down at her polished nails peeking out of the most exquisite bejewelled, impossibly high sandals. Her body was draped in a soft taupe velvet gown, ruched at the bust; it was so well tailored it made Meg's waist impossibly small.

Staring into the mirror, this time Meg actually smiled at her reflection, somehow recognised herself beneath the glamour and hype. Unlike before, Meg had used her voice, told the dressers and make-up artists the colours she preferred, the ideas *she* had for her hair—and now she gazed in awe at the transformation.

She stared at the Meg that Luca had always known was there.

But as Luca knocked and gently summoned her, though there was nothing to touch up, nothing to fiddle with, she hesitated before stepping out, knowing that tonight she wasn't just escorting Luca to the ball, but possibly entering his future…stepping into a world that was so impossibly different and wondering if she had what it took.

He answered her question without speaking—his eyes telling her with certainty that, not only was he proud to be by her side tonight, but he knew she was nervous, promising her with the most tender of embraces that he would be there for her through it all.

'You look stunning,' he affirmed. 'Everyone is going to love you.'

'You don't look too bad yourself.' Nerves were forgotten for a moment as she glimpsed her *date*, almost had to pinch herself to believe that she was with him.

Always immaculate, always beautiful, tonight he was breathtaking. His hair was swept back off his face, making him look even more haughty, more aloof if that were possible, his exquisitely tailored suit just divine, accenting his broad shoulders, his heavy silk cravat beautifully knotted, and for once he was cleanly shaven, his skin flawless. His mouth was full and completely kissable, so she did, and her expertly applied make-up was happily forgotten as her lips met his, Luca's expert touch delivering all the confidence she needed to face the night.

'We must go....' Reluctantly Luca pulled back a touch, his arms still around her waist, encircling her, holding her exactly where she wanted to be. 'But first...'

'Can we?' Meg broke in, with all the enthusiasm of a child with a brand-new toy, sure she would never, ever be able to get enough of him! Their lovemaking was an utter revelation. She felt as if she'd spent her life with the wrong set of keys, every door, every lock a challenge—until this afternoon, until Luca had produced the master key and let her into a world she'd barely glimpsed! Showing her over and over the delights of her own body, showing her over and over the magic of his.

'You are incorrigible.' Luca laughed. 'I wasn't actually talking about making love.'

'Oh.' Meg pouted as still he held her.

'There will be time for that later; anyway...' seeing her crestfallen face, Luca made a joke '...you would ruin my hair.'

'This won't, though.'

She couldn't believe her own boldness, her own assuredness in his want for her—but heard his gasp of delighted shock as she sank to her knees. For Meg it made her impromptu decision the right one—*this* was how she could be; *this* was how she was with his trust... She took him in her mouth and all Luca could do was take what she gave him so willingly, couldn't offer a protest against something so divine, couldn't even coil his fingers in her carefully styled hair, just stood to rapid attention, his moans of pleasure shuddering into one long sigh as she completed her delicate task.

Stunned, incredulous but eternally grateful, he pulled her to her feet.

'You are a bad girl,' he attempted to scold, but his eyes were smiling.

'You'd better get used to it, then!'

Meg's first walk on the wild side put them impossibly behind schedule, of course, and by the time they *finally* made it to the door, they were already late. Luigi knocked to check that everything was okay.

'*Di due minuti.*' Luca called, and Meg frowned, throwing her lipstick into her tiny jewelled purse and expecting to race out of the door. 'I've told him we would be two minutes, Meg.'

'But I'm ready….' she called, her voice trailing off as Luca now halted her.

'What I was trying to say, before I was, er, diverted.' Pulling out a slim black box, Luca opened the tiny antique clasp and Meg caught her breath at the beauty of the two jewels that glittered on the plush velvet. Impossibly beautiful, two huge diamonds sparkled in the light, each twinkling at the end of the finest white-gold chain—and she'd have recognised them anywhere.

'They're the jewels I'm supposed to have stolen!'

'The very same.' Luca smiled. 'These were my grandmother's.' Gently Luca lifted them from where they rested, but, reeling, Meg stepped back.

'I can't wear them.' She shook her head. 'Luca, these are your family jewels. I can't possibly wear them tonight—what if I lost one? What if—?'

'They are your jewels,' Luca interrupted. 'This is my gift tonight to you.'

'Luca, no, I can't possibly—'

'You like them?' he interrupted.

'Of course—they're beautiful.'

'And I want you to have them, so there is no problem.'

Spun into confusion, Meg shook her head. 'It's too much, too soon, Luca.'

'Not for me.' He stared back at her. 'And this is not about making you stay, or showing you all you could have—I know you are not that superficial, Meg. I want you to have them because, whatever happens between us, it has been more special than I can say. This gift is yours with no expectations, nothing more than—' He gave a frustrated shrug. 'I would not give these to just anyone—you might not know that, but my family will. I want you to walk beside me tonight and for them to know how precious you are to me. Please, accept them.'

So she did, overwhelmed not just at his generosity and the sentiment behind them, but the apparent fact that Luca felt as strongly as she did—that the feelings that had swept her away since she'd first laid eyes on him had carried him with her, had been as strongly felt by Luca too.

'They're beautiful,' Meg breathed, watching the light capture them in the huge antique mirror above the fireplace, but, as captivating as they were, when Luca came behind her, his hands locking around her waist, burying his face in her neck and kissing his way down over her shoulder, Meg closed her eyes on the image in the mirror, focussing her mind solely on him.

'So are you, Meg.'

She felt it—for the first time in forever she felt beautiful, not just on the outside but somewhere deep within, as if he'd reached inside and polished the rough stone of her heart into a diamond that sparkled more magnificently than the ones he'd just given. This time when he offered his arm, when he checked that she was ready, for Meg there was no hesitation, just anticipation, nowhere in the world she'd rather be than beside this stunning, intriguing man.

Niroli had pulled out all the stops for this most special day—and by evening it was the royal family's turn to thank them, to acknowledge the people of Niroli before the celebrations continued long into the night.

Across Niroli, preparations had been made to feast and party late into the night, to celebrate the riches the fertile soil brought them each year—but first, as was tradition, many of the islanders had come to wait outside Niroli Palace where their royal family would appear, acknowledging the people of Niroli before greeting their guests for the ball.

It was a glittering line-up. The women were lavishly dressed, exquisitely made-up and dripping in gemstones, their opulent perfumes mingling as they gathered on the steps of the palace, whilst the royal men stood suave and resplendent in their tuxedos as the crowd cheered.

This Feast, though, Luca had explained as they'd made their way through the palace, was tinged with sadness. Despite the exuberant crowds, despite the buzz of excitement, for the people of Niroli the fact their king was too weakened to attend made the celebrations bittersweet.

What he didn't add was that tonight, more so than usual, the eyes of Niroli were upon him.

Could Prince Luca Fierezza rule them?

Could the black-eyed wild child they had all simultaneously adored and berated through his reckless youth really be their king?

Their answer was a resounding yes—the cheers deafening as Luca and the stunning, mysterious woman beside him joined the family on the steps.

'Trust Luca!' The crowd nudged and cheered. *Trust their Luca* to add an extra dash of glamour to the night. 'Who is she?' It was the question on everyone's lips—who was the gorgeous stranger at Luca's side? Who was this woman who chatted amicably with Princess Laura? It was a question that would have the whole town talking and guessing long into the night!

For Meg, awkward in crowds, nervous of eating in front of strangers, the night was illuminating. Despite the grand company she was keeping, despite the endless conveyor belt of food that would normally have had her breaking out in a cold sweat, with Luca beside her, it wasn't just bearable—it was enjoyable! It was as if he'd reached inside her and turned on a switch, everything brighter, sweeter, more vibrant—everything just so much easier with him beside her.

'You are enjoying yourself—yes?' They were dancing now—Meg, who didn't know whether or not she could, because she'd never attempted a formal dance, was still none the wiser as to her skill because Luca's lead was so skilled, so effortless, he more than made up for her lack of experience.

'I am.' Meg beamed up at him, drunk on a single glass of wine and the intoxicating presence of him. 'It's all wonderful, the people, the music, the food…' Her eyes caught his. 'You.'

'Tonight, I enjoy myself too.'

'You don't normally?'

He didn't get to answer, the dance finished and the floor broke into applause. 'Come.' Luca took her hand and guided her off the floor. 'It is time to introduce you to some more people.'

'More kissing strangers?' Meg gave a tiny little sigh. It would surely take her forever to get used to the effusive Italian greeting of kissing on both cheeks. 'I guess it's so easy for you but—'

'Believe me—' Luca grinned '—on many occasions it is less than easy. My family are not all beautiful.'

This one was, though!

There was a familiar feel to the woman who stepped forward at Luca's bidding. Slightly taller than Meg, she was dressed in a sheath-like golden dress, her thick, honey-blond hair fell heavy and immaculate and without introduction Meg knew she was royal. There was a timeless elegance about her, not just from what she was wearing, but from the way she carried herself, and when Luca introduced her Meg knew where she'd seen her.

'Meg, this is my cousin, Princess Isabella Fierezza.'

The name was as familiar as the face and instantly Meg placed her—Princess Isabella Fierezza frequently graced the pages of glossy magazines, a darling of the paparazzi. The fascination with this stunningly beautiful woman carried around the world, whether sipping coffee in a bar or lying on a sun-drenched beach, her image was newsworthy.

'Please, call me Isabella.' As charming as she was elegant, Isabella dispensed with titles, pulling Meg into the inner sanctum of the royals with surprising ease, and after a moment or two of awestruck awkwardness Meg started to relax, so much so that she didn't mind a scrap when Luca had to excuse himself to attend to a duty dance.

'How are you finding it all?' Isabella asked in excellent English. 'We're a difficult lot to get used to, I'm sure.'

"Everyone's been charming,' Meg answered truthfully. 'Though, I have to admit, I was nervous at first.'

'It will take a while to get used to it.' Isabella nodded her understanding. 'Especially at the moment—the interest in our family is always intense, but never more so than now. There are many eyes watching us….' Was it sympathy in her own eyes as she smiled over at Meg? 'Luca does not like the press—he still seems to wonder why his life is newsworthy. It will be more so now!'

'Because of the king's health.' Meg checked, but surprisingly Isabella shook her head.

'Because there is nothing the press like more than the possibility of a new princess.'

'We've only just met,' Meg responded with a smile, not sure if Isabella was teasing her as Laura had, or was somehow testing her—but she was wrong on both counts.

'You are wearing the Royal House of Niroli jewels, Meg.' Isabella nodded graciously to a rather red-faced couple who were coming off the dance floor, then turned direct hazel eyes back to Meg's. 'Understand that I will not be the only one to notice.' For a second Meg thought she was being warned, that there was something underhand to Isabella's comments, but again she was mistaken. 'If you need to talk—if you would like another woman to talk to when it all gets too much, and,' she added, 'it *will* get too much, then I would be more than happy to help you. Unlike Luca I am used to the press—I know how to work them. Sometimes it is better not to dodge them—'

'Don't believe a word she tells you!' Luca was back, for Meg's sake talking in English as he good-naturedly teased his cousin. 'I was never *that* bad.'

'Oh, yes, you were, Luca—' Isabella smiled, carrying on

the joke '—but I'm too much of a lady to talk about your past. Anyway, why would I scare her off when she's absolutely charming?'

'From my cousin—that was high praise, indeed,' Luca said *much* later when they were back in his apartment, Meg utterly aching and exhausted but reeling from the wonderful night they had shared.

'I liked her.' Meg nodded, sitting up in bed wearing nothing but a smile and talking nineteen to the dozen as an exhausted Luca attempted to close his eyes. 'She's stunning.'

'She works at it,' Luca mused. 'You could learn from her. Not like that!' He laughed as she nudged him angrily in the ribs. 'I'm not talking about how she looks—Isabella manages the press well, manages to be royal and work too.'

'She works?'

'In tourism.' Luca nodded. 'She does well for Niroli...' He didn't get to finish, falling asleep mid-sentence, his expressive face relaxing, dark lashes fanning his cheeks. Given it was 3:00 a.m., Meg probably should have done the same— should have flicked off the night light and cuddled up beside him, only she didn't want this day to end....

Didn't want to close her eyes on the magic she had found.

Nothing.

Waking up, wrapped in his loving embrace, her whole body exquisitely tender from the passion of the day before, Meg took a moment to work out what was worrying her....

Nothing.

Not a single thing on her mind was big enough to detract from what she was feeling now, and as he opened his eyes and smiled back at her Meg knew he was feeling it too.

Safe.

Two ships coming in from the storm at the same time, holding each other as they reached solid ground—revelling in the peaceful harbour they had found.

'Good morning,' Luca greeted her in English.

'*Buongiorno*,' Meg answered, stretching luxuriously, doing absolutely nothing to retrieve it as the sheet slipped from her warm, relaxed body, just sharing a slow, lazy kiss before the busy day invaded.

'Can't we stay in bed for a while?' Meg grumbled as Luca reluctantly climbed out.

'Impossible!' He gave a dramatic Latin gesture but, given he was naked, it merely made Meg giggle. 'We will be expected in the dining room for breakfast.'

'With your family?'

'Don't worry.' Luca waved away her anxiety. 'It will be very informal. There is no need to dress up or worry about make-up and such things.'

'Please!' Meg rolled her eyes. 'Don't send me in there unarmed. I somehow can't picture your cousin Isabella wrapped in a shabby dressing gown, wearing last night's make-up.'

'Probably not,' Luca conceded, 'but it will be very relaxed. No doubt there will be a prolonged discussion about who behaved worst last night….' Seeing Meg's slightly frantic expression, it was Luca's turn to laugh. 'You, Miss Donovan, were impeccable, unlike Countess Arabella….'

'Which one was she?' Meg frowned. 'The one in the salmon-coloured dress who—?'

'Well, she was leaping like a salmon!' Luca grinned. 'But, no, Countess Arabella was the one…' His voice trailed off as there was a knock at the door and he went to answer it. Meg settled back on the bed, still smiling at the many memories from last night. Frankly, for such a dignified bunch, some of their behaviour had been shocking to say the least.

'Your cousin Isabella was nice. She said...' But Meg's voice trailed off as Luca re-entered the room and she saw his unusually pale face, the carefree features of moments ago replaced—his face taut with tension, lines she had never seen before grooved around his eyes as he sat on the bed beside her. 'What's happened?' Meg gasped. 'Luca, what's happened?'

'It is my grandfather, the king...' Meg's mind jumped to the obvious conclusion but, without her even asking, Luca refuted it. 'No, it is not that. He has summoned me.'

'Summoned you?' Meg frowned, not just the language but the whole concept unfamiliar, that a grandfather *summoning* his grandson could cause such a shocked reaction. 'What for?'

'I am about to find out.' He let out a heavy breath as if willing himself calm—and Meg realised then just how huge this was for him.

'This isn't a regular event, I take it?'

'*No.*' He gave a brief shake of his head. 'The fact he has summoned me means that it is royal business that he wants to discuss. I knew this day was coming, I just never expected it now.'

Luca dressed quickly—but the informal attire he had deigned suitable a matter of moments ago was replaced with a suit, his tousled hair smoothed back, a quick grimace in the mirror as he decided if he had time to shave, but another rapid knock at the door put paid to that decision.

'Wait here.' He gave her a thin smile as he kissed her distractedly. 'We'll go down to breakfast together once I have spoken with the king.'

'Are you okay, Luca?' She captured his hand as he went to go and for a second he held it, held it so tightly it actually hurt.

'I don't know,' Luca admitted. 'I don't know what I am hoping to hear when I speak with him. Wait here for me, Meg.' He said it again, only this time with entirely different meaning, pulling her into his arms for the briefest of embraces that protocol would allow, before he went to learn his fate.

'Always,' Meg answered, but it fell on deaf ears, Luca closing the door behind him and heading off to meet with the king, heading off to find out his fate, and as she lay back on the pillows, staring at the ornate ceiling, only then did it dawn on her.

It wasn't just Luca's future that was being decided, but her own.

## CHAPTER FOURTEEN

*EVERYTHING* WOULD CHANGE if Luca was chosen as heir.

Meg knew that.

Somehow she understood that the pressure that would placed on him, on *them*, would increase dramatically if Luca was to be King; understood that they wouldn't be afforded the luxury of a normal dating process—but, Meg pondered, nothing about their relationship to date *had* been normal, and not just because of Luca's status.

Because of the man himself.

The second he'd walked into the kitchen at the casino he'd been constantly on her mind: filling her senses, confusing her, angering her, thrilling her. Like a drug addiction, like the disease that had once consumed her, Luca was *all* she could think about—only there was no danger in this obsession.

Despite the blizzard of emotion Luca so easily triggered, still he put peace into her soul. A peace she'd never really known.

He made her strong.

Strong enough to deal with whatever the future threw at them; strong enough to handle whatever fate had in store.

Almost.

One look at his stricken face as he walked back into the apartment and Meg knew that he was devastated, knew that whatever he'd been told hadn't been pleasant—only time hadn't allowed her the luxury of knowing his true choice in the matter.

'It will be okay.' Crossing the room, she put her arms out to him—whatever the king's verdict, it truly didn't matter, it was the effect on Luca that was her primary concern, and she wanted to impart that, wanted to hold him as he told her his fate.

'Don't!'

The force, the venom in the single word he spat out was so unexpected, so completely out of step with the man who had left just a short while ago, that Meg stepped back as if he'd hit her.

'You have to leave.' He didn't look at her as he said it, *refused* to look at her as he gave her the order, delivered with gusto the one scenario, since the king's summons, that she'd never envisaged.

'I have to leave?' She could barely get the word out, couldn't fathom the change in him. 'Luca, what on earth did he say to you?'

'The truth.' Only now did he look at her, eyes that had recently adored her now unfamiliar as they eyed her with contempt. 'That you are not fit to be Queen. That if I continue to date you then I relinquish any right to the throne.'

'I don't understand…' She was so bemused at the complete change in him, it didn't even enter Meg's head to be angry and, plunged into confusion, she struggled to make sense—to make *him* see sense. 'I didn't steal the jewellery, though, Luca. We sorted that out.'

'Did we?' Luca checked. 'Or is this some magnificent ruse you and your friend have concocted?'

She couldn't believe what she was hearing, couldn't

believe the change in him. Last night he had held her, loved her, promised to be there for her—yet at the king's bidding *everything* seemed to have changed.

'Luca, you know I had nothing to do with the theft. You *know* that,' she reiterated. 'We went over this yesterday—'

'Yesterday is over,' Luca interrupted, shrugging his broad shoulders, splaying his hands open and cruelly dismissing what they had so recently shared. 'Yesterday we were caught up in attraction, lust. Today things change, responsibility catches up.'

'What about your responsibility to me?' White-lipped, she confronted him.

'We have known each other a few days.' Again he shrugged—again he twisted the knife. 'As the king pointed out—I have been a prince all my life.'

'And a bastard, too.' Anger was broiling now. Anger at the way he was treating her, yes, but Meg's anger was turned inward on herself—that she had trusted him, that she had *chosen* to believe him, the bitterest of all pills.

'You will leave now. The royal plane is in use with dignitaries, but there is a charter flight in an hour. It will take you to—'

'I'm not flying anywhere.' She raked a hand through her hair. 'I'll get the boat.'

'You'll do as I say.'

'Never again!' Meg flared, but still she had to know more, to make some sense of this madness. 'What did he say to you, Luca? Please tell me what he said.'

'You really want to know?' Finally he faced her. 'I could be King of Niroli or have you—but never both.'

'So you chose Niroli?'

'Of course.' He gave a scornful laugh—mocked her,

humiliated her, and for Meg it was more than enough, already she was turning away, only Luca hadn't finished with her yet.

'What do you expect here, Meg?' He was shouting now, but it barely sunk in, her mind cruelly slow to process each vile word, like a huge sticking plaster being slowly ripped off the raw surface of her heart. Why couldn't he just end it—just rip it off in one burst instead of prolonging the agony, exposing her raw wounds, so slowly, so roughly they bled all over again? 'You were acting like a *puttana* in the bar the night I met you, a common backpacker, first scrubbing pots in the kitchen, gambling and flirting with rich businessmen—'

'Enough!' Trembling but somehow firm, she raised her hand, halted his hideous tirade with one of her own. 'Whatever you think of me, Luca, I don't want to hear it, because your opinion doesn't matter to me any more.' She thought she was going to vomit, right here on his bloody royal carpet—cold nausea engulfing her—but she refused to suffer any further indignity. She headed to the bedside, the rumpled sheets they had made love within mocking her now, and took a sip of water from a glass by the side of the bed that had been hers for a fraction of time. The nausea receded but a new visitor arrived, one that she'd suppressed for so long, one that she'd never dared act on—till now.

Swinging around, Meg splashed the remains of the glass in his face with as much venom as if she'd spat at him.

'Guttersnipe!' Luca hissed. 'I will tell the king his assessment was correct.'

'Why?' She'd never asked before—never had the courage to confront, but that much he'd given her at least, anger a powerful precursor to courage. Only it wasn't just Luca she was asking the question, her eyes ravaged with all the pain the world had inflicted in her twenty-five years. 'Why, when you could have just slept with me, did you have to make me love you? Why did you have to do it to me all over again?'

'Again?' His eyes narrowed at her question. 'What do you mean again? You cannot compare me to your parents.'

'Can't I?' Meg rasped. 'Why is it that the people who are supposed to care about me, the people who are supposed to love me, are the very people who hurt me? Why did you have to do this?' She thumped her fist to her chest—more Italian in her actions than him. Raw, untapped emotions were unleashed now, her voice rising with each and every passing word. 'I trusted you, Luca—you made me trust you! You're worse than my parents!'

'Worse? How can you say that? Did I starve you? Did I ignore you?' He was attempting to match her fury, but he couldn't. Attempting to justify, but, for Meg at least, he never could.

'Far worse,' Meg said finally, the screaming over, cool detachment in her voice as her contemptuous eyes gave him one final glance. 'At least my parents never pretended to care.'

'Your backpack is in the car….' Luca's complexion was grey, his voice abrupt when he spoke, but he wasn't shouting any more, wasn't even looking at her now. 'Luigi will take you to the airport.'

'I'm leaving on a boat.' Meg stood perhaps not firm, but resolute, the defences she had let him take down snapping into delayed action, her back straightening, tears drying up, and somehow she managed to face him.

'I want my winnings.' She held out her hand—if he thought her nothing more than a tart, then she'd act like one! 'Heaven knows, I've earned them!'

* * *

Luigi took her to the Port of Niroli where she'd arrived such a short while ago—yet it felt as if it had been a lifetime away. As if she were a criminal being deported, Luigi escorted her onto the boat. How she wanted to book a cabin—to curl up in a ball and hide—but she refused to go there again. Refused to even set a foot in the black hole she'd worked so hard to dig herself from.

It had been a lifetime—Meg realised. She'd arrived in Niroli a frightened girl, but was leaving now a woman.

A proud woman.

'Cheese focaccia and a café latte, *grazie*.'

It was the last thing she wanted, yet Meg knew as she ordered it was the most important meal she'd ever eat—the first big step towards moving forward.

Taking her order, Meg made her way onto the deck, sat at one of the white Formica tables and forced herself to carry on with living, and if her nose occasionally ran, or tears were streaming out from under her glasses, if the man opposite was giving her curious looks from over his newspaper as she sniffled her way through her meal, it really didn't matter.

Somehow she'd get through this. When the acute agony of the moment had given way, somehow she'd assimilate it, somehow she'd manage to relegate the last few days to a brief holiday romance. One day, Meg decided, she'd even look back with fondness, gaze at a map and remember dancing and romancing with the Prince of Niroli, perhaps watch the foreign news with a pensive smile....

Just not yet.

The tears were starting again, the gargantuan proportions of the task ahead starting to overwhelm her, because, no matter how much time might dilute the pain, no matter how much it healed, right now she was stuck in the present—his vicious words still stinging in her ears, the brutal force of his rejection still ricocheting in every nerve.

God, she knew she looked a sight, but wouldn't that man stop looking? He wasn't even being discreet, just blatantly staring.

Taking a bite of her food, Meg wished she'd ordered water to wash it down, every morsel sticking in her throat as she struggled to begin her future and, reaching in her bag for her purse, Meg decided to do just that and then take the opportunity to move to another table.

But first she'd have a quick look.

Rarely did Meg need to be reminded these days of her painful past—eating, self-nurturing, coming so much easier, but this morning a few life lessons were needed, and she'd utilise every means available to get her through.

Unzipping the wallet part of her purse, Meg's fingers slipped inside, and she frowned as the well-thumbed photo didn't come to immediate reach, more desperate now as she started to unzip each segment. It was gone; she must have dropped it. Frantically she tried to remember when she'd last seen it…the night she'd met Luca. Panicking now, Meg tipped out her purse's contents onto the table—but everything else was in order….

'Scusi?'

Meg tried to ignore the man opposite. Still frantically looking for her photo, she was in no mood to be chatted up, but as he gestured to the newspaper in his hands she realised why he had been staring. There on the front cover, almost unrecognisable in her happiness, she stood resplendent by Luca's side.

'This is you? Yes?'

'No.' Meg shook her head and told the twisted truth. 'She just looks similar.'

Thankfully she'd lost her audience, his attention diverted by a seaplane dipping precariously low on the smooth sparkling ocean, the whole top deck watching as it drew in for landing, but Meg couldn't have cared less, more relieved when her table mate excused himself and, camera in hand, headed to the rails to get a few shots for his album. But curiosity overrode her, and, reaching over, Meg turned the paper around, staring at the image and trying to believe it had only been yesterday. That the radiant, smiling face was hers, that Luca, proud, dignified and gazing down at her with nothing but pride and tenderness in his features, could possibly be the cruel beast she had witnessed this morning.

SCANDALO AL PALAZZO.

Meg's eyes jerked from her and Luca's picture as the headline caught her eye. What scandal?

Some of the guests might have kicked up their heels, but that had been long after midnight, long after any article would have been written and the paper put to bed.

Curious now, wondering what she might have missed, Meg turned the paper around and opened the first page—her inquisitiveness replaced with frozen horror as she stared at the images in front of her. It didn't matter that the article was written in Italian, because Meg knew without translation what had been said—a true case of a picture painting a thousand words. Because there, staring back at her, frail and emaciated, was the fragile, bewildered woman she once had been. The photo she had carried to remind her of her most private pain was a salacious piece of gossip now. The awful realisation sank in that she hadn't lost her photo…it had been stolen.

It was as if the universe were coming out in sympathy—as her heart lurched and Meg's world literally stopped, so too did the boat, the vehicle shuddering as the engines cut, everything falling silent as Meg tried to take it all in.

'Signorina Donovan?' The hesitant tone to the captain's voice, the fact he was addressing her by name, momentarily dragged Meg's eyes away from the article. 'I am sorry to disturb you—this really is most irregular—' He gestured out beyond the deck to the seaplane, bobbing gently on the calm water, as Meg attempted to focus on whatever it was the captain was telling her.

Maybe there had been an accident, perhaps she needed to move…. Gathering up the newspaper, her bag, she tried to stand on legs that seemed to be made of cotton wool, tried polite conversation with a mouth that didn't know how to move, a mind that simply didn't know how to respond.

'He wonders if you would join him. We have a small boat that can take you and naturally we would wait—'

'I'm sorry.' Meg gave a helpless shake of her head. 'Join whom?'

'Crown Prince Fierezza!' When Meg clearly didn't react in the way the captain expected, when, instead of jumping to attention, Meg sat back down, the captain's voice became more insistent. 'This way, *signorina*—he has asked to meet with you.'

'No.' She didn't care that the whole boat was taking pictures, didn't care that the captain was practically dancing on the spot with anxiety—didn't even particularly care that Luca had made this dramatic gesture and landed a seaplane beside the boat, because she had nothing to say to him.

Nothing at all.

'*Signorina*, you cannot just refuse, when our prince requests—'

'*Your* prince,' Meg interrupted. 'Luca Fierezza is *your* prince, not mine. I have absolutely no desire to speak with him.' She cleared her throat, wished, wished, wished she'd made it to the bar to get her bottle of water before all this had happened, and that she *had* booked the tiny cabin and was away from all the curious stares. 'I'm not leaving this boat,' Meg said firmly. 'So if you could kindly pass on that message, then we can start moving again.'

The captain looked as if he were about to have a seizure, Meg's response, or lack of it, clearly diverging from protocol, but he got the message when proudly she headed towards the bar, absolutely refusing to look over her shoulder, to look back on *all* she was leaving behind... focused instead on all she was heading to.

At twenty-five years and four months, Meg grew up.

Not that she'd been immature, not that she'd shirked responsibility for herself—with the cards she'd been dealt Meg had never been afforded that luxury—but in facing her past, somehow she embraced her future.

No, she wasn't perfect and, yes, she'd make mistakes—but from now on each and every one would be her own; the cards she'd been dealt had long since played out.

'*Uno champagne, grazie!*' Meg said to the bar man.

Who cared if it wasn't even midday?

Who cared if the Prince of Niroli was waiting for her to come over?

Who cared what anyone thought? Sitting down at her lonely table, placing a napkin over her knees and taking a sip of her champagne, Meg took a deep breath and smiled at the world.

Her best *was* good enough for her.

'May I join you?'

Well, if he was going to land a seaplane, then it wasn't *that* unexpected that he'd board the boat, and Meg kept her smile in place, gestured for him to sit, a glint of triumph in *her* eyes at Luca's bemused expression.

Because he was a prince, because *nothing* like this had happened on the boat, new strategies were being put in place. The gawking passengers were all relegated to the hull of the boat to give the couple some semblance of privacy, but their cameras aimed, their eager faces all watching on as Meg's plastic cup was removed and replaced with two glass flutes and the boat's best champagne was poured into them. A hastily prepared antipasto platter was placed in front of them and when there was nothing more the boat could pull out to impress, nothing more that could be done, with a flick of Luca's impatient wrist the hovering staff melted away until finally it was just the two of them.

'You are okay?' Luca asked, his voice tentative, glancing down at the open newspaper, then tearing his eyes away.

'Do I look okay?' Meg asked.

'Actually, yes.' Luca gave a slightly bemused frown. 'You have seen…' His voice trailed off and Meg completed the difficult sentence for him.

'The newspaper—yes, I've seen it. I haven't read it as such, but I can imagine what it says. "Shocking past of future Queen—from famine to feast".'

'Surely you're not okay then…' Luca attempted. 'After this morning—'

'Oh, sorry.' Meg fixed him with a steely glare. 'Were you expecting to find me in the foetal position in a cabin, or perhaps with my fingers down my throat—?'

'Meg, please!' One very well-manicured hand tried to halt her, but Meg wouldn't be silenced.

'Well, sorry to disappoint you, Luca. You know, for the past couple of years I've spent my time dreading I'd relapse, dreading how I'd react in a crisis—well, you've actually done me a favour. Since you walked in that kitchen, my life's been nothing but hell and I haven't gone back—if I can survive Niroli I can survive anything. I might even get a T-shirt printed saying just that!'

'Please—do not be facetious. Do not try and make light of this. This photo, this *article*, this disgusting piece of journalism is the reason I sent you away this morning. This is why it was so imperative that you leave—this is the very thing I was trying to protect you from, hoping you would not see.'

'Really?' There was a slightly shrill note to her voice, a disbelieving edge that had Luca frowning. 'Or were you hoping your subjects wouldn't see it?'

'No.' Immediately he shook his head. 'The king summoned me this morning because his press secretary had seen the first version of the papers.' He gave an angry gesture at the filthy paper. '*This* is what I was trying to prevent you from seeing.'

'But you can't!' His frown deepened at her strange answer. 'How can you save me from it? How can you prevent it, Luca, when it's already happened? Like it or not, this *was* me! And if some prison guard wants to make a small fortune raking up my past—'

'It was Jasmine.' He let the words sink in for a moment before softly continuing. 'This is what your friend did to you, Meg.'

And it was so much worse than a drunken mistake, so, so

much worse than a thief trying to cover her tracks, that Meg's bravado left her then, her body racking in quiet spasms as tears begged to be let out, as the world hurled yet another blow.

'This is the price you will have to pay if you are with me, Meg.'

'Would have paid,' Meg wretchedly corrected. 'This is the price I would have paid for you, Luca…but not now. I guess you'd better go and find yourself a more suitable queen….'

'There will be no queen….' Luca grabbed at her hands, but she pulled them away, didn't want him to touch her ever again. 'Because I am not going to be King. He didn't summon me with an ultimatum. That is what I told you so you would leave, so you would never know…'

'Why would you lie?' Meg begged. 'How, after everything we went through, could you think that would be…?' Her voice petered out, watching as his dark, expressive eyes stared at her image in the paper, and finally she saw it.

Saw the shock and pain in his features.

The same shock and pain she felt each and every time she saw the photo herself—but there was something else in his eyes too that took a moment or two to register.

Fear.

The fear of seeing someone you love so very, very ill, and all the guilt, however misplaced, that came with it.

'It was a long time ago, Luca.'

'You told me you will never be recovered.' This time when he reached out for her hands she let him hold them. 'I knew you had been sick, I knew you struggled, but seeing that photo—' It was Luca's eyes filling with tears, Luca struggling to contain his emotions, and Meg understood then what had happened—the terror that had struck him this morning. 'You said you never wanted to go back there—when I saw this photo, I just lost it. All I could think of was getting you away from Niroli—I didn't want to be the one to send you back there!'

'You never could,' Meg said softly. 'That part's up to me.'

'Whether I am a prince or a king the press will always want a story. This is just the start—next it will be that you are adopted, the sister of Alessandro…all your past slowly revealed with only worse to come in the future. Every time you put on weight, or lose an ounce, all your family secrets—'

'Every family has got them,' Meg broke in. '*No* family is perfect.' And, seeing his pain, she spoke a touch more softly. 'Not even royal ones.'

'*Especially* not royal ones!' Luca gave a thin smile, but Meg shook her head.

'Every family has their secrets, their rows, their shame. Well, everyone with an iota of zeal in them. That's why people like gossip—it helps when you find out that the future King of Niroli was dating an anorexic—' he winced at her use of past tense but didn't interrupt '—that Princess Laura—'

'Was beaten by her husband.' This time he did interrupt her, joined Meg in saying the truth out loud, and by boldly shining a light on the dark, murky past, somehow brightened it, chased away the shadows that distorted the images and shrank them to more manageable proportions.

'What *did* the king say this morning, Luca?'

'He said that there was already too much scandal attached to my name—that he'd warned me that one more slip-up, one more piece of scandal, and I would not be considered as the successor.'

'I'm sorry,' Meg said, staring down at her hands, the

vastness of what he was telling her hitting home, and even if it wasn't her fault, somehow she had been a part of his demise, but Luca refused to accept her apology.

'I'm glad.' Luca smiled over at her, but she didn't believe him for a second, knew he was just putting on a front, trying to say the right thing....

Until she looked up.

It was as if a genie had sprinkled some magic dust on him, or some Hollywood surgeon had somehow performed the speediest of makeovers whilst she hadn't been looking, because, staring back at her, looking younger, happier, *sexier* than she had ever seen him, was Luca Fierezza.

Well, maybe not sexier, Meg thought to herself, her mind working on minor details before she cleared her mental in tray to deal with the big tasks that were surely coming to hand—Luca Fierezza had always oozed sex appeal. That had been the problem from the start!

'You're not even a tiniest bit disappointed?'

'No.' Luca shook his head, but his eyes crinkled at the side as he thought a bit deeper. 'Maybe a little,' he admitted. ' I have this huge ego, you see—I have to be the best. I guess when the new king is crowned, or if I feel sorry for myself on New Year's Eve one year...'

'Woe is me.' Meg smiled at his confusion and quickly translated. 'You'll be thinking "poor me".'

'I like the first one,' Luca said stoutly. 'Yes, for five minutes every now and then it will be "woe is me", but, that is a small price to pay for freedom.

'I don't want to be King,' Luca said firmly, his hand gripping hers tightly. 'I told the king that—I said that even without this latest scandal that would have been my decision....' He stared down at the paper, his mouth tightening in a thin, angry line before speaking again. 'I hate them for what they did to you. I don't know how I can stop it.'

'Luca,' Meg said gently, 'do I look like I'm mortified? Do I look as if the world has just ended?'

He stared at her for the longest time, taking in the champagne, the half-eaten sandwich, then, slowly removing her sunglasses, he revealed her reddened eyes.

'Don't pretend it didn't hurt.'

'I'm not,' Meg said softly. 'It hurt like hell, but I *am* okay. Better than okay, actually—I know that I can bounce back now! Of course this hurt me, Luca—' she gestured to the picture '—but it was the change in *you* that was agony.'

'I was trying to protect you.'

'I didn't want you to protect me, Luca,' Meg said sadly. 'I just wanted you to stand beside me.'

'And I will,' Luca urged, 'if you'll let me.'

'I don't think so.' Meg glanced over to the deck, to the passengers all clicking their cameras, thrilled to be witnesses to this most exciting moment and, no doubt, Meg thought with a healthy dash of cynicism, aching for the boat to start so they could get to land and sell the photos! 'If we're together, what happens next time, Luca? Next time the press have their blood up, or you're summoned by your grandfather?'

'There won't be a next time,' Luca started, wincing at the hollowness of mere words, knowing it would take so much more than that to convince her.

'The things you said to me this morning—'

'Were to make you leave—to make you hate me, if that was what it took. It was the only way, or so I thought. Then, when you'd gone, Isabella came to see if you were okay with the newspaper, to see if she could help.'

'She wanted to help?' Meg blinked at the thought that

Isabella, that the stunning, beautiful Princess Isabella, had been prepared to help her through this, that, instead of being furious or angry, she had actually been prepared to be there for her.

'Isabella didn't know you had gone. She came in full of advice, said that we should go to the beach this afternoon—be photographed together happy and carefree—that this would soon pass, but all she was really concerned with was how *you* were, how you were coping with it all. I knew that in trying to help you I had deeply hurt you. When you said I was worse than your parents…' He paused, hoping, praying that she'd intervene, tell him it had been spoken in haste, only she didn't.

'You hurt me deeply, Luca.'

'I know—and I will regret it forever. I will try to make it up to you forever. I was never ashamed of you, Meg. I was scared for you.'

'Truly?'

'Truly.' Luca nodded. 'In fact nothing would make me prouder than responding to the press by telling them that you are my future wife.'

'Wife?'

'Princess Megan Fierezza!'

'It sounds terrible.' Meg giggled, but it faded midway, the magnitude of the moment catching up, and it was all too confusing, too big, too much to take in, and she started to cry instead. 'I don't know if I can trust you again. You're asking me to lay all my cards on the table—'

'Not yet,' Luca interrupted. 'Don't say anything till I have revealed mine….' Meg frowned in confusion, anger almost as he stared at an imaginary hand of cards, laying his first on the table.

'A king of hearts,' Luca said, but Meg angrily shook her head.

'This isn't a game, Luca.'

'I've never been more serious,' Luca said. 'I show you all that I have in my hands, a potential king that really doesn't want to be one. What about you?'

'A heart,' Meg gulped, 'that doesn't know if it can trust you again.'

'What number?' Luca insisted. 'What number is this heart?'

'Two.' Meg plucked a number from air again—no idea where he was leading, but at least in playing along with Luca she had time to think.

'Well, I have a queen of hearts—' Luca took a deep breath '—only she is not happy. What is your next one?'

'Three of hearts,' Meg said, staring boldly at him now. 'Who's not ashamed of her past—and not particularly proud of it either—but learning to deal with it. You?'

'Knave.'

'Sorry?' Meg let out a little laugh. 'You mean the Jack! The scoundrel, the reprobate—'

'The knight in shining armour?' Luca countered. 'If you'll let me be?'

'Four of hearts,' Meg said, evading the question and smiling at his frown.

'You bluff?'

'Nope.'

'What else?' Luca asked.

'It's your call.'

'What else?' Luca insisted.

'I don't know.' She stared at her imaginary hand, tried to fathom what should come next—the joker, perhaps, smiling in the face of adversity, ignorant of the tremendous problems they faced. 'Ace of hearts…' she attempted, but Luca shook his head.

'No, you don't!' The soft pad of his thumb wiped away the single tear on her cheek that had strayed. 'You cannot have that one, because I hold it here. So don't try to bluff me, Meg, because I can read you. I know you are strong, I know you are proud, and I know that you will be okay without me—but I also know you would be so much better with me, as I would be with you. I know that with this hand I will always win.'

'How?' Meg begged. 'How do you know that?'

'This is a royal flush.' Luca placed his imaginary cards on the table and the strangest thing of all was that she actually looked—looked at all he was holding, all he was offering. 'Which is the best combination of all—no one can beat that.'

'No one?' Meg checked.

'Together these cards beat all others.' Luca took her pale, trembling hands and warmed them in his. 'Together we can beat anything.'

She screwed her eyes closed, blinded with indecision, frantically trying to process her thoughts, but when she opened them Luca was still there, still smiling, still patiently waiting for her answer.

'I need lipstick!'

*'Scusi?'* Clearly it wasn't what he was expecting her to say, but he accepted it without question, handed her her bag and watched in bemused wonder as she ducked behind the beastly newspaper and painted on a glossy smile. 'Better?' Luca checked when she came out from behind.

'Much.' Meg beamed, but her eyes were glittering with tears. She felt happy, scared and nervous all at the same time as she looked out at the frantic passengers. Tired of patiently waiting, they were starting to get restless, and Meg knew that it was time. Taking a deep breath, she held it in her lungs, reaching out for Luca as they prepared to jump together. 'We should get back to the palace.'

'You're sure?' Luca checked, relief flooding his face as he captured her hand in his.

'Very.' Meg nodded, nerves strangely settling as she stood up and he slipped his free hand around her waist and guided her out to the cheering crowd, cameras flashing, a hundred well-wishers capturing this precious moment.

As *their* Luca brought forth his future bride.

# EPILOGUE

'IS EVERYTHING to your satisfaction, Your Royal Highness?'

'*Sì.*' Luca nodded, barely glancing up from the magazine he was reading as the air steward refreshed his glass, but when she asked the same question of Meg, used her very new, very unfamiliar formal title, Meg could only manage a blush, cringing as the steward melted away.

'We're supposed to be going to Australia to escape all this.' Meg gulped. 'I'll never get used to it.'

'I'm sure if you ask she can find you a seat back in economy,' Luca drawled, but, seeing Meg's rigid expression, he stopped teasing her.

As Luca had feared, the press had been merciless and, seeing the needless anguish it was causing, tired of the constant barrage of intrusion, he had made a decision—a huge one: he was leaving Niroli to start a new life in Australia on the Gold Coast where he already had more than a few business ventures.

'They've got a passenger list,' Luca explained. 'My title's on my passport—of course they're going to use our titles, but once we get to Australia we'll just blend in.'

'I doubt it.' Meg stared over at her new husband and,

despite her nerves, found herself smiling—Luca could never 'just blend in' even if he didn't use his title, or reside in a palace. Even without his bodyguards or legions of adoring subjects, Luca would always stand out from the crowd, would always turn heads wherever he went.

'Won't you miss it?'

'Miss what?' Luca shrugged. 'Having my private life sprawled over the magazines? Being told how to behave, how to react?'

'Your family,' Meg pushed, sure he was putting on a brave face, that walking away from Niroli and all he had there, all that he *was* there, surely couldn't be that easy. But as he took her hands in his and gazed so deeply into her eyes it was as if he were inside her, Meg realized, with clarity so bright it blurred the edges, that he wasn't putting on a front—that here, *anywhere*, with her was where Luca wanted to be.

'You are my family,' he said solemnly. 'You come first, last and always, Meg.'

The intensity of his love was overwhelming, but it didn't daunt her now—it soothed her. The strong backdrop he provided was a delicious constant for all that would follow— life's journey an exciting adventure, not a daunting passage, with Luca by her side.

'What do you think *your* family make of it all?'

'I have no idea,' Meg admitted. 'First they had Alex's bombshell to deal with, and now this!'

'I joked to your father on the phone that when I asked for your hand that he wasn't losing a daughter but gaining a princess. Do you know what he said?' Luca didn't wait for her response. 'That he already had one.'

Meg's eyes filled with tears at the thought of seeing her parents and brother again, showing them the proud, beautiful, happy woman she had finally become—and all thanks to love.

Their love and Luca's.

\* \* \* \* \*

# The Tycoon's
# Princess Bride

## NATASHA OAKLEY

# CHAPTER ONE

HER Royal Highness, Princess Isabella of Niroli knew from the flashing pinprick of green light in the far right-hand corner of the conference room that she was being watched.

And she didn't like it. Not one bit.

She straightened her spine in one tiny, barely perceptible movement and let absolutely no emotion appear on her face. She was used to surveillance. Telephoto lenses were aggressively focussed on her every time she stepped out of doors and even the fairly basic security system in her family's fourteenth century castle was considerably more sophisticated than the one protecting Domenic Vincini's inner sanctum.

Even so…

That blinking green light made her feel irritated. She twisted the fine platinum bangle of her wrist watch so the diamond encrusted face was uppermost and looked at the time.

How much longer was she prepared to wait for Signore Vincini to put in an appearance? Five minutes? Ten? How many before she appeared too desperate?

Maybe it was already too late to think about that? Maybe by forcing this meeting she'd already undermined her bargaining position? Shown her hand too early, as her cousin Luca would say?

But…

She *wanted* this deal. Badly. It felt personal. *Was* personal. So much effort had gone into it—and for such a long time now. Two years spent carefully courting the Vincini Group of hotels, nine months of concentrated negotiations…

And, in all those months, she'd not once met Signore Vincini, the power behind the Vincini Group and the man who would ultimately make the decision.

She'd been warned that he was a man who could not be forced…or cajoled. Rumour had it that he worked like an automaton and made his judgements without reference to anything other than the 'bottom line'. In recent years he'd stopped visiting his proposed investments or, indeed, the existing hotels he owned across the Mediterranean, yet he somehow managed to keep a finger on the pulse.

Back on Niroli that had sounded exaggerated. Surely a development the size of the one they proposed would warrant a more personal involvement…but, what if it was true?

Perhaps her 'charm offensive' was, at best, pointless and at worst…

*Damn.*

She didn't want to think about failure. Isabella stared unseeing across the width of the conference room. There was so much resting on her ability to bring this deal together—not least her own future on Niroli. Her hand moved to twist her watch round once more. She'd give him another five minutes and then—

'Your Royal Highness?'

Isabella turned at the sound of a hesitant voice. The quietly handsome man who'd ushered her into the room twenty minutes earlier let go of the door handle and unconsciously flexed his fingers.

'M-may I offer you something to drink, Your Highness?'

'Nothing, thank you.' She smiled, and then watched with resignation the slow blush that moved up from his neck.

Why did men react like that? She'd chosen her clothes so carefully in the hope she'd be seen as something other than an elegant coat hanger. There wasn't much else she could do, short of sticking a paper bag over her head and wearing a bin liner—which probably wouldn't help her be taken seriously either.

'S-signore Vincini wondered…if…' he cleared his throat '…I might assist you? R-rather than keep you waiting any longer.'

Her eyes flicked up to the pulsing green light. Was Domenic Vincini watching this? Somehow she felt certain he was—an all-seeing omnipotent being. 'I'll wait.'

'I've been asked to say that Signore Vincini is delayed indefinitely. He sends his apologies and—'

'Then I'll wait *indefinitely,*' she said, cutting him off, her voice uncharacteristically crisp.

Isabella watched the nervous bob of his Adam's apple and allowed herself to feel a moment's sympathy, but not so much that she'd do as he wanted. She couldn't.

Whatever Signore Vincini felt about her being here, there was no point in trying to explain the complex rivalry that existed between Niroli and Mont Avellana to this man. He wouldn't understand.

No one born away from the islands would appreciate the depth of mistrust. It had been built over centuries and was practically sewn into the fabric of daily life. And, in her opinion, it was time it stopped.

She picked up her briefcase and set it out on the table. With practised fingers she manipulated the combination lock and opened the case out. 'Perhaps I might have a glass of water after all?'

A sharp frown snapped across Domenic Vincini's face as his half-sister perched her bottom on the edge of his wide desk. 'Is there something you want?'

'I've come to talk to you.'

'I'm busy,' he said, retrieving the papers she'd dislodged.

'You're always busy.' Silvana picked up his letter opener and idly ran her fingers over the pewter point, the fact that she was messing with his things was as irritating as her being here. 'You must know you can't keep her waiting for ever. She's obviously not going anywhere until she's spoken to you, so why put off the inevitable?'

'*She*' being Her Royal Highness, the Princess Isabella of Niroli. His eyes flicked over to the closed-circuit television screen on his desk. 'It was her choice to come without an appointment—'

'You wouldn't have given her one if she'd asked.'

Domenic sat back in his chair and looked at his half-sister. 'Because it's unnecessary,' he agreed smoothly. 'Eduardo can tell her everything she needs to know.'

'She's waiting to talk to *you*.'

'Even a Nirolian princess must have met with disappointment before.'

What was it about Princess Isabella that made everyone think it necessary for him to immediately stop what he was doing? As if he didn't know. He rubbed a tired hand over his face. She had the kind of smile that made the paparazzi scramble and strong men falter.

'Can't you sit on a chair like a normal person?' he snapped.

'No, if I did you'd ignore me. This way I know I've got your attention.' Silvana returned the letter opener to his desk and studied him for a moment. 'It would take ten minutes of your time. You do want to build on Niroli, don't you?'

'Mildly.'

She let out her breath in one go. 'You're being offered nine thousand two hundred acres with forty-two miles of waterfront. This isn't a take-it-or-leave-it kind of offer, it's a fantastic opportunity.'

'It's an option—'

'It's more than that and you know it. *Damn it,* this is what you said you wanted. Years ago. This was the grand plan.'

Something to rival Sardinia's Costa Smeralda... He remembered.

'Actually, it's better. It's on *Niroli.* Twelve years ago, when we first started talking about a luxury purpose-built resort, no one thought that a remote possibility. It doesn't get more perfect than this,' his half-sister continued, her expressive hands moving as quickly as she spoke. 'Luca Fierezza's casinos already bring in the kind of clientele we need. As does the annual opera season and the very fact Niroli still has a monarchy brings a certain charm. This is everything you and Jolanda talked about doing.'

*Together.* They'd talked about doing it together. And on Mont Avellana. 'I'm considering it—'

'What you're doing is letting it slip through your fingers— and I don't understand why. If we don't take up the opportunity soon, then Princess Isabella will look elsewhere.'

'That's her prerogative.'

Silvana let out an exasperated scream. 'This deal is worth billions—'

'This deal will *cost* billions,' Domenic slid in quietly.

'Which you knew when you began negotiations.'

His eyes narrowed. *True.* He'd known that, but this was *Niroli*. The arguments for and against buying the land were so personal, and so interwoven, he couldn't tell which side they fell.

'So what's changed? It's not as though you're miraculously prepared to consider developing the land we have on Mont Avellana—'

With an abrupt movement Domenic sat forward. Just the mention of his birth-island caused images to flash through his mind with fierce rapidity. It hurt. Still. He picked up his fountain pen and twisted it between long, lean fingers.

Silvana bit her lip. 'I'm sorry.'

'It's nothing.' Domenic's voice sounded rough even to his own ears. *Nothing?* How could he say that? Traumatic memories crowded round, fresh and clear. He could see the fire licking through the roof. Hear the shouting. Even taste the bitter, acrid smoke in the back of his throat.

And he could smell the burning—indescribable, but unforgettable…

In the air, on his clothes, in his hair.

He swallowed painfully. After four years there should be a way of managing his experience. He ought to have found a way of keeping control and…

'I shouldn't have said that. I'm sorry. I didn't think.'

*Focus on the practical.* Time had taught him to concentrate on the matter-of-fact rather than his emotions. And the fact was Mont Avellana wouldn't seduce Europe's rich and famous away from Sardinia, Sicily and a fast-developing Niroli. It had the white sandy beaches, but little else when compared to its nearest neighbour.

Domenic set his pen down on the table with meticulous care. 'Are you angry I've not developed the palazzo?'

'Of course not,' Silvana said a little too quickly. She climbed off the desk and walked over to the water cooler. 'It has to be your decision. Whatever you feel is right…'

He watched as she pressed the button to fill a cup with ice-cold water. *His* decision to make. So why did he feel as though the empty palazzo was a quiet rebuke?

'Do you want any?' she asked with a look over her shoulder.

Domenic shook his head and spoke quietly. 'Mont Avellana lacks the infrastructure of—'

'I know. Nothing's in place.' Silvana walked back and pressed a light kiss on the top of his head.

*But…?* He waited for the 'but'. However sorry she might be, he knew his half-sister too well to think that the conversation was over.

'And I agree. Totally.' She smoothed a hand across his shoulder. 'Mont Avellana probably isn't right for us.'

Still he waited. The rest of the world tiptoed round him, fearful of saying anything that might remind him how much he'd lost. But Silvana had no such sensitivity. She just ploughed in and told him what she thought—even though she'd been standing beside him when his life had fallen apart.

*Perhaps because she'd been standing there…?*

'Jolanda wouldn't blame you for reacting to market circumstances, you must know that. So why haven't you signed? What's going on, Dom? This could all have been settled weeks and weeks ago.'

Domenic twisted his pen and watched the light play on the sleek metal. The 'why' was complicated. If he'd been the kind of man who believed his problems could be solved by therapy, no doubt his analyst would have had a field day on the 'why' of it.

'And why keep Princess Isabella sitting in the conference room for twenty-five minutes?'

'Eventually she'll speak to Eduardo,' he said with assumed nonchalance.

'And if she doesn't?'

Domenic shrugged. 'I dislike having my hand forced.'

Silvana sat herself in the chair on the other side of his desk. 'That's not what's happening. She's en route to Niroli and stopped off as a courtesy to—'

'That's what she told you?' he asked.

'She hasn't had to. Everyone knows she's been at the wedding in Belstenstein as King Giorgio's representative. She wore a Mariabella Ricci dress in the palest pink. Absolutely fabulous.'

Domenic stood up and walked slowly over to the large picture window with its view of the painfully modern rooftop garden. *Jolanda would have hated the angular lines.* He should never have allowed it. He looked over his shoulder. 'Perhaps a reasonable percentage might also know Rome isn't *en route* to Niroli from Belstenstein.'

'She might have other business in Rome.'

'Unlikely.' Domenic smiled grimly. Now, if there'd been a film première in Rome this weekend, a fashion show…

'You're deliberately missing the point.'

'No, you are.' He turned. 'If I decide to build on Niroli it'll be because I believe it'll be profitable. No other reason. If I decide not to, it's because I believe it won't be. But, before I commit myself to a decision either way, I want to know why Luca Fierezza has decided to concentrate on projects away from the island.'

Silvana's mouth dropped open. 'How the...*hell* do you know he's going to do that?'

'I make it my business to know. It's why I'm very good at what I do. And if he's moved his attention elsewhere there'll be a good reason for it—and I'm not about to pour billions into a development on Niroli without knowing why.' Domenic ran a finger around the neckline of his black T-shirt as the fabric irritated his neck.

'You could ask Princess Isabella.'

His right eyebrow jerked up. 'You think she'd tell me? The very fact *Princess* Isabella has made the time to come here is suspicious,' he said, sitting back down.

'Why do you say "Princess" like that?'

Domenic looked at the television monitor and at the beautiful woman sitting at the far end of the conference table. She offended him on pretty much every level, but he hadn't realised his voice reflected his private feelings so clearly.

'It can't be because she's Nirolian royalty,' Silvana spoke into his thoughts. 'You've done business with Prince Luca perfectly happily.'

'He has an excellent track record in business,' Domenic countered. 'Princess Isabella, on the other hand, does not. She owns one small and moderately successful hotel—'

'It's beautiful!'

'And her cousin, Nico Fierezza, is responsible for that. Out of the entire Fierezza family she's the only one who floats about Europe with an entourage in tow. And, frankly, I object to doing business with someone whose involvement rests on an accident of birth and her ability to fill a designer dress to perfection.'

'That's very unfair,' Silvana said quietly. 'Eduardo says he's been impressed by her commitment to this project. And he says Princess Isabella's been an active participant from the very beginning.'

'Her *name* might appear in the paperwork, but I seriously doubt she's had more to do with it than crossing her ankles at the occasional meeting.'

'Domenic—'

'If she'd walked in here quietly, without drawing attention to herself, I'd have had more respect for her. As it is…'

Silvana shook her head. 'I don't see how she could do that. She's as much a brand as the Vincini Group.'

'A brand?'

'You know what I mean. She's photographed all the time, everywhere she goes, everything she does,' Silvana said, standing up and smoothing the creases out of her linen skirt. She met his eyes, daring him to contradict her. 'And it's not because she's the granddaughter of a king that there's an entourage waiting down in the reception hall and a bodyguard outside the conference room…'

His eyes followed her as she walked towards the door, and he wondered why his staunchly republican half-sister had suddenly become such a vocal defender of Princess Isabella.

'It's because she's got paparazzi crawling out from behind skirting boards to get a shot of her. People love her. If she wears a dress by a certain designer that designer is made.'

He knew that. Everyone knew that. It was difficult to pass any newsstand without seeing her *face* on something.

'Even without Luca's casinos, Dom, Niroli has the potential to be a very glamorous resort simply because she's prepared to lend her face to it. You ought to think about that for a minute.'

Domenic rubbed his forefinger against the spike of pain in his temple.

'And I think you're wrong to leave her sitting there. It's a mistake,' Silvana said from the doorway.

Domenic let his hand fall. 'If you feel that strongly about it, why don't you speak to her?'

She stopped. 'Me?'

'On my behalf. Why not?' He looked across at her.

'Because I'm responsible for the interior design of our hotels. I've never had anything to do with acquisitions and I wouldn't know what to ask.'

'Find out why she's here. You're good at drawing people out.'

'Domenic—'

'And you're family,' he cut in firmly.

Silvana moved a small way back into the room. 'I can't—'

'Find out why Luca has decided to focus on his casinos in Queensland.' Domenic stretched out his arm, feeling the usual stiffness in his elbow. 'And try and get some indication of who the old king intends to nominate as his successor.'

'Do you think that might have something to do with Luca's leaving?'

'It's a possibility.' Domenic sat back in his chair and twisted his pen between his fingers once more. 'It's also a variable and I like as few of those as possible, particularly where King Giorgio's concerned. The man's a snake.'

His half-sister nodded. 'I'll do my best, but you may still need to talk to her yourself if she's here for anything more than a simple hello,' she said, shutting the door behind her.

Domenic swivelled his chair round so he had a better view of the monitor—and of Princess Isabella.

Why was she here? Why *now?* After months of being content to leave the complex negotiations in the hands of a skilled team, why had she decided to come to Rome? Silvana might buy the idea that she had other business, but he didn't. And the longer she was prepared to sit waiting for him, the more he doubted it.

Domenic locked his fingers and rested them against his mouth thoughtfully. The timing of her visit had to be significant. Within twenty-four hours of Domenic's hearing that Luca Fierezza had left Niroli, Princess Isabella was sitting in his conference room. It spoke of some kind of 'damage limitation'.

Perhaps…

Or perhaps not.

He sat back in his chair. Truthfully all he really wanted was a sound business reason to decline the offer. Something that would allow him to hold up his hands and tell the world it simply wasn't meant to be.

Instead he was confronted by the public relations coup that was Isabella Fierezza. More entrancing than any woman he'd ever seen in a suit. What was it about the way she wore a pair of cream trousers and matching jacket that made it instantly bewitching?

She moved her hand to twist the diamond stud in her ear and his eyes helplessly followed the movement. Was he supposed to be honoured by her visit? Dazzled by her beauty?

If it was the latter, he *was* dazzled. Undeniably. She had a…luminosity about her. An inner glow that lit her features from the inside. Business aside, it made him want things, remember things that were no longer part of his reality.

Please God Silvana would be able to stave off a meeting. There was something particularly painful about the sympathy of a beautiful woman.

And Princess Isabella *would* feel pity. She had that kind of softness about her that told him it was inevitable—and he hated sympathy. He found it even more distressing than an ignorant person recoiling from him.

Domenic shifted uncomfortably in his chair and reached forward to switch the monitor off. Then he pulled his hand across his face once more, before picking up his pen.

## CHAPTER TWO

ISABELLA sat back with a sense of achievement and took a moment to admire the room she was in. The hexagonal shape of the sitting room was unusual, but it was the light streaming in from the high windows that made it so stunning. It bounced off the glass bowls filled with fresh flowers and shone off the reflective surfaces of the furniture.

'Domenic will be another five minutes,' Silvana Moretti said, sitting in the armchair opposite. 'I'm so sorry.'

It didn't matter. She *was* going to meet him. That was the important thing. If, after today, everything came crashing down around her at least she'd know there was nothing else she could have done. 'I came prepared to wait.' She smiled, intending to charm. 'And it's so wonderfully cool in here I might decide to stay for ever.'

There was an almost imperceptible hesitation. 'My brother insists on an ambient temperature in all our hotels.'

For one second Isabella wondered what Silvana Moretti had decided not to say, but when she looked again she thought she must have been mistaken.

'The summer months are sweltering,' the tiny brunette continued smoothly, 'particularly in the city.'

Isabella smiled her agreement, but every sinew in her body was straining to hear Signore Vincini's approach.

'All of the bedrooms at the Villa Berlusconi are air-conditioned for that reason, but none of the public areas. Perhaps that's something I ought to address.'

'I've read about the Villa Berlusconi. I know my brother was impressed by the sensitive conservation of—'

'Nico Fierezza is a talented architect,' a masculine voice cut in. Deep, smooth and incredibly sexy. Impossible not to register that. Her stomach clenched in recognition.

Isabella pulled air into her lungs. Please, God, she had to do this well. Too much was resting on it for her to feel totally confident in her ability to pull it off.

'I've seen some of his more recent work in Milan, and it's equally impressive.'

'Nico has a…' Isabella turned to face the man she needed to impress, stopping as her breath caught at the back of her throat.

*Dear God.*

Her eyes took in the scar that ran from his forehead to a point perilously close to his left eye. '…real affinity for old…' *buildings.* She'd meant to say 'buildings', but her voice didn't hold out that long.

'Domenic, this is Her Royal Highness, Princess Isabella,' Silvana said, moving towards him. She rested a hand on his arm. 'My brother, Domenic Vincini.'

Her voice sounded muffled as Isabella struggled to meld her expectations of Domenic Vincini with the reality. A second scar, raised and vivid, ran the length of his cheek and touched the puckered scarring of a severe burn.

Domenic Vincini was a burns survivor. Why had no one told her that? Did they know?

Skin that had wrinkled like paper disappeared beneath the soft fabric of his long-sleeved T-shirt. *Severe burns.* The truth of that imploded in her mind. Whatever had happened to him? When? And why?

Her role as an ambassador for numerous charities meant she'd seen and spoken with many burns survivors. Their stories were, without exception, harrowing. People who'd emerged from a living nightmare to face months of skin grafts and painful rehabilitation.

Her voice caught as sympathy flowed through her. 'Signore Vincini.' Then she forced her legs to move. 'Thank you so much for finding the time to see me.'

But she'd been too slow. She knew it by the flicker in his brown eyes. There was a slight hesitation before he reached out his hand to meet hers.

'Domenic.' His voice was crisp, his handshake firm.

Isabella kept her gaze firmly on his face, sheer willpower stopping her from looking to see whether he also had scars on his hands. 'And I'm Isabella. I was particularly anxious to talk to you personally.' His skin felt smooth beneath her fingers. Strong. Warm.

'So I've been told.'

'You need to see these photographs, Domenic,' Silvana said.

Domenic Vincini had a hard face, strong and uncompromising and, right now, it looked particularly unyielding.

'Why?' he asked, releasing her hand.

Isabella lifted her chin a fraction more, refusing to be intimidated by his monosyllabic question. 'Because the proposed citing of the resort is on the south coast—'

'I'm aware of that.' His voice sliced across hers.

'Which means it has spectacular views of Mont Avellana,' she said, as though he hadn't spoken.

His eyes flicked towards his sister and then back to her. 'And you think that might help swing my decision in your favour?'

'In favour of the project. Yes, I think it might.'

'Then I'd better see them.' Domenic turned away, angry at himself for having so little control over his emotions, angry at Silvana for putting him in this position.

If he'd thought his feelings about Niroli and about Mont Avellana were complicated, his feelings about Princess Isabella were even more so. He should have all the natural antipathy of a self-made man towards a woman who'd made a career out of her hereditary title, but nothing could have prepared him for the feel of her hand in his.

The lightest touch from her fingers had sent long-forgotten impulses coursing through his body. Hot, raw need. Painful in its intensity. In that second he'd known the agony of wanting to pull her into his arms, feel her body warm against his—and of knowing it was an impossibility.

She moved towards the sofa, seemingly oblivious to the thunderbolt that had shot through him. Once he might have been able to attract a woman like Isabella Fierezza, but no longer. He'd seen the shock in her hazel eyes when she'd looked at him. The instinctive recoil.

'Shall we sit down? Make ourselves comfortable?' Silvana asked, her eyes casting a reproachful look in his direction. He deserved it, he knew, but he felt so helpless. Like a dinghy out of control he could only react to the power of the storm raging inside him.

Isabella turned and smiled at him. Her eyes shone with gentle kindness—and it shamed him. If he hadn't seen her instinctive reaction to him he might have been able to convince himself she could see the man beneath the scarring, but he'd long since accepted that would never happen.

Women who claimed an attraction to him were, in reality, attracted to his money. And for good reason. His money was the most attractive thing about him since the fire. The tragedy had robbed him of everything.

'May I see the photographs now?' he said, without moving and his voice stripped of any warmth.

'Of course.' Isabella perched on the edge of the sofa and gracefully crossed her ankles. 'I realise your time is limited.'

She looked up suddenly and he felt the blood pump round his body. Her eyes were wide, a little questioning, as though she'd noticed the way he was looking at her.

Domenic sucked in his breath and willed his body to relax.

'Do you want an espresso, Domenic?' Silvana asked, moving round him to sit in one of the armchairs. 'I was about to send for some?'

'Please.' He dragged a hand through his hair. The very fact that Silvana had judged it necessary to stay for this meeting was an indictment of his behaviour. His half-sister walked over to a small telephone and spoke quietly.

Isabella leant forward and unzipped the inner pocket of her briefcase, pulling out a presentation file. Her fingers were long, thin, with perfectly manicured nails. *High maintenance.* That was what Jolanda would have called a woman like Isabella Fierezza.

'Why do you think I need to see photographs of Mont Avellana?' He was aware of Silvana beside him, felt her tension as though she doubted his ability to manage this situation.

That should have been criticism enough, but the charm and ease that shone from Princess Isabella exacerbated it. In her company he felt ill-bred and boorish, but he was hanging by a thread. This was the best he could do. 'I know what the island looks like.'

His brusqueness was rewarded with a smile that had his blood pressure soaring. 'You were born there. I know.'

'And you think that has something to do with my reluctance to commit to your proposal?'

She reached up to finger the diamond drop that hung in the hollow of her throat. A tiny movement and the only thing that betrayed any sort of nervousness. Domenic wished he could bite back the question. The words were acceptable enough, but his tone had not been.

'Your reputation would suggest not,' Isabella said quietly. 'Certainly my team thinks it's an irrelevance.'

'But you disagree?'

'I think it might be a factor in it,' she said, meeting his eyes and holding his gaze.

He liked her ability to do that. And, in his experience, it was rare. The vast majority of people would have buckled beneath his acerbic tongue by now, certainly wouldn't have issued so obvious a challenge.

'I know it would affect mine if our situations were reversed.'

Silvana sat in the chair beside him. 'There's no doubt many people on Mont Avellana will feel betrayed if we build a luxury resort on Niroli.'

'And I can understand that.' Isabella let her hand fall from the diamond. 'Niroli is in my blood in the same way as, I imagine, Mont Avellana is in yours—'

'Whatever I might feel about my birthplace, Niroli has an established tourist industry which Mont Avellana lacks. Your team is right—anything else is irrelevant. Emotions have no place in business.'

Yet wasn't that *exactly* what he was doing here? Mixing

his emotions in with what should be a purely business decision? Even if they were not for the reasons Princess Isabella was supposing.

The door opened and a waiter walked in carrying their coffee on a small tray. Silvana looked up and smiled her thanks. 'Domenic's quite right when he says there's very little in the way of an established tourist industry on Mont Avellana.'

'I'd heard that.'

'There've been two decades of consistent under-investment,' Silvana said as the door shut. 'Several years ago now, Domenic bought the Palazzo Tavolara with the intention of turning it into a Vincini hotel but the timing has never felt quite right.'

*Palazzo Tavolara.*

Isabella knew that Domenic Vincini now owned the Palazzo Tavolara. She'd thought she was resigned to that, but her reaction to hearing Silvana refer to it was completely instinctual.

She'd been brought up to feel resentment. Taught to believe the Palazzo Tavolara had been stolen from the Fierezza family. Tension expanded in her head. It was almost like a time bomb waiting to go off at any moment.

'Certainly we couldn't consider building a resort there,' Silvana continued, passing across an espresso. 'Funnily enough, Domenic and I were talking about that earlier this afternoon.'

Isabella scarcely heard the final sentence. She reached out for her coffee and sipped, grateful she had an action to hide behind.

Domenic Vincini might be able to leave his emotions out of his business decisions, but she couldn't. Emotion was at the heart of everything she'd ever done. She was only here at all because she loved Niroli, she felt as connected to it as if it were by umbilical cord.

And, deep down, she didn't believe he could separate his life into neat compartments either. He'd been born on Mont Avellana. He couldn't have escaped being shaped by the war that had driven their two islands apart.

Domenic leant forward to pick up his own coffee. 'Perhaps that wasn't the most sensitive comment, Silvana.'

His voice held a different tone, which cut through her thoughts. Isabella looked up to find he was watching her and she had the strangest sensation he'd known exactly what she'd been thinking. Understood what she was feeling and, more surprisingly, had empathy for it.

'I don't think my sister is aware that the Palazzo Tavolara was built by the Fierezza family,' he said dryly.

The hard glitter had disappeared from his eyes. They were kind and entirely *different* somehow.

'Oh, hell!' Silvana said, her hand coming up to cover her mouth. 'I'm so sorry. I didn't think.'

Isabella shook her head, not needing or wanting Silvana to feel awkward. 'Both sides of the conflict had land and property confiscated.' She searched out the unexpected warmth in Domenic's eyes. 'I've only seen photographs of the palazzo, of course. I was told it was badly damaged during the war?'

'It's structurally sound, but many of the original features were looted. She's wounded, but still very beautiful.'

He smiled and she found her own mouth curve in a genuine response. Domenic Vincini was a man of contradictions, it seemed. 'I'm glad. It was my grandmother's favourite home.' She hesitated. There probably would never be a more perfect opening to say what she'd come to say. 'I understand your family, too, had land confiscated?'

'Land you're now offering to sell me back. The irony of it

hasn't been lost on me.' Domenic picked up his espresso. His eyes glinted above the rim of his cup. 'Is that why you're here? Because you've only just realised the connection I have with Niroli?'

She swallowed painfully, unsure of what she felt about him. She was unsure, too, how to answer that question. There was so much she could have said about why she'd come to Rome and *why* she was so anxious to stop this deal disintegrating around her.

Isabella looked up into his dark eyes. He was calmly waiting for an explanation. She'd forced a meeting on him and now couldn't think what to say.

And, yet, it was all so clear in her head. She was here to offer him a common sense solution to something she suspected was the real issue behind the delays.

*But she might be wrong.* All reports about the way Domenic Vincini did business suggested she was. Isabella fingered the diamond stud in her ear. It was too late to back down now. She'd made her decision when she'd arranged to come to Rome rather than fly directly home.

'No,' she said quietly, but quickly gaining confidence. 'Though I admit there was more concern over your family's connection to the resistance than the land we confiscated from your mother's family.'

She knew by his body language that she had his attention. 'The Vincini name is remembered…and—'

'Hated?'

Isabella shook her head. 'Resented. Deeply.'

His mouth twisted. 'Then why approach us? There are many consortiums who would be interested in what you're offering.'

Vaguely she heard Silvana murmur his name, but she

ignored it. This was between the two of them. 'But few have the client base you do…or the reputation for excellence. I want something that will rival the Costa Smeralda. Exceed it.'

He roughly set his espresso cup down on the table and she feared she was losing him. Her heart thumped against her rib cage. 'I want Niroli to be the first choice for Europe's rich and famous.'

'I accept that what *we* are would complement Niroli, but, as you've already said, my family have owned land there before and had it snatched away. What guarantees have I got?'

'My grandfather is fully supportive of this venture.'

'Long term that's no guarantee. Times change.'

Monarchs changed. And King Giorgio was elderly. He didn't have to say that for Isabella to know what he was thinking. Nor could she give any guarantees. Six months ago she'd been certain what lay ahead for Niroli. But, now…everything was changing so quickly—and her position with it.

'That's true. But, like Mont Avellana,' Isabella began carefully, 'Niroli was damaged by the war of independence. It was costly in terms of lives and money and I don't honestly believe anyone wants to see that kind of violence again.'

Isabella saw the slight narrowing of his eyes. Whether that was good or bad she couldn't tell, but she knew he was listening intently. 'And I don't believe you think it's likely either. If you did you'd have said no months ago.'

Almost he smiled. There was the tiniest quirk of his mouth, quickly suppressed.

'But if our situations were reversed I think I'd find it difficult to contribute to Mont Avellana's success, particularly if I thought it might have an adverse effect on Niroli. We've all been pretending the old prejudices don't exist, but I think everyone in this room knows they still do.'

She stopped. For a moment there was silence. Isabella looked from brother to sister and back again, trying to gauge their reactions. 'For the past two years I've been told you would not be interested in anything other than the profit margin, but…'

'But you don't believe that?'

Isabella moistened her lips. 'I think if that were true you'd have signed by now. We're a sound investment. The only real negative I can see from your perspective is that we're Niroli.'

He sat back in his chair and touched the tips of his fingers. The eyes that watched her were thoughtful.

'Domenic was concerned that Luca—'

He stopped Silvana with a shake of his head. 'What are you proposing?'

The intensity of his gaze unnerved her, but she resolutely held out the presentation file she'd had resting on her lap. He needed to see how beautiful Mont Avellana looked from Niroli. How romantic.

Domenic leant forward and took the file from her. His fingers hesitated before he flicked open the top cover.

'That's the view that your hotels would look out on.' She knew that the image was a powerful one. Caught just as the sun was rising.

He said nothing, but he pulled a hand through his hair. Isabella didn't stop to try and analyse what Domenic was feeling, she ploughed on. 'Anyone looking out on that each morning will want to go there. Even though I've been taught to feel…' She waved her hand and searched for the word that would convey her family's anger at having to give up sovereignty of Mont Avellana.

'I understand,' Domenic said.

Isabella swallowed. 'Even though I've heard so many terrible stories about Mont Avellana I've always wanted to go there. And if I feel that, how much more will people who haven't been taught to think as I have?'

Her words pooled in the silence.

Domenic looked back down at the image, then his fingers turned the page. Photograph after photograph. Isabella knew she'd caught the magical beauty of Mont Avellana.

'I was thinking that the proximity of the new development to Mont Avellana could work to the advantage of both. Why shouldn't there be boat trips from the resort across to the cave I've read about, for example?'

'Poseidon's Grotto,' Silvana clarified, her eyes on her brother.

'How do you know about that?'

'It's in my grandmother's diary.' Isabella looked from one to the other. 'I was thinking we might build links with the best of the local restaurants, certainly develop the diving opportunities. It's the obvious thing to do because Niroli already draws a significant number of diving enthusiasts.'

Domenic looked up. 'Encourage diving among the wrecks?'

'Yes.'

In the silence that followed Isabella felt as though she could hear her heart beating. A solid thud. She watched as he flicked through the file once more and forced her hands to remain relaxed in her lap.

She'd never wanted anything quite so much, or been so entirely unsure of the ultimate outcome.

# CHAPTER THREE

'So, ARE you optimistic?'

'About Domenic Vincini?' Isabella looked up from the newborn baby in her arms as Bianca curled herself in the corner of the sofa. 'Truthfully?' She grimaced. 'I've no idea. He's a difficult man to read.'

Her friend laughed. 'So I'm told. I'm sure you managed him brilliantly. All men are putty in your hands.'

'Not this one.' She smiled. 'But it was worth a try. If he doesn't sign on the dotted line now I think I'm going to have to accept he's not going to. Niroli has nothing to offer him he doesn't already know about.'

'What will you do then?'

'Don't know. Move. Start again.' She shrugged. 'I'm sure I'll think of something. I should probably have left Niroli years ago anyway.'

'Like your sister?'

'Perhaps.' Isabella looked back down at the sleeping baby, his tiny mouth pursed in seeming concentration.

She envied Bianca this. Husband, home, baby… Was it wrong to feel so dissatisfied with her life? To want something so spectacularly 'normal'? 'Fabiano's beautiful,' she said, stroking the soft skin of his cheek.

'When he's asleep.'

Isabella placed her forefinger against his hand and marvelled at the reflex action that brought his tiny fingers round it. 'You don't mean that. He's a little miracle. Aren't you?' she said softly, stroking the fingers.

Fabiano's tiny mouth pursed tighter and then he hiccupped, his body racked with the sudden onslaught. 'Oh, darling,' Isabella murmured, moving him to rest against her shoulder. Her hand moved rhythmically against his back. 'Does that hurt you, little one?'

Bianca smiled, watching. 'You ought to be a mother. You're a natural.'

'Chance would be a fine thing. The men I meet are too interested in my money and title.' She kept her voice light, but it was an effort. Fabiano's body was warm against her chest and he smelt of baby and talcum powder. There was nothing more perfect than that clean newborn smell.

She also loved the way his legs were still tucked up underneath him, much as he would have been in the womb. He was achingly perfect. Isabella rubbed her own cheek against the softness of his head. *The chance would be a very fine thing*.

'Tell me about Domenic Vincini. What's he like?'

*Like?* Isabella's hand moved soothingly across Fabiano's back. She thought for a moment. Like no one she'd ever met before. Just not an easy man to sum up in a few words.

She'd expected someone powerful—and he was, but not in the mould of her brother Marco, or her grandfather. Not like that at all. He was… She frowned. He was confusing. She wasn't at all sure what she made of him.

'Is he ugly?'

'Ugly?'

Bianca shrugged. 'I thought he was badly scarred. I'm sure I heard that.'

'He is. But, not ugly.'

*Not ugly at all.* She frowned. But not precisely attractive either. More charismatic. Certainly confusing. She wasn't at all sure whether she'd liked him. At first she'd been certain she didn't and then almost certain she did.

He'd been brusque. And he'd been kind.

*And his eyes…*

Deep, deep brown. Fearsomely intelligent. He looked like a man who would have an opinion on most things. Strong.

*A man who was not overly impressed by her.* She smiled and kissed the top of Fabiano's head. After a weekend of being fêted and photographed that had made a change.

Domenic Vincini hadn't tried to hold her hand too long. He hadn't pawed at her—or stood too close. He hadn't been obsequious or overly complimentary. In fact, he'd not been complimentary at all.

'He's got a scar that goes from here to here.' She moved her hand down the side of her face. In fact, he'd had two scars. Deep set, but not fresh. 'They're not ugly, but they're very noticeable.' In fact, they were shocking—partly because without them he'd have been spectacularly attractive.

Isabella lifted Fabiano off her shoulder and settled him back in the crook of her arm. 'And he's got a burns scar on his neck. Keloids—is that what they call them?'

Her friend pulled a face. 'You'd be more likely to know that than me.'

'Do you know how he got them?'

'In a house fire.' Bianca pulled her legs up tight against her chest and wrapped her cotton skirt around her ankles. 'I think.

At least that's what everyone says. His wife and baby died in it.'

*Died?* Had Bianca really said that? Isabella looked up from Fabiano.

'Several years ago now.' Her friend twisted her hair back into a high topknot. 'I don't think I ever heard the details because it was a good couple of years before my time. Stefano would know more than me since his parents now live a few kilometres from where it happened. I could ask him about it if you like?'

Isabella shook her head. 'No one had warned me. It came as a bit of a shock.'

'I suppose it's the kind of thing people tend not to talk about because they don't know what to say.'

'Even so…' Surely someone would have thought to have mentioned something so significant. Luca? Surely he knew?

Bianca smiled, attuned to her thoughts. 'You need more women on your team if you want that kind of information. Perhaps I should have said something, but it's not exactly relevant when it comes to a business deal and I didn't think.' Fabiano stirred and let out a piercing scream. 'There he goes,' she said, reaching for her son. 'He's hungry again. Not surprising really. He's slept for almost four hours.'

Isabella handed Fabiano across and watched with a pang as Bianca concentrated on latching her baby onto her left breast. Her friend's face momentarily contorted and then she looked up with a smile. 'He's on.'

'Good.' She looked away, mainly because it was painful to watch something so intimate. It tightened the knot of dissatisfaction within her just that little bit more.

'Do you have to fly back to Niroli tomorrow? It seems such a long time since I saw you.'

Isabella smiled. 'You'd soon get tired of having paparazzi camped outside your door.'

'I wouldn't. I—'

The door opened and a maid came forward with a note. 'There's been a letter delivered for Her Royal Highness,' she said, nervously holding out a heavy cream envelope.

'Thank you, Caryn.' Isabella held out her hand and raised her eyebrows in Bianca's direction. 'Who'd write to me here?' She slid a finger underneath the gummed flap and pulled out a single sheet of paper. Handwritten in strong, black strokes.

'Well?'

'It's from Domenic Vincini.'

'How does he know you're here?'

'I told his sister.' Isabella frowned as she read on. There wasn't much to take in. Short, precise…and very much to the point.

'Silvana?'

Isabella looked up. 'That's right. She was at the meeting today.'

'I like her. She's his half-sister, you know.'

*No, she didn't know.* She frowned. Another thing she hadn't been told.

Bianca inserted a finger to detach Fabiano from her breast. She switched sides. 'What does Domenic want then?'

'Dinner.'

Bianca's eyebrows shot up. 'I told you they all become putty.'

'No, not that.' *Definitely not that.* 'Business.'

'That's great!'

*Was it?* Possibly. Isabella wasn't so sure. All of a sudden she felt as though a million butterflies had been loosed in her stomach.

\* \* \*

Domenic knew the minute Princess Isabella arrived. On the monitor he saw the sudden surge of paparazzi towards her, watched the practised smile, the quiet skill of her bodyguard in detaching her.

He pulled a hand through his hair and wondered, for perhaps the hundredth time, what he was doing this for. Silvana had been in favour, but then Silvana would favour anything that would coax him back to Mont Avellana.

And who was to say she wasn't right? At some point he was going to have to face his demons. Although this time his demons would have to wait. There was nothing that couldn't be delegated.

Switching off the monitor, he stood up. Pausing only to straighten the report he was reading so that it rested at right angles to the desk, he picked up his jacket and headed out towards the lift.

*Not a date.* Not by any means a date—but he felt nervous, like his teenage self going to meet Jolanda. So many years ago now. Eighteen. No. Nineteen. *Nineteen years.*

Domenic unrolled the sleeves of his white shirt and shrugged himself into his dinner jacket. He had to keep at the forefront of his mind that this was business. Business was what he did best. The lifeline that had kept him breathing in and out day after day…

But it didn't feel like business when he stepped out onto the sixth-floor *terrazzo*. The combination of lemon trees, white flowers and Roman lamps that decorated it made it appear almost bridal. If there'd been time he would have asked that they removed the candles from the single dining table. It created entirely the wrong mood…

He turned at the sound of footsteps, braced to see her again. Where was the wisdom in this? But, there was no time to think about that now as his *maître d'* opened the door and ushered the princess out.

And she looked like a princess. Her rich honey-blonde hair was piled on her head, soft tendrils left to frame her face. *God, but she was beautiful*. Like a May morning. Fresh, and full of promise.

Domenic's feet seemed leaden. He knew he ought to move towards her, to welcome her…but his feet refused to move.

The warm summer breeze caught at the light silk of her dress. She looked different from this afternoon. More relaxed… Approachable and incredibly sexy. In a different life he would have wanted to kiss her. And he knew that her lips would feel warm. Totally seductive.

He stepped forward. 'Your Royal Highness.' His voice was low, but clipped.

'Isabella. Please.'

*Isabella.* She reached out her hand and he took hold of it. Her palms were warm and her fingers were cold. He looked up—and her eyes were like molten toffee.

*Bad idea!* This was a truly bad idea. At some deep, fundamental level he responded to this woman. God only knew why. Perhaps it was nothing more than recognition of her undeniable beauty? Perhaps a consequence of his celibacy?

But he knew it was more than that. It felt like a meeting of souls.

She was looking at him, her black-lashed eyes taking in the scars on his face. Seeing the slashing red ridges that would always remind him of failure. Of loss.

Domenic pulled in a breath, difficult in the still heavy air. 'Thank you for coming at such short notice.'

And then she smiled. If he thought he'd been suffering

before, he knew now that was nonsense. Her smile ripped through all his defences. He ached for a woman like Isabella.

Loneliness was part and parcel of who he was now. It was part of his day-to-day existence, but it felt like a razor slicing through flesh to be on the receiving end of a smile like that.

The breeze tugged at the corkscrew curl that brushed against one of the the long silver-coloured droplets that hung at her ears. His eyes followed the length of her neck, helplessly taking in the small hollow at the base of her throat.

He would not allow his eyes to travel any further. Not to the matching necklace with the equally long droplet that nestled between her full breasts…

*Oh, God.*

This felt like a reawakening. For four years he'd scarcely noticed whether the people around him were male or female. He noticed competence, general efficiency…

He never registered perfume. *Never.* But he knew that from this moment Isabella Fierezza would always be associated in his mind with the scent of vanilla and musk. It hovered on her skin, enticing and beguiling.

'I was pleased I could come. I fly back to Niroli tomorrow morning.'

Domenic released her hand and stepped back. The *maître d'* moved to guide Isabella towards the table. As she walked away from him he had the most perfect view of her bare back. His eyes followed the line of her spine until it dipped behind the light silk of her dress.

A wise man would back away now, but perversely he liked to feel the pain. It felt right that he should suffer…

'This is beautiful,' she murmured, looking out towards the *Trinità dei Monti.*

It was more than the perfect symmetry of her face; it was

something that shone from inside her. Something that meant he reacted to her in a way he'd never done when seeing a photographic image of her.

'I love the feeling of being on top of the world. To watch what's going on without being seen.' She looked back and smiled, unfazed by the fact he was studying her so closely. 'I have a small private terrace at the Villa Berlusconi where I can watch the early evening *passeggiata*. Everyone dressed up and eating *gelato*.'

Domenic swallowed and took a step back. 'Privacy, I think that's called.'

And she laughed. 'You're probably right,' she said, sitting down. 'I have precious little of that. My fault, of course.'

Which was exactly what he'd thought about her. A woman that courted publicity, loved the attention she got. But nothing was ever quite as it seemed, was it? There was a wistful edge to her voice, hidden by a quick smile and a determined cheerfulness.

He took the seat opposite and nodded at the *maître d'* to offer to pour wine into her glass.

'I would prefer mineral water. Please.'

'Don't you drink?'

'Rarely.'

He understood so much more than she'd put into words. He heard the finality in her 'rarely'. Understood that Princess Isabella was always on duty, constantly aware that a picture of a high-profile and inebriated royal would be syndicated around the world.

A simple movement of his wrist had the *maître d'* remove both their wineglasses.

'Please, don't let me stop you—'

Domenic shook his head. 'I'm no great lover of alcohol these days.' And a clear head this evening was a necessity.

She looked at him as though she had a question forming, but had thought better of asking it. He was grateful for that. What would she think if he'd told her that, particularly in the early days, anything that numbed the pain, even for a few hours, was welcome?

She looked away, out over the darkening skyline and then back. 'I do have to break my rule occasionally, though.' She smiled. 'My cousin Max is a passionate advocate of Niroli's Porto Castellante Blanco and he'd never forgive me if I refused a glass when there was an opportunity to publicise it.'

'We stock it here. If that's your preference I can—'

She smiled again, her teeth white and perfect. 'You do?'

'It's an excellent wine. Dry. Good with fish.'

Her smile became almost impish and he felt his gut tighten yet further.

'I know it's sacrilege to say it, but I've never really liked it.' Her hand brushed at the hair floating across her cheek. One single strand of warm honey-gold. 'Nor am I particularly fond of rainbow mullet, even though it is our signature dish and, I'm sure, perfectly delicious.'

Domenic gave a crack of laughter, simply because it was so unexpected.

'Or squid. Which is totally revolting.'

He smiled, feeling his body relax. Almost. He would never be able to entirely relax around Princess Isabella. No man could. 'I believe we're having Spicy Rack of Lamb with Sweet and Sour Caponatina, but, of course, if there's something else you'd prefer…?'

'That sounds perfect,' she said quickly. 'It was thoughtless of me to express any opinion before I knew what your chef had prepared for me.'

Domenic smoothed an invisible crease out of the starched white tablecloth. She had manners as charming as her face. 'The price of royalty?'

'I made a deal with the devil when I was too young to know what it would mean,' she said, pulling herself straighter in her chair. He watched the tentative smile and wondered at the vulnerability behind it. 'It's too late now to start complaining that I have no anonymity and that people go to extraordinary lengths to impress me.'

'And it would be rude to disappoint them?'

'Hurtful,' she agreed. 'And why do that if you can avoid it?'

*Why?* She stated it as though it were a fact. Domenic sat back in his chair. 'Do you ever want to kick over the traces?' he prompted. 'Rebel? Do something entirely for yourself?'

'Often. I thought I'd schedule it in as some kind of midlife crisis.'

She was joking, but there was a clear underlying core of truth in her words. Isabella Fierezza's life was one of duty.

And, right now, her life was chafing. The façade she presented to the world was almost perfect, but he knew more than most what it felt like to hide.

Domenic Vincini was easy to talk to. *Very easy.* She hadn't expected that, but then from the very first moment of setting eyes on him he'd defied expectation.

She'd deliberately set out to make him feel comfortable— and she was fairly sure she'd succeeded. More unexpected was that she'd been able to relax herself. She pushed a spoon into her melting chocolate cakelet and let the rich dark chocolate ooze out onto the white plate.

Luca had said that he was a trustworthy businessman. Right at the beginning when she'd had to fight with her grandfather for the possibility of approaching the Vincini Group he'd told her that. And he was right. Domenic was certainly trustworthy. She felt confident that whatever she said would go no further.

There were precious few people she could say that about. She'd learnt the hard way that the nicest of people could be corrupted. Letters, gifts, conversations. Nothing was sacred.

She closed her eyes as she tasted the rich perfection of the chocolate sauce. Dark, smooth and not cloyingly sweet. It was yet more proof, if more were needed, why she wanted the Vincini Group behind Niroli's luxury resort. Everything that happened within one of Domenic Vincini's hotels was flawless from the minute you walked through the door to the minute you left.

'Good?'

'Food fit for the gods,' she said with a smile. 'How do you find your chefs?'

His eyes glinted. 'That would be telling.'

She laughed. Then, scared though she was to hear the answer, it was time to find out why he'd decided to ask her back. Isabella snatched a quick breath and asked the question before she lost her nerve. 'What did you want us to discuss?'

Domenic rested his spoon down on the edge of his plate and rubbed a hand across his face. His fingers smoothed over the deep scars that scored down the left hand side of his face.

It was strange, but until that moment she'd almost stopped noticing them. Now her eyes searched out the puckered skin that ran down the left side of his neck, clearly visible because he chose not to, or could not, wear a tie.

*Ugly?*

Perhaps. But the story behind the scars was likely to be

uglier still. She'd heard experts talk about the 'hidden scars', the ones that didn't show on the body but were buried deep in the psyche of burns survivors.

Quite deliberately she pulled her eyes away and concentrated on taking another mouthful of her dessert.

'The photographs you brought me were…interesting.' She looked up again. 'And I agree with you that anyone sitting out on their terrace each morning would want to visit Mont Avellana…'

'But?' she prompted when he paused.

He looked at her, and then smiled, a slow tilting of his mouth. 'It's not going to be easy for people who've habitually mistrusted each other to put that aside—even if it does mean jobs and increased prosperity.'

Isabella laid down her own spoon. 'I was thinking I could invest my own money in a handful of projects on Mont Avellana. It would be—' she broke off, searching for the right words '—a show of trust.' She wrinkled her nose. 'That's not quite right. A show of commitment.'

Another pause while he considered it. Isabella almost didn't dare breathe in case she missed his reply.

'That might help.' He picked up his mineral water. 'This is indelicate, but I have to ask. Would that be Fierezza family money? Or money from your personal funds?'

'Does it make a difference?'

'I think it does.' His eyes met hers above the rim of his glass and the expression in them was almost apologetic. 'Fierezza money promised now might not be forthcoming if Niroli should have a new king in the near future.'

Isabella reached up and pulled at her earring. She might have expected a response like this if she'd paused long enough to think about it. Marco's decision to relinquish his claim to the Niroli throne had far reaching consequences. It spread uncertainty like ink in water. 'I have a personal fortune.'

'Forgive me…' Domenic's strong hands splayed out on the white tablecloth '…but you'll need considerable funds at your disposal if you're to make any kind of impact on Mont Avellana.'

She felt the familiar prickle of irritation. Did he honestly think she didn't know that? Why was it so hard for anyone to take her seriously? 'I'm aware of that!' She met his gaze squarely. 'How many millions are you thinking I'll need?'

'I would think one and a half would be a reasonable starting point.'

'Then we don't have a problem.'

Domenic smiled and she fancied she could detect the supercilious superiority she found in so many men, particularly those in her family when he asked, 'Immediately available?'

*Damn it!* She wasn't an idiot. 'Certainly.'

His right eyebrow rose at that. 'Have you done any kind of feasibility study?'

'There's no point unless you're committed to Niroli.'

'Which still requires me to trust you.'

'Yes.' And that was the crux of the issue. Did he? Could he? Her heart thudded and she willed her breathing to stay steady.

'Have you ever been to Mont Avellana?' he asked after a moment.

Isabella brushed a hair off her face. 'No.'

'No,' he repeated.

'You haven't visited Niroli either.'

She watched a slow smile start at the edge of his mouth. He sat back in his chair. His dark eyes didn't leave her face. 'I'm prepared to sign on one condition.'

'Which is?'

'You need to visit Mont Avellana. Yourself.'

Isabella couldn't have been more shocked than if he'd stood up and yanked the tablecloth from beneath their plates. 'I can't do that.'

'Why?'

'It wouldn't be safe.'

'In what way?' he asked, mildly.

She thought of the stories her grandfather had recounted, the horrors of a brief but vicious war. 'No member of my family has been there since nineteen seventy-two.'

'Which is rather the point.' He sat forward again. 'Silvana says that people follow where you lead. If you visit Mont Avellana you'll immediately raise its profile.'

Isabella felt as though her stomach were about to climb into her throat.

'And if you're serious about bringing our islands closer, I can't think of a more effective way of achieving it.'

Her mouth felt dry. 'If I come you'll sign?'

'Yes. Whether you ultimately decide to invest in projects of your own on Mont Avellana or not.'

She was so close to pulling off the biggest deal in the history of Niroli. So very close. She could smell the victory. See the disbelief on the face of the sceptics who'd said it wouldn't happen.

'How long for?'

'Long enough for people to notice you're there. Shall we say two weeks?'

'I can't possibly stay that long!'

He shrugged.

'Three days. I could manage that.'

'A week.' Domenic smiled. 'And that's my final offer.'

Isabella reached up and pulled at her earring. 'Is it safe? For me, I mean?'

'As safe as it is for you anywhere I imagine.'

At that she laughed. He could have no idea what her life was like. 'I need protection everywhere I go now. Even on Niroli.'

'There's no reason you can't travel with your usual entourage.'

*Go to Mont Avellana?* Could she? Her grandfather would be apoplectic.

Isabella pushed back her seat and walked over to the edge of the *terrazzo*. She could hear laughter and the smoky sound of jazz carried along on the night air.

*Mont Avellana.*

Marco wouldn't hesitate. Luca, Alex…they'd all defied the king when his will had crossed theirs. Could *she?*

The big difference was that she was a woman. In his grandsons he tended to see defiance as strength and leadership potential. In his granddaughters it was less attractive. Perhaps even less so in her than in Rosa.

'Where would I stay? If I came?'

'There are two obvious choices—' He broke off as the *maître d'* returned to clear the table.

As soon as his footsteps disappeared, Isabella turned. Domenic hadn't moved. He was sitting, watching her, his face calm as though he knew her decision had already been made.

'Silvana is prepared to offer you the use of her home for the duration of your visit, although we would have to change the venue of my father's party. Or…' his voice was bland '…you could stay at the Palazzo Tavolara.'

She knew she must have betrayed some emotion when he added, 'Unless you would find that awkward.'

Isabella returned to the table and sat opposite him. Staying there wouldn't be 'awkward', but it would be strange. Good or bad, she couldn't possibly say. For years she'd longed to see what it looked like. 'Is it habitable?'

'Yes.' His long fingers picked up a grape from his plate. 'And its advantage over Silvana's villa is that it's secure. Our intention—' He broke off. '*My* intention when I acquired it was for it to be a luxury hotel and the perimeter security is already in place. It's been designed to keep photographers, bona fide fans and stalkers out.'

'That sounds better.'

He nodded. And then, 'Will you come?'

There was no choice. Not if she wanted to stay on Niroli. 'Yes. Yes, I will.'

'Good.'

It was as if someone had opened a floodgate to emotions she didn't know she possessed. Almost like one of those moments in a film where images flashed through a character's mind. *Mont Avellana. Her grandfather. War.* Her voice faltered. 'Will you be there?'

'Silvana will be there. You can liaise with her directly, or your people can speak to her people…' He smiled. 'Whichever suits you best.'

Isabella took a moment to assimilate that. 'I'd prefer it if you were there.' Though why she thought that would help she didn't know. Perhaps because he seemed so calm. Rocklike.

He'd started to shake his head even before she'd finished speaking. 'There's no need.'

'But—'

'No.' His eyes were shuttered. 'That isn't going to be possible. I'm sorry.'

# CHAPTER FOUR

IGNORING the book on her knee, Isabella stared almost constantly from the window during the short helicopter flight from Niroli to Mont Avellana. Logically she'd not expected any dramatic change of scenery, but it still surprised her to see the almost familiar rocky cliffs and long stretches of white sandy beach.

'Equally beautiful' was how Bianca had described the islands. Isabella loosened her seat belt and tucked her novel in the bag beside her. Her friend had also told her that the people were welcoming, relaxed…

Which under normal circumstances they probably were, but Bianca didn't come to Mont Avellana as the granddaughter of a king they'd fought a war to get rid of. She came as the much-loved wife of one of their own. That would have to make a rather enormous difference to how they'd be treated.

'Your Highness…'

She looked up. Isabella snatched a quick breath and then let the air out in one calming stream. Not that it worked. Her heart was pounding from pure fear.

*Please, God…help me.*

A week. That was all this was. She could do that. A week

of smiling, of looking pleased to be here, and then she could go home. Back to Niroli secure in the knowledge she'd just brokered the biggest deal in their entire history. And for all his blustering her grandfather would be pleased…

She left her bag on the seat beside her and stood up. The skeleton team she'd brought with her quietly went about their business as though this really were the everyday kind of goodwill visit they were all pretending it was. There were even the usual jokes.

Isabella tried to look coolly confident as she waited for the steps to be positioned, but, inside, she felt like a little girl caught up in a vortex. *Why was she doing this?*

Did she even believe Domenic would keep his end of the bargain?

Yes, she did. She was certain he would. And that was the point. He *would* sign on that dotted line and her future would be assured. Her position in Niroli cemented…

Her bodyguard moved alongside her. 'Ready, Your Highness?'

She snapped to attention and stepped out into the familiar noise of whirring blades and the tremendous wind they created. Soft white linen trousers flicked around her legs, wind caught at hair that had been captured into a curling ponytail especially to deal with this moment. This was what she did. And she did it well.

*Her Royal Highness, Princess Isabella of Niroli—reporting for duty.*

Her heels made no impression on the baked hard ground as she stepped down onto Mont Avellanan soil. The first member of the Fierezza family to do so since nineteen seventy-two. She knew how newsworthy a moment that was, the message her arrival would send out across the Mediterranean.

Isabella held back her flicking ponytail and looked towards the palazzo—a seventeenth century gem, set against the backdrop of a cobalt sky and a hard lump settled in her throat.

There were no words to describe how she felt. She'd expected to feel emotional, but she'd underestimated just how emotional. Knowing her paternal grandmother had loved it here gave the place a special meaning. Made her feel as if she might cry.

'This way, Your Highness.' Her bodyguard urged her forward towards the waiting group. Tomasso's intention, no doubt, was to lead her away from open ground, but his words reminded her that her hostess was standing in the full heat of the sun. Isabella tore her eyes away from the palazzo. There'd be time later to look and think about what her family had lost.

'Come inside,' Silvana shouted above the whirr of the blades. 'Roberto and Gianni will see to your entourage. Let me get you something cool to drink.'

Isabella said nothing because she couldn't. It felt as if she were stepping off a precipice—which was pure nonsense. Nothing terrible was likely to happen to her inside the palazzo. Outside…on the streets of Mont Avellana? That was, perhaps, a different matter.

She smiled and glanced over her shoulder at Tomasso, whose eyes were darting about the enclosed grounds.

'The pool is through there.' Silvana pointed through an archway. 'It's completely private should you wish to use it during your stay. Jolanda planted trees that would screen it from any prying cameras and they've grown up beautifully.' She led the way across the lawn and up a set of wide steps.

'Jolanda?'

'Domenic's late wife. She was passionate about gardens. Always insisted he put thought and money into them before

anything was done to the buildings because they'd take longer
to become established.'

Isabella glanced round. Domenic's wife had been called
*Jolanda*. And she'd had a hand in the design of the palazzo's
gardens. Had the house fire in which she'd died been here?
Her eyes wandered looking for signs of damage but the white
limestone looked completely untouched.

'Domenic is waiting for us in the grand salon.'

'He's here?' She looked back at Silvana. 'I thought he was
unable to…spare the time.'

'No, he's here. Against his will, maybe, but he can't resist
my mother when she really wants something.' Silvana turned
her head and smiled. 'Even though he likes to think otherwise, his sense of family runs like steel through his personality. He would have come out to meet you in person, but he
finds the intense heat at this time of day hard to cope with.'

'I'm sure…'

'Burns survivors generally find it difficult to regulate their
body temperature.'

'Yes, I know that. I'm glad he didn't feel he had to.' She
was so close to asking Silvana what had happened, but she
stopped herself at the last moment. It felt wrong to intrude
on what was an intensely private grief.

*But Domenic was here. On Mont Avellana.*

Silvana led the way through the loggia with its beautifully
decorated wall paintings and into a living room, painted in
the deepest red.

'The *salottino rosso*,' Silvana murmured. 'I'm so proud of
this room. I think the colour is very effective. And this is the
entrance hall.'

It was simply furnished. Isabella's eyes immediately took
in the family emblems that ran around the top of the walls.

*Her* family emblems. The palace in Niroli had similar decoration in the magnificent dining hall. She glanced across at Tomasso, keeping step beside her, wondering if he'd noticed the similarity.

'And through here…is the grand salon.'

Isabella stepped through into an immense room, decorated with what she recognised as being a late-seventeenth-century fresco and a truly magnificent Nirolian fireplace. An incongruous touch of home.

She walked towards it and ran her hand along the marble mantelpiece.

'It dates from the seventeen hundreds, I believe,' Domenic said coming up behind her.

Her pleasure at hearing his voice came as an immense surprise. Isabella spun round on her high stiletto heels. 'I think so. The shape is quite distinctive.'

'It's one of only two that survived the war.'

It was ridiculous what a difference his being here made to how she felt about being on Mont Avellana. She could feel the tension seep from her bones. 'It's a beautiful example. I'm so glad it survived.'

Domenic looked different from the last time she'd seen him. Less austere. More troubled.

'I apologise for not coming out to meet you.'

'It's extremely hot,' Isabella said quickly, 'and there was no need.'

His hand moved into a fist at the side of his body, then unclenched. Isabella noticed it and recognised it for what it was—anger.

She looked up into his strong face. He might want many things from her, but sympathy wasn't one of them. She could understand that. Though it was what she felt.

Anyone looking at Domenic Vincini would feel pity. He was a man in his mid thirties, tall, lean and toned…with the kind of natural sex appeal that came from confidence in who and what he was. A man who had driven his business to a level of unparalleled excellence.

A man who would seem to have it all.

So…it was a shame to see his face slashed down the left-hand side. Incredibly sad to know his body had been mutilated by fire.

But it was even more difficult not to feel intense pity when you realised he'd lost the people he'd loved in that tragedy.

Isabella deliberately turned away, intending to give him privacy. She couldn't change his past, but she could respect his wishes now.

Tomasso stood looking out through one of the windows. Whatever he saw obviously satisfied him because he gave her a slight nod and walked out of the salon, shutting the door quietly behind him.

'We have a great many bodyguards stay at our hotels,' Silvana remarked, 'but few seem as conscientious as yours. Most would have given a room in a place like this no more than a cursory look.'

'Tomasso's been with me six months. Before that he was assigned to Luca.' She smiled. 'I think I'm a relief.'

That and the fact that Tomasso knew she was frightened. Never spoken of, but understood all the same.

Domenic moved over towards the fan and sat down in one of the enormous sofas that looked so tiny in the huge proportions of the room. 'Why "relief"?'

'Because I do as I'm told. I don't disappear for hours on end without telling anyone where I am.'

He gave a sudden crack of laughter. 'And Luca does?'

'Of course. You've met him. He hates being accountable to anyone and—' she shrugged her shoulders '—I suppose he doesn't feel as vulnerable.'

Silvana indicated the sofa opposite and Isabella sat down, ankles neatly crossed, hands folded loosely in her lap. She looked across at Domenic and found him watching her, a strange expression in his dark eyes. *Speculation?*

He had an odd way of doing that. Of looking deeper than any man she'd ever met before. Most were too overawed or dazzled or a combination of both to listen to what she actually said.

'Can I offer you a drink?' Silvana moved towards the doorway. 'I fancy a Caffe Shakerato since it's so hot, but we can offer you espresso, lemonade, mineral water…'

'A Caffe Shakerato would be lovely. Thank you.'

The expression in Domenic's dark eyes sharpened, but he said nothing.

Silvana's hand rested on the doorknob. 'If you'll excuse me, I'll organise that and make sure your entourage are being taken care of. Roberto and Gianni should have everything in hand, but…' She opened the door and looked a little startled to see Tomasso standing there. 'Ooh! Excuse me.'

Domenic smiled. He leant forward and picked up a wooden dice that had been left lying on the low table. He turned it over in his fingers as the door clicked shut. 'I suppose you get used to tripping over the bodyguard.'

'Eventually.'

The door clicked shut.

'But never quite?' His eyes flicked up. Dark, dark brown. 'Do you want to drink a Caffe Shakerato or are you merely being charmingly polite?'

'No, I—' She broke off as she took in the glimmer of laughter. 'I was given a choice,' she said with dignity.

'So you were,' he agreed, tossing the dice into the palm of his other hand.

'I stated my preference.'

'Did you?'

The warm understanding and soft laughter in his eyes made her smile. 'Almost.' And then she watched his smile broaden—and when he did that she stopped seeing the scars. She just felt power. A connection.

'Thank you for coming,' he said quietly.

'Did you think I wouldn't?'

'Not having met you. No.'

*Which meant what?*

'Once you've said you'll do something, I suspect you always do it.' He placed the dice back on the table. 'Did you encounter any opposition?'

'Yes.'

Domenic smiled. It would have been a miracle if she hadn't. She might be more amenable than Luca when it came to cooperating with her protection officers, but there had to be something steely about Isabella Fierezza for her to be here. He could only imagine how resistant King Giorgio would have been to the idea.

Strange that she could stand up to a formidable man like her grandfather and yet didn't feel able to state a preference for the everyday things of life.

The door clicked open and Silvana returned. 'Everything seems to be happening perfectly smoothly without me. I've brought my file in. I thought we could go through your itinerary—'

He stopped her. 'There's no hurry.'

'No, please.' Isabella smiled the smile she habitually hid behind. It was socially perfect and it irritated the hell out of him.

*Say what you think,* he urged silently. Say that you've just arrived and would like to drink your drink first. Say that you'll let her know the places you want to see in due course. *Tell her.*

'I'm not at all tired and I should like to know what you want me to do while I'm here.'

His half-sister shot him a look of triumph, but he was convinced she didn't have much to feel triumphant about.

What you saw when you were confronted by Isabella Fierezza was a consummate professional. She could be bored, tired, angry, sad, deliriously happy…and no one would suspect. There was just the tiniest chink in the façade when she'd said she felt 'vulnerable'.

And he'd noticed it—and he'd never feel quite the same about her again. In that moment, in his mind, she'd stopped being a princess of Niroli and had become a woman.

'Tonight there's a fund-raising ball at the Palazzo Razzoli.' Silvana flicked over a sheet. 'I've arranged for cars to collect us at eight-thirty.'

'Is that far from here?' Not by so much as a tremor did Isabella's well modulated voice betray any emotion. Domenic searched for a hint of something in her wide eyes. Was a fund-raising ball something she'd enjoy going to? Or not?

'Less than ten kilometres.'

Isabella nodded. There was no dangling earring to distract him. This afternoon she'd chosen pearl studs, small, round, with a luminosity that brought out the soft creaminess of her skin.

But he didn't need an earring to distract him. *She* distracted him. Simply by being. The way she spoke. The way she moved. The way she said one thing when he was certain she meant another.

His hands fisted against the fabric of the sofa. *The way she looked.* He'd have been wiser to have stayed away.

Silvana flicked over a second page. 'There's a guest list of more than five hundred, so that's an excellent start in making sure everyone knows you're here.'

'Who is going with me?'

Her eyes didn't travel in his direction. It was pitiful that he wished they had. Once upon a time he would have taken her to the charity event. *Danced with her.* He'd have been able to let his hand slide round her slight waist and pull her up close against his body.

'Silvana and her husband.' She looked at him then. Wide-eyed. Beautiful. 'They'll take great care of you,' he said, his voice husky.

His half-sister was oblivious to what he was feeling. 'It's formal evening dress. Dinner jackets. Long dresses—'

'And if you wouldn't mind wearing a tiara and a couple of insignias…' *He'd had enough.* Domenic stood up and walked over to the door, ostensibly to look for their drinks. The timing was perfect. He stepped back and let the maid come through, indicating the central table.

There was something that felt very wrong about what they were doing to Princess Isabella. Behind the sophistication and regal poise there was a woman. He wanted to tilt her face up so he could see into those beautiful eyes and read what she was really thinking.

'The tiara is fine. I never travel without one,' Isabella stated calmly into the slightly awkward silence he'd created, 'but an insignia is more of a problem.'

'I don't think anyone will expect you to wear an insignia. Dom, I—' Silvana looked up and caught the amusement in his eyes. 'Was that a joke?'

Above her head he looked across at Isabella, whose eyes were smiling. He'd not realised eyes could do that. 'Yes, a joke. It was irresistible. I'm sorry. I'm sure Isabella will be able to work out what she should wear by herself.'

'If there's anything specific you might like to tell my stylist,' Isabella said softly. 'Sometimes there's an unwritten code and I'd hate to offend anyone.'

Domenic sat back down and stretched out his legs. He believed her. A natural diplomat.

'If a hostess always wears red it would be a mistake to wear it, too.'

*Particularly if you couldn't help but look better.*

'Don't you think?' she said, turning to look at Silvana. Her words a gentle balm.

'I'm not aware of anything, although Imelda Bianchi does tend to wear red. Perhaps it would be better to avoid it since she's a very…fashion conscious woman. Other than that, the tickets have cost five thousand euros and everyone is looking forward to meeting you.'

The maid passed Isabella her drink and he watched her curve her long fingers round the fluted glass. The fine gold chain she wore at her wrist slipped back and blinked in the light.

'Thank you,' he said, receiving his own glass from Olivia. He sipped the creamy iced drink.

Isabella let her glass rest untried on her lap. 'And tomorrow?'

'Is Sunday.' Silvana smiled. 'I thought church. We could go to mass at the *Cattedrale di Caprera,* followed by a reception at—'

'Enough!' It was almost as though Isabella was a conquest of war and she was to be paraded around the entire island. 'Why not give Isabella a list of your suggestions? And you,' he said, looking at Isabella, 'can decide which ones seem most appropriate for what we're trying to do here.'

There was a moment's stunned silence and then Silvana shut her file with a snap. 'No problem.'

'I'm sure whatever you've arranged will be perfectly fine with me.'

Domenic stood up and walked over to the window, starring out at the piazza. Damn it! He didn't believe her. Not for a minute. She had to have a preference, some kind of *feeling* about what she was being asked to do.

He wanted to shake her with frustration. She was too perfect. Too beautiful.

*And unhappy.*

He turned. 'Were you serious about wanting to encourage tourism on Mont Avellana?'

Her eyes widened. 'Yes. Yes, I was. Am.'

'Then,' he said, sitting back down, 'you might like to visit some of our attractions while you're here? Rather than merely go to parties and shake the hands of the great and good?'

Isabella glanced across at Silvana, her curling ponytail swinging. 'That would be useful.'

As breakthroughs went it was small enough, but it felt good. 'Do you have any idea what you'd like to see?'

Again her ponytail swung. This time as she shook her head. 'On Niroli I work by instinct. I encourage what interests me.'

He was getting somewhere. 'So that explains the opera…?'

Isabella's face lit into a genuine smile. 'I love it. Particularly if it makes me cry.'

He nodded. Somehow that didn't come as a surprise. 'And marine life?'

'Less so.' A hand moved up to brush a stray hair from her cheek. 'But that's important, don't you think? Local festivals, traditions… I think we should treasure those.'

Domenic set his glass back down on the table. 'We might not have opera here but we do have plenty of local festivals, excellent climbing, diving, walking, scenery…'

He stopped and made sure he had eye contact. She had to hear this. Understand what he was trying to say. 'But it's enough you've come to Mont Avellana,' he said, quietly. 'Whether you ultimately decide to invest your money in projects here, you've healed a lot of hurt by being here.'

He rubbed a hand over his face. 'I hope that you'll have a pleasant stay with us.'

'Th-thank you.'

'Now, if you'll excuse me I need to speak to Toby Blake in Melbourne. If I leave it much longer he'll be asleep.'

Silvana looked as if she wanted to protest, but didn't. No doubt surprised by his outburst.

He didn't dare to look at Isabella. 'Silvana will take care of you, I know.'

He needed to get away from here, focus on work. It didn't matter what Isabella thought, or Isabella felt… It didn't matter if Isabella was happy. At least, if he were to stay sane, it shouldn't.

# CHAPTER FIVE

ISABELLA pulled open the floor-to-ceiling doors that led onto the balcony and walked out to lean against the marble balustrade.

It was late—or very early, depending on your perspective—and it was hot. That still, heavy kind of airless night. It was a lot like being home on Niroli.

Except there was silence. And she loved that. After the bustle of the charity ball, silence was the most perfect thing.

It had been a long, long evening. She'd smiled, she'd laughed—she'd done everything anyone could have reasonably expected of her… In fact, everything she always did.

'Are you sure you don't want any help with your dress or hair, Your Highness?'

Isabella turned and walked back into the bedroom, resting her hand on one of the posts of the enormous four-poster bed. 'I can manage by myself, thank you, Mia. It's a simple enough dress.'

Her stylist smiled. 'Good night, then, Your Highness.'

'Good night.' Isabella watched her leave and sat down on the edge of the bed. She wasn't a fool. When her normally meticulous stylist was prepared to let her take care of her own clothes there must be a strong reason. Particularly when she'd sat up to nearly three in the morning for her to come back to the palazzo.

Isabella smiled. She hadn't missed the look that had passed between Mia and Tomasso. They were in love. She was sure of it. And that meant there'd be more changes for her in the near future. Tomasso would be taken off her staff and she'd have another Chief of Security watching her every move.

But, to look on the bright side, at least this one hadn't fallen in love with her. Isabella eased her feet out of her high sandals and wriggled her toes, before padding back across to the open doors.

That was where she wanted to be. Outside. Breathing in real air and listening to nothing. If she really followed her inclination she'd put on her swimming costume and go for a swim.

*No!* If she really followed her inclination she wouldn't bother with the swimming costume. Just skin and cool water. That would be perfect.

And completely inappropriate for a woman like her.

The palazzo's security had won high praise from Tomasso, but it was never worth taking the chance. Some exceptionally determined photographer would find a way of circumventing it.

As her mother had always said, being a princess brought both privilege and responsibility. And she was a very good princess. Day in, day out, that was what she did.

She walked back through and pulled the curtains across. Unlike other members of her family who took the privileges and left the responsibilities. Marco. Luca. Though to be fair, neither Alex or Luca had ever expected or wanted to be king.

And Marco had fallen in love. Deep down, wasn't that what she wanted for herself?

But all that left her precisely where? Everything was shifting about so much she wasn't sure where she fitted in any more.

Isabella glanced back over at the balcony. It was so hot. And she was so restless. With sudden decisiveness she picked up her sandals off the bed and walked barefoot out of the bedroom and along the wide landing towards the staircase.

The first hint she wasn't alone came from the glimmer reflected in the hall mirror. Like a moth she followed it—and found a lamp left alight in the beautiful sitting room. She moved over to switch it off and noticed the doors had been left open to the *terrazzo*.

Holding her sandals with one finger, she moved to look out. Somehow it wasn't a surprise to see Domenic Vincini sitting there. Alone. Still as an image in a photograph. And sad.

Isabella hesitated in the doorway for a moment, wondering whether she ought to go quietly back up to her room. He was staring out across the darkened gardens, his hand loosely wrapped around a half-empty wineglass, which told her he must have been there sometime.

The decision not to intrude was taken away from her. He looked up, his face half in shadow. 'Isabella!'

She stepped out into the moonlight. 'I'm sorry. Am I disturbing you?'

'No. I'm…' Domenic stood up and he gestured towards the still-almost-full bottle of wine on the table.

She nodded. 'Yes, I see.'

He set his glass down on the table. 'Is there anything you need? Is your room comfortable? I—'

'It's lovely.' Isabella tentatively walked forward, her sandals in one hand and the fabric of her long skirt caught up in the other. 'I thought I'd get some air. It's so hot and I don't feel like sleeping yet.'

'Parties don't exhaust you?'

Her smile twisted. 'Some peace would be nice.'

Domenic ran a hand around the back of his neck. 'Would you like to join me?'

The invitation seemed wrung from him, but Isabella nodded. 'I'd like that. Thank you.'

In fact, she'd like that very much. Their dinner together had been like an oasis in a life that felt increasingly difficult.

Why was that? Nothing amazing had happened. He'd talked. She'd talked. But it had all felt so easy. There'd been no sense of having to watch what she said for fear it would end up twisted.

After an evening like tonight she really needed that. Constant scrutiny and the need to watch everything you said had a way of wearing you down.

She sat down on the second wrought iron seat and took a deep breath. The air was rich and spicy with the scent of orange blossom. So like home. She'd merely exchanged a secluded balcony for a wide *terrazzo*. Solitude for company.

'I'll fetch a second glass.'

'No, I…' If there'd been time she'd have stopped him, but he'd turned away almost immediately and didn't hear her.

Isabella sat back in her chair. It was so quiet. She could get used to this. Her suite of rooms within the Villa Berlusconi were her private sanctuary, but there was always a hubbub of noise until the early hours.

She smiled wryly in the darkness. She had to take some responsibility for that. Without her active encouragement there probably wouldn't be the plethora of smart cafés and street performances.

But here the silence was so complete she could almost hear the thump of her heartbeat. And it was lovely.

'I would have brought the water in something more elegant, but I couldn't find anything suitable.'

Isabella turned to see Domenic carrying a large earthenware jug, the kind that was more likely to hold flowers.

'There must be something better in one of the cupboards, but I haven't the first idea where to look. To be honest I did well to find the glasses.'

She felt a bubble of laughter form in the pit of her stomach. 'How long is it since you were last here?' she asked as he set the pitcher down on the table and then the glass.

'A year.' He sat down. 'I find it difficult to come back.'

'To the palazzo?'

He shook his head. 'Mont Avellana. I love it and hate it here in pretty much equal measure. I only come when I really have to.'

Isabella stashed her sandals beneath her chair and wiggled her toes. 'Because of the fire?'

She watched the convulsive movement of his throat, so near the damaged skin that ran its length.

'Yes, the fire.'

Pain ripped through his voice and Isabella wished she'd not spoken without thinking. Of course he'd want to be as far away as possible from the place that had taken everything he valued most. 'Do you need to come?'

'Yes and no. Every year I say I won't, but then I change my mind. It's my father's birthday in a few days' time. Once a year he likes to have his entire family around him—sons, daughters, grandchildren… It seems little enough to ask.'

But one of those grandchildren would be missing. Domenic's child. So that was what Silvana had meant when she'd said family was 'like steel running through him'. He would come, every year, even though it hurt him to do so.

Domenic continued. 'I'll fly back to Rome the day after. Visit over for another year.'

Which would leave her alone here. It didn't help to remember that was only what she'd expected when she'd first arrived.

'Wine or water?' He held up the bottle of wine. 'This is imported. Sardinian. Sella & Mosca Alghero "Le Arenarie". You might like it. It's light, a little lemony. Not as dry as your Porto Castellante Blanco.'

Isabella held out her glass. 'Please.' He poured some wine into her glass and she took a tentative sip. 'It's nice,' she said politely.

He laughed, a sudden bark. 'Why do you do that?'

'What?'

'Say what you think I want you to say, rather what you really think.'

'I don't—'

His right eyebrow shot up.

'Maybe. Sometimes,' she said in response. 'It's a habit.'

'Tip it away if you'd prefer water.'

'No, I'll drink it,' she said, resting her hand on her glass as though she thought he might take it from her. 'My sister would never forgive me if I did anything as sacrilegious as throw it away. Do you know how much love is lavished on grapes?'

'No.'

'More than many parents give to their children.' She took another cautious sip. 'This isn't too bad.'

'Damned with faint praise.' Domenic lifted his own glass, catching sight of his rolled up shirt sleeve. He put his glass down again and went to unroll it.

The sudden movement drew her eyes to the puckered and discoloured skin on his forearm. 'Don't. Please.'

His hand hesitated.

'Not on my account, anyway,' she said quietly and deliberately turned her face away to look out across the garden. She lifted her head back to catch the gentle night-time breeze on her face.

'Is saying the socially preferable thing a learnt habit or are you a natural pleaser?'

She turned her head to look at him, glad to see he'd left his sleeve rolled up. The skin on his arm was dark brown and wrinkled to a point midway down his forearm. But his hands were beautiful. Strong, sculptural, unblemished in any way.

'It's a long story,' she said with a shake of her head.

'I'm not going anywhere.'

She shook her head again. To explain that would be to explain the dynamics of her family and that was private. Too private to share, however lovely a garden and cooling the night breeze.

However fabulous a listener the man she was with happened to be.

He seemed to recognise that because he smiled and it occurred to her that it wasn't only his hands that were beautiful. 'How was it tonight?'

'At the ball?'

He nodded.

'Truthfully?'

'Of course.'

'Well…' She smiled and set her glass down on the table. 'I'm assuming you don't want fashion details…'

'Er…not particularly.'

'Though you might be interested to know Imelda Bianchi did wear red.'

'Which made your blue the perfect choice.'

*Socially and aesthetically perfect.* Domenic took another sip of wine and let the tang of lemon bite against his tongue.

No woman should look as beautiful as Isabella. Her hair was a million shades of corn and gold. Warm. Rich. Stunning. And she, or her stylist, had clipped her heavy curls back off her face with a barrette of pale blue gemstones set on wires to look like dancing cornflowers. The tiniest sapphire drops hung in her ears, nothing at her neck or on her wrist. Simple. Unaffected. And she'd have made every other woman look like an overdecorated Christmas tree.

'It's always a good idea to know in advance what your hostess is likely to wear. I learnt that very early on in my career.' Isabella toyed with her wineglass. 'Fashion among women is a competitive business.'

'You make it sound like war.'

She looked up. 'It's gamesmanship. And some of it comes from men, I think. "My wife is more attractive than your wife", "I can afford to buy my wife better jewels".' She wrinkled her nose. 'That kind of thing.'

Isabella Fierezza was a cynic. The next time he saw her smiling from a magazine cover he'd know what was really going on behind those amber-flecked eyes.

Domenic sat forward to refill his glass. 'What did you think of the Palazzo Razzoli?'

'Now that was beautiful. And Vittore and Imelda had clearly gone to a lot of effort and expense to make it a wonderful evening. They'd even laid a mirrored dance floor across the ballroom.'

'Tacky.'

She laughed and he found he loved to hear it. 'Well…

tricky anyway. It was considered spectacular, but I gave it a wide birth. There are some photographs of me I don't want circulating on the World Wide Web.'

'Where there many photographers there?'

'Lots. I shouldn't think there'll be anyone on Mont Avellana who won't know I'm here by the end of the weekend.'

'Excellent.'

'Mission accomplished,' she said lightly.

And it was, so why did he feel as if he'd stolen something from her?

'Is it true that the Bianchis were once a noble family?'

He almost choked on his wine. 'Is that what he told you? Vittore's grandfather was a mountain shepherd.'

'Imelda did. Or implied it.' She frowned. 'I wish people didn't feel they had to do that.'

'She wanted to impress you, I suppose,' he said, watching her over the rim of his glass. 'Why does it bother you so much?'

'It implies that they think that matters to me.'

He smiled. Isabella was nothing like the woman he'd thought she was. He'd love it if he could introduce her to his father. Would she be prepared to meet him? An elderly republican and the granddaughter of the man he'd helped depose?

He shook his head. It wouldn't be right to put her in that kind of an awkward position. But he was fairly sure they'd like each other. His father would certainly love her. Aside from anything else he knew a beautiful woman when he saw one.

'I also wish she hadn't shown me the bullet holes in the courtyard wall—'

Domenic sat forward. 'She didn't!'

'Apparently it was caught in crossfire in the August of

nineteen seventy-two and Vittore thinks it should be kept for posterity. Some kind of warning against human frailty, I believe.'

Her eyes twinkled with suppressed amusement and Domenic felt himself relax back in his chair. 'And what did you say?'

'That it was always wise to remember the mistakes of the past.'

*The consummate professional.* His finger stroked around the rim of his glass. 'Where was Silvana when all this was happening?'

Isabella let the laughter out. 'Two feet away from me and she performed an excellent rescue mission. Smooth, swift and practically undetectable.'

He laughed.

'Your sister is very lovely.'

'You didn't grow up with her.'

'Neither did you I hear.' Isabella looked up at him with a slanting expression.

'Not until I turned fifteen. No.'

'Silvana told me.'

How much had she told her? He didn't want Isabella's view of him distorted by other people's gossip, malicious or otherwise.

A memory speared into his head, fresh and clear—and for the first time it didn't hurt him to remember. Jolanda had laughed up at him. Teasing. *'Women talk, Dom. Of course I know if you so much as smile at another woman.'* He'd known then that he never would smile at another woman because he'd found the one he'd wanted.

And they'd been happy together. It was all too easy to forget that and simply remember the grief that had come later.

'Did she tell you why?'

'No. I merely said something about you two being close and she said it was surprising since you hadn't lived with them until you were fifteen.'

*Ah.*

'I'm sorry. I didn't mean to pry.'

'It's no secret.' He sipped his wine. 'My mother grew up on Niroli. Then at eighteen, she went to Rome to study and met my father. After a very swift romance they married and she came to live on Mont Avellana. I think they were reasonably happy for the first couple of years, until my father's politics got in the way.'

'I'm sorry.'

'It's not your fault.' He smiled. 'They can take full responsibility for their own mistakes. I was a "sticking plaster" baby, I think, born to keep a marriage together, but in the end my mother left and took me to London.'

'Did she marry again?'

Domenic shook his head. 'She was a good Catholic girl and felt she'd failed her vows. Lived the rest of her life between a rock and a hard place.'

Why was he telling her this? The last person he'd told any of this to was Jolanda. It was simply that he wanted Isabella to understand something about his relationship with his family. And God only knew why that was.

He shifted in his seat. 'She died when I was fifteen and I came back to live with my father and his new family. My father is a bad Catholic and had no such scruples in creating one.'

'Did you know him well?'

'Not then. I was uprooted and landed unceremoniously on his doorstop. Fortunately my stepmother is a rather special woman.'

Isabella said something under her breath. He smiled, almost sure she'd sworn.

'I thought I'd had it tough.'

Surprisingly it hadn't felt so tough, even at the time. And it certainly wasn't when viewed through what had happened to him since. He took a sip of his wine. 'What happened to you?'

'Boarding school. Nothing in comparison to you, but I hated it. I'd never been away from home before and I missed my mother. I only started to settle and make some friends after my sister was born. The fact that she wasn't the "spare" heir everyone was hoping for made me feel better.'

*The poor little rich girl.* No doubt that was where some of her vulnerability stemmed from. Curious that someone as beautiful as Isabella Fierezza should carry with her a feeling of not being quite good enough.

'And then Rosa turned out to be the cutest baby with a halo of dark curls.'

'So you forgave her for being born?'

'Naturally. I drew her hundreds of pictures to decorate her nursery because I was worried she'd forget who I was.'

'And became firm friends.'

She hesitated. 'Eventually. Seven years is a lot between children. Since my parents' accident we've been much closer, though it has to be by e-mail. Rosa works in New Zealand.'

'I'd heard that.'

'It's such a long way away.' Isabella rubbed at her arms. 'It must be incredibly late. What time is it?'

'Half past four. Just after.'

'I'd better try and get some sleep. I've got mass to go to in the morning.'

'Only if you want to.'

Isabella smiled and shook her head. 'That's not how this game is played,' she said, pushing her chair back.

His hand snaked out and stopped her with a light touch. 'I meant what I said earlier. It's enough you're here.'

She looked slightly shocked, a suspicion of a blush along her cheekbones. 'Thank you.'

'I mean it. Just by being here you'll have raised the profile of Mont Avellana.'

Isabella gave a choking laugh. 'It's what I do.'

*Yes, it was.* And she did it well. But where did that leave time for Isabella Fierezza the woman? When did she ever do something because it was fun?

Domenic put down his glass. 'Come with me. I've got something I'd like you to see.'

He stood up.

'What?'

'The sunrise. There's no point staying up until morning if you miss the best part of the day.'

'See the sunrise?'

'Come and see. It's particularly beautiful from the gardens.'

*Could she?* 'I'd like that. If you're sure Silvana won't mind if I'm fit for nothing in the morning.'

'She won't mind.'

Why did an innocent thing like staying up all night and watching the day begin feel a little wicked? Isabella caught the flash of his smile and reached down for her sandals.

'Leave them. You won't need them. It's across the lawn.'

Barefoot. In an evening dress. *With a man who made her feel special.*

Isabella glanced sideways up at him. Standing to his right you couldn't even see the scars. Dressed in loose-fitting linen trousers and a white T-shirt covered with an open shirt, he looked relaxed and sexy. A little dangerous.

And they were going to watch the sunrise together.

She felt happy. Everything seemed brighter. The moon shone that little bit stronger. Scents in the air were intensified. The grass felt softer and looked greener.

'Do you often stay up all night and watch the sunrise?'

'I often stay up until the early hours. It's cooler at night and I like it. And without air-conditioning it becomes even more appealing.' He turned his head towards her and she caught sight of the scars down his face. 'But I don't deliberately stay up to see the sunrise any more.'

The expression in his eyes made her feel a little breathless. 'Why?'

'Because they can't be watched alone.'

Her stomach rolled over. 'I suppose that's true.' Although that was exactly what she did do. Camera in hand, she loved to see the day begin. But he was right—it made you feel lonely when there was no one to share that kind of breathtaking beauty with.

Domenic led her through the archway and along the side of an impressive pool, all the more stunning because of the view from it. One side was shielded by the trees Silvana had mentioned. The other was a huge mass of barely undulating sea. Miles and miles. A strange, dark and eerily beautiful world.

'Will you ruin your dress if you sit on the grass?'

'I shouldn't think so. It's so dry.' *And she didn't care.* This felt a little like magic. As though she'd walked into one of the films she loved to watch.

She settled herself comfortably and stretched out her legs, one foot resting across the top of the other.

Domenic sat beside her. 'If we'd planned this better we should have brought rugs to sit on. Jolanda and I used to bring out cappuccinos and doughnuts and make it an early breakfast.'

'Here?' Isabella glanced up at the trees. The trees his late wife had planted but not lived to see grow.

He shook his head. 'We had a small balcony. Barely room for a table and a couple of chairs. In the beginning. All this came later.'

'You must miss her.'

'Every day.' His voice was low. 'I miss them both.'

Isabella's hand felt the softness of the grass beside her. She was here because they couldn't be.

And it was too awful to talk about why they weren't here.

'Look.' Domenic pointed out to sea. 'He'll have been out all night.'

She followed the line of his finger and there, on the horizon, was a white fishing boat. Isabella pulled her knees up to her chest and kept watching. She could feel the breeze that came off the sea tug at her hair, taste the salt on her lips.

It felt as if everything were waiting, trembling on the brink of something. First she heard a lone gull, and then slowly it was joined by other birds. Isabella held her breath. And still it wasn't morning.

Just the two of them. No one was watching. There was no reason to be here but that they wanted to be.

'What was Jolanda like?' she asked quietly, almost too quietly to be heard although she knew he had. She felt him tense beside her.

'She was…' Domenic raised a hand to shield his face. 'She was fun.' He pulled the air into his lungs and continued. 'She had a way of making the little things seem special. We could do absolutely nothing and I'd feel like I'd had the best time.'

Isabella looked back out to sea. High in the sky the

feathery cirrus clouds had turned all shades of pink. It was dramatic and it was beautiful, but she scarcely saw it.

That was what she wanted for herself. Someone who, when it was all over, would sit there and say that she'd made the world a better place for them.

'I miss being part of her life. I miss the dreams we had together.' He looked at her. 'And I wonder all the time what life would have been like if they hadn't died. Our daughter would have been five in October.'

Isabella felt the lump in her throat stopping her ability to swallow. And she felt ashamed. She'd allowed self-pity to colour her life and yet she had nothing to be unhappy about. Not in the larger scheme of things.

So her life wasn't perfect. Whose was?

'What was your daughter's name?'

'Felice.' His voice deepened and the emotion he was feeling ripped through her. 'Felice Alisa.'

*Oh, God.* Isabella couldn't do this. It hurt too much to think about what had happened to him. To them.

One single teardrop spilled out and ran down her face, leaving a glistening trail. How did he bear it? How could he go on day after day after day…?

Then she felt a hand rest gently on top of hers. His. Warm. Comforting. Isabella looked up, her eyes glistening.

'Thank you for asking the question and for listening to the answer.'

Another tear tipped over and spilled down the path the first had made.

'No one lets me talk about them.' Domenic raised a hand and gently brushed away the tears on her face. 'And if I don't talk about them I'm scared I'll forget how incredible they were. How lucky I was to have them in my life.'

'I'm sorry you lost them,' she said, her voice broken. There was nothing she could say that would make it better. Nothing that could put it right.

Domenic lifted her hand from the grass and cradled it in his lap, his fingers stroking the length of her palm. Isabella shivered and he moved to wrap an arm around her.

*Two lonely people watching the sunrise.*

It was too precious to spoil with words. The simple act of holding each other was enough. More than enough.

Then the first suspicion of orange filtered into the sky, gradually spreading. Brighter. Stronger. It was a huge shame she didn't have her camera with her, but she wouldn't have traded this moment for anything.

Isabella looked up at Domenic's profile and noticed the hint of stubble. It would be easy to reach up and touch the roughness of his face, feel the bristles against her fingers. He was so close she could feel his chest move when he took a breath. It was the first time in almost a decade someone had held her. Just held her.

'We'd better get back,' he said against her hair.

Isabella closed her eyes and tried to imprint on her memory how wonderful this felt. *She didn't want to go back.*

'I'll talk to Silvana and tell her you need sleep more than mass today.'

'I don't think I could risk closing my eyes in prayer,' she said, allowing him to pull her to her feet. 'I'm not sure a snoring ambassador of peace and tolerance would be quite as effective.'

'Perhaps not.' He kept hold of her hand as they walked across the grass back to the *terrazzo*. Once there, he released it and Isabella bent to pick up her sandals.

'Isabella?'

She turned, clutching her sandals against her waist. 'Yes?'

'My family's having Sunday lunch together. Would you care to join us?'

And not go to the afternoon reception that had been pencilled in?

She looked at his face, impassive but for the tiny pulse beating in his cheek.

'If you'd prefer not to I'd completely understand. My father's mellowed over the years, but his politics—'

'I'd love to. Thank you.' Then she stepped forward and pressed a light kiss on his scarred cheek.

# CHAPTER SIX

ISABELLA had kissed him on the cheek.

Watching her with the sunlight glinting on her hair, it was difficult to believe it had happened. God only knew how much that simple gesture had meant to him. Acceptance. Friendship. At least that was what he chose to believe.

Domenic reached a hand up and ran his fingers down his ravaged face, reminding himself that she could only have done it out of pity. She'd hardly have been overcome by passion.

*Beauty and the beast.*

Domenic smiled. He wasn't holding his breath for that kind of happy ending. He didn't even want it. He reached out and picked up a fig from the platter in front of him. He'd had his chance at happiness. It had been wonderful, but now it was over.

Everyone said that time was a great healer, but everyone didn't know what they were talking about. Time passed. That was all. Nothing changed. Every morning he woke up and the realisation seeped through him that he was alone.

Jolanda was still dead. Felice would never be older in his mind than the nine months she'd been when fire had ripped through their home. To try and recreate what he'd already had would be a betrayal of what he'd felt for them.

Leastways that was what he wanted to believe he felt. Thinking that would make it easier to accept he'd never have that kind of happiness again. Domenic moved back further under the shade of the pine, his skin prickling with the heat. He'd never have a woman like Isabella Fierezza look at him with any kind of desire.

Silvana slid alongside him. 'She's lovely.'

'Who?'

His half-sister bit into an almond sweet. 'The woman you're watching.' She looked up, finishing her *sospiri d'orani*. 'You know, you do go for very up-market women. First Jolanda, now…'

Domenic dragged a hand round the back of his neck. If Silvana had noticed how fascinated he was by Isabella, then he could be certain his stepmother had done the same. He glanced over to where she was seated, grandchildren around her. She looked up and smiled. Then they both looked at Isabella.

For a moment. That was all he'd allow himself. But he could hear her voice. He didn't need to look at Isabella to know how her hands moved when she was trying to explain something, or how her eyes sparkled when she found something funny.

It was a mistake to have brought her here. It had been the impulse of the moment. But now, whenever he returned, he'd know what it felt like to see her among the people he loved.

He'd wanted to show her the real Mont Avellana. The inner world. The world that people who came searching for white sand and warm sea would never experience. But more than that, he wanted her to have a memory that was something other than the chink of crystal and the flash of diamonds.

And she seemed to love it. He'd wondered how a princess

of Niroli would manage when her wine came in a rustic pitcher and her food was simple. But nothing, it seemed, fazed Isabella.

She'd looked at the huge platter of suckling pig and Mont Avellanan veal, both cooked in the old stone oven in the backyard, and had asked about the wood they'd used in the cooking of it. In one fell stroke she'd won another army of admirers as they'd fiercely contested the use of sumac, moving on to consider the merits of fennel on a grill when cooking sea bass.

His father was in a particularly expansive mood, but she seemed able to take him in her stride. Just as easily as she had the three generations of Vincini family seated along the series of rustic tables. Not by so much as a flicker did she appear anything other than delighted to be where she was and talking to the people around her.

It was a rare gift.

*And he was lying.*

It wasn't a mistake to have brought her here. Nor had it been the impulse of the moment. It had been the impulse of many moments. Beginning when he'd switched on his monitor and seen her look directly into the camera. She'd known she was being watched. And he'd known she didn't like it but would stay as long as it took to get what she wanted.

Isabella was here because he liked her. When she looked at him she seemed to see him and not the scars. She looked him in the eye and he felt good about himself.

And when he looked at her he saw goodness. And loneliness. He saw that, too. Loneliness that reached in and touched him, forging an unexpected bond.

His eyes pulled round to look at her again—because he couldn't help it. Honey-gold curls captured in a low ponytail by a wide band of red, small studs in her earlobes and a cotton sundress that made her look fresh and cool despite the searing heat.

She was a public relations dream. Exactly what he'd told her he wanted. A woman who could do something for Mont Avellana in exchange for what he could give to Niroli. But everything was changing for him…

His father moved his hand in a sweeping motion. 'The whole notion of monarchy is outmoded.'

'You might not like it, but that doesn't make it outmoded,' she said in her husky voice that made his body heat in a way that had nothing to do with weather. 'How many times have you seen something done purely for expediency in the short term because the politician knows they won't be there to be accountable for that decision even five years later?'

'Democracy may be flawed, but it is a better system than leadership awarded by virtue of birth. What right have you to rule over other people?'

'Personally? None. I'm a victim of primogeniture,' she said, reaching for a fig. 'As a woman in a family of so many men I'm unlikely to become the Queen of Niroli but, if it were my birthright, I'd aim to find the middle ground between the two systems. Take the best of both.'

His father made a noise that was suspiciously like a grunt. 'But your wealth isn't earned.'

If Isabella needed any help from him he'd have given it, but Domenic knew from her slanting smile that she was in complete control. The steely core he'd always known she possessed was shining in his vocally aggressive family. And his father was mesmerised by her as he'd known he would be.

'And the land you own?' She glanced around at the stone villa set against a mountain backdrop. 'Isn't this all inherited?' She smiled at his father's silence and Domenic smiled to see it. 'We're all born to different circumstances. I believe our responsibility is to live as best we can. We should make the most of the opportunities we've been given.'

*Not at all the woman he'd first thought she was.*

Domenic met his stepmother's eyes and read the compassion in them. They both knew Isabella Fierezza would never contemplate a man like him. It didn't matter how good her hand had felt in his. How soft her skin. Or that he knew what her lips felt like against his cheek. He pushed back his chair. 'It's too hot for me now. I'm going to sit under the pergola.'

Silvana looked up. 'I'll come and keep you company.'

'There's no need.' Domenic glanced across at his stepmother. 'If Princess Isabella needs me…'

Lucetta nodded. And he knew she understood. Her hand fell on her eldest grandson's head. Domenic pulled his hand across his face. Lucetta understood that, too. There was a child missing. And she'd always be missing. Best he remembered that before he started to hanker after a romantic dream.

Domenic was exactly where Silvana had said he'd be. Isabella pushed the baby onto one hip and held onto the doorframe so she didn't slip on the high step down.

'What are you reading?' she asked, walking beneath the vine covered pergola.

He turned at her voice, unguarded, and for that second she could see…something that made her feel breathless. Then it was gone. He held up his novel.

She forced a smile. 'Blood and guts.'

'You've read it?'

'I've heard it talked about. I've been asked to take Carlo to find somewhere cool. The sun's so hot.'

He turned his book over so that it rested on the seat beside him. 'By who?'

'Silvana,' she said, her hand moving to hold Carlo's bare foot. 'She said I'd find you here.'

He nodded, but said nothing as she sat in the chair opposite.

'Are you feeling all right?'

'Nothing I'm not used to,' he said, running a hand across his face.

Isabella's eyes flicked to the darkened skin showing starkly against the white of his loose shirt. No, she supposed it wasn't. Hiding from the scorching heat of high summer would be part and parcel of his experience.

She settled Carlo across her lap and gave him her finger to hold. He pulled it firmly against his mouth and rooted as though he were at a breast. 'He's just been fed and your cousin says he should sleep now.'

'He looks tired.'

'Yes, but still hungry.' She looked up suddenly and caught him watching them, the expression in his eyes unbearably sad. It was gone in an instant. Isabella glanced down at the baby cradled against her as a new thought occurred to her.

This must be difficult for him. 'Would you rather we sat somewhere else?'

'No.' He shifted in his seat. 'It's cool here and Carlo will sleep.'

Which wasn't what she'd meant and he knew it. Isabella bit her lip and let the silence stretch out between them. She listened to the chirruping cicadas in the bushes, wishing she'd taken Carlo somewhere else. She might be fighting the deep seated ache for a baby of her own, but he was missing Felice. She should have thought.

Domenic moved to pick up his book again, but didn't. His fingers rested against the spine. 'Has my father offended you at all?'

'Of course not. Why?'

His smile twisted. 'He isn't particularly good at seeing anyone's point of view but his own.'

'Who is?' Isabella watched as Carlo's eyes gently closed, his little round face completely sated. He was so lovely. 'Your father reminds me of my grandfather a little. They probably don't have an opinion in common, but they have the same innate certainty they're right.'

'You sound fond of him.'

'Grandfather?' She looked up. 'Yes, I am. He's honestly one of the most remarkable men I've ever met. I suppose you don't have a particularly high opinion of him…'

His mouth quirked and she didn't need him to say anything. It wasn't surprising that someone who'd been born on Mont Avellana would feel that way. Perhaps his treatment of what he'd seen as a satellite island hadn't been fair.

'But he's my grandfather.'

'Of course.'

'And I love him.' Isabella twisted one of Carlo's dark curls in her fingers. 'I've seen a different side of him. Did you know he can make a paper aeroplane that can fly across the entire dining hall? Or that he can recite Wordsworth in the most perfect English accent? And that he carries a picture of my grandmother with him everywhere he goes, even though she's been dead more years than she was alive?'

Domenic smiled. 'No.'

'I don't think everything he's done has been right, but I do believe he's done them honestly. And I know he loves Niroli.'

'And that's all that matters?'

'It's important if you happen to be the sovereign of it, don't you think?' Her hand moved to rest on Carlo's tummy and she felt his chest move up and down. 'And the last two years have been an incredibly painful and difficult time for him.'

'I can imagine.'

She looked up. There were probably few men on earth who could truly empathise. First her grandfather had lost the wife he loved, then a grandson and, finally, both sons.

'Difficult for you, too.'

Isabella slid her finger into Carlo's limp hand. She loved the feel of his tiny fingers. So perfect. So small. 'Sometimes I don't believe it's happened. My father was such an experienced sailor. I keep thinking it's all been a stupid mistake and everything will go back to the way it was…' She stopped herself, suddenly aware of what she was saying—and to whom.

'I know that feeling.'

'I'm sorry, I—'

'Were you close to your parents?'

She rushed to answer him. 'Yes. Though my father was…very private and difficult to know. At least with me.'

And he'd been completely dominated by his own father. That was the one thing that had constantly annoyed her about him.

'But he would have made a good king, I think.'

'And your mother?'

'Would have been a charming and beautiful consort.'

Domenic smiled, his face becoming instantly softer.

'She was my best friend.' Warm memories crowded round her, comforting her as they always did. Though now there was the nip of pain when she thought about how much it would have meant to her mother to have known her second son was alive and happy.

*A surgeon.* She'd have been proud of that. Proud of Alex's decision to continue with a life that made him happy. Hopeful of grandchildren and a chance to play a meaningful part in his life.

'Is she why you decided to settle on Niroli?' Domenic asked, startling her out of her thoughts.

Isabella gave a shocked laugh. 'No. Though she was what made it bearable. In the first couple of years anyway, before I found something I could do.'

'You didn't want to come back?'

She shook her head. 'I wanted to do a degree in English and Spanish, but I needed my grandfather's permission.'

'And he refused?'

Sitting there under a shady vine, a warm little body heavy in her arms, it was easy to forget how angry she'd been.

'What did your parents do?'

'Nothing. It wasn't their decision to make. I suppose that's what I was trying to say to your father. You have to live as well as you can within the circumstances you find yourself. My mother taught me that. She was the most gracious woman.'

Carlo snuffled and Isabella looked down with a smile. This was what she wanted. If she could choose. A family of her own. People to love and who would love her. Maybe if she'd had more courage at nineteen she'd have had that now.

'I had to have the king's permission to live anywhere but Niroli. And my grandfather didn't give it.'

A frown snapped across Domenic's head. 'Why?'

'Because he believed it wasn't necessary to educate women to the same standard as men. His own marriages were arranged, my parents' all but. I think he honestly believed that would be my future.'

'Marriage to a European prince?'

Isabella's fingers buried themselves in Carlo's soft curls. 'Fifty years ago that would have been my lot, but princes are more inclined to marry for love than bloodlines.'

'Are you disappointed?'

'Having now met most of the eligible princes across Europe, I don't think so.' She looked up and smiled. 'But I was very angry Marco had permission to live in London when I was refused it.'

'I can see why.'

Isabella felt Domenic's anger on her behalf. 'I was silly though. I could have defied him and done exactly what I wanted. The only power he has over me is my place in the succession, and since my cousins will inherit ahead of me...'

Her tone must have given away more than she'd intended. 'A victim of primogeniture.'

She smiled at the echo of her own words. 'Years ago I used to try and argue it out with my father, but he only ever said that it was the way it was and there was nothing to discuss.'

'Did he want you to marry a nameless prince?'

'He never expressed an opinion other than to tell me my face would be my fortune.'

Her father was a quiet voice at the back of her head that undermined everything she tried to do. It didn't matter how hard she worked, how much she achieved, his voice was still in her head telling her that her value was entirely based on her ability to look 'pretty'.

Even now. Two years after his death.

And it was even worse now because he wasn't alive for her to show him how wrong he'd been.

'Isabella?'

'I'm here.' She looked round at Lucetta's voice.

The older lady stood in the doorway, her round face thoughtful as she watched them. 'Is Carlo asleep?'

'Soundly.'

'And snoring,' Domenic added.

Isabella smiled down at him, loving the little grunting noise he made.

'Then come and lay him down inside. You'll make yourself too hot if you have to sit and hold him all the time he's sleeping. Silvana shouldn't have asked you to do this. Come.' Lucetta encouraged her to come in. 'We keep a cot up in the little bedroom. And we can put a fan on him to keep him cooler.'

Reluctantly Isabella walked inside and through into a narrow, oblong room. A simple wooden cot was against the far wall, already made up and waiting. Lucetta rested her plump hand on the carved end. 'My father made this for my eldest son.'

'It's lovely.' Isabella carefully laid Carlo on his back, slightly disappointed when his eyes didn't open in protest.

'He was a talented carpenter. He also made us the most beautiful rocking horse, but that was lost in the fire at Domenic's home.'

Isabella looked round.

'Has he told you about the fire?'

'A little.' Then, 'No. Not really.' Not about the fire. He'd spoken about Jolanda. About Felice. But not about the day itself. Nothing about how he'd got his scars.

'Come with me. I want to show you something.'

Isabella glanced back at the sleeping baby and then followed Domenic's stepmother into her cosily furnished sitting room. It was a room full of nick-nacks. Tiny crucifixes mingled with homemade cards and mismatched photo frames.

'Now…' Lucetta walked towards a table in the corner and reached towards the back, selecting a photograph standing in a black lacquered frame. 'This one is of Domenic taken five years ago.'

For a moment she didn't realise the significance of what Lucetta had said. But then her eyes travelled to the image and she looked back up at Domenic's stepmother. She was standing with her hand clutching at the small cross at her neck.

Isabella looked back down at the photograph. Domenic before the scars. Before the fire. Before tragedy had taken away the laughter.

'And this is another one. Of him with Jolanda,' she said, passing across a second picture, this time in a red plastic frame. 'That was taken the year before she got pregnant with Felice.'

Isabella held one in each hand. Jolanda had been small and dark. Elfin features surrounded by a cloud of black hair. Laughing.

And Domenic had been one of the most charismatically good-looking men she'd ever seen. Strong, handsome and supremely confident.

She concentrated on the smooth skin that stretched over a tanned face. The short-sleeved T-shirt that showed the arms of a sportsman. The sexy glint in his eyes.

A compelling and supremely attractive man.

How much harder did that make the scarring to deal with? To look in the mirror and see someone he didn't recognise? To be treated differently?

Isabella looked back up at Lucetta. 'What did happen?'

Lucetta took the photographs from her listless fingers and

looked at them. 'Fires are not that uncommon here. The smallest spark will set it off during the summer months.'

She placed them back on the table. 'The fire started in the middle of the day. No one really knows why exactly. Jolanda and little Felice must have been asleep because no one raised the alarm until the fire had pretty much taken hold.'

Isabella felt as though someone had reached inside her and taken hold of her heart. Long icy fingers gripped round and squeezed until she thought she'd cry out in pain. 'And Domenic?'

'Had been at the palazzo. Looking to do some grand thing or other. Great ones for plans, those two. Came back for lunch and found the place ablaze.'

Isabella felt sick.

'Everyone rallied round. Did what they could. Planes flew over with sea water to douse the flames, but it was all too late.' Lucetta pushed back a lock of grey hair. 'They'd have been dead from the smoke before Domenic even got there.'

'How did he get burned?'

She shook her head. 'He was like a madman. Wouldn't listen to anyone and far too strong to be held. He broke a window and went in.'

And who could blame him when the people he loved had been inside? Isabella wrapped her arms around her middle and hugged hard. She'd seen firsthand how indomitable the human spirit was, but how did anyone recover from an experience like that?

'He didn't even make it as far as the staircase.' Lucetta squeezed Isabella's cold hands, then turned and walked towards her kitchen.

Isabella followed, wondering what Lucetta thought her relationship with her stepson was. 'Did he have to be rescued?'

She nodded. 'He was in a coma for the first two days and then, when he came back to us, we had to tell him Jolanda and Felice had died.' Lucetta pulled open her large fridge and pulled out a glass jug of homemade lemonade. She set it down on the kitchen table, turning away to find some glasses.

Isabella rubbed her hands over her bare arms. She didn't want to hear any more. Not from Lucetta. She thought about the night before. The quiet and the peace of the sunrise and how he'd thanked her for letting him talk about Jolanda.

She reached up and brushed a tear away before it started. But Lucetta wasn't finished with her yet.

'Jolanda was a lovely girl,' she said, pouring lemonade into a glass. 'Shouldn't have really looked at a boy like Domenic. Not with her family's money. And until he met her Domenic was a little bit wild…'

She handed across a glass. 'It was her family that were the hoteliers, you know? Of course, Domenic has taken it all onto another level, but the start of it was Jolanda's grandfather. Bought his first hotel in nineteen thirty-seven. Held onto it through the war.'

'Did they blame Domenic for the fire?'

'No. No, not at all. It was no one's fault. But Domenic blames himself for her being on Mont Avellana even though that was very much her decision. She loved it here.'

Lucetta filled a second glass. 'The Palazzo Tavolara was going to be the start of something much larger on the island. I don't know what she'd have made of this idea of building on Niroli. Not a lot, I suspect.'

Her words left Isabella feeling confused—on so many levels. She was trying to absorb too much information too quickly.

'Why?'

'Because her dream was for Mont Avellana,' Lucetta said, reaching for a tray.

Isabella stood with her hands clasped around her lemonade. 'Then why hasn't he developed the palazzo into a hotel?'

'He finds it difficult to be here. We all know that. But he can't quite bring himself to sell it either.' Lucetta placed a crocheted circle with small beads on it over the top of the lemonade and set the jug on the tray beside the empty glasses.

'The place is hanging like a millstone around his neck.' She picked up the tray. 'Would you mind taking Domenic out a glass of lemonade? The step down is difficult carrying a tray.'

*Would she mind?* Actually, yes. For reasons she couldn't even begin to understand she felt…nervous. It was almost as if she'd been given a small window into his soul and she wasn't quite sure what she wanted to do with that information yet.

So many questions—and no possibility of asking them.

Isabella picked up the glass and walked slowly back to the shady pergola. Back on Niroli it had seemed all so straightforward. The Vincini Group was the perfect match for…

And then she stopped.

The *Vincini* Group. Why was it called that if its origins lay with Jolanda's family? There was so much she didn't know about him.

*And so much she wanted to know?* Isabella shook her head. She felt as if cold water had suddenly started to run round her veins in place of blood.

She couldn't be falling in love with Domenic Vincini. That wasn't possible. *Was it?* There were hundreds of men who'd come to her at a click of her fingers and she was falling for a man whose heart was buried with his dead wife and child.

A man whose scars were both inside and out. A man who sought solitude and a life away from the limelight.

Isabella stopped in the doorway.

'Is that for me?'

She swallowed. 'From Lucetta. She asked me to bring it out,' she said, moving nearer.

'Thank you.'

'You're welcome.' Most often, when she was talking to him, she wasn't aware of the scars at all. But now, having seen what he'd looked like before the fire…she was reminded.

'Is Carlo still asleep?'

'Yes.'

She looked at the ridged scars running the length of his face and wondered what had happened to him inside that burning house. Had glass exploded in his face? Had he fallen?

And what percentage of his body had been burnt? Looking at him now, all she could see was the puckered skin at the base of his neck. How far did it spread across his body? *Would it change the way she was starting to feel about him?*

Domenic laid his book to one side. 'What did she tell you?'

Her eyes flew guiltily back up to his face. 'What?'

'Lucetta. What did she tell you? And don't say "nothing",' he added with a tight smile as she started to reply.

Isabella sat down on the seat opposite, wondering what and how much to say.

'Did she talk to you about the fire?'

'Would you mind if she had?' Isabella asked cautiously.

His hand moved across his face and Isabella recognised she'd seen that mannerism many times. It was what he did when he was uncertain and thoughtful.

He shrugged nonchalantly, but his voice was bitter. 'I wish people didn't feel the need to but, I suppose, it's an unrealistic expectation.'

'She loves you.'

'I know that.' Domenic drained his lemonade in one go and placed the glass down on the table. 'It's why I come here.'

Isabella sipped her lemonade, feeling the ice cube knock against her teeth. This conversation felt a lot like stepping through a minefield, uncertain where to tread and what to probe, but there were things she needed to know. 'Is it true Jolanda wouldn't wish you to build on Niroli?'

'Why do you say that?'

'Is it?'

Domenic stood up restlessly and walked over to the edge of the pergola and looked out towards the granite mountain. 'Niroli wasn't an option when Jolanda was alive.'

'But if it had been?'

'Jolanda loved Mont Avellana,' he conceded, his hand moving across his face once more. 'She had a passion and a vision for this place. She loved the fact it was an island and a world unto itself. She loved the patchwork of local dialects, the different cultures and customs concentrated into such a small area.'

'Do you think she would have minded?'

Domenic turned to look at her. 'Yes.'

*Yes.* A simple, straightforward answer. Isabella placed her glass carefully down on the table, hugging her knees against her chest.

'Perhaps. Jolanda wanted to make Mont Avellana *the* tourist destination in the Mediterranean. It was her dream and she was passionate about it. It didn't matter to her that there's only the tiniest of airports and that the only way to drive across this island is via an inconvenient web of twisting local roads. I think she'd have been sad more than anything else.'

'So why haven't you done it? You could have developed the palazzo and—'

'I've had other projects.'

Isabella waited, watching as he moved to sit back down. The silence stretched out.

'It was never the best option for us, but Jolanda wasn't particularly interested in the financial payback. She'd been born to money and never thought about that side of things because it had always been there for her. What she wanted was to be part of something from the start. She wanted to put down roots in a place and really belong.'

'So…has not doing something with the palazzo been a financial decision or an emotional one?' Isabella prompted when he stopped.

'A little of both. I would find it hard to do it without her.' Domenic's mouth twisted. 'And things have undeniably changed since we bought the palazzo. Niroli wasn't the tourist destination it is now, for a start. If there's to be a magnet in this part of the world it won't be Mont Avellana.'

'But if you know she'd have hated you to be part of any development on Niroli, why am I here?'

'Honestly?'

She nodded.

He smiled. 'Because you said you wanted to create something that would rival the Costa Smeralda.'

Isabella frowned, not understanding.

'It could have been her speaking,' he said, softly. 'She wanted to create exactly that. And then you said you could do something for Mont Avellana and it seemed a good compromise.' He shrugged, picking up his book and shutting it.

She was here to salve his conscience by doing something for the island his late wife had loved so much.

'Is it enough?' Isabella looked across at him, struggling to find the words to ask what she wanted to know. She bit her lip. 'I don't want you to commit to Niroli if you feel you're betraying her memory. I know we had an agreement, but—'

'I've given you my word. The papers are already with my lawyers. When I'm back in Rome on Thursday, I'll sign.'

That should have made her feel euphoric—but it didn't. In her entire life, she'd never felt quite so muddled.

And she'd think more about why that was when he wasn't there to see it.

# CHAPTER SEVEN

DOMENIC stood and watched Isabella's car drive down the heavily rutted track—her bodyguard beside her, motorcycle outriders forward and back and Silvana following behind in her own car.

*And he wished that it had been him going with her.* For the first time in four years he felt left behind.

This evening she would walk through the narrow cobbled alleyways and arches of Caprera. She would watch the sunset and eat *gelato*. Everyone would be charmed by her and he wouldn't be there to see it. He wouldn't share it with her. See her face. *Hold her hand.*

A shadow fell across him and his stepmother reached out a hand and tucked it into his arm. 'Come and have something more to eat.'

'No. No more.'

'Come anyway.' Her eyes were fixed on the short procession. 'Come,' she said, pulling on his arm, and they started walking back towards the stone villa. 'She's a good woman. Your father is impressed. Very impressed.'

Domenic looked down at Lucetta. 'With a Nirolian princess? Surely not?'

She shook her head. 'You shouldn't mock him. You know Alberto has only ever wanted what was best for Mont Avellana. And your Princess Isabella is certainly turning the world's eyes in our direction. Exactly as you knew she would when you asked her to come here…'

'And you don't like it?' he asked, picking up on something indefinable in her tone.

'It doesn't matter what I like.'

Domenic's smiled twisted. 'But that didn't stop you telling Isabella that Jolanda wouldn't have wanted me to build on Niroli.'

She gave a significant sniff.

'You shouldn't have done it. Isabella offered to release me from our agreement.'

'That would be the best thing for you. You shouldn't do business with her.' Lucetta stopped walking. 'I think she's a lovely woman doing a remarkable job…but she's not for you, Domenic.'

'Luc—'

'Don't.' His stepmother crossed her arms in front of her. 'Don't even think of lying to me. I can see the way you watch her and I'm worried for you.'

Domenic squinted up to the clear blue sky. 'I won't marry again.'

'That worries me, too. Jolanda wouldn't have wanted you to live like you do. She wouldn't want you lonely. No wife. No *children*.' Pain must have flicked over his face because she added quickly, 'I know I'm not supposed to say that to you. We all pretend…but, Domenic, Felice is in your heart until the day you die whether you have other children or not. And love stretches. If you have other children some day you will love them with all your heart, but you won't love Felice any less.

'I want to see you happy…but…Princess Isabella?' She shook her head sadly. 'No. She is not the wife for you.'

Domenic's hand moved against the ridged skin of his neck. 'You don't need to say this,' he said, more roughly than he'd intended.

'Think about her life. What it is like. Isabella Fierezza lives in a goldfish bowl. The only reason she could be here today without photographers straining to get her picture is because no one would have dreamt she'd be here.'

Because her itinerary stated she'd be at the Cattedrale di Caprera. He knew that. And her Chief of Security had been nervous in spite of it.

'That's not a life for you. Paparazzi chasing your picture when you even struggle to go to your father's party because of the way people stare.'

No, that wasn't a life for him.

'I want you to find a nice Mont Avellanan girl. Make a good home and stop pushing yourself to make more and more money that you don't want or need.'

Domenic pulled a hand through his hair. Lucetta saw too much, but how he felt about Isabella was an irrelevance. It changed nothing.

*He had to believe that.* On Thursday he would fly back to Rome and everything would go on as before.

'What Isabella is doing,' Domenic began quietly, 'she's doing because I want something for Jolanda. That's it. Niroli is business. Good business. And I'll run it at a distance like all the other hotel complexes we have around the Mediterranean.

'But…' His throat worked. 'Jolanda loved *this* island. I've not forgotten…and I saw a chance to do something in Mont Avellana. Maybe I can develop the palazzo into some kind of a hotel? Maybe a restaurant? I don't know yet. Something.

'But, I honestly believe Jolanda would have understood what I'm doing. Disappointed it wasn't what we planned...but understood. If I can't make her dream happen in its entirety at least I can give her something.'

*This was about nothing else.*

His feelings for Isabella were just that—feelings. And feelings could be conquered. *Damn it,* he was living, breathing proof of that.

Lucetta might hope he'd marry again. Might wish he'd have another child some day. Children. But that wasn't going to happen. It had taken years to find any kind of peace. It would take an incredible kind of courage to risk loving again and he wasn't that brave. Losing the people he'd lived for had broken him.

But, in all the suffering, he had learnt something about life. He knew how precious it was. How vital it was that you grabbed every day and lived it to its full potential. And he wanted that for Isabella. He wanted to see her happy.

Lucetta took hold of his arm. 'Just be careful, Domenic. Hmm?'

*Home.*

The thought slid into Isabella's mind the minute the palazzo came into sight. A place of refuge.

Strange she should feel like that about the Palazzo Tavolara when she'd never felt like that about the Palace in Niroli. Being in the fourteenth century fortress made her feel confined and...tired somehow.

She was tired now. Her face hurt from smiling and her feet ached from the beautiful Rodrigo Brambilla shoes. As soon as the high gates shut behind her she felt her body relax and a sense of peace pervade her soul.

It was getting harder and harder to play the part of Princess Isabella of Niroli. And that probably had a lot to do with Marco's decision to relinquish the crown. She glanced out of the window, watching the shadows. How could he have done this to her? Had he even thought what the consequences of his actions would be for her?

Isabella bit her lip as guilt slipped in. *Of course,* she hadn't been a factor in his decision. He'd given up the throne for the woman he loved. For Emily. She even thought he'd made the right choice.

But…

'Are you tired, Your Highness?'

Isabella turned her head to look at Tomasso. 'No more than you, I imagine.' She smiled, outwardly calm. 'At least I got to eat ice cream.'

Her companion smiled. 'I wouldn't swap.'

The car pulled smoothly to a stop and the door opened. Isabella twisted in her seat and climbed out with a practised flick of the legs.

'What would you like done with the flowers, Your Highness?'

Isabella turned her head to look at the beautiful bouquets she'd been presented with. 'Could you see if there's a local hospital or hospice nearby that would like them?'

'Certainly, ma'am.'

She skipped up the wide steps, hoping that Domenic would be there to meet her. She wanted to tell him about the man who'd bowed so low his toupee had slipped, and about the woman who'd been so shocked to see her that she'd walked straight into one of those twisting lampposts.

Silly things. Things she couldn't normally tell anyone…

But everywhere was quiet. Mia walked down the staircase

towards her but her eyes were fixed on something behind. *Someone.* Isabella didn't turn round. She knew without looking. Tomasso. A gentle ache gripped her heart. Her Chief of Security had someone waiting for him. She had no one.

Where was Domenic? She wanted to see him.

'That all went well, I think, but I'll be glad to get out of these shoes,' she said with one foot on the stairs. 'Good night, Tomasso. And thank you.'

'Are the shoes particularly uncomfortable?' Mia followed her up to her room with its pale rose-coloured walls and eighteenth-century furniture upholstered in a rich plum.

'Very.' Isabella slipped them off and walked over to the elegant balcony and looked out. There was no glimmer of light anywhere. No indication that Domenic had stayed up in the hope of seeing her. No indication that he'd stayed up to enjoy the cool of the night either.

He was nowhere to be seen and she felt a rush of disappointment. She'd hoped to see him. Talk to him.

'We have a message for you, Your Highness,' Mia said from the depths of the room behind her. 'Signora Cattaneo is staying on Mont Avellana for a few days.'

Isabella turned back into the room. *Bianca.* Here?

'She's staying with her husband's parents.'

'That's fantastic.' It was more than fantastic. Isabella pulled the pins out of her hair and ran her fingers through the lacquered curls. 'Is Stefano with her?'

'She didn't say so, ma'am.'

Which probably meant he wasn't. Stefano would be unlikely to take time off at such short notice but, in a way, that made it better. She rarely had any time with her friend alone now. 'I'll contact her first thing. It's too late to do it now.'

As she spoke she looked out through the double doors. 'I'd like my white trousers and…oh, anything comfortable and cool. I really don't mind. I think I'll read on the balcony for a while.'

She wouldn't be able to sleep yet awhile. *Where was Domenic?*

'I've left an outfit on your bed, ma'am.'

'Thank you. Thank you very much.'

'Good night, ma'am.'

Isabella heard the click of the door and walked back into her bedroom, sliding down the zip of her pale green dress.

She couldn't quite believe it. Bianca was here on Mont Avellana. She might not have many friends she could trust implicitly—but those she had were very precious.

She pulled on the loose white cotton trousers and silk caftan top, before laying the pistachio wrap-over dress on the bed. Mia would have to do something clever about the creases if she was ever to wear it again. Though that was unlikely if any of today's photographs found their way into the world's papers.

Goodness, she was tired! Aching feet, aching face… Isabella stepped out on the balcony again, leaning on the balustrade. She couldn't go on living like this. Day after day, city after city, handshake after handshake.

She needed to make some decisions about what she wanted. Maybe she should have taken the opportunity to talk to her old school friend about Luca being removed from the succession when she'd been in Rome…but it had been too recent…and she'd felt too angry. With her grandfather, with Luca and with the situation as a whole. But this time she would.

Isabella lifted her hair off the back of her neck and felt the breeze cool her warm skin.

Isabella wandered aimlessly back out to the bedroom and over to the desk. The leather cover of her grandmother's diary was shiny from where she'd turned it over in her hands so many times. She picked it up and glanced back towards the balcony.

*Where was he?*

Domenic might have decided that he wouldn't spend another evening on the *terrazzo,* wouldn't watch another sunrise, but she…wanted to smell the mimosa, eucalyptus and oleander that hung in the air.

More than that, she wanted to take back some special memories of this place and lock them deep inside for the difficult times ahead. Because they were coming.

Queen Eva's slyly triumphant face when she'd learnt it would be one of her grandsons on the throne told her that. Her grandfather's second wife couldn't have been more delighted. And now it wouldn't even be Luca. It would be Nico…

The doors that led out to the *terrazzo* were open. Isabella padded across the warm stone, loving the feel of residual warmth against her feet. There was the sense of being insignificant against a vast sky and of being able to breathe.

Being at the Palazzo Tavolara had the feel of being in an oasis. She stepped out onto the lush lawn. A miracle in such an arid climate. She'd never seen it happening but a lawn like this would need watering daily. Why did Domenic keep ownership of something that must be a huge financial drain if he had no intention of turning it into a hotel?

The only answer must be that it had an emotional connection for him. Memories of his late wife must be bound up in this place.

Isabella walked through the archway towards the swimming pool. The grass was soft against her bare feet.

Cool. The cotton of her trousers flapped against her legs and she listened for the sound of the cicadas still chirruping. She might not have the courage to slip into the water without her clothes, but she did have enough to dangle her feet in.

She wasn't sure what stopped her walking. A sound. Something. An inner feeling that she wasn't alone, maybe? But her feet slowed and she approached the final archway cautiously, and then stopped. Listening.

*Nothing*—but her heart was pounding as she started walking again. Through the arch...

*Domenic.*

Here.

In the moonlight she couldn't see much more than the outline of his body. A shadowy figure. But she knew it was him. Her stomach immediately did a compete roll-over. She pulled a hand through her curls and stepped out of the cover of the bushes.

He was swimming down the length of the pool and didn't see her. His arms moved smoothly through the water, scarcely making a ripple. Long, clean strokes.

And then he reached the end and did an underwater flip and powered his way back the other way. The same easy stroke, the same clean movement through the water. She went to stand at the end of the pool.

Domenic's hand touched the tiles at the end and he looked up. His face was shuttered. Not pleasure. Not anger. He was resigned.

To what?

To her interrupting his solitude or her seeing how scarred his body was? Curiosity surged through her. For Isabella everything stilled. There was just this moment in all of time. Just the two of them in all the world.

Water glistened on his olive skin. His thick hair was slicked back off his face and the arm he held out the water looked strong and healthy. Unblemished.

With one easy movement he pulled himself out of the water and stood before her. He was…

*Male.*

That was the word that sprang into Isabella's mind. He was unbelievably male. Strong. Powerful. And intensely beautiful.

Water droplets hugged the dark hair on his chest and her eyes followed the narrow line that ran across a muscular stomach until it dipped behind his tight swimming shorts. She couldn't help but notice the firm bulge and her blood sang in her ears.

*He wanted her.*

In this moment, here and now, he wanted her. It gave her the confidence to look lower. There were scars on his legs. White, feathery lines that must have come from exploding glass. A complex web that burst across the darker colour of his skin.

She looked up and into his dark brown eyes. He was watching, looking for her reaction. Waiting.

Isabella moistened her lips with the tip of her tongue. 'I-I couldn't sleep.'

'We both seem to have a problem with that.' Domenic turned and picked up a large white towel resting on a sun lounger. He held it in his hands, not attempting to cover the puckered skin of his burn scars.

They were there, too. Cruelly disfiguring. Just touching his neck and spreading out across his shoulder and down his left arm. Then in one deliberate movement he swung the towel across his shoulder.

Isabella swallowed and then sat down on the edge of the

pool. As though his being here changed nothing she rolled up her trouser legs and dangled her feet over the edge.

The water felt warm, baked by the sun, but still refreshing. Her nail varnish shone dusky pink through the ripples.

'You ought to go in,' Domenic said from somewhere behind. 'The water is lovely.'

Isabella didn't turn round. She could hear the rasp of the towel on his skin as he dried himself. 'I rarely swim.'

'Why?'

'I'm not particularly good at it. Somehow I never managed to learn how to breathe properly.' She moved her feet in the water.

'It's the same principle as out of it.' She could hear the smile in his voice and knew he'd relaxed. Whereas she...*she* was pulled as taut as a bow string.

'Not for me. I must hold my breath somehow and I end up with a stitch.' She pulled her feet out of the water and stood up. Acutely conscious of being here so late. Of him. Of having not brushed her hair or checked her make-up.

Domenic had put on a loose T-shirt and dragged on a pair of jeans, presumably over his wet swimming shorts. He held out his towel. 'Do you want this?'

'Thank you.' She took it and carried it over to a lounger, placing her diary on the small table beside it. The dark brown leather had one spot of water on it and she smoothed across it with her fingers.

'What's that?' he asked, sitting on the lounger next to hers.

'My grandmother's diary. Queen Sophia. My grandfather's first wife.'

Domenic nodded.

'Do you remember me telling you that she loved this place? My grandfather brought her here soon after they were married and they stayed throughout that first summer. Until she had to go back to Niroli to give birth to my father, actually—'

She broke off. She was gabbling. Stupid.

'I remember. She wrote about Poseidon's Grotto.'

'I thought it might be fun to read it here, so I brought it with me. I—' She stopped, mesmerised by the expression in his dark, dark eyes. More pupil than iris.

*He did want her.* She could feel it. Tension hung in the air like a tangible thing. It was real. Living. Vibrant.

And it scared her. It was like catching a wave and knowing you could do nothing but ride it out and see where it took you. Too powerful to be controlled, and that frightened her.

Never, ever, had she been out of control.

'May I?' Domenic held out his hand for the diary.

'Of course.' She brushed her hair out of her eyes. 'Y-yes, of course. It's quite hard to read. Her handwriting is very small and…'

*Shut up! Just shut up!*

Isabella held out the notebook and saw his hand move towards it. Long, beautiful fingers. Tanned skin. Tiny sun-bleached hairs standing up on his forearm.

And her fingers were millimetres from his. So close. One slip and they'd be touching.

Yesterday he'd held her hand, but this felt different. This wasn't about friendship. Or being lonely. It was about wanting and need. It was power and passion.

'How old was Queen Sophia when she came here?'

'Eighteen.'

'Young.' He opened the diary. 'When did she die?'

Isabella hugged her knees. 'Giving birth to my father. My grandfather was heartbroken. He really loved her. And she him.'

Domenic's dark eyes flicked up. 'I've not heard very much about her.'

'No, well…' Isabella picked up his towel and started to dry her feet. 'He married again and his new wife found it difficult. I think he took the easy path.'

'Does he speak about her at all?'

Isabella shook her head. 'No. But he gave me that. About eighteen months ago. Told me to keep it safe.'

The subtext being it wouldn't be safe in the hands of his second wife. That fitted with everything Domenic had heard about Queen Eva. By all accounts, she was a thoroughly dislikeable woman.

'And my father had a portrait of her. It hung in his dressing room. I think he liked to look at her, but didn't like anyone to see him do it.'

'Where's the portrait now?'

'Packed away waiting for Marco to decide what he wants to do with it.'

*Primogeniture.*

There was nothing fair about that. Domenic watched Isabella's hands twitch against his towel. She could never have expected to inherit. She wasn't the eldest child…but there was an edge to her voice that told him she was angry with her brother.

Whether that was due solely to his lack of action on their parents' possessions he couldn't tell. He only knew that every instinct in his body was prompting him to gather Isabella up and hold her close. Protect her. Shield her from whatever was troubling her.

She was inexpressibly lovely. Warm and kind. And he knew that each moment he spent with her meant he slipped just that little bit deeper in love. Millimetre by millimetre, centimetre by centimetre. She only had to turn her head and look at him to have every nerve ending in his body standing to attention. And when she smiled he responded with all the testosterone at his disposal.

It was a painful kind of pleasure. It would be so easy to ask if she'd like to see the grotto her grandmother had evidently loved so much. He'd be able to spend time with her alone but he knew it wasn't wise.

Here, within the perimeters of the Palazzo Tavolara, they were cocooned against reality. The real world wasn't so forgiving. Lucetta was right when she said there was no possible future for him and the Princess Isabella of Niroli.

He knew it. This idyll would end. It would end when he travelled back to Rome.

But it was so tempting to spend all the time he could with her. And Isabella would love Poseidon's Grotto. They could take a picnic…

Domenic shifted uncomfortably, his erect penis pushing against the rough denim of his jeans. He was being foolish.

But…

But when she'd looked at him, *really looked* at the discoloured and puckered skin on his shoulder, the scars that crisscrossed his body, there'd been no repulsion in her eyes. *None.*

It had been the most intensely sexual moment of his entire life. Her eyes had travelled down the length of his body. She'd seen every imperfection, must have seen his arousal…

And she'd not rejected him.

Seeing that had created an explosion in his head. She'd looked at him with curiosity. Even *desire?* Was that possible? Just the thought of her eyes on his body had the blood pumping through his veins, pounding in his eardrums.

It took every ounce of willpower he had to behave naturally around her. 'Did Marco inherit everything?'

Her eyes flashed up at him. For a moment he thought she'd not answer and then she relaxed again. She tucked her hair behind her ears and lifted her knees up to her chest. She looked younger than her twenty-eight years. Apprehensive. Rather as if she were staring out into a future and uncertain what it might hold. He wished he could help her. Really help her.

'Yes, of course. Everything that doesn't belong to the Crown. Marco inherited my father's personal effects. Rosa and I were given my mother's jewellery. Pieces that she'd brought into her marriage from her own family. Most of her jewellery belongs to my grandfather and will pass to his heir.'

Her fingers carefully untwisted the rolled up cotton of her trouser legs. Domenic watched the rhythmic movement, amazed by how uninterested he was in who would become King after King Giorgio's death.

Three weeks ago it had bothered him intensely. Rumours and counter rumours had started to come out of Niroli. Some of them so outrageous they defied belief…

She smoothed her hand down the fabric and wrapped it round her feet. 'I don't resent it,' she said, looking up. 'I inherited from my maternal grandfather. It's how I have money to invest in Mont Avellana. He was very generous to all of us.'

But that didn't make it any easier for her to see her mother's jewellery given elsewhere. That had to hurt. Domenic watched the muscle pulse in her cheek, the shadow of something in her eyes.

She might not resent Marco for inheriting the bulk of her parents' estate. As she said, she was independently wealthy. He'd checked it…

But…she *was* troubled. Perhaps angry with Marco for stepping aside from the succession? It would be ironic if he discovered, now he was morally committed to building on Niroli, that he'd been right to be concerned about who would be the next king.

Prince Luca seemed unlikely now. *Prince Nico?* What kind of man was he? Strange to think that Isabella, as the eldest granddaughter, would be the queen-in-waiting now if Niroli had adopted the Danish approach.

Setting aside his republican beliefs for a moment, he thought she'd have made an excellent queen. Every time she spoke about Niroli she lit up from the inside.

When had Nico Fierezza first left the island? Domenic tried to do a rapid calculation and failed. He'd no idea…but it had been years ago. Marco, too, had made his life elsewhere. But Isabella had stayed. And worked. And planned for her island home.

'Would you have wanted to be Queen?' he asked, watching her face. 'If your grandfather changed the rules of succession?'

'He won't.'

'But if he did?'

Isabella looked away. 'There's no point even thinking about it hypothetically. My grandfather believes there's strength in tradition…and he has an old-fashioned view of the role of women.' Her fingers plucked at her cotton trousers.

'But would you want it?'

Isabella hesitated and then answered quietly, 'Yes.'

'Does he know that?'

'Quite possibly but we've never talked about it. Nico will be the next crown prince.'

'Not Prince Luca?'

She shook her head. 'Not now. One scandal too many.' Her

fingers continued to pluck at the fabric of her trousers. 'I think if Luca had been prepared to…*flatter* grandfather, for want of a better word, everything would have been fine.

'But Luca isn't that kind of man. He's too honest. He was never going to fawn about Grandfather like he wanted him to. At least, that's my take on it. It's all irrelevant now. Luca's in Queensland and barred from the succession. Did you know that?' she asked suddenly.

He nodded. 'Suspected it, anyway. I've been paying close attention to who will succeed King Giorgio. Prince Luca is to marry an Australian girl, I gather.'

'Megan,' she said, with a slight smile. 'Despite what you may have read about her, she's lovely. He'll be very happy, I think, and Nico will be the next king. At least, he's been summoned back to Niroli…'

'Will he come?'

Isabella tucked her hair behind her ears. 'Eventually.' She looked up. 'I think he'll take his time. He says he's got work commitments but it's more than that.'

Domenic watched the emotions flicker across her face.

She hugged her knees closer and rested her right foot on top of her left. 'Nico finds Niroli too confining. He's never going to be happy living back on the island. I can't see it. He's…fearless. I think that's the best word to describe him. I can't really explain him because I don't understand him. But Niroli is far too insular a place for him. And, of course, he loves his work—'

'He's brilliant,' Domenic cut in.

'He is—and he'd have to give that up because no ruler is allowed a separate profession.'

'Can he refuse?'

'He can.' Isabella chewed her lip. 'And in many ways Max

would make the better king. At least he loves the island but...'
She shook her head. 'Nico won't refuse. He's a little like you
in that his sense of family is central to who he is. He'll come.
And I'm sure he'll be a good king.'

Isabella's fingers pleated the soft cotton of her trousers,
clearly troubled.

'What does that mean for you?'

She turned her head to look directly at him, shock showing
in her beautiful eyes—as though no one had ever thought to
ask her the question. Then she smiled at him and he slipped
another millimetre towards loving her. 'I-I don't know. In the
short term, perhaps, nothing. But everything will change
eventually. For one thing, Nico will have to marry and his
wife will assume my royal duties. All I'll have is my secular
career.'

Isabella stroked one finger over the dusky pink nail varnish
on her big toe. Domenic followed the movement with his eyes,
content to listen, knowing there was more. Even her voice had
the ability to curl his insides into a hard knot of wanting.

'That's why I came to see you. In Rome.' She glanced up. 'I
thought...if I could get you to sign then there'd be a real reason
to stay on Niroli. I've always thought bringing all the strands
of our tourist ventures together was a good idea. It just became
more important when Marco chose Emily over the Crown.'

Her hand moved to rub her arm, the silver threads in the
silk of her kaftan shimmering in the moonlight. 'I think
Marco made the right choice. I do. I really do. It's only...'

'His decision altered your life,' Domenic finished for her.
Too many people, it seemed, were thoughtless in their treatment of her. Had anyone even noticed how she was feeling?

'Yes. Yes, it has.' She moistened her lips with the tip of her
tongue. 'But that could be exciting.'

He could easily imagine her racking her brain to think of a way to secure his involvement in her project. He'd known when she'd sat in his conference room that it was important to her without guessing at the reason why.

He laid the diary back on the table. And her ideas for Mont Avellana had sprung from her grandmother's description of the island. An island she'd been frightened to come to…

But she was here. Searching for something that she could invest in, something that would give her life purpose. Domenic pulled his hand across his face, his fingers feeling the scar tissue.

Queen Sophia had loved Poseidon's Grotto. And he knew Isabella would, too.

But…

It touched so close to Jolanda's dream.

A muscle clenched in his cheek and his question came out as a bark. 'Would…you like to see your grandmother's grotto while you're here?'

'I asked Silvana about that. When I first arrived. She said she didn't think it would be possible.' Isabella hesitated. 'She said you've consistently refused all offers to turn it into a tourist attraction.'

And he'd refused to develop the palazzo. Domenic's mouth twisted into a wry smile. 'I'd like to show you. I think you'd love it.'

'I-I would. My grandmother describes it as being like a mystical kingdom.'

Her eyes were wide…and very beautiful. Domenic deliberately looked away. 'Has my sister left you much free time?'

'How long will it take?' Isabella asked. 'I have slithers of time each day, but all of Tuesday is free.'

'Because of my father's party?'

Isabella nodded. 'Silvana thinks there'll be lots to oversee on the day before. She's busy again on Wednesday, of course, but I'm being taken on a tour of the island…to get an overall feel of it, so that doesn't involve her anyway.'

'Tuesday, then?'

'Are you sure?'

'Of course. Would you mind going early? Before it gets too hot?'

'N-no, not at all. Whatever suits you best.'

'Perhaps eight?'

Isabella nodded.

'I'll wait for you on the *terrazzo*.'

Her hands bunched against the towel in her hands. 'Domenic…'

He looked across at her, watching the expressions work over her beautiful face.

'Silvana told me the grotto was one of Jolanda's favourite places—'

He stopped her. 'It was.' Jolanda had found the caves awe-inspiring. Strangely it didn't hurt remembering that. 'It's a magical place. It might even be what you're looking for. Though I meant what I said. I'm committed to the resort on Niroli regardless of what decisions you make.'

'Thank you.'

Isabella still seemed sad to him, the expression on her face wistful. 'Whatever happens with the succession, you will always be the granddaughter of a king,' he said softly. 'Nothing will ever take that away.'

She said nothing for a moment, resting her head back and looking up at the night sky. 'When my grandfather dies I'll be merely a cousin of the king. I won't have any specific royal duties. I didn't mind so much when it was Luca. Silly! It's exactly the same now it's going to be Nico,' she said, standing up and folding the damp towel in half. 'Where shall I put this?'

It was like shutters coming down on her confidences. As though she'd suddenly realised she'd said too much, been indiscreet.

Domenic swung his legs off the lounger and looked up at her. He could feel her sense of isolation—and no one knew more than him what a bleak place that was to inhabit. 'You can trust me not to repeat anything you say.'

Her hands stilled. 'I know that.' She spun round. 'I do know that. It's only I never…I never talk about my family. I-I hope you know I didn't mean that I don't like Nico, or that he won't be a good king when his time comes, it's just…I don't know him as well and…'

Domenic stood up and reached for her hand. Her fingers twitched inside his and he watched as she bit down on her lip to stop it trembling. Inside him something snapped. The way she was feeling about herself was wrong. He'd do anything he could to change that. She had to know that her value wasn't defined by her relationship to someone else. Isabella was worth more than that. So much more.

And he didn't have the words to tell her. His free hand moved to cup firmly around the back of her neck, drawing her closer. He heard her shocked intake of breath, saw the widening of her eyes, but the feel of her soft hair on the back of his hand was more potent than any drug.

He felt her swallow.

'I-I'm used to working with Luca. Because of the c-casinos and…'

She was so beautiful. *Luminous.* Domenic moved the pad of his thumb along her jawline…because he couldn't help it.

Her skin was soft, smooth and unblemished. His thumb touched her lips, full, red and trembling. He hadn't felt like this in the longest time.

*He wanted her beyond reason.*

It was as though everything about her was filling his senses, stopping his brain from functioning normally. He only knew that he wanted her so badly he ached. He wanted to comfort her, hold her, *love* her.

Her lips were so close to his. So close. He could feel her breath on his face. Warm. Sweet. His nostrils were full of the scent of vanilla that hung about her hair.

And her eyes met his, looking up at him. Almost black. Her eyelashes heavy with the tears she hadn't cried.

'Domen—'

Her husky voice breathed his name and he responded. Helplessly. His world shrank to this moment as he bent his head to kiss her. Her lips were warm. Responsive.

It was like a bolt of electricity shooting through his body.

He wanted to bury himself within her. Feel her respond to him. Hear her call out his name.

Her hand twisted out from his and she rested her palm against his chest. Both his cupped her face, tilting her head back as his tongue slipped inside her mouth. Warm and moist. He needed to taste her, had to…

His hand moved round to the small of her back and he could feel the warmth of her skin through the fine silk of her top. *Dear God…* He hadn't held a woman, kissed a woman, since Jolanda. Not since the fire…

Reality screamed in his head. *What was he doing?* This was madness. She couldn't want this. Domenic pulled back with an abruptness that left Isabella reeling. He reached out and steadied her.

'I'm sorry.' He pulled a hand across his ravaged face, feeling the ridges beneath his finger. 'I shouldn't have done that.'

'W-why?'

He sensed the question rather than heard it. The man he'd used to be could have comforted her like that—but not now. Not him. A woman as beautiful as Isabella belonged with someone equally beautiful. She needed to be with a man who could take her to charity balls and fund-raising dinners. She needed to be able to walk barefoot on the beach without any thought of finding shade. She needed a man who could bring her laughter.

*Children.*

His mind was suddenly filled with the image of her holding Carlo. The gentle expression on her face as she'd looked at the sleeping baby. The way she'd stroked the top of his head and curved her fingers round his plump foot.

Isabella would want children. Perhaps most women wanted children at some point during their lives? Certainly Jolanda had. Domenic pulled a hand up to cover his eyes.

Like a montage, memories flooded through him. Jolanda holding Felice. Jolanda blowing kisses on the soles of Felice's feet. Jolanda asleep on the bed with Felice lying spread-eagled beside her.

Happy. Laughing. He could see Felice's round face lighting with joy when he walked through the door. The small white rabbit she'd slept with each night.

*Until the fire.*

Until the fire.

Domenic's hand balled into a fist. Everything he loved had been snatched away that day. Jolanda and Felice had died in a smoke-filled room but he might as well have died with them.

He didn't have the courage to risk loving again. If he carried on with this…*madness,* Isabella would destroy him.

'Your work with your charities will continue.' His voice seemed to grate as he forced out the words. 'And the resort will happen. It's up to you to see that it benefits Niroli's economy at large.'

Domenic consciously relaxed his hands. This was difficult. Everything about Isabella made him want to gather her up in his arms and kiss her until she couldn't do anything but respond to him. He wanted to feel her body against his, feel the weight of her breasts in his hands. Instead he was going to walk away. And he was going to do it now.

'And encourage our islands to work together,' she said, wrapping her arms in front of her.

'That, too.' He forced a smile. 'If you achieve any kind of harmony you'll have done more than any Nirolian royal has managed in two hundred and fifty years.'

'I will.' Her dark eyes looked cloudy. Confused.

Domenic glanced back towards the palazzo. 'It's late. I should go in. Good night, Your Highness.'

# CHAPTER EIGHT

ISABELLA put on her sunglasses, as much to hide her eyes from Bianca as to shield them from the sun.

'What did Domenic do then?' Her friend reached out for the suntan spray and aimed it at her legs.

'Nothing. He left. He muttered something about all the things I could do to benefit Niroli and went inside.'

'*After* he kissed you.'

'Yes.'

'And you've not seen him all day?'

'No. Silvana and I went to see a bird sanctuary this morning but he wasn't at lunch and he's supposed to be out this evening.'

Bianca set the bottle down on the floor beside her sun lounger. She wrinkled her nose. 'Sounds to me like he was running away.'

It had sounded like that to Isabella, too. But *why?* Why run away from something that had felt so natural and right?

'And he called me "Your Highness". He hasn't done that since I first met him.' Isabella closed her eyes against the prickle of tears. She didn't even know why she was so upset. She'd known him for a mere handful of days. They'd shared one kiss…

*One.*

She didn't understand why it felt so precious. She only knew that when he'd walked inside she'd never known rejection like it. Or what it really meant to be alone.

Because it had been rejection. It had been in his eyes.

'Maybe he's got a problem with the royal thing,' Bianca said. Isabella could hear her settling back down on the lounger. 'You know, it would be amazing for a Vincini to be in a relationship with a Fierezza.'

'I know.'

'You're up against centuries of rivalry. Stefano said there were a fair few pokes at Domenic when he first starting doing business with Prince Luca, simply because of his close connection to King Giorgio. It wasn't well liked on Mont Avellana.

'And you know yourself how many concerns were raised on Niroli when you decided to approach the Vincini group. Old prejudices run deep. He must be aware of that. I don't know why it isn't bothering you more. *Hell,* just think what your grandfather would say!'

King Giorgio would quote the rule book at her. Recent events meant that she knew it verbatim. 'No marriage is permitted if the interests of the island become compromised through it.' She was on dangerous territory. She knew it. There was no point starting a relationship with a man who was forbidden to her.

Only...

Only she'd never felt like this before. She'd never met anyone who seemed to want to know her. They were all fascinated by the princess, when she wanted someone to love the woman.

Her grandfather probably wouldn't understand that either. Certainly not when the man in question was a Vincini.

Isabella turned her head and looked at her friend through her dark lenses. 'Then why did Domenic kiss me at all?'

Her friend laughed. 'Don't be silly. You're beautiful. He's a man.' Bianca lifted a hand up to shade her eyes from the sun. 'You must have had men kiss you before in the heat of the moment…?'

'Of course.'

*But rarely.* Most were in awe of her royal status—and those that ventured so close had never stopped so abruptly. Or so strangely.

Isabella frowned. It hadn't felt like a kiss in the 'heat of the moment' either. Certainly not one that should be regretted. It had come out of a feeling of closeness. A real *connection.*

She'd told him things she'd not confided to a living soul. Not even her sister knew she'd be glad to succeed their grandfather. She certainly hadn't even hinted to Rosa that, with Nico as the future king, she was scared of becoming obsolete and angry she'd been trained to fulfil a role that was no longer hers to occupy.

But Domenic had effortlessly understood. He even seemed to understand the knife edge she lived on—one half of her embracing her royal duties and the other feeling trapped by it. He'd seen past the carefully packaged image she presented to the world and found *her.*

*And she knew him.* Which was why she knew Domenic had pulled back for altogether more complicated reasons than her family background. There were probably many strands to it…and that was what scared her.

'Maybe he feels guilty about asking if you want to see the grotto? If his wife loved it there so much,' Bianca offered beside her. 'And, if he does, he'll certainly feel guilty about kissing you. Perhaps he still feels married in his head?

'You know I've not heard of him getting involved with anyone since his wife died. And he must have had plenty of opportunity because he's so incredibly rich.'

Isabella pushed her sunglasses up on top of her head. 'Bianca!'

Her friend shrugged. 'It's life. Rich men are always targeted by women who like the things they have and are prepared to put up with them. But there's never even been a whisper of a rumour about him. I'm sure I'd have heard if there was. He seems to like to be alone.'

Domenic was fiercely alone. Inflexibly and determinedly. Only sometimes she seemed able to cross the divide. Isabella set her glasses back on her nose and lay back. Perhaps Bianca was right and Domenic felt guilty. The sun warmed her skin but didn't touch the cold knot that had settled inside her.

'He's probably got that thing survivors get sometimes,' Bianca continued. 'I read about that somewhere. Apparently people who've been through a sudden tragedy find it difficult to allow themselves to live normally. They almost think they should have died.'

Isabella immediately thought of the photograph Lucetta had shown her. Standing beside Jolanda, Domenic had looked like a very different man—and those differences were not entirely due to the physical scars. The changes in him went deeper.

'And, he *must* have body issues.' Bianca sat up abruptly and Isabella opened her eyes to see why. Her friend reached for her iced water and sipped. 'I don't know what proportion of his body was burnt in that fire but I'd heard he's had skin grafts and the like. Hell, I've got issues about the way my body looks after having Fabiano. I imagine burns scarring must be worse.'

Isabella closed her eyes again, safe behind the dark lenses. Bianca's words conjured up the image of a scared and grieving widower, with an inbred distrust of her family—and she was right.

Only…when she was with Domenic it didn't feel like that. It felt a lot like coming home.

How did she make him feel?

Last night she'd been so conscious of her own reaction to the scars on his body she hadn't really thought about how difficult it must have been for him. In some deeply private place she'd been worried she might find the sight of them unattractive and she'd been flooded with relief when she hadn't.

Had she hurt him? Had he been uncomfortable? But then he'd gone on to offer to show her Poseidon's Grotto. Was he regretting that as much as the kiss?

'What are you going to do?'

Bianca's question forced her to open her eyes again. She wasn't sure what she was going to do. Truth be told, she wasn't even sure what she wanted. Everything was so confused in her head. All she really knew for certain was that when he'd pulled away from her it had felt as if something very precious was being taken away from her. And she wasn't ready for that to happen.

'Bel?' Bianca prompted.

'I don't know.' Isabella pushed her glasses back onto the top of her head. 'I suppose I'll see what he does next.'

'And if it's nothing?'

'Then it's not meant to be. I suppose that might even be for the best.'

She'd never stepped outside of what was expected for her as a Princess of Niroli—it seemed unrealistic to expect she'd do it now.

Isabella picked up her camera and thought about what lenses to include in her bag. Her grandmother had talked about the long walk down to the grotto so she didn't want to overburden herself with equipment.

On the other hand, there was nothing worse than seeing something and knowing it would make the most perfect shot and not having the right lens.

Always assuming she got there.

Isabella bit on her bottom lip. What would she do if Domenic wasn't there? Worse still, what would she do if he was there to tell her he'd changed his mind, that he thought it would be a mistake? That had to be a possibility.

She swung her bag over her shoulder and headed for the door with ten minutes to spare. She had to try and do what she'd told Bianca she would—she'd be guided by him.

Whatever his feelings for her, she *did* want to see the grotto. For as long as she remembered, she'd been told she bore an uncanny resemblance to her paternal grandmother and being given her diary had only fostered that feeling of connection. Staying at the Palazzo Tavolara, walking where she'd walked, was rather special.

She pushed the door open into the sitting room, her eyes immediately looking out towards the *terrazzo*. The doors were open, but there was no sign of Domenic. She pulled her bag up higher on her shoulder, feeling foolish.

Isabella glanced down at her wristwatch and then back at the empty *terrazzo*. It wasn't quite eight. There was still time.

'You're early,' Domenic said, coming up behind her. 'I'm sorry I've kept you waiting.'

And immediately she was covered with uncertainty.

She pulled on the strap of her bag and turned to look at him. It took a moment before her eyes adjusted to the comparative gloom inside. He looked casual and relaxed. Sexy. 'Are you happy for me to take pictures of the grotto?'

He moved closer and the jagged red lines on his face stood out starkly. 'As long as you don't include me in any of them. Are you ready to go?'

Isabella nodded. 'Are you sure you still want to do this today? I-I can always—'

'I want to,' he said, cutting her off. 'Is your security team happy for you to go alone, or do we need to wait for someone to join us?'

'No. I mean, we can go alone.' The words were out of her mouth before she felt a sudden wash of confusion. Perhaps he didn't want to be alone with her? Hadn't expected it? In twenty-eight years she couldn't remember *ever* having felt like this.

It was a mixture of excitement and paralysing fear.

'Only it is possible to get to the grotto by boat.'

'Do many people do it?'

Domenic shook his head. 'I own the mooring. But it's not as secure as it is closer to the palazzo. I'm happy to wait for a body-guard to join us, if you'd feel safer.'

She didn't want that. For the first time she really understood why Luca evaded his protection. She wanted to be alone with Domenic. Just the two of them.

She moistened her lips. 'I'm sure it'll be all right. It's not a controversial place for me to be. Everyone knows I'm looking at potential tourist sites.'

He nodded and reached down to pick up a bag from the floor. 'What did you think of the bird sanctuary yesterday?'

'It was lovely,' she said, flicking her hair back off her shoulder.

Domenic's face changed. A far softer smile than she'd ever seen him give curved his mouth. 'I hate it, too.'

'I didn't say that.'

A wicked glint lit his dark eyes. 'But you thought it. And I agree.'

She choked on a laugh. No one ever saw through her like that. Everyone took what she said at face value. But not Domenic...

*Not Domenic.*

'We should think it's lovely.'

'I don't see why.'

'What they're doing there is important. It's only I don't know enough about it to make it interesting. That's my fault, not theirs.'

He glanced down at her and the expression on his face had her stomach feeling as if a million ants were let loose inside. And all at once she was glad she was here. Spending time with Domenic *was* a good idea. *It was.*

'I can't imagine Silvana enjoyed it much either. She's probably seen more of Mont Avellana in the last few days than in the rest of her life put together.'

'She does seem more suited to city life.'

'She is.'

It was on the tip of her tongue to ask which he preferred, but even that seemed a sensitive question. She already knew he'd lived on Mont Avellana until the fire had robbed him of his family. And that Jolanda had loved it here.

What she really wanted to know was whether he was still actively mourning his late wife. And how much of his reluctance to be with other people was because of his changed appearance and how much was because he was missing her.

Impossible questions.

They'd walked beyond anything Isabella recognised. Although it all seemed so familiar. Very like home. Everything about Mont Avellana was. The smells were the same, the flora and fauna...

'Please say if you want to stop to take any photographs,' Domenic said, following the line of her eyes as she was looking intently at some grasses. 'We've plenty of time.'

Isabella turned her head. 'I was just thinking this could be Niroli. I suppose I should have expected everything to be the same.'

'Disappointed?'

'No.' *Not at all.* She pulled at her camera strap. It was more that it made her sad that their islands had been so suspicious and resentful of each other.

Was that why he didn't act on the feelings she was sure he felt for her? Because she was sure he felt something. Sometimes when his eyes rested on her…

She tucked her hair behind her ears in a gesture she hadn't done since she'd left her teenage years. 'But I shan't take a picture unless it's something a little different.'

Jolanda's stunningly orchestrated gardens had long disappeared. Unerringly, as though he'd done it many times, Domenic led her along a narrow path through a pine forest until they emerged and Isabella could see the bright blue of the sea. As they walked closer to the cliffs the wild coastline took her breath away.

Instinctively she reached for her camera. 'Do you mind?'

'No. I don't mind.' He turned his face towards the sun and Isabella concentrated on finding the lens she wanted.

She squinted out across the sea towards a small island. 'Where's that?'

'Teulada. It's uninhabited.'

Isabella concentrated on getting her shot. Then she turned to look at him. 'There's a building on it.'

'That's a Spanish watchtower.'

'Spanish?'

'Niroli wasn't the only invader to come our way,' he said with a smile. He was doing that more often now. But…it was the kind of smile that held a hint of sadness, an underlying regret. 'It was built in the sixteenth century to protect against Arab raids.'

'It's beautiful,' she said, turning back to take another couple of shots. Strangely she was glad to be doing something familiar, something that always gave her comfort.

There was silence for a minute, but she knew his eyes were fixed on her profile rather than the distant island.

'How did you get interested in photography?'

Isabella put down her camera. 'I think it was probably a reaction to being photographed so much.'

He held his hand out to hold her bag while she released the lens from the camera. 'When I first started attracting attention I was very shy and found it difficult. My mother bought me my first camera. She thought it might help.'

'Did it?'

'Yes.' She smiled. 'Much to my surprise, it did. I started focussing more on what they needed from me to get a good shot.'

'Which explains why the world's press loves you.'

'I don't know about that. But I do try and make their job as easy as possible. If you don't it can be very painful.'

She knew Domenic thought about that, but she was grateful he didn't ask her to elaborate. If he was curious it would be easy enough to find the photographs she wished had never been taken.

He wouldn't though. He wasn't that type of man.

'Your pictures of Mont Avellana were stunning,' he said into the silence that stretched between them. 'I don't think I told you.'

It felt good to be praised by Domenic.

'Thank you.' She tucked the lens into its felt lined box and tucked it away in her bag. 'I'm getting better all the time. Some of my pictures are being used in Niroli's advertising campaign.'

'I didn't know that.'

'My favourite is the one of the amphitheatre.' She smiled up at him. 'But then, I like everything about that place. It has a real sense of history and I love to feel I'm connected to the past.'

Her foot stumbled on a rock and Domenic's hand shot out to steady her. It was warm against her skin and her breath caught in her throat. She was so attracted to this man. On every level there was.

'Careful. The path does get a little treacherous.'

Isabella's eyes searched his for a similar kind of awareness. It was there. She was sure of it. A telltale muscle pulsed in the side of his cheek and his smile was almost frozen in place.

'We can't rival your amphitheatre,' he said, his hand dropping back by his side. 'But you ought to get Silvana to take you to the ancient city of Chia.'

'What's there?' she asked, her voice breathless.

'Until nineteen seventy-five, people thought nothing. The records showed Chia as the capital of the Roman province of Mont Avellana but it was abandoned when they left and, over the centuries, was completely covered by sand.'

Domenic turned away. 'It needs some serious investment,' he continued, 'which our government have not given to it, but it's a fascinating place. So far scholars have identified the temple and the Roman baths but the site is far more exten-sive than that. And the mosaic-tiled floors are very exciting.'

'I-I'd be interested in that.'

'Tell Silvana. In fact, I will. I'd like you to see it while you're here.'

Isabella walked in silence. Some part of her must have been hoping that he'd offer to take her himself because she felt hurt—and that was foolish. Domenic was flying back to Rome on Thursday.

She had so little time with him. So little time to discover what it was that was drawing her to him. She brushed a stray hair off her face and took a shaky breath. 'Shall I send you my photographs when I get back to Niroli? Perhaps you could use them. Or give them to someone who could?'

He glanced across at her, his brown eyes warm. Isabella rushed into speech. 'Yesterday I managed to get some beautiful ones of the flamingoes on the salt flats. And the marshland had egrets and purple heron. I don't think they're so special. The light was fading by then, but I'll know better when I get home and look at them properly.'

He smiled. 'You really are passionate about photography, aren't you?'

'It's one of the few things I take seriously. I think about it all the time. It's become something of an addiction—'

Isabella broke off as she took in the steep steps carved into the limestone cliff. They stretched on and down towards a small cove. So beautiful.

Mutely, Domenic held out his hands to hold her bag. 'There are five hundred and seventy-three steps down.'

'You've counted?'

'Jolanda did.'

Isabella looked up, scared to ask the question and frightened to hear his answer. 'Does it hurt you to be here without her?'

'I thought it would, but, no. No, it doesn't.'

She knelt down to rest the lens case on the ground. 'I'm glad.' She was more than glad.

'How did Queen Sophia describe it in her diary?'

Isabella stood up again and trained her camera on the cliff face, bringing the steps into sharp focus. 'She says they took so long climbing back up they were late for dinner. I didn't imagine anything like this though.'

'It's quite impressive.'

Everything was impressive. Isabella had to concentrate on the steps as she walked down them. So many were uneven and there were places where it would have been easy to fall.

Domenic stopped in front of her and pointed. 'Look over there.'

Her hand automatically reached out to steady herself and she touched his back. It felt as if every hair on her arm stood to attention. Her fingers splayed out and she looked at the whiteness of her hand against the oatmeal colour of his linen shirt.

*What was happening to her?* She'd never been like this about a man. Not even the Rt Hon Justin Leagrove-Dyer had made her feel so reckless—and yet she'd been so infatuated with him. For a time. Until she'd discovered he'd been interested in her money more than her.

Slowly she removed her hand and looked where Domenic was pointing. Just appearing from behind a jut of rock was a long stretch of white beach strewn with juniper plants. High sand dunes gave way to the dramatic cliffs behind.

She immediately went for her camera and Domenic laughed. It was the first time she'd heard him do that. Rich and warm. She looked up into his face and her breath froze.

His smile faded and his eyes flicked to her mouth and back to her eyes. *He was going to kiss her again.* She knew it. She didn't dare breathe and every thought she had was concentrated on willing him to do it.

*Kiss me. Kiss me. Please kiss me.*

His hands seemed to reach out for her, resting on her shoulders. Slowly, very slowly, he moved closer, his mouth touching hers.

It was exactly like last time. But the response his kiss provoked was like nothing she'd ever experienced before. It was gentle and demanding at the same time. Comforting and exciting.

Her hand fisted in the linen of his shirt. Her head was full of his name. Over and over.

Then she felt him pull away and heard the small groan she gave from the base of her throat. His thumb brushed against her bottom lip and he eased back further.

'Isabella…'

She opened her eyes.

'*Oh, God.*' His mouth swooped down on hers. His tongue flicking between her lips. Demanding. Seducing.

It wouldn't have mattered if she'd known a telephoto lens was trained on her. She wanted this so badly. It seemed Domenic's kiss was everything she'd been waiting for. Like the fictional sleeping princess, she felt alive because of it. Alive as she'd never felt before.

Moments later it was over. Domenic had pulled back again and Isabella was left feeling exposed and shaken. She reached out to take hold of his hand, his fingers instinctively interlocking with hers.

His hand was darkly tanned against the pale skin of hers. *His beautiful, beautiful hands.* So sexy.

'I can't seem to help but kiss you,' he said quietly.

Isabella struggled to find her voice. 'Is that a problem?'

The expression in his eyes made her want to reach for him. 'I think so.'

'Why?'

His eyes flicked to her mouth and her stomach clenched in response.

'Because it can't lead anywhere.'

'But why?'

He shook his head and then said quietly, 'We can talk about it later. Not now. I don't want to talk now.'

And neither did she. She didn't want to discuss what her grandfather's reaction would be to discovering she'd begun a relationship with Domenic Vincini. She didn't want to talk about Jolanda...

Domenic kept hold of her hand and led her down the final run of steps. His fingers felt so good against hers. Jolanda was dead...but she was *alive*. He had to see that.

And she needed him. Really needed him. The knowledge burst in her head like a sudden crack of lightning.

And he needed her.

Isabella held her breath as they approached the mouth of the cave. Her expectations were high but she hadn't even begun to appreciate the beauty of what she would see once inside.

She looked up at Domenic and found he was watching her, looking to see her reaction. Despite everything she smiled. 'This is unbelievably beautiful.'

'Come with me.'

They took the narrow path that led along the side of the natural lake. Rudimentary lighting had been placed in crevices along the wall. Presumably a remnant of Jolanda's plans for the grotto.

Isabella pushed the thought of Domenic's late wife aside. As long as he was choosing to hold her hand she was happy.

More than happy. Even her inability to take a photograph of what she was seeing failed to spoil the experience. Without additional lighting she'd never begin to capture the eerie beauty of the stalagmites.

It was like stepping into Tolkien's Middle Earth. Extraordinary and perfectly beautiful. No artist could have carved anything as beautiful. And around it all there was dark, still water.

'This is the second largest freshwater lake in the world,' Domenic said, his voice rumbling. The grip on her hand tightened. 'The tide can only reach so far. Certainly not enough to salt the underground water.'

Isabella felt a little as if she were walking in a church. She felt the same sense of awe.

'Through here is the largest of the chambers.'

A cavernous space opened up before her, more breathtaking than anything that had gone before. 'It's incredible,' she whispered.

'Yes, it is. When you think about it there had to be a reason why your ancestors went to the trouble of building the steps down here.'

'Did they?'

He nodded. 'They're as old as the palazzo.'

'I'm not surprised my grandmother loved it so much. She planned on organising an orchestral concert here.' Isabella looked round and searched out the large flat area Queen Sophia had described. 'There I imagine.'

Domenic's fingers moved against hers. 'That would be beautiful.'

Her head was suddenly teeming with ideas. She could see the grotto lit with lanterns. Maybe even sculptures set into the alcoves and reflected in the dark water.

If Domenic was prepared to let her do it.

She shivered.

'Let's go and have some lunch before we attempt the climb back up. I brought something down with me.'

Isabella said nothing. Her time with Domenic wasn't over yet, but she could sense she was on borrowed time. He led her back out from the grotto and they stood for a moment blinking in the bright sunlight.

The heat was steadily climbing. She looked across at him, searching for signs of discomfort. Maybe the stiff breeze off the sea compensated.

Domenic released her hand and shrugged his small rucksack off his right shoulder. Isabella sat down and pulled out her camera, fitting the telephoto lens to it before turning back to look at the entrance to the grotto.

And, then, she took a picture of Domenic. Forbidden…but irresistible.

If he noticed he didn't say anything. His concentration was entirely on the picnic he'd brought with him. 'The focaccia is stuffed with sausage, ricotta, chard and red peppers.' He set it on a stone and added prosciutto, olives, tomatoes, fresh mozzarella and a large bottle of water. 'Are you thirsty?'

Isabella nodded.

He reached inside his bag and pulled out two plastic tumblers. His fingers brushed against hers as he handed it across. 'Not exactly fit for a princess,' he said with a tight smile.

'That would depend on the princess.'

He looked up from pouring the water. He'd understood exactly what she was trying to tell him. She watched him swallow and every fibre of her being wanted him to throw the bottle aside and kiss her again. Kiss her…and never stop kissing her.

'Have you thought about what King Giorgio would think? What he might do?'

Unbelievably it didn't matter. Didn't matter at all.

'It can't happen, Isabella. *We* can't happen.'

Her throat felt dry and it was suddenly difficult to swallow. She didn't know how to handle this situation. She wasn't even sure what she was fighting because he hadn't told her. He broke the focaccia apart and handed her a section of it.

'I'm not needed on Niroli now,' she said, painfully. Did she dare suggest she might even like to live in Rome? What would he say if she did?

'But you're still a Fierezza.'

She would always be that.

Domenic settled himself on the sand and looked out towards the craggy island with its oversized watchtower. 'We'd started to build there. Jolanda and I.'

Isabella forced down the piece of bread that had stuck in her throat.

'The idea was to make a holiday island. Very exclusive. Individual villas, each with access to their own private beach.'

'How far did you get?' Isabella managed to ask.

'Just one villa. The plans were all in place but then there was the fire and everything was shelved.'

*The fire.*

Isabella pulled her knees up to her chest and hugged them to her. Was he trying to explain why he didn't want to be with her?

'You ought to carry on with it.'

There was a pause and then, 'I think so. And, maybe, the palazzo, too.' He turned his head to look at her. 'What would you do with it if it were yours?'

'I'd live in it. Part of it, anyway.'

'On Mont Avellana?'

'If it were mine,' she said, watching the gentle lap of the

water. 'And I'd build a restaurant in the grounds with views of the sea.'

But it wasn't hers. And soon, very soon, she'd leave Mont Avellana and she'd never return. 'Would it be different if I wasn't a Fierezza?' she asked on a burst.

Domenic turned slowly. 'You are.' He pulled a hand across his face. 'My father invited you to his party, didn't he?'

She nodded.

'And you've decided not to come.'

It was a statement not a question. Isabella's eyes didn't leave his face.

'Haven't you?'

'Yes.' Part of her had wanted to go; only Tomasso had expressed grave reservations. And, of course, she knew what the repercussions would be when she got home.

'I should never have kissed you.'

Words of protest formed in her head but they didn't make it out of her mouth.

'And you know I'm right,' he said quietly.

# CHAPTER NINE

ISABELLA had had ample time to make her decision. Sitting on the balcony, long into the evening, looking out across the formal gardens. Then this morning over a solitary breakfast of persimmons and prickly pears…

She needed to go to Alberto Vincini's birthday celebration—and, though she was frightened, she would go.

Over the years it had apparently developed into a major social event, and drew both personal and political friends from all over Mont Avellana. She was completely aware of how big a statement she'd be making as far as the world's press was concerned.

It would be a grand gesture.

Tomasso had warned her that republican activists might use the occasion to draw attention to their political goals. And she knew what her grandfather would think when he saw the inevitable photographs.

But against that was the way she felt about Domenic Vincini. He'd made a unilateral decision about their future and she wanted him to see how little she cared about the politics of their respective families.

She also wanted to catch him off guard. Make him act without thinking.

Isabella deliberately chose a simple gold droplet to wear in her ears, rather than a flashier diamond.

'Would you like the matching necklace, Your Highness?' Mia asked twisting the final strand of hair up into a complicated twist of curls.

'Not if I'm wearing the flowers,' Isabella answered, watching as Mia placed three red roses in the honey-gold curls. The deepest shade of the petals picked out the exact colour of her long shift dress.

That, too, had been chosen for its simplicity. It was deceptive, though. Its high price tag was warranted by the clever cut, which meant the silk hugged her curves and dipped low on her back.

There was a firm rap on the door and Isabella turned her head.

'The car will be brought up to the front of the palazzo in ten minutes,' Tomasso said from the door.

Isabella nodded and gave her reflection a final look. 'Thank you.' She smiled up at Mia. 'Thank you, too.' Then she stood up and smoothed out the silk of her dress. It fell in soft folds around her ankles. 'I'll be down in a moment.'

She walked over to the balcony and looked out across the gardens as the door clicked shut behind her. *Jolanda's garden.* Was Domenic's love for his late wife another barrier? *The main one?* She didn't *know.* At the back of her mind she did wonder whether she was about to incur her grandfather's wrath for nothing.

Isabella turned abruptly and walked out of the room. It didn't help to think like that. Tomorrow Domenic was flying back to Rome. *Tomorrow.* There was very little time left.

Tomasso met her at the bottom of the dramatically beautiful porphyry stairs and led her out towards the car. Isabella gave him a brief smile and slid into the back seat, while he walked round to the other side.

'Ready?' he said, sitting beside her.

She nodded.

'Not surprisingly there's already considerable press interest in your going to the Vincini party. Do you still wish to use the main entrance?'

Isabella straightened her spine. 'It's not a secret I'm going, so let's not make it difficult for them to get their photographs.'

Then she looked back at the palazzo. It would be so easy to turn back now. She could plead a headache, even send a message that she'd decided it would be unwise...

The car surged forward and Isabella switched into professional mode. If nothing else she would at least have made the biggest gesture possible to heal the rift between Niroli and Mont Avellana.

*But she was hoping for more.* So much more.

They passed through familiar-seeming countryside. Along tiny roads with sweeping views of vineyards and wheat fields. And on through a city of wide tree-lined roads and imposing eighteenth century houses. Then they took the main road and headed out towards the coast.

Tomasso sat impassively by her, but she wondered what he was thinking.

'The villa is immediately round this bend, Your Highness.'

Isabella didn't need the warning. She could see the lights hung throughout the garden. Her car slowed and she heard the shout as the gathered photographers realised she'd finally arrived.

Fear gripped her. And excitement. That, too. It was a heady potion. For the first time in her life she really felt as if she was taking control of her destiny and finally stepping out from beneath the shadow of her family.

'Here we go.' Tomasso opened his door and walked round to open hers.

Isabella allowed herself one deep, steadying breath and then she smiled. She flicked her legs and stood gracefully, not needing the hand Tomasso offered her. Her performance was faultless. No one would have been able to guess how hard her heart was slamming against her rib cage.

'Your Highness, does King Giorgio know you are here?' one voice shouted louder than the rest. Mostly she could only hear her name above the general hubbub. 'Isabella.'

She paused as the cameras flashed.

'Princess Isabella!'

'Are you aware Alberto Vincini actively fought for independence from Niroli, Your Highness?'

Isabella turned to look at the woman whose voice was more insistent, her questions specific. It was a face she recognised, one of the pack that followed her everywhere.

'Giovanna,' she said, pulling the reporter's name from the recesses of her memory. 'In the years you and I have travelled together, we've seen the consequences of all kinds of violent conflict. I think anything that promotes understanding and peace is something that should be grasped, don't you?'

'And King Giorgio?' the steely-haired reporter persisted.

'Is keen for there to be good relations with Mont Avellana.' That, at least, was true. The fact that he'd prefer them to be on his terms was something that didn't need to be said here.

Silvana came into the small summer sitting room and shut the door. She perched on the arm of one of the chairs, slipping off her shoe to rub at her foot. 'Isabella's doing amazingly. I've seen her in action over the past few days, but what she's doing tonight is phenomenal.'

Domenic looked up from his book. 'I don't know why you're surprised.'

'And that from the man who said her chief skill was filling a designer dress to perfection…if I remember rightly!'

Domenic said nothing, merely running his hand down his face. Before he'd met Isabella he'd certainly undervalued what she did and how much she contributed. This time, though, he feared she had a different agenda.

'Dad's incredibly pleased she's come. He's taken it as a personal compliment.'

'It is.'

'Is it?' Silvana's right eyebrow rose a fraction. 'I'd have thought the compliment should go elsewhere.'

Domenic knew his sister glanced across at him but he kept his eyes firmly on his book. Silvana wanted him to have the fairy tale but the real world wasn't so kind. A twenty-first-century version of *Beauty and the Beast* would have a very different ending.

'Dad's introduced her to practically everyone,' Silvana said, slipping her foot back into her sandal and walking over to a side table. 'She must have shaken so many hands this evening she's in danger of getting repetitive strain injury.' She poured out a couple of glasses of wine and handed him the slightly fuller one, then sat down. 'How long are you going to stay in here?'

'I always keep a low profile at these things.'

'Not like this.'

Domenic felt a spark of pain in his right temple. He raised a hand and moved it in concentric circles, hoping it would ease. It was difficult enough knowing Isabella was here, walking about the gardens, talking to his father's friends, without Silvana's version of the Spanish Inquisition.

Particularly when he wanted to be with her.

'You ought to be out there making sure Isabella's okay—'

'You do it.' He closed his eyes at the brusqueness in his voice.

'No. She's put herself on the line for you. I'm not a fool. I have seen the way you look at each other.'

'You don't understand—'

'I understand perfectly.' She stood up. 'So *what* if someone asks you how you got burned? This is self-indulgent, Dom. The truth is you're too bloody scared to get on with living and out there is someone more amazing than you deserve!' She walked across to the door, shutting it with a decisive click.

Domenic was left in semi darkness, just the light from a single lamp. He rubbed his hand across his face. Then he shut his book and stood up to pace restlessly towards the French windows. He looked out and listened to the soft music and the laughter.

Even with Jolanda he hadn't felt like this. He'd never experienced this…uncontrolled attraction he felt for Isabella. He'd not known what it was to physically desire someone so much that it consumed him.

But being with her was impossible. It was a line he couldn't cross—for very many reasons.

But wasn't the problem that he'd already crossed it? He was already in love with Isabella. He'd fought against using the word 'love', but he knew it was the only one that would do justice to the intensity of what he was feeling.

And he was running scared. A woman like Princess Isabella of Niroli didn't belong with a man like him. And she'd realise that eventually. One day she'd leave him and he knew he wouldn't survive a second loss.

She was lonely. Certainly confused over her future. Maybe she even felt a misplaced sense of pity for him? He raised a hand to rub his temple. He couldn't bear that. Not *pity*.

The door opened suddenly and he turned expecting to see Silvana again. Instead he saw Isabella. His book fell to the floor and he stared at her.

She looked…like…

He swallowed. She looked too beautiful to rightly belong in this world. Domenic couldn't put words on it. Her beauty lit her from within. It was so much more than the dark red column of her dress and the twisting curls piled on her head. More even than the curves of her body or the fullness of her lips.

And he knew, with complete certainty, that whatever she did, wherever she went, he would love her until he died. It was like suddenly stepping into a beam of light.

He loved everything about her. The way she looked. The way she moved. The way she spoke. The way she thought…

*He loved her.* Simple as that. And it was a love that would rip him apart.

Isabella let go of the handle and quietly shut the door behind her. 'Silvana said I would find you here. Sh-she said this was the perfect place for sanctuary.'

'Do you need it?'

She smiled and her eyes sought his. He could read the plea in them. His hands balled by his side.

'A little. My face is beginning to ache from smiling.'

'Are people being friendly?'

'Very.' Her fingers strayed up to one of the gold teardrops hanging from her ears. 'But there's dancing and saying no is becoming harder.'

Domenic reached down to pick his book off the floor.

'Do you have to say no?'

The deep red silk of her skirt seemed to shimmer in the subdued lighting as she walked. 'It's not obligatory, just wiser. And there's no one out there I wish to dance with.'

Her eyes were wide and soft like velvet. Domenic turned away to pick up the book and carefully placed it back on Silvana's colour-coded shelves. His mind was full of images of what it would be like to dance with her. How wonderful it would feel to have her body pushed up against his.

She glided over to one of his sister's most uncomfortable chairs and sat down. She reminded him of how he'd first seen her in his Rome offices—tightly controlled, a little nervous...and impossibly beautiful. Everything in him was straining to go to her. To let his hand cup her face and to tell her that everything was all right, that he loved her and wanted them to be together.

*But that wasn't possible. It would never be possible.* If she looked at him clearly she would see that.

'Have you been in here all evening?'

He steeled himself to tell her the truth. 'I came in when I heard you arrive.'

He knew he'd hurt her...but he'd intended to. She needed to see for herself how futile their attraction was. He wanted her to be the one to pull away because it would make it easier for him to accept it *was* futile.

But it was painful to see the fleeting expression in her eyes. 'Isabella...' He said her name on a groan. That single word was full of yearning, of everything he wasn't prepared to tell her.

'Please come out and join the party. Dance with me.'

'That's not possible. There are too many people with mobile phones who wouldn't be able to resist taking a photograph.'

Her fingers moved to twist the gold droplet again. 'We could just talk.'

Everything was warring inside him. What he wanted, what he thought was right for her. Guilt. Fear.

*Mostly fear.*

'And everyone would stare and whisper behind their hands.'

He turned his back to her. Silvana had placed lights artistically across her garden and huge lanterns with large creamy candles in them surrounded the pool. Romantically beautiful, particularly when it was combined with the music from Mont Avellana's premier orchestra.

And, more than anything in his entire life, he wanted to walk there with her. He wanted to hold her hand and for everyone to know she was his. *His.*

'They're doing that anyway. But everyone seems to like my dress, so it could be worse.'

Her dress was stunning. *She* was stunning. But she wasn't the woman for him. Lucetta was right. Isabella's lifestyle was one he couldn't embrace. Domenic's hand reached out for support and he rested it against the window frame. A light breeze tugged at his hair and he could feel it brush against his face.

'You might come and share the load.' He heard her stand up, move towards him. Her voice was low and hesitant. 'People will talk. You can't stop them.' There was a long silence. 'Please don't hide yourself away.'

'I'm not hiding.'

'Domenic—'

His control snapped. 'Go out and enjoy the party if you want to, but leave me here. I'm tired of watching people's eyes try hard not to wander down to my neck.' He turned round. 'I hate seeing the shock and repulsion. What do you think they'd say if they thought ours was anything other than a business relationship?'

Isabella kept walking towards him. He could hear the soft rustle of her skirt and smell the faint scent of her perfume.

She stopped centimetres from him. Her eyes were half challenge, half fear. Then she lifted her right hand and gently stroked it down his face. Her forefinger traced the long scar from his eyebrow to his nose. Then she meticulously traced the second, which ran from the centre of his cheek to his jawline.

His body jerked in response. Then she stepped closer still. He could feel her breath stroking his skin. Her fingers moved against the burns scarring on his neck. The discoloured and puckered skin he hated to touch himself because he remembered the pain...and how much he had lost.

'I don't care what they say. I wish this hadn't happened to you,' she said, her voice husky. 'But you got these scars because you loved your wife and daughter enough to risk your life.'

Her voice was barely more than a whisper. And she was so close he could see each individual eyelash. They swept down across her pale cheeks and then she looked up into his eyes.

'There's nothing unattractive about that.'

Inside he was screaming.

'I need you.'

It was like a siren's call, impossible to resist. He could feel his body warming, every male instinct responding.

He knew how it felt to hold her. And he knew what it felt like to push his tongue past her lips and into the softness of her mouth. He knew what she tasted like.

He knew how her body moulded itself against his. And he

knew how her back curved and the warmth of her skin felt beneath his fingers. He *knew*.

'Dance with me.'

It wasn't a request. More a dare. Isabella waited for him to respond.

Suddenly his mind was flooded with an understanding of how Adam had been unable to resist Eve's offer of the fruit of the tree of knowledge. He knew his survival depended on his turning away…but he couldn't.

Didn't.

His hands reached for her and she seemed to be in his arms before he realised how it had happened. He pulled her closer. And closer. Every line of her body was pressed up against his. He didn't even care that the hard length of him was pushed up against the softness of her belly.

And then there was the music. Scarcely remembered Mont Avellanan pieces he couldn't have put a name to if he'd tried but they filled his senses. Her body moved against his and he felt his final resolve buckle.

His hand slid around her waist and he let his fingers feel for the bare skin of her back. He wanted that. He wanted to slide his hand around and cradle the weight of her breasts. Instead he let it slide down over her buttocks, pulling her in hard against his arousal.

'Isabella.' His voice was husky and broken. He had no resolve left. He wanted her. Needed her as much as it seemed she needed him.

And then she kissed him. An echo of what she'd done before when she'd kissed his cheek. But this time she kissed his neck. Her lips were moist and warm against the part of his body he despised the most.

He hadn't allowed himself to cry since his mother died,

but he could have cried now. Certainly lifted his head and howled at the moon.

Sexier than anything that had gone before. Isabella Fierezza was here to claim him. Deliberately she'd stepped over the line…

It would have been so easy to give himself over to the sensations of the moment.

But this was the most photographed woman in Europe. He couldn't do it. Her life was played out on too big a stage. And in the full glare of publicity.

She would want a life he couldn't give her.

Her hair smelt sweet and brushed against his cheek and he allowed himself to bury his face in it. He wanted to remember. His whole body responded to her scent and he felt her breath catch.

'Isabella.' *Oh, God. Isabella.* He wanted everything to be different.

She raised eyes that tempted. Her breath brushed across his lips. She was so close. Very close. If he dipped his head he could kiss her again.

Warmth seeped into the hand resting low on her spine and sensations flowed down the one holding her hand. He'd not danced for years but it seemed it was something one didn't forget. Domenic's hand tightened its grip on hers.

Isabella looked up and smiled and the last fingernail he had on restraint crumbled. He loved her and he was powerless to resist her. The truth of that flowed through him as though it were part of the almost Middle-Eastern-sounding folk music they were moving to.

Tomorrow he *would* leave. He would suffer every time he saw her picture, every time he read her name…

But tonight he would hold her.

She curved into him as though she'd been designed to fit there. Her hair brushed softly against his cheek. And she smelt as he imagined heaven would.

Then she raised her face towards his. Her eyes rested on his lips but she didn't move any closer. Just waited—knowing that the movement towards her had to come from him.

And, *dear God,* he wanted to.

He wasn't aware of closing the distance between them, only of knowing that he had. His mouth fastened on hers and he felt the tremble that ran through her body. That first kiss was questioning, almost as though he were testing himself to see whether he could resist her.

But one touch and he was lost. He heard the small guttural sound in the base of his throat and his whole body surged with power. It was primeval. Conquering.

His woman. *His.*

It was like a shot of pure heroin. He wanted more. He wanted her closer.

Years of rigid control, of complete numbness, were gone in a moment. He wanted her more than he'd wanted anything in his entire life. It was all the more urgent because he knew that he couldn't slide his hand under the fine spaghetti straps of her dress. He couldn't lower his head to take her nipple in his mouth…

*Dear God…* He'd not prayed to anything since the fire, but he was praying now. He wasn't sure what for. Whether it was strength to resist or strength to grasp what she was offering. He simply didn't know.

But he knew, with absolute certainty, she'd no intention of stopping him from doing anything he wanted. Isabella had walked into this room with the express purpose of offering herself as a gift.

It didn't matter that the doors to the secluded swimming pool were open and that a stray reveller might conceivably come that way. It didn't matter that there was the distant sound of conversation and laughter...

In fact, that only made this feel more raw. More essential.

Her hands moved to cradle his face, her fingers splayed out against the scarring on his face. 'Please don't say you shouldn't be doing this.' She breathed the words against his lips. And then she kissed him.

# CHAPTER TEN

ISABELLA could feel Domenic's indecision. Then she felt the tremor that ran through his body and she deepened her kiss. It was a moment before his arms tightened convulsively round her.

His tongue wound round hers, teasing and coaxing at the same time. He couldn't leave her tomorrow. She wouldn't let him.

She wanted him to be a part of her life. She needed him to talk to her, to make the huge changes being imposed on her life seem unimportant and petty beside what she was feeling for him.

She wanted him. Wanted this.

It was like a sudden surge of power to know that she wanted him in her life more than she wanted anything else. If he wanted her to leave Niroli she could do it…for him. And she'd do it without any sense of regret…because she'd know that what she was walking towards was better, more exciting, than what she was leaving behind.

But she could only do that if he wanted her, too.

Her hands snaked up to bury themselves in his thick brown hair. Holding him close. Then closer still.

She knew the minute he took a mental step back from her.

'You're being searched for.' His voice was strained, his breath coming unevenly.

Then she heard someone in the distance calling her name. She raised a shaking hand up to her bruised lips.

The voice called again. 'Your Highness? Princess Isabella?'

'That's Angelo. He's Tomasso's deputy,' she whispered, her eyes not leaving Domenic's face. 'They consider this a high-risk situation and Tomasso mobilised the entire team.'

'You probably shouldn't have come.' His hand brushed her cheek, inexpressibly tender.

'Princess Isabella?'

There was going to be no escape—and they both knew it.

Domenic's smile twisted and his eyes glinted down at her. 'You have more in common with Luca than they thought.'

She found her mouth curved into an answering smile, even though she wished Angelo a million miles away. 'If I were like Luca I wouldn't have been found. He has a gift for disappearing.' Then she turned her head and called out. 'I'm here.'

Her bodyguard came into view and stood in sight of the open doors. He looked flushed and a deep frown cracked across his forehead.

'I'm sorry to have worried you,' Isabella said quickly, walking towards him. 'I should have told you where I was going.'

She looked behind her to where Domenic was still standing. His evening jacket was open, his dress shirt open at the neck, his scars clearly visible…and he was the sexiest man she'd ever seen.

He was the only man she'd ever want. Could ever want. Because she loved him. *Loved him.*

Somehow she'd fallen in love with Domenic Vincini. And her happiness depended on his loving her back. Her grand gesture was no longer about being given the opportunity to explore a mutual attraction. It was about spending a lifetime together. Sharing a future.

*And it probably always had been.* Nothing was ever going to matter as much as the next few minutes.

Isabella swallowed painfully, acutely conscious of Angelo standing within hearing distance. His face might be turned away and his expression impassive, but that didn't mean he wasn't listening.

She moistened her lips and tried to steady her breathing. 'Come out to the party,' she said huskily. 'I want you with me.'

'I'm better here.'

Domenic was distancing himself again as surely as if he'd turned and walked away. He was looking at her as he might a pleasant memory and she wanted to scream at him, make him understand it didn't have to be like this.

Behind her she could hear Angelo reporting that he'd found her. 'Would it really matter if they took your photograph?' she said, softly.

His hand reached out to hold hers and he moved his thumb across her palm. 'I would hate it.'

'Dom—'

'You go.'

Domenic let go of her hand and Isabella wasn't left with much alternative but to do as he said. She smiled for Angelo's benefit, but inside the cold knot of fear she'd arrived with had returned.

She didn't know how to fight Domenic's resistance. Instinct told her she was going to have to break it down piece by piece.

Isabella stepped outside and walked past the oversized lanterns by the edge of the pool. She didn't look back but she was aware that Domenic watched her go. All the way. And she had no idea whether he would follow her.

Angelo fell into step beside her, saying nothing.

She glanced up. 'I'm sorry.'

'We were worried.' It was as close to a rebuke as he would dare.

'I know.' Isabella lifted the front of her skirts to negotiate the steps that twisted down to the large white marquee. Small white lights had been looped across the vast tented ceiling and beyond it she could see the sea, a warm rosy moon reflected in the water. It was so beautiful her heart ached.

Everywhere there seemed to be people. And noise. The moment she appeared the general hum rose a notch and Angelo remained solidly by her side, ready to protect her if the need arose.

She refused to look back towards the villa. She'd needed him to care about her enough to ignore the hurtful comments and come with her. *She needed him to love her.*

'Did you find him?' Silvana asked, coming to stand beside her. 'I wish he'd—' She broke off as her attention was caught by Domenic appearing at the top of the steps.

Isabella followed the line of her vision and her heart stopped beating.

Both women watched as Alberto insistently called him across to join the group of men he was talking with. Domenic's eyes met hers and a frisson of awareness tingled across the space between them.

'I don't know what you said but I'm glad it worked,' Silvana said quietly. 'Sometimes I think we should have been harder on him when he first came out of hospital. Made him face people and the crass comments.'

The tiny brunette looked up as the noise of a helicopter drowned out the sound of the orchestra. 'I think that's someone trying to get pictures of the party. That's the second time it's been over in as many minutes.'

'Your Highness?' Tomasso moved swiftly alongside her. 'Perhaps you might like to move out of range?'

Isabella obediently turned towards the lighted marquee. A huge buffet table groaned under goat's cheese, Arab inspired flat breads, roasted peppers shining with olive oil, salami and rice timbales. Marzipan had been carefully fashioned into the shape of strawberries, figs and prickly pears.

'Is it after you?' Domenic asked, coming across the marquee towards her. His eyes looked back to where the helicopter was still circling overhead.

'Probably.' Her chest felt tight and her voice sounded a little breathless. 'If I keep out of sight maybe it'll go away.'

The eyes that met hers were smoky. What she wanted to do was touch him, dance with him, but already she was aware of eyes turning to look at them.

And he'd told her he wasn't ready for that.

Domenic's hand moved to hold his neck, apparently conscious of their stares.

The helicopter circled overhead and the sound of the blades drowned out the orchestra. 'I think I should go. My being here is beginning to cause a problem. W-will we get a chance to talk back at the palazzo, do you think?'

She could see his throat work painfully. 'Isabella...' He broke off and tried again. 'What would we say?'

'We could—'

'What?' His voice rose and she saw the conscious effort

he made to lower it. 'Arrange to meet in Rome? Or do you think I could visit you on Niroli?'

Tears stung the back of her eyes.

'This isn't going to happen.'

Isabella bit down hard on her bottom lip. *Finally,* she'd fallen in love. She'd met the man she wanted to spend the rest of her life with…and she was fairly sure he was in love with her.

But that wasn't enough. Domenic wouldn't let her into his life. And tomorrow he'd be gone.

The helicopter turned and made another circuit. Everyone had stopped what they were doing to look. Isabella blinked hard, fighting back the tears.

'Are you wanting to leave, Your Highness?' Tomasso asked, coming to stand beside her.

This scenario wasn't new. Many, many times she'd been covertly led away from intrusive reporters but she'd never found leaving anywhere so difficult. 'I think so.'

'Very good, Your Highness.' She was aware of his quietly voiced instructions to a colleague. Her car would be brought up to the villa. In minutes she'd be speeding away…

'Silvana is staying on Mont Avellana until you leave.'

Domenic's eyes seemed to hold hers and her throat felt dry and ripped raw.

'And I'll have my lawyers contact yours about moving forward with the resort.'

She nodded, knowing her voice wouldn't work. *This couldn't be it. It couldn't.*

'Your Highness…' Tomasso stepped in closer. 'Your car is ready.'

It was only a full decade of royal experience that meant she smiled as she walked away.

\* \* \*

Domenic turned his car into the long sweeping driveway of the palazzo, pleased to see every window was in darkness. He'd half expected Isabella would be waiting for him.

At least, he *should* have been pleased to see it was in darkness. It was what he'd told her he wanted.

And there was nothing to be gained from a long and painful goodbye. Nothing that needed explaining.

The tyres made a satisfying crunch on the gravel as he pulled the Ferrari to a stop outside the central main doors. Normally he would take it round the back to the garages, but tonight he felt too weary.

*Or too heartsore?*

He'd allow himself a short sleep and then he'd leave for Rome. He might even be gone before Isabella was awake. It would be best if he was gone before she was awake. He glanced up at the window of her bedroom. Heavy lace panels billowed out of the open doors leading onto her balcony.

Domenic gripped his car keys so tightly they left marks on the palm of his hand. He pushed open the heavy doorway and walked into the darkened entrance hall. A sudden flash of white had him looking upwards.

And he knew what he would see. *Who.*

Isabella stood up from the stair she'd been sitting on. She'd changed into a simple white T-shirt and skirt and no longer seemed like a woman who graced red carpets across Europe. She looked approachable, fresh and beautiful.

*His.*

Against the ornate backdrop of the dramatic central staircase she even looked a little out of place. Her hair hung loose and softly about her face. Her lips trembled.

He put a foot on the bottom stair. 'I thought you'd be asleep.'

'No.'

Happiness came crashing in around him and scared him with its power.

'Did Alberto enjoy the rest of his party?'

'He's still going.' Domenic climbed the rest of the stairs until he stood level. 'His particular friends won't leave until after breakfast.'

'Did the helicopter return?'

'No.' He pulled his hand across his neck. 'No, it didn't.'

She nodded. 'It followed my car back here, and then left. I-I hoped it wouldn't.' Her eyes hovered on his mouth and he felt as if a hand had reached inside him and squeezed his heart hard.

'He was glad you came.'

'I came for you.' Her words hit him with the force of a sledgehammer. Her brown eyes met his.

'Isa—'

She stopped him. 'Don't! Please don't tell me it's not a good idea.'

Domenic reached out a hand and flicked the nearby switch. Light flooded the upper landing and picked out the tiny crystal flecks in the stone staircase. 'Even though it isn't? This isn't some kind of a game. Take a good look at me, Isabella.'

Her eyes remained steadily on his face. 'I love you.'

'No! Really look at me.' His hand pulled open the neck of his white shirt. 'Look at it.'

'You're scarred,' she said quietly.

His let the fabric go and violently dragged the same hand through his hair.

'It doesn't make any difference. I still love you.'

Domenic pulled in a breath. 'You think you do, but you're living in some kind of fantasy.'

'I think you should have more faith in me,' she said on a spurt of anger. 'I know what I'm feeling.'

'This is madness!'

'Why?'

'You want me to list the reasons? Really? Do you really want me to do that?'

Isabella moved towards him for the first time, resting her hand on his arm. Even through his dinner jacket her hand seemed to touch his skin. 'There are solutions to all of them.'

He shook his head. 'Not this one,' he said, with a gesture at his face.

'I love you. I want to be with you.'

'You say that now, but sooner or later you'd leave me. You'd get tired of people whispering every time they saw us together. Tired of having to look at a face like this. I've had enough pain in my life. No more. I don't want any more.'

Isabella's chin came up and she met his eyes. 'So you've decided you have to leave me first? Is that it?'

'It's not like that—'

'It's exactly like that! *Damn it!* Aren't you stronger than that? Braver?' She drew a shaky breath and her hand reached up and touched the side of his face. Her palms were cool against his cheek. She stepped closer and stood on tiptoe. 'Who managed to convince you no one could love you?'

'I—'

'They lied, Domenic. I love you. *You.*'

Her hair brushed the underside of his jaw as she let her hands run down across his shoulders and slip inside his jacket. Slowly, deliberately, she took the weight of his dinner jacket and pushed it off his shoulders.

He felt a shudder pass through his body. It felt as if every negative comment he'd overheard was warring with what she was telling him. Was it a weakness in him to want to believe?

The bow tie he wore but hadn't tied followed his jacket. Then she reached up and kissed him. His lips seemed to have taken on a will of their own. 'Let it happen,' she murmured against his mouth. 'Just let it happen.'

He wanted to, with every fibre of his being.

His hands moved of their own volition, pulling her in hard against his arousal. 'This is madness.'

'Be mad.'

Domenic ran a finger along her collarbone and pressed a kiss against the pulse at the base of her neck. Her head fell back and he ran the tip of his tongue up the length of her neck.

Then he found her mouth. Warm and sensual. He'd kissed her before. Each time had been memorable but *this* time he knew it was the prelude to something more. This time it seemed to reach into his soul and draw it into her.

He heard the moan rip from her throat and he felt the answering surge of power within him. His hands buried themselves in the sweet smelling softness of her hair, while hers fisted in the fabric of his shirt.

Another moment more and he'd make love to her on the landing. Laughter bubbled up inside him and he pulled away. 'We—'

She placed a hand over his mouth. 'Don't speak.' Her eyes were gleaming. She took hold of his hand and led him towards her bedroom.

This *was* madness. He knew it as she shut the door behind them…but forgot it when her hands reached up to unbutton his shirt. Her fingers stroked down his ribs, pushing the cotton aside.

Her eyes locked with his as she slowly moved up to caress

the bare skin of his shoulders. One side smooth, the other puckered and twisted. He tensed and she stood up on tiptoe to kiss his mouth while her fingers smoothed out the tension.

'Trust me.'

And, unbelievably, he did. Slowly she eased the cotton over his shoulders and let her fingers trail down his arms.

'I've never seduced a man before.' Her fingers moved to link with his. 'I'm not sure I know how to do it.'

He stared into her eyes for a moment and then moved. Her lips were warm and trembling as he kissed her. He could feel her nervousness and it made him love her more. He hadn't believed that was possible either.

'Am I doing it right?' she whispered against his lips.

'I'd say you had it about perfect.' He inhaled deeply and moved her hands to rest on his chest. Her fingers splayed out and then she let them slide down the narrow line of hair that ran down the hard plane of his stomach.

The muscles of his stomach quivered and he kissed her again. His own hands ran down her arms and reached for the bottom of her T-shirt. For a moment he hesitated. Her eyes met his and then she stepped back and raised her arms.

Domenic pulled her top over her head and his eyes fell on the deep pink of her nipples pushing up hard against the white transparent material of her bra. He let the T-shirt fall onto the floor and moved his thumb to brush against the tip.

Her white teeth bit down on her bottom lip and she shivered. 'Are you sure you want this?' *Want me,* he added silently.

Her answer was to reach in front and unclip the central fastening of her bra. It fell open and his hands smoothed it away.

Dark nipples against pale skin. Round, full breasts. He

watched amazed as she moved closer so they brushed against the darker skin of his chest. She looped one finger into the top of his trousers and pulled him towards her. 'Take me to bed.'

## CHAPTER ELEVEN

ISABELLA woke quite suddenly and knew she was alone in the bed. She rolled over, taking the sheet with her. Domenic was standing by the doors to the balcony, lost in thought, and he'd been up long enough to have pulled on his trousers.

All her euphoric certainty of the night before evaporated. 'Have you been awake long?'

'I haven't slept,' he said without turning round.

Isabella sat up and pushed her hair back from her face. They'd made love—but it changed *nothing*. 'Domenic?'

'Go back to sleep.'

She flicked her long legs out of bed and padded across to him, wrapping the sheet around her as she went. Then she laid her cheek against his bare back and put her arms around him. 'You're still going, aren't you?'

He nodded and she felt a huge sob well up inside her. 'Why?'

He turned and pulled her up close against him, rubbing his face against the top of her head. 'I think you know that—'

'I could go with you.'

'Not without bringing the world's press with you. A-and I can't live like that.' Domenic dragged a breath in and let his hands rest on her shoulders. His fingers were warm on her skin and then he let the palms of his hands slide down her arms. 'We need to talk.'

They had to be the most frightening words in the universe. They didn't need to talk. They needed to kiss and to hold each other...

Isabella let him lead her back towards the bed. Why was he doing this? He loved her. She knew it. He might not have said the words, but she'd seen it in his eyes, felt it.

His hand stretched out to cup her face and he drew her in for a kiss. It was soft, healing...but far too brief. Domenic pulled back and looked into her eyes. 'Should we have taken precautions?'

Her mind took a moment to shift into gear. Precautions? She didn't know what he was talking about. And then she understood. A baby. He was asking whether they might have made a baby together.

And she felt numb. 'No. At least, yes.' Isabella pulled a hand through her tangled curls. 'I suppose it's possible...but, no. I don't think so. It's not the right time of the month.'

And the dreadful truth was she wouldn't care if she was pregnant with his baby. Particularly if it kept him with her. Was that wicked? To wish she had a way of tying him to her?

'I didn't think. I'm sorry...'

Isabella looked down to where he'd laid his hand over hers. Long, beautiful fingers stretched out on hers. He moved his thumb in an agonising sweep across the back of her hand.

'We didn't plan on last night.' She swallowed, trying to force down the hard ball of unshed tears that were wedged at the base of her throat. 'It just happened. We were—'

His thumb moved again. 'I should have thought about it, but Jolanda was the only woman I've ever made love to.'

*Until last night.* Isabella looked up. She hadn't expected

that and yet, the more she thought about it, the more she thought she should have done.

'I've never had a lifestyle where I've needed to carry condoms in my top pocket. I'm sorry.'

'You wouldn't be here if I thought you were.' Her voice cracked. 'W-was it difficult? To be with me, I mean?'

'No. No.' His hand moved swiftly to hold her face, his thumb brushed the sensitive skin beneath her right eye. 'But I should have thought about the possibility of making you pregnant.'

'You won't have.'

The thought of having his baby made her melt. Why couldn't he smile at her and tell her it wouldn't matter? Why couldn't he say he loved her and wanted to build a family with her?

'I can't believe I've been so thoughtless.' Domenic turned away and walked restlessly back towards the French doors.

She sat further back on the bed and covered her body with the sheet and watched him. This felt a little like dying inside. It was crueller, harder, because she'd allowed herself to hope.

'When are you going?' Her voice was hollow, completely toneless.

'Today. Now.'

Pain licked through her.

'I think it's best.'

'For who exactly?' The question burst like the cork from shaken lemonade. 'It's not best for me.'

His eyes settled on her face. Then he sat down on the edge of the bed. 'Do you want children?'

'Yes.' Isabella gasped in air. 'One day. Not straight away necessarily but, yes, I'd like children.' His children. She desperately wanted to have his children.

'I don't.' He pulled a shaky hand through his hair. Then

his eyes searched hers for understanding. 'I don't ever want children. I couldn't…do that. Not again.'

The words seemed to back up in his throat so he couldn't get them out. Isabella sat forward. 'I know it would be difficult—'

'No, you don't know!' There was shocked silence as his voice echoed around the room. 'I'm sorry. But you don't know. You couldn't.' His hand balled into a fist as he punched his frustration. 'Every morning I wake up and I feel sick inside because I couldn't save them. It's a living nightmare. And it keeps going on and on. Day after day.

'I keep breathing in and out, pushing myself to keep on going, because I don't have an alternative. But don't think I haven't thought about it. I've thought about it.

'In the early days I even tried drinking myself into oblivion. It feels like I'm being dissected piece by piece. I'm not…*able*…' he pulled the word out with immense difficulty '…to do everything again.'

'It would be different—'

'You belong with someone who isn't…*tortured* by memories they can't control.'

'I could help and we could take things slowly. We—'

'I don't want to love you.'

Isabella felt the effect of that like a gunshot. He didn't want to love her. Didn't *want* to. She looked up, her eyes stinging.

'You're right. This is about being brave enough. *Strong* enough. And I'm not strong enough to live with the risk of losing you.' His teeth clenched together and a pulse flickered in his cheek. 'I can't have children with you and watch them grow and think about the one I couldn't save. I can't do that.'

'It wasn't your fault.'

His eyes were shining and then one tear welled up and rolled slowly down his cheek in one glistening trail. Isabella felt a searing pain as she watched, powerless to do anything to help him. *Powerless to change it.*

'I don't want to love anyone or anything so much that I can't face losing them. I…' His voice cracked and he raised a hand to cover his eyes.

Isabella moved on pure instinct. She pushed the sheet aside and went to him. Her arms went round him and she cradled him into her, her cheek resting against the scarred tissue of his shoulder.

She knew something about pain. The loss of her parents had been sudden, dramatic and disorientating. She knew what it felt like to wake and be flooded by fresh grief.

Her arms tightened about him. Then she pressed small kisses against his chest. She heard him groan and his hands tangle in her long curls. He tipped her face up and he kissed her.

Isabella made an incoherent little sound as his fingers skimmed her bare back, gossamer light. She wasn't sure what she was thinking, or even if she was thinking at all.

Isabella arched against him and his mouth firmed over hers. Her lips parted involuntarily at the pressure of his mouth and his tongue was ruthless.

*This felt desperate.*

He might not want to love her but he couldn't resist her. If she just had a little more time. Time to convince him it was already too late to decide he didn't love her. Didn't *want* to.

He pulled back like a man drowning and she'd never seen him look so bleak. Often, in repose, his face fell into lines of sadness, but this was something more.

Her hand went out. 'Domenic—'

'If I kiss you any more I'll make love to you again,' he said, catching her hand and holding it.

'Would that be so bad?'

'And you could have my baby in nine months. This is already complicated enough. I need to go.'

Isabella felt an unbelievable sense of desperation. Her fingers convulsively closed round his. 'Not yet. Don't leave me yet.'

She could feel the tension in his hand. The war that was going on between what he wanted and what he felt was right. 'You could just hold me—'

Domenic shook his head. 'If I did that I'd kiss you and when I kiss you I want to make love to you.'

'I want you to. I won't get pregnant.' Tears ran silently down her face. 'I won't.'

'You can't know that. Not for sure.' The muscle pulsed in the side of his jaw. 'Isabella, I can't be what you want. And I need to go while I still can.'

Inside she felt raw, as though she'd been flayed until she had no skin left. 'Spend the day with me.' Her voice was as broken as she felt. 'Just one more day.'

The grip of his fingers on her shoulders tightened and words tumbled out of her mouth. 'Don't leave me like this. We could spend it here in the grounds of the palazzo. No one would see us. One more day before we let the world back in.'

The muscle pulsed in the side of his cheek. 'I need to go.' He stood up and let his hand slide from hers.

Isabella watched as he picked up his shirt and walked out of the room. For a moment she felt nothing—and then the pain splintered through her like shrapnel.

Domenic pulled his hand over his face and walked over to the water cooler. Isabella's letter sat on the desk unopened.

Missing her felt like a physical ache. It was a constant, gnawing pain. He took the cup back to his desk and sat looking at the cardboard backed envelope.

He knew what was in it. Photographs of the morning they'd spent at Poseidon's Grotto. Could he bear to see them? To remember?

Could he bear not to?

His fingers ripped open the top and a sheaf of glossy prints fell out onto his black desk. Beautiful, *beautiful* pictures.

There were the steps down the limestone cliff. The view out across to the Spanish watchtower. A seabird soaring high in a bright blue sky. He really ought to pass them on to someone who could contact her about using these images. Certainly if they decided to build the grotto up into a tourist attraction…

Isabella had a real talent. He'd been there and had seen the views she'd taken, but he hadn't seen it with her eye for detail. He hadn't noticed the shadow cast by the juniper plant. The changes of colour across the limestone cliff.

He wished he could tell her.

Then he came to the last in the sheaf and he stopped breathing. A photograph he hadn't known she'd taken. One he'd forbidden. His hand splayed out on top of it because it was almost too painful to look at.

Isabella had taken a picture of him. He was concentrating on unpacking their picnic, unconscious of the camera. And she'd spared him nothing. He could see the twisted skin of his neck, the slashes across his face. And yet it was a picture taken with love.

Every image she captured seemed to ring with truth and passion. It started when she made a decision to take a picture.

Understanding hit him like a sledgehammer. *He was such an idiot.*

He'd thrown away the chance of unconditional acceptance because he was too afraid of rejection. She'd seen him, *really seen him,* and she still loved him.

Loved him enough to push aside centuries of resentment between their islands. Loved him enough to face the criticism of her family. Loved him despite the superficial scars on his face and the deeper trauma that had forged his personality.

She had told him. 'I love *you*'. And on some level he'd heard the stress she'd placed on the word 'you'.

Domenic turned the photograph over and saw the three words she'd written on the back. 'I miss you.'

Isabella stepped out of the car into the flash of cameras. For the past ten days the attention on her had been constant. Exhausting. News that she'd clinched the biggest deal in Niroli's history had spread like ink through water.

Her success had even gone some way to pacifying her grandfather. He'd been inclined to think her contact with the Vincini family had been a necessary evil.

She stopped while a young girl nervously presented her with a bouquet of yellow roses and forced herself to smile. It was important to her that her grief remained private. But she longed to move away from Niroli and find some anonymity.

It was funny that, having achieved what she'd thought would enable her to stay on the island, she'd no desire to do so. The truth was she wanted to be where Domenic was.

But more than that. She wanted a quieter life. Her time on Mont Avellana had taught her so many things about herself. Now her 'duty' to Niroli didn't require her to travel so many air miles she'd prefer not to.

She wanted to pursue her photography and take it to a new level of creativity. She wanted to allow more time and space for friends.

And it was possible. For the first time in a decade, it *was* a viable choice. All this was Nico's responsibility now. He could promote Niroli's film industry. He could shake the hands of the producer, director, director's wife...

Isabella moved on down the line while the cameras flashed all around her. She responded appropriately to Signore Lanza's comments about not forgetting his cinematic roots now he'd moved from smaller art-house movies to big-budget films. And she stopped to allow the gathered photographers to capture her image alongside the 'A'-list actor who played the central character.

As she was about to move inside the carefully restored art deco building she looked back at the lines of people banked up either side of a sweeping red carpet. She lifted her hand to give a final wave...

And then she saw him. Domenic. Darkly handsome in black dinner jacket, his shirt open at the neck, his hands thrust deep in his dinner jacket.

His eyes looking directly at her.

For a few seconds nothing made sense. There was a part of her that wondered whether she might have conjured him up because she wanted him with her so badly.

Around her the crowds disappeared into a blur of indistinct colour. He was here. *Domenic was here on Niroli.*

'Your Highness.' Tomasso was urging her inside but she felt her feet moving the other way.

'Excuse me,' she murmured, walking back down the broad steps. 'I'm so sorry, excuse me.'

Domenic was held back from her by a low-slung red rope. Police and security guards lined the sides and banks of reporters were clustered to her left. In some strange way she was aware of it all but she kept looking at Domenic's face, trying to read the expression in his eyes.

Why was he here? Had he changed his mind? Was he here for her?

She stopped a few feet away from him.

His smile twisted into a kind of wry apology. His eyes were holding hers. 'I thought it was time I was…braver.'

'Past time.'

'Am I too late?'

Isabella shook her head as a tremulous happiness quivered inside her. 'No.'

Lights flashed all around them but Domenic was unflinching. With a glance across at one of the security guards he climbed over the low roping. 'I got your message. I miss you, too.'

There was a sudden cheer and excited whispering as people in the crowd caught a glimpse of what was happening. Isabella felt a bubble of laughter. 'What are you doing?'

'Doing what I should have done at my father's party.' He stopped in front of her. 'I love you.'

Isabella couldn't breathe. She couldn't quite believe he was here…or what he was saying. Most of all she couldn't believe what he was saying.

'I love you more than I fear this.'

She gave a sudden laugh and reached for his hand. The crowd went berserk. Reporters pressed forward and Tomasso gestured security guards to create a ring around them. 'Your Highness,' he prompted. 'We need to move inside.'

Isabella kept her eyes on Domenic. 'You know they'll be able to lip-read everything you've said.'

He smiled and her stomach flipped over.

'Your Highness. Please.' Tomasso became more insistent.

Laughter spilled over. She'd never felt happiness like this.

'Princess Isabella!'

She turned to look at Tomasso and then back at Domenic.

Her fingers felt small and safe within his hand. 'Shall we go inside?'

His eyes flicked down to their joined hands. 'I'll go anywhere you go.'

It was a promise. All the way back up the red carpet she didn't take her eyes off him. It was too incredible he was here with her. There were shouts and cheers. People calling her name and asking her his.

Tomasso cleared the path before them and led them into a small office immediately off the grand entrance. As the door shut behind them Isabella suddenly felt shy. She looked down at his shiny black shoes.

'I wasn't sure you'd forgive me for being such a fool,' he said quietly.

Isabella reached up and touched the scars on his face. 'I thought this was your worst nightmare?'

'So did I. But then I discovered losing you was a worse one.'

She let her thumb brush against his bottom lip. He took it into his mouth and nibbled against it. Isabella gave a sob of sheer happiness and his arms closed about her. 'I love you. I love—'

And then he was kissing her as though she was the most precious thing in his world. 'Marry me?' he said, pulling away. 'Be my wife? Have children with me?'

'Children?' Her hand splayed out on his chest.

His eyes were warm and his touch gentle as they brushed away the single tear that tipped over onto her cheek. 'Sometime. When you're ready.'

'I'm ready,' she said on a husky whisper. 'But you—'

'Nearly lost the best thing that had ever happened to me. Silvana said that.'

'She did?'

He nodded. 'At my father's party.'

There was a sharp knock at the door. 'Princess Isabella?'

She brushed her fingers beneath her eyes. 'They want to start the movie. Is my make-up all right?'

'You're beautiful,' he said, hanging back.

Her hand came back to rest in his. 'Come with me.'

'I don't have a seat.'

Isabella felt her laughter bubble over. 'They'll find you one. It's the only advantage I know in being in a relationship with a princess.'

'There are others.' His hands spanned her waist and turned her. 'Are you going to marry me?'

'Oh, yes.'

His eyes moved over her face. 'Even if you have to leave Niroli?'

'Even then.' She reached up to kiss him. 'Yes, please.'

# EPILOGUE

Away from the streetlights the night sky was a million dots of light. Isabella felt small, insignificant…and perfectly happy.

She turned her head as she heard Domenic walk up behind her. He pulled her against his body and she felt his arousal hard against the small of her back. Then he bent his head and placed a kiss at the base of her neck.

'Tired?'

Isabella turned within his arms. 'Not really.' Her smile was deliberately teasing and she watched the laughter glint deep in his brown eyes. She reached up a hand and smoothed back the hair from his forehead, then let it run down the side of his face.

He caught it, and held it against his chest. 'You have to know…'

Beneath her fingers she could feel the steady beat of his heart.

'I want you to know that I've never done anything in my entire life I've been more sure of.'

Isabella understood what he was trying to tell her. There had been moments during their simple church wedding and at the family gathering at Silvana's villa when she'd wondered how much of his mind was on Jolanda. And little Felice.

'Jolanda helped make you the man I love.'

His fingers tightened around hers. 'I was happy then. I'm happy now.' His eyes moved to her lips. 'And I didn't think I'd ever be happy again.'

She'd thought she didn't feel any kind of fear at being the second wife of a man who had so deeply loved his first one, but in that moment she realised Domenic had been wiser than her. Seen more.

He placed a kiss against her lips and pulled back to murmur, 'I love you. With everything that I am and everything that I have.'

And when he kissed her again she felt a new warmth spread through her body. A feeling of total acceptance. Of simply being right for him because of who she was.

His hands moved against the fine silk of her wedding dress and spread out across her buttocks, pulling her in closer still. She threw back her head and laughed, giving him access to the long column of her throat.

She breathed his name as he kissed down her neck and sought out the pulse at its base. 'I love you, too.' Her eyes sought his. 'With everything that I am and everything that I have.'

He smiled at the echo of his words and then he found her hand to lead her back towards the villa. 'Are you sorry we chose to come here?'

'To our own private island?' Isabella moved in closer and placed an arm about his waist, loving the feeling of his body so close to hers and the warm sand beneath her bare feet. 'Whatever we decide to do and develop, we must always keep Teulada for ourselves. Our own little bit of paradise.'

His fingers moved in her curls. He led her up onto the wide raised decking and pulled her down onto a pile of cushions. Far out across the dark sea were the lights of Niroli, clearly visible now they were out beyond the jutting limestone cliffs of Mont Avellana.

It looked beautiful. Romantic. But Isabella knew there was nowhere else she'd rather be.

Domenic kept his eyes on her profile. 'I wish your family could have been there for you today.'

'Yours were.'

'But your brother. Sister.'

Isabella shook her head. 'Marco's Emily is pregnant and doesn't want to fly. And I don't want to make Rosa's life difficult. I know she loves me. That's enough.'

'And King Giorgio? Niroli?'

She turned to look at him. 'I'd give up more than that to be with you.'

'I wish you hadn't had to.'

Isabella pulled herself up on the cushions and moved into his arms. 'It won't be for ever. When Nico arrives everything will change again. Once Grandfather is happy that Niroli will be in safe hands after he's gone he'll lose much of his anger.'

Domenic pressed a kiss on the top of her head. She looked up at him and smiled. Her eyes took on a teasing glint. 'Now stop talking…and kiss me.'

She watched his eyes darken and her stomach tightened in anticipation as he bent his head to do just that.

\* \* \* \* \*

TURN THE PAGE TO DISCOVER
MORE ABOUT

THE

*Royal*

HOUSE OF NIROLI

## THE RULES OF THE ROYAL HOUSE OF NIROLI

**Rule 1:** The ruler of Niroli must be a moral leader for the people and is bound to keep order in the Royal House. Any act which brings the monarchy into disrepute through immoral conduct or criminal activity will rule a contender out of the succession to the throne.

**Rule 2:** No member of the Royal House may be joined in marriage without previous consent and approval of the ruler. Any marriage concluded against this rule implies exclusion from the house, deprivation of honours and privileges.

**Rule 3:** No marriage is permitted if the interests of Niroli become compromised through the union.

**Rule 4:** It is not permitted for the ruler of Niroli to marry a person who has previously been divorced.

**Rule 5:** The ruler forbids marriage between members of the Royal House who are blood relations.

**Rule 6:** The ruler directs the education of all the members of the Royal House, even when the general care of the education of children belongs to their parents.

**Rule 7:** Without the approval or consent of the ruler, no member of the Royal House can make debts over the possibility of payment.

**Rule 8:** No member of the Royal House can accept inheritance nor any donation without the consent and approval of the ruler.

**Rule 9:** The ruler of Niroli must dedicate their life to the Kingdom. Therefore they are not permitted to have a profession.

**Rule 10:** Members of the Royal House must reside in Niroli or in a country allowed by the ruler. The ruler can give permission for Royal House members to live elsewhere, but the ruler must reside in Niroli.

# THE ORIGINS OF THE RULES OF THE ROYAL HOUSE OF NIROLI

The Rules of Niroli have dictated the lives—and loves—of the Fierezza family for centuries. In a recent speech the ageing King heralded them as the backbone of the monarchy, provoking speculation that, as unrest begins to bubble away under the surface of the Nirolian people, the Royal House is pulling its traditions even closer. The Rules may be deemed old-fashioned, and even out of touch, but to this day they have never failed the turbulent Fierezza family! As a whole, the Rules are designed to provide unity and continuity for the island of Niroli. They ensure that the Royal Family conducts itself with dignity—to set an example for its subjects—and keep all the Fierezza firmly under the control of the monarch.

## The Rules

*Rule 1: The ruler must be a moral leader. Any act which brings the Royal House into disrepute will rule a contender out of the succession to the throne.*

Origin: King Alvaro II, who ruled for forty years in the sixteenth century, was a pious and devoted ruler. He added this rule, claiming that he believed that a King of Niroli could have no greater calling than to ensure that he provided a moral compass for the Royal Family and his subjects.

*Rule 2: No member of the Royal House may be joined in marriage without consent of the ruler. Any such union concluded results in exclusion and deprivation of honours and privileges.*

*Rule 3: No marriage is permitted if the interests of Niroli become compromised through the union.*

Origin: Both rule 2 and rule 3 come from the time that the Fierezza dynasty was first formed, when it was considered essential that the King maintained control over his family and who they married, so that any union would strengthen the illustrious House of Niroli.

*Rule 4: It is not permitted for the ruler of Niroli to marry a person who has previously been divorced.*

Origin: Another ruler, King Benedicio, who was concerned with the morals of the Royal House considered that it was vital that anybody marrying into it had a spotless reputation. Following Prince Francesco's attempt to marry a divorced European countess with a dubious past in 1793, King Benedicio deemed it necessary to add this rule.

*Rule 5: Marriage between members of the Royal House who are blood relations is forbidden.*

Origin: Many royal houses have suffered from inbreeding, as cousins, and even nieces and uncles, have married each other across the years. King Dominico I declared in 1752 that to keep the Fierezza bloodline strong and healthy, this practice would not be tolerated in the Royal House.

*Rule 6: The ruler directs the education of all members of the Royal House, even when the general care of the children belongs to their parents.*

Origin: In common with most of the ruling houses of Europe, it has always been considered vital that all members of the Fierezza dynasty are brought up with an education which prepares them for their role in the Royal House of Niroli.

*Rule 7: Without the approval or consent of the ruler, no member of the Royal House can make debts over the possibility of payment.*

Origin: A relatively recent addition to the rules, this was added in 1950, when Ricardo Fierezza, an inveterate gambler, found himself in huge financial difficulties after he banked on certain deals coming to fruition that subsequently failed. In order to avoid any more scandals of this nature, the Royal House decided that a rule governing the Fierezzas' financial conduct was in order.

*Rule 8: No member of the Royal House can accept inheritance nor any donation without the consent and approval of the ruler.*

Origin: In the early years of the Fierezzas' rule over Niroli, King Pietro faced a possible usurpation of his throne from his younger brother, Prince Guiseppe, following the latter's acceptance of a huge sum of money from the King of Aragon, Alfonso V. Alfonso wished to gain control of the increasingly wealthy island, already famed for its trading ports, and was prepared to pay Guiseppe to raise an army and buy the support of any dissident nobles. After his defeat, in 1427, Guiseppe was exiled and King Pietro added this rule to ensure that there could be no repeat of this kind of rebellion ever again.

*Rule 9: The ruler of Niroli must dedicate their life to the Kingdom. Therefore they are not permitted to have a profession.*

Origin: Another rule that is a relatively new addition. As the administrative machine has grown, the kings of Niroli have found themselves less burdened with the machinations of state. In 1897, King Adriano, a scholarly and shy ruler, consulted over the possibility that he would take up a teaching post. It was decided that the ruler of Niroli must be absolutely dedicated to the island and that involvement in other professions was undesirable and detrimental to the long-term survival of the monarchy.

*Rule 10: Members of the Royal House must reside in Niroli or in a country approved by the ruler. However, the ruler **must** reside in Niroli.*

Origin: As the Fierezzas' lifestyles became increasingly jet-set, this rule was added as a pre-emptive measure to ensure that the ruler of Niroli would always be able to control the whereabouts of his family. In addition, it was felt that it should be enshrined that the monarch, as part of his dedication to Niroli, must live on the island to provide a focus and a symbol of unity.

## A BRIEF HISTORY OF NIROLI

Niroli has a colourful and fascinating history filled with ancient rivalries, rebellions and the fight for the ultimate prize —the crown of Niroli.

The Fierezza family has ruled since the Middle Ages and is one of the richest royal families in the world, having founded its fortune on ancient trading routes, thanks to Niroli's prime position to the south of Sicily. Thanks to these links, it has traditionally been seen as the 'Gateway to the East'.

Since the establishment of the Fierezza dynasty, Niroli has thrived as an important European port, situated on major trading routes for spice, wine and perfume. However, while Niroli has prospered, it has a turbulent history right up to the modern day, and after a civil war in 1972 Niroli lost control of the neighbouring island Mont Avellana, which has become a republic. In addition to this, a group of bandits, known as the Viallis, who are ex-Barbary corsairs, formed a resistance against the monarchy. The height of their rebellious activity was in the 1970s and a few remaining Viallis still live in the foothills of the Niroli mountain range.

# NIROLI – A TOURIST'S GUIDE

## The Island of Niroli

With all it has to offer, who would not be tempted by a holiday on the beautiful island of Niroli? The climate is very agreeable, particularly to the south of the island. There are beautiful sandy beaches, especially around the new development area on the south coast which has been built to attract tourists. In this area you will find luxurious five-star hotels, casinos, restaurants, bars, etc., perfect for a relaxing and sophisticated holiday.

## Things to See

The island also has a rich and varied history—don't miss the chance to explore its wonderful Roman ruins. In the north east of the island, there is a Roman amphitheatre where concerts are still performed today, particularly during the festivals celebrating the grape- and olive-picking seasons. There are also many fine castles to explore. Visitors must see the stunning main town of Niroli. If you enter the port by boat it is particularly impressive, as you see the town sprawling up the hillside in front of you, with the historic old town to your left and the palace just in view. Do wander round the old town and soak up the atmosphere, as well as stopping at the numerous charming shops and exclusive boutiques.

## Things to Do

For those who are into more active pursuits, there are plenty of opportunities for diving and swimming, then afterwards relax in the wonderful spa and beauty treatment area on the east coast. To the west of the island you can walk and climb in the mountains and take in the stunning views across the Mediterranean. The central part of the island is devoted mainly to agriculture, with the vineyards extending to the rolling foothills of the mountains. There are also olive groves, orchards and livestock and Niroli is deservedly famous for its fine olive oil and wonderful wines.

# NIROLI – ISLAND PRODUCE

Niroli is a sun-drenched and idyllic Mediterranean isle. Thanks to the now-extinct volcanoes, Nirolians enjoy lush and fertile conditions in which to grow a wonderful range of produce, famed the world over, and Niroli is surrounded by an abundant and generous sea which provides wonderful local fare.

## Oranges

Niroli is famous for its orange groves of Cattina, which produce a particularly sweet-flavoured fruit. **Oil of Niroli** is extracted from the orange skins. Niroli has a floral, citrussy, sweet and exotic scent, which is used to make perfume, aromatherapy oil and health and beauty products; it has special healing, rejuvenating, soothing and restorative properties which make it especially popular for relaxation and anti-ageing treatments and scar reduction therapy at the Santa Fiera Spa, which has an international reputation for the excellence of its products.

## Olives

Green olive trees flourish on the rocky limestone soil in the fertile Cattina Valley.

The fruit is prized by cooks and the island exports olives whole, pitted, stuffed and marinated.

**Niroli Virgin Olive and Orange Oil** is a delicacy; infused with the zest of local oranges, it is particularly delicious when drizzled over fish, seafood, chicken, asparagus or pasta, and you can sample all of these dishes in Niroli's excellent array of restaurants.

### Grapes

The Niroli vines produce the queen of white grapes. Cultivated since Roman times on the slopes of the Cattina Valley, and ripened by summer sun and storms, these grapes are harvested to make **Porto Castellante Bianco**, a dry white wine with a crisp, citrussy bouquet, which makes an especially good accompaniment to fish dishes.

### Marine life

The seas around the island of Niroli are fertile fishing grounds, filled with bass, bream, tuna, red snapper, squid, shrimp and scallops. The fishing fleet goes out daily to catch the local sea's fine bounty. Natives and tourists alike savour these catches and the island's speciality dish of **Rainbow Mullet**, which is marinated in Niroli Virgin Olive and Orange Oil, then lightly grilled.

The Santa Fiera Spa also makes excellent use of an abundance of marine algae in its skin and beauty treatments.

### Volcanic Mud

The volcanoes on Niroli are now extinct, but the area around them is still a rich source of volcanic mud, which is a mixture of rainwater and volcanic ash formed at the time of eruption.

The Santa Fiera Spa specialises in volcanic mud baths and masks as health and beauty treatments, which are reported to rejuvenate and revitalise the skin, drawing women from across the globe keen to take advantage of its miraculous properties!

## CAROL MARINELLI

recently filled in a form where she was asked for her job title and was thrilled, after all these years, to be able to put down her answer as 'writer'.

Then it asked what Carol did for relaxation and, after chewing her pen for a moment, Carol put down the truth—'writing'. The third question asked, 'What are your hobbies?' Well, not wanting to look obsessed or, worse still, boring, she crossed the fingers on her free hand and answered 'swimming and tennis'. But, given that the chlorine in the pool does terrible things to her highlights, and the closest she's got to a tennis racket in the last couple of years is watching the Australian Open, I'm sure you can guess the real answer!

# CAROL MARINELLI
## QUESTIONS & ANSWERS

### Did you enjoy the experience of writing about Niroli?

I adored it. I had never written about royalty before and was a little bit nervous (read "terrified") but have been bitten by the bug now!

### Would you like to visit Niroli?

I just did. I can see Niroli as clearly as if I've been there on a recent holiday—I just don't have the endless souvenirs I usually collect. Also, on the plus side, I didn't have to shake the sand out of everything on my return.

### Which of the 'Rules of Niroli' would you least like to abide by?

Oh, dear—all of them—I have read and agonised over them and am putting up a shaky hand up to admit I'd be the last to abide by any of them.

### How did you find writing as part of continuity?

Fantastic! Writing is so lonely at times it's wonderful to have the excuse to chat, in depth, to other authors about my characters and how terribly my hero is behaving as I attempt to whip him into shape for my lovely heroine. It's a rare luxury.

### When you are writing, what is your typical day?

Er, I cannot lie—I don't do typical very well! My characters seem to live in my head and refuse to come out till they're ready and then they run like the little gingerbread man as I try to chase them and get the info down. That said, I am just coming up for air, after finishing a Medical™ romance, to the usual chaos and catch-up that occurs at the end of a book and I swear that once I've tidied my study, seen how much my children have grown, reacquainted myself with friends who think I've disappeared…I *am* going to get organised.

**Where do you get your inspiration for the characters that you write?**

Everywhere—my heroes and heroines are sort of mine and I grow them from scratch, but the sub-characters could be a lady at the coffee shop that makes me laugh or a posh guy at a restaurant frantically checking the bill to see if he's been diddled out of a few pence—I love watching people.

**What, in your opinion, makes a great Modern™ hero?**

Gorgeous men are everywhere (perk of the job—I'm *forced* to observe), but I honestly don't know what it is that flicks that switch and makes OK into yum! I just know him when I see him and I try to capture it in my book.

**Tell us about the project you're working on at the moment.**

I'm not—I'm cleaning out my study, remember. Saying that, it's a Modern™ and I've just been introduced to my hero and heroine. They popped in for a visit last night and I now have my opening scene: an international airport—he's Russian (double yum), she's pregnant and… Oooh, my study may have to wait!

# MORE ABOUT
# NATASHA OAKLEY

## NATASHA OAKLEY

told everyone at her primary school she wanted to be an author when she grew up. Her plan was to stay at home and have her mum bring her coffee at regular intervals —a drink she didn't like then. The coffee addiction became reality and the love of storytelling stayed with her. A professional actress, Natasha began writing when her fifth child started to sleep through the night. Born in London, she now lives in Bedfordshire with her husband and young family. When not writing, or needed for 'crowd control', she loves to escape to antiques fairs and auctions.

Find out more about Natasha and her books on her website natashaoakley.com

## NATASHA OAKLEY
## QUESTIONS & ANSWERS

### Did you enjoy the experience of writing about Niroli?

I hugely enjoyed the experience of writing my Niroli book. It felt rather like being given the pieces of a puzzle in a plastic bag and being asked to fit them together to make a complete picture. There were days when I found it extremely frustrating but, overall, it was very satisfying.

### Would you like to visit Niroli?

Of course—but I would time my visit to avoid the full heat of summer. My Celt skin is inclined to burn and I wilt in hot weather. Although I might rely on Domenic's air conditioning and arrive in time for the opera festival held each year in the Roman amphitheatre. I'd certainly take the boat across to Mont Avellana and visit Poseidon's Grotto. I'd also try Niroli's famed "Red Mullet" and wash it down with a glass or two of Porto Castellante Bianco.

### Which of the 'Rules of Niroli' would you least like to abide by?

Rule 10, I think.

*Members of the Royal House must reside in Niroli or in a country allowed by the ruler. The ruler can give permission for Royal House members to live elsewhere, but the ruler must reside in Niroli.*

It seems reasonable for the ruler to live

in Niroli—but why should they have jurisdiction over every other member of the family? I think I'd develop an overwhelming desire to go and live somewhere inappropriate!

**How did you find writing as part of a continuity?**

Coming from an acting background I love sparking ideas off other creative people. It's the one thing I really miss from my old life. Carol Marinelli, whose Luca I borrowed for my book, was truly delightful. I'm also comfortable with "direction" and working out a way to incorporate the given Niroli "facts" felt a lot like that.

**When you are writing, what is your typical day?**

My day starts at 6.00 in the morning and is a mad rush to get my five children off to school with the appropriate books/ lunches/homework/games' kits…

By the time I return home, just after 9.00, I feel like I've been through the mangle. I manage to answer my e-mails, check the Pink Heart Society blog, maybe post something on my personal blog or do a bit of research, before going for a sleep. Usually I wake up in time to do all the house jobs and still write for a couple of hours before I pick my youngest child up from school at 3.20pm.

Then it's manic—but what actually happens depends on the day of the week. Everything eventually calms down by about 10.00pm and that's when I start work. I'm an evening person and I like to write when the house is quiet. If I'm on "deadline" I'll work until the early hours…which means I'm not at all ready when 6.00am comes round again!

**Where do you find the inspiration that shapes your characters?**

I have absolutely no idea! I reckon it's magic—and it's probably best not to look too closely. I suspect it's a complete melting pot of people I've met, stories I've read, films I've seen, interviews I've heard…

**What, in your opinion, makes a great hero?**

Setting aside the superficial things—Hugh Jackman's body, Alan Rickman's voice, Rufus Sewell's eyes and Toby Stephens' hands—I'd say a great hero is someone who believes in you. A strong someone who'll be on your side whatever life throws at you.

It's also great if he can look at you in the morning, when you're still wearing make-up from the night before, and manage to convince you he still thinks you look beautiful.

**Tell us about the project you're working on at the moment.**

I'm writing Willow and Daniel's story. Daniel is a single dad who's struggling with his wayward daughter. I've made him an auctioneer, which is entirely self-indulgent because I love auctions. Willow is a bad-girl-come-good...and now she's come back to the English village she grew up in. It's about overcoming prejudice and discovering what's really important in life. At least, I think it is...

# THE OFFICIAL FIEREZZA FAMILY TREE

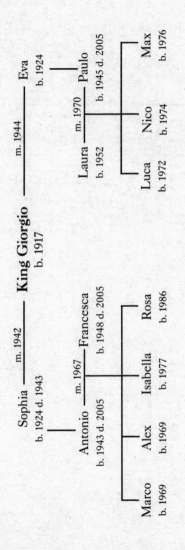

Sophia — m. 1942 — **King Giorgio** — m. 1944 — Eva
b. 1924 d. 1943     b. 1917     b. 1924

Antonio — m. 1967 — Francesca
b. 1943 d. 2005    b. 1948 d. 2005

Laura — m. 1970 — Paulo
b. 1952    b. 1945 d. 2005

Marco
b. 1969

Alex
b. 1969

Isabella
b. 1977

Rosa
b. 1986

Luca
b. 1972

Nico
b. 1974

Max
b. 1976

Turn the page for an exciting glimpse of

*Expecting His Royal Baby*
by
Susan Stephens

the first story in the addictive next volume in
the Royal House of Niroli collection

*The Royal House of Niroli:*
*Innocent Mistresses*

Available in March 2011
from Mills & Boon

# PROLOGUE

As HE WATCHED the tiny dot appear through the clouds the ambassador of Niroli's throat dried. What if this precious heir to the throne should perish? And with Nico Fierezza's addiction to extreme sports that seemed extremely likely; if not today, then some day soon. The ambassador's nerves refused to steady even when the dot turned into six feet four of solid muscle and Nico hit the ground on target. Only Nico didn't *hit* the ground, he landed like a cat.

As someone took away his parachute Nico lifted off his helmet and stared straight at the ambassador. He had detected the distinguished visitor in the same instant he had located the cross hairs on his jumping target and was relieved to see that duty rather than disaster had brought him to the field.

He maintained a distance between himself and the bickering and power play surrounding his grandfather, King Giorgio of Niroli. The Fierezza family had ruled Niroli since the Middle Ages, but Nico was a self-made man. Niroli, a tiny island set like a jewel in the Mediterranean, was prosperous and beautiful enough to attract the glitterati from every part of the world, which was enough in itself to keep him away. He had built up his own architectural practice in London free from royal privilege or favour and could state categorically that everything he owned he had earned.

He had been drunk on adrenalin when he'd landed, feeling invincible because he'd survived against the odds the highest jump without oxygen ever recorded, but calm reason had kicked in reminding him that, like any emotion, euphoria was a dangerous deception; it clouded the mind.

Tucking his helmet under his arm, he started forward with his usual purposeful stride. He couldn't account for the insatiable force driving him. He'd had a happy childhood, idyllic compared to most, with a mother who adored him and poured all her love into the family. Perhaps that was it, Nico thought, halting at a point where he and the ambassador could have some privacy, perhaps men like him came with an inborn gene that insisted they must break away from everything that was feminine and soft and loving and drive themselves to the limit just to know they were alive. His father had done this, taking his yacht to the limit of its capabilities, killing himself along with his brother and sister-in-law. It was a miracle his mother had survived and was a lesson he would never forget.

As the ambassador approached Nico ordered himself to go easy on the man, but there could be no compromise. He might be the grandson of the king, but he neither asked for nor expected any favours. 'Ambassador?' he said curtly as the portly man arrived.

'You recognised me…' The ambassador gave a nervous laugh.

'Of course.' Nico's voice was clipped and controlled. As always he was polite, toning down his need to know in deference to the other man's advanced age. 'My mother?'

'Is quite well, sir. Your grandfather too….'

Nico's brow furrowed. Why the hesitation? As if he

didn't know. 'His Majesty wishes to see me.' It was a state-ment rather than a question. Nico never wasted his breath on unnecessary questions.

'That is correct, sir.'

The ambassador was distracted briefly by the whoops of celebration from other skydivers in the competition. Nico's had been a landslide victory, but he remained un-moved, his thoughts hidden behind his slate-blue gaze.

As he stroked one hand across the sun-bleached hair he kept aggressively short, Nico had no idea how intimidating he appeared to the older man. Lean and tanned from work-ing outside in all weather, Nico Fierezza towered a good six inches over the ambassador. It didn't matter that an archi-tectural scheme had been conceived in the clinical sur-roundings of his high-tech office—Nico liked to see his cutting-edge designs up close. So while the ambassador's hands were soft and white, Nico's were weather-beaten and rough, and the ambassador hardly seemed to have a beard in contrast to Nico's black, piratical stubble. But the ambas-sador worked for a wily monarch and was used to handling every type of situation. He had recovered from his trot across the airfield and his shrewd grey eyes missed nothing. He rested super alert like a pulsing brain as Nico began to speak.

'Please tell His Majesty that I will attend him the mo-ment my business allows.'

As a cheer went up and calls rang out for Nico to join the other men on the podium he made a holding gesture with the flat of his hand.

The ambassador weighed the facts. Nico Fierezza was easily the best of all the men there. Surely, he must be feel-ing the same charge they did, the same adrenalin rush? And yet he appeared to be in no hurry to join the celebrations and there was no hint of self-congratulation in his expression. He'd heard this grandson to the king was a stranger to emotion, and it seemed the rumours were true. Nothing could have suited his purpose better. King Giorgio was eager to put an heir in place before his health deteriorated further, and this man had all the qualities they looked for in a monarch. He put duty first and chose to reveal nothing to the outside world. There wasn't a woman alive who could cause Nico Fierezza embarrassment. The ambassador maintained his impassive expression, but inwardly he was already celebrating.

'Please apologise to His Majesty,' Nico continued, 'and tell him that I will attend him in Niroli at the earliest opportunity.'

The ambassador dipped his head. Compromise was an easy thing with victory in sight. 'His Majesty will understand. He has empowered me to ask you to attend him at a time convenient to yourself.'

The hint of a smile fed into Nico's stern gaze. Since when had King Giorgio been any more accommodating than he was? His grandfather had to be desperate to see him if he was prepared to wait. 'It may be one week, or two,' he said, 'but no longer than that.'

'That's excellent news,' the ambassador said. 'I'm sure His Majesty will be delighted.' A flicker in Nico's eyes warned him not to overstate the case. 'Perhaps if we could settle on a date,' he added.

'I'll let you know.' Nico's voice had turned hard. His message was clear: one concession was enough for today. 'If you'll excuse me, Ambassador…'

As he strode away Nico didn't see the ambassador dip into the type of bow he normally reserved for the king.

# CHAPTER ONE

THERE WAS A single white rose on a coffin splattered with raindrops....

It made Carrie sad to see the tender bloom lying on the brass plate that spoke to a world that would never read it: the name of an aunt who had never loved her. But love could not be controlled at will, and Carrie had loved her aunt in spite of the woman's rejection of her. Sad as she was, Carrie was glad there were some things words could never destroy and that love was one of them.

'Carrie Evans?'

Carrie turned to find a man standing behind her. He was sheltering beneath the oily spread of a black umbrella, which made the shadows on his saturnine face all the deeper, adding to his air of gloom. There were only four people at her aunt's funeral other than herself—the minister and three undertakers—and it was hard to feel brave as the small group peeled away to allow her some privacy. Lifting up her chin, she gazed squarely into the face of the man. 'I'm Carrie Evans. Can I help you?'

'Sorry, miss… I tried the house.'

Carrie didn't know the man, but she could guess what he had come for. He was here to serve papers evicting her from her aunt's house on the instructions of relatives who hadn't been to visit Aunt Mabel in Carrie's living memory. A solicitor had rung her yesterday to explain.

*Yesterday, the day when everything in her life had changed for good....*

Carrie was twenty-five, but she looked much younger. Her complexion was pale and she dressed conservatively, keeping her luxuriant hair scraped back neatly in a practical twist. She found the lush tresses an embarrassment. Her natural hair colour was a rich golden red that painters called titian, and she believed it better suited to an actress or a glamour model. She had even thought about dying her hair a pale shade of brown, but the upkeep would have been too much on a secretary's salary. Her eyes were large and cornflower-blue and were perhaps her most expressive feature. Widely set and fringed with sable lashes, they were quick to darken with emotion, but could turn steely when there was something or someone to defend.

The man addressing Carrie saw a capable young woman, a little too plump to ever be called stylish, but determined, nonetheless, he concluded.

'I have already cleared my belongings from my late aunt's house,' she told him without rancour, 'and as soon as we're finished here I will collect my suitcase and deliver the house keys to my aunt's solicitor....'

She couldn't do any more, and he felt some sympathy for her. He'd heard she had nowhere to go since her aunt's heirs had turned up and laid claim to the house where she lived. 'You're so well organised,' he said, trying to soften the blow for her, 'I hardly need to give you this....'

'I think you do,' she told him.

Her tone was serious and exposed his attempt to console her for the sham it was. She held his gaze as she reached for the documents he was carrying and, as he handed over the eviction notice, he couldn't help thinking that, in spite of the downturn in her fortunes, the young woman in front of him possessed a quiet dignity that commanded his respect.

She had forgotten how cold and bare her attic room was. The eviction notice allowed her twenty-four hours to clear out her things. She neither wanted nor needed twenty-four hours. She missed her aunt, but she was pleased to be leaving such a sad and lonely place. Her aunt's house could so easily have been filled with love and laughter if only Aunt Mabel had been able to forget that Carrie's father had chosen Carrie's mother over herself.

But things could be worse. Carrie's mouth tipped down wryly as she totted up the facts. She was jobless, homeless, single and pregnant.

Carrie's wry smile turned into a smile of true happiness when she thought about her baby. The pregnancy was a source of great joy to her that nothing could dim. She was going to have someone to love; someone who would love her, someone she could care for and champion. The only problem was her baby's father. He would have to be told. He had a right to know, Carrie thought, even as her stomach clenched with apprehension.

Unfortunately, her baby's father was the hardest and most unfeeling man she had ever known. He was about as approachable as a tiger with a thorn in its pad. He was also the man she was in love with, the man she had loved since the first moment she had set eyes on him; the only man she could ever love… The same man who barely knew she was alive. And the longer she left it, the harder it would be to tell him that he was about to become a father.

Crossing her arms over her stomach in a protective gesture, Carrie determined she would not allow anything to stand in the way of her baby's future happiness, certainly not her own lack of nerve. She had to face up to him and she would. She didn't want anything for herself, but she did want recognition and security for her child. Her baby's father was a very wealthy man and she wondered if he could be persuaded to set up a trust fund to provide for college fees when the time came.

Before Carrie had learned she was pregnant she had dreamed of leaving the office where she had worked as a secretary to try and turn her hobby of painting into a profession, but that was out of the question now. She planned instead to find some cheap accommodation and work until the baby came. Her goal was to build up a small nest egg so that one day she could buy a modest property with a child-friendly garden. A solid base was important. She didn't want a child of hers to be pushed from pillar to post as she had been after her parents' tragic accident. She might be homeless today, but not for long.

Nico Fierezza. It was the only name the King of Niroli had allowed to be spoken in his presence for days, and he had just been informed that his grandson Nico was on the final flight path to Niroli.

Nico piloting his own jet… King Giorgio's mouth curved with appreciation. Nico lived the life he would have enjoyed had not royal duty claimed him. And now the only task remaining in his long and eventful life was to tame this wild grandson of his and persuade him to accept the throne.

Tame Nico Fierezza? King Giorgio's eyes clouded over. Even a king might find that a challenge. Then his crafty gaze brightened. Maybe there wasn't a man alive who could tame Nico Fierezza, but a woman might…

are proud to present our...

# Book of the Month

## Walk on the Wild Side
## by Natalie Anderson

### from Mills & Boon® RIVA™

Jack Greene has Kelsi throwing caution to the wind
—it's hard to stay grounded with a man who turns
your world upside down! Until they crash with
a bump—of the baby kind...

Available 4th February

*Something to say about our Book of the Month?*
*Tell us what you think!*

millsandboon.co.uk/community
facebook.com/romancehq
twitter.com/millsandboonuk

# These hot-blooded, hard-hearted desert sheikhs have chosen their queens!

**The Desert Sheikh's Defiant Queen**

4th March 2011

**The Desert Sheikh's Innocent Queen**

1st April 2011

MILLS & BOON

www.millsandboon.co.uk

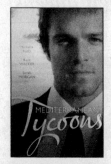

# Is the *It* girl losing it?

At the helm of must-read *Snap* magazine,
veteran style guru Sara B. has had the joy of
eviscerating the city's fashion victims in her
legendary DOs and DON'Ts photo spread.

But now on the unhip edge of forty, Sara's
being spat out like an old Polaroid picture:
blurry, undeveloped and obsolete.

After launching into a comic series of blow-ups,
Sara realises she's made her living by cutting people
down…and somehow she must make amends.

**Available 21st January 2011**
www.mirabooks.co.uk

# THE Balfour LEGACY

## EIGHT SISTERS, EIGHT SCANDALS

### VOLUME 1 – JUNE 2010
*Mia's Scandal*
by Michelle Reid

### VOLUME 2 – JULY 2010
*Kat's Pride*
by Sharon Kendrick

### VOLUME 3 – AUGUST 2010
*Emily's Innocence*
by India Grey

### VOLUME 4 – SEPTEMBER 2010
*Sophie's Seduction*
by Kim Lawrence

8 VOLUMES IN ALL TO COLLECT!

# THE

## *Balfour* LEGACY

### EIGHT SISTERS, EIGHT SCANDALS

**VOLUME 5 – OCTOBER 2010**
*Zoe's Lesson*
by Kate Hewitt

**VOLUME 6 – NOVEMBER 2010**
*Annie's Secret*
by Carole Mortimer

**VOLUME 7 – DECEMBER 2010**
*Bella's Disgrace*
by Sarah Morgan

**VOLUME 8 – JANUARY 2011**
*Olivia's Awakening*
by Margaret Way

8 VOLUMES IN ALL TO COLLECT!

## MODERN

### TAMING THE LAST ST CLAIRE
by Carole Mortimer

Gideon St Claire's life revolves around work, so fun-loving Joey McKinley is the sort of woman he normally avoids! Then an old enemy starts looking for revenge and Gideon's forced to protect Joey—day *and* night…

### THE FAR SIDE OF PARADISE
by Robyn Donald

A disastrous engagement left Taryn wary of men, but Cade Peredur stirs feelings she's never known before. However, when Cade's true identity is revealed, will Taryn's paradise fantasy dissolve?

### THE PROUD WIFE
by Kate Walker

Marina D'Inzeo is finally ready to divorce her estranged husband Pietro—even a summons to join him in Sicily won't deter her! However, with his wife standing before him, Pietro wonders why he ever let her go!

### ONE DESERT NIGHT
by Maggie Cox

Returning to the desert plains of Kabuyadir to sell its famous *Heart of Courage* jewel, Gina Collins is horrified the new sheikh is the man who gave her one earth-shattering night years ago.

## On sale from 4th March 2011
## Don't miss out!

## Her Not-So-Secret Diary
### by Anne Oliver
Sophie's fantasies stayed secret—until her saucy dream was accidentally e-mailed to her sexy boss! But as their steamy nights reach boiling point, Sophie knows she's in a whole heap of trouble...

## The Wedding Date
### by Ally Blake
Under no circumstances should Hannah's gorgeous boss, Bradley, be considered her wedding date! Now, if only her disobedient legs would do the *sensible* thing and walk away...

## Molly Cooper's Dream Date
### by Barbara Hannay
House-swapping with London-based Patrick has given Molly the chance to find a perfect English gentleman! Yet she's increasingly curious about Patrick himself—is the Englishman she wants on the other side of the world?

## If the Red Slipper Fits...
### by Shirley Jump
It's not *unknown* for Caleb Lewis to find a sexy stiletto in his convertible, but Caleb usually has some recollection of how it got there! He's intrigued to meet the woman it belongs to...

## On sale from 4th March 2011
## Don't miss out!

*Available at WHSmith, Tesco, ASDA, Eason
and all good bookshops*

*www.millsandboon.co.uk*

# THE DRIFTER & TAKE ME IF YOU DARE
(2-IN-1 ANTHOLOGY)

## BY KATE HOFFMANN & CANDACE HAVENS

### The Drifter

Charlie Templeton is a wanderer, an adventurer. But one thing scares him: the chance that he's permanently lost the woman he loved, the woman he left. He's going back to Eve...

### Take Me If You Dare

Mariska Stonegate's new man is secretly a CIA agent on the run. And he'll do just about anything to stay alive, including seducing Mariska one hot, steamy night at a time!

# AMBUSHED!
## BY VICKI LEWIS THOMPSON

Gabe Chance is blown away by the feisty redhead who unexpectedly lands right in his bed and, soon enough, his heart! He realises that Morgan's everything he wants, but she may be attracted by his ranch...

# SURPRISE ME...
## BY ISABEL SHARPE

Seduced by his fantasy woman. She's overlooked his intellect and dodgy haircut. He's totally in love; until he realises *she thought she'd climbed into bed with his bad-boy brother*!

## On sale from 18th February 2011
## Don't miss out!

*Available at WHSmith, Tesco, ASDA, Eason and all good bookshops*

*www.millsandboon.co.uk*

0211/14

**Desire™**

**2 in 1 GREAT VALUE**

**MASTER OF FORTUNE** by Katherine Garbera

Astrid Taylor was the only woman Henry Devonshire wanted. But mixing business with pleasure could cost Henry a fortune.

**MARRYING THE LONE STAR MAVERICK** by Sara Orwig

He needed a wife and fast. And his lovely new assistant would do just fine.

**BACHELOR'S BOUGHT BRIDE** by Jennifer Lewis

When his new wife slammed the bedroom door in Gavin's face, he realised his feelings for her were very real. But was it too late?

**CEO'S EXPECTANT SECRETARY** by Leanne Banks

Betrayed by his lover, CEO Brock Maddox discovered she'd been keeping an even bigger secret.

*Series – Kings of the Boardroom*

**THE BLACKMAILED BRIDE'S SECRET CHILD** by Rachel Bailey

Nico Jordan's world shattered when his lover Beth married his brother. Seven years later, Nico wants answers. But that's not all he wants!

**FOR BUSINESS...OR MARRIAGE?** by Jules Bennett

She had one month to plan Cade's wedding. And one month to change his mind.

**On sale from 18th February 2011**
**Don't miss out!**

*Available at WHSmith, Tesco, ASDA, Eason and all good bookshops*

*www.millsandboon.co.uk*

0211

# LORD OF THE DESERT
## BY NINA BRUHNS

When historian Gillian visits Rhys's grave to settle a dispute for his descendants, she is shocked and enchanted by the immortal's charm. But his master plans a dark fate for her...

# GUARDIAN
## BY LINDSAY McKENNA

Nicholas de Beaufort is ordered to return to his human form to guard Mary, a woman with a special purpose. Unsure of his new mission, Nicholas is only certain of the scorching lust Mary ignites in him!

### ON SALE 18TH FEBRUARY 2011

# SINS OF THE FLESH
## BY EVE SILVER

Calliope and soul reaper Mal are enemies, but as they unravel a tangle of clues, their attraction grows. Now they must each choose between loyalty to those they love or loyalty to each other—to the one they each call enemy.

### ON SALE 4TH MARCH 2011

### Don't miss out!

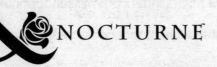

NOCTURNE